Equinox

EQUINOX

by Kurt
Maxwell

ARBOR HOUSE   New York

For Joanne and Margaret—
sisters and best friends

Manufactured in the United States of America

10 9 8 7 6 5 4 3 2 1

Library of Congress Cataloging-in-Publication Data

Maxwell, Kurt.
   Equinox.

   I. Title.
PR9199.3.M417E6   1987   813'.54   86-26538
ISBN: 0-87795-860-2

Designed by Laura Hough

THE BEGINNING:
Bremerhaven, June 1944

Sometimes years can pass without a noteworthy event—and sometimes the events of a single day can change your life so thoroughly that from that day on you will be a stranger even to yourself.

June 4, 1944, was such a threshold day for Paul von Fontana. On this last day when all seven young men of the special cadet class K1 were still alive and united, bombers of the British Royal Air Force performed a daylight raid on the German U-boat base at Bremerhaven.

At the time of the attack Paul von Fontana, along with the six other special cadets in his class, was attending a lecture on underwater plotting. Their guest-instructor on this day was the celebrated U-boat ace Lieutenant Commander Fiebig. His boat, U-27, was in Bremerhaven for provisioning.

The U-boat pens were separated from the instruction bunker by a long underground tunnel, and the entire installation was protected by thousands of cubic feet of concrete. But the force of one particular explosion was such that the classroom shook like a depth-charged submarine. Desks, bodies, and plotting tables were flung through the air; the lights went out, and when the emergency lamps came on, Fiebig was the only one on his feet.

"Up, up!" he yelled. "Get up, you cowards. If you leave your post every time a bomb falls nearby I certainly won't want you on *my* boat." Fiebig was a seasoned warrior of twenty-five years of age, while the cadets were only eighteen or nineteen.

Above them, the air-raid siren was still wailing, and they

continued to hear and feel the thunder and shock waves of more bombs.

Fontana crawled to the wall and stood up slowly. His friends were stirring among the tumble of furniture. He helped Attila Benn, and together they freed Herbert von Dornier, whose head was bleeding. The blood dripped on his white cadet uniform and painted crimson medals on his white chest.

The four remaining cadets were stirring now, but Carl Stolz suddenly let out a piercing scream. "My arm, it's broken!" he yelled, and Fontana crawled over a desk to get to him.

Fiebig told them to pull themselves together. He added, "I'll take a look at your arm, Stolz, and damn you if you're just being an old woman."

At that moment the door was ripped open, and Major von Helm shouted, "Commander, your boat! The pen's been destroyed."

Fiebig stared at the major for a terrible moment, then he raced out of the classroom and down the dimly lit corridor. Until that day, no bomb had been capable of breaching the ten-meter-thick concrete shells of the North Sea U-boat pens.

Major von Helm looked at his boys. "Dornier, are you all right?" The major was their home-form officer, and they all loved and admired him dearly.

"Yes, sir!" Dornier straightened up.

Fontana said, "Carl Stolz broke an arm, sir. We need to—"

Major von Helm held up a hand to stop Fontana. Then he pointed at the door. "Wait outside. I want a word with you."

Fontana stepped into the tunnel. Cracks had opened up in the concrete ceiling, and airborne grit was so thick that he could not see beyond the first standby light on the wall.

Major von Helm came out of the bunker and closed the door. With great urgency he said, "Now listen, Paul. Do exactly as I say. You are in big trouble. Shh——never mind. I'll tell you later. For now, use this chance to get away. Run and hide in my apartment at the villa. Run!"

"But, major—"

"It's about Franziska."

"Your cousin? What—"

"Yes, yes. Now run. I'll see you later."

Fontana darted through the tunnel, away from the U-boat pen. By the time he reached the aboveground entrance, the bombardment had moved south to the city of Bremen itself. He ran along the embankment road, then turned into a side street.

Numerous warehouses were on fire and acrid smoke billowed and rolled along the ground. Fire bells clanged everywhere. But no one stopped him and ten minutes later he crossed Stadtpark and entered the Ribnitz property through the gap in the living wall of boxwood.

The villa lay whole and peaceful in the afternoon sun. One of the maids was hanging laundry. Paul greeted her and went brashly striding along the raked gravel path. He had almost reached the side entrance to the major's flat when the butler appeared on the terrace and called, "Yes, lieutenant?"

Paul slowed only fractionally to say, "Major von Helm has asked me to wait for him at the flat."

The butler was a dignified old man, with white, Bismarckian mutton chops that touched his starched collar. He cocked his head, then said, "Very well, lieutenant. Should I get the key for you?"

"I know where it's kept, Klixbuell."

The butler watched as Paul reached into the flowerpot on the windowsill.

The guest apartment at Villa Ribnitz was elegantly furnished with English and French antiques. Persian carpets lay on the gleaming hardwood floor. Trying hard not to think of Franziska, who was most likely upstairs and alone, Paul sat down on the sofa in the living room to wait.

Major Dietrich von Helm had been the hero and mentor of his class of special cadets for three years now. What Paul and his colleagues admired about Helm were his openness and his courage. His courage was exactly the opposite of that of men like Fiebig. It was a courage of the intellect and of conviction rather than of blind obedience.

Paul suspected that the major belonged to the growing anti-Hitler movement. Von Helm had trusted the cadets with his personal convictions, and because of their family backgrounds each of them understood why it was up to the Wehrmacht to stop Hitler. In return for his trust, the cadets had given him the fierce loyalty young men reserve for their heroes.

Suddenly he was far too excited to sit still. He leaped up and was pacing up and down the room nervously when Major von Helm walked in the door. He was pale and his breath came quickly.

"Paul, this is urgent—sit down."

Fontana returned to the sofa, while the major remained standing. "You are in great trouble, Paul. Now don't lie to me. Have you been—what's this about you and my cousin? Servants know everything, Paul."

Fontana sat very still. The blood drained from his head and his heart seemed to have stopped. He stared at the major in panic, and the silence was nothing if not an admission of guilt. Stupidly he croaked, "Franziska, sir?"

Von Helm groaned and pulled up a chair. Before sitting down he took off his uniform tunic. Except for moments like this, and of course for the sight of his left hand permanently gloved in leather, one was not aware of his artificial arm.

"Paul," he said angrily, "when we came to Bremerhaven for the U-boat course—remember the party for you cadets here at my uncle's house?"

Paul nodded.

"Yes, yes. Of course you remember! And when I introduced you to Franziska, didn't I tell you she was engaged to Commander Fiebig? *Engaged*, you great ass, and a *von Ribnitz*. What makes you think you can put horns on Fiebig? All of Germany knows his name. He is the biggest thing since Gunter Prien and Scapa Flow. Now here's his chance to marry into a wealthy, titled family, and you think you can poach in his territory?"

Major von Helm leaned back in his chair and said tiredly, "You see, that's what I call stupid. Do you know what you are risking? Shall I tell you what has happened as a result of your little dalliance?"

Paul straightened and tried to speak. On the second attempt he got out, "But I love her, sir. We love each other. It's not just a dalliance!"

"Paul!"

"He beats her. I've seen the bruises . . . sir."

The major stared at him. For a while both men sat completely still. Then Paul pointed at his thighs. "Here, front and back."

Major von Helm took a deep breath, then said, "I'll speak with her and her father. Let me deal with that."

"What can *you* do? If she marries him . . . he doesn't love her. He is despicable. She hates him. He is a very rough—"

The major held up his hands. "Enough of that. Listen to me . . . the result of all this is that you will have to leave the country right away. I have made arrangements for you to go to France—Cherbourg. You must leave tonight."

"Sir? I don't understand. What . . . why?"

"I have learned that Fiebig has filed a claim with the Gestapo accusing your father of publishing anti-Nazi propaganda. Could that be? Was your father a writer? Speak, speak—quickly, Paul!"

Fontana felt numb and helpless. He had the strange impression that he was dreaming and that nothing was important because if things became unbearable he could will himself to wake up.

In this dream he said, "He was not really a writer. Even if he did publish a few things . . . he asked some questions in public. Letters to the editor. But he was a *farmer*. There is the estate in Thuringia, and we had a house in Cologne."

Paul saw his father's face up close; the dark hair accurately parted, the strong nose, the smooth-shaven chin, and the creases in the cheeks.

The three of them, mother still instructing the servants in the kitchen, were about to eat supper in the dining room of the Cologne house. Then mother sat down too, and his father would cut the bread—silver-handled knife stroking the large brown-crusted loaf in cruciform before slicing it.

The bread was always the same—dark rye with coriander—baked by a Thuringia baker from family estate grain. But his memory was not so much of the bread and the quick ritual blessing as of his father's face hollowed out by the angle of the ceiling light above the table, and, in shadow on the wall behind him, the row of portraits of the Von Fontana line—a straight, unwavering line going back to a time long before the Germanic Federation. Before the plague and the peasants' uprisings and Dürer and Handel and Bach and Bismarck and the Junkers.

And certainly before the current ghastly deformity of the Third Reich, the megalomaniacal vision of an autodidact with bad breath, pudgy hands, and a talent for large-scale murder. A mad actor with millions of devoted followers.

The family house in Cologne—a beam and granite affair dating back to 1625. Now, having seen the way bombs fall—graceless, pendulous, in a screaming arc—it was easy to imagine the bomb that had happened to fall on number 3 Schaafenstrasse in the middle of the night.

"Number three?" the fire marshal had asked when Paul had come back from the tank course. The marshal ran his finger down a long handwritten list. He turned a few more pages, then shrugged. "It's not even on here. I'll put it down now."

But the house was gone of course; even if, with the stone-age way the inner city looked, it was hard to pinpoint the location where it had stood. And where his parents had died . . .

Paul blinked and said to Major von Helm, "The letters to the editor would go back ten years at least, but it's possible that Fiebig has something on my family." He saw the look in Major von Helm's eyes, and suddenly understood the seriousness of what he had just said.

"You must leave. There is no time to lose. What's at stake is not only your life, but also the security and success of my organization . . ." The major broke off, then added, "I hope it's not too late. At any rate you must leave tonight."

"I should have told you earlier. But it never occurred to me. Letters to the editor. Surely they must see that it's just Fiebig pointing a jealous finger."

Major von Helm stood up. His left arm struck the chair back with a harsh metallic sound. "Good luck, Paul. Always remember what we spoke about."

Paul was aghast. "But what about my life here?"

Von Helm answered impatiently. "Paul, wake up. If you don't move quickly there will be no life left for you at all. Cherbourg is the best place for you. We expect an invasion in Normandy any time now. I want you to surrender to one of the western Allies as soon as you can. Any of them—Americans, British, Canadians. POWs don't end up in Nazi concentration camps." He reached into his tunic pocket and handed Paul two stamped and signed forms with the Wehrmacht eagle on the letterhead.

Paul unfolded them. One was signed by Major von Helm, the other by an illegible hand.

"Your orders," said von Helm. "Now listen closely. It may save your skin. One of these forms is Field Marshal Rommel's request for you as cadet observer to his staff. He—"

"Erwin, *the* Rommel?"

"Of course, who else? Now don't interrupt. Rommel knows about your dilemma. He is prepared to help you. He likes you. He met you during the Panzer course last fall, and he was much impressed. No one will argue with that; when Rommel calls, people go. The second form is your travel orders and your temporary release from my supervision. So there—I'm even giving you a car and a driver. Are your things still in the locker at the U-boat school?"

Fontana nodded. "But I can't just leave without saying goodbye to *anybody*."

"Such as who? Your colleagues—I'll tell them about Rommel's request, and they'll be pleased for you. By the way, Carl Stolz is in the infirmary, and Atilla Benn's head is patched. Dornier is just fine. You four are very close, I know."

Fontana took a deep breath and asked, "What about Franziska, sir? Could I . . . would it be possible for us—"

"Paul, we've just agreed on how stupid you were to get into this mess in the first place." But then the major's face was lit up by a grin, and he said unexpectedly, "Oh, what the hell. You may use this flat tonight. I'll get your things and have them in the car for you. Give me the key for the locker. All right, Paul. Final offer: three o'clock at the far entrance to the Stadtpark. Corporal Richter will drive you to Cherbourg. Good luck." He offered his hand, and Paul von Fontana grabbed it, shook it in embarrassment and gratitude and love.

Von Helm freed his hand and punched Fontana playfully on the shoulder. "Take care of yourself—whatever happens. And remember: we no longer want to *win* this war. We must do what we can to *end* it. Perhaps you can find an opportunity to speed things up from the other side. Use your good judgment."

Fontana watched the major take the tunic off the back of the chair and put it on, left sleeve first. The injury had ended his outstanding flying career less than two years ago.

When the last button was done up, the two men faced each other for the last time.

The golden afternoon sun slanted through the window. It filtered through the leaves of the dieffenbachia and the decorative palms behind the ottoman and fell not on the major's face but on his chest.

Medals gleamed: the Knight's Cross under the collar, the gilt wound badge, the Luftwaffe honor clasp in the buttonhole, the Special Services clasp.

Von Helm laughed. "Napoleon had the right idea. He said, 'Give me a warehouse full of medals and I will win you any war.' Paul, honors are only worth something if you respect the authority that bestows them. The only reason I wear these things is so as not to be conspicuous."

Paul nodded. Save for the gold lanyard and the brass buttons, his tunic was white and bare like a field of snow. He said, "I don't know how to thank you, sir."

"No need to, Paul. A favor that as it happens might save your skin. Maybe sometime in the future, when all the grotesque nonsense and buffoonery is over—who knows, maybe you can return it."

"Yes, sir."

"Stop calling me, 'sir.' Call me Dieter."

Paul cleared his throat and nodded.

Von Helm said, "Chin up, Paul. The war is almost over; the Fascist clock is almost run down. If you have a choice, go to the Americans. Who knows, perhaps you might even be able to settle there. They're going to be the new leaders—not Europe anymore. There is a moral strength that comes out of American innocence that will form a new wall for the world to lean on. According to Canaris, anyway."

"America." Thinking of adventure, Paul had to grin.

Dieter von Helm said, "That's been Franziska's dream for a long time now. She must have told you. She used to talk my ears off about how the American Constitution was the best thing ever written."

"She is an idealist," said Paul.

"This will be the last time that you'll see her. Perhaps forever, you understand? Tomorrow morning I will have her moved back to Stralsund. I'll think of a reason to tell her father. It's safer there, anyway."

Paul nodded. He saw visions of New York and Arizona, boyhood dreams of the Wild West. He asked, "How do the Americans see us?"

"Your own guess is as good as mine. But it's pretty obvious, isn't it?" With a final look at Paul, the major said, "Good luck, whatever happens." And he walked out the door.

Franziska must have been listening behind the servants' entrance because as soon as her cousin was gone, she came in to stare at Paul, wide-eyed and speechless.

Her rich black hair was pulled back into a silver clasp from where it cascaded to the large white collar that covered the shoulders of her linen dress. Paul could not look away from her face, from her eyes that mirrored the loss and confusion in his own heart.

He walked towards her, and she broke from her spot and threw her arms around him.

Paul's memory of their last night together would forever be hazy, like an impressionistic canvas or a multidimensional piece of art filled with shapes and colors, movement and sounds—filled with whispers and dreams where the wish to die alternated with the Statue of Liberty and cowboys riding herd in a fiery Texas sunset. At one point, when the moon had moved around and was shining through the window and illuminating her face on the Persian rug, when her cornflower-blue eyes seemed almost black in her face, she said, "America—I envy you and I wish you so much success. Will you write to me?"

He leaned closer on his elbows and asked, "Franzi, we knew that this could not last, didn't we?"

She placed a finger on his lips.

And the clock moved on. It was nearly three when he freed himself from her arms, got up and moved over to the pile of his clothes.

From the dark, Franziska watched. Every garment put miles between them.

In a whisper, so that he had to strain to hear, she said, "You know nothing about me, and now there is no time left."

Paul put on his socks and stepped into the uniform pants.

Franziska said, "I grew up on the estate in Stralsund on the Baltic Sea. I remember the evenings in the fall, the mist rolling in and blending with the smoke from the potato fires. I used to play in the dunes, huge dunes of the finest sand you've ever felt. And I had a Shetland pony. His name was Albert . . ."

Paul was knotting his tie, but his hands were unsteady. They fluttered like birds frightened by the pounding of his heart.

She whispered, "And because my mother died when I was still very small, I always had nannies and governesses. Mostly English girls. My favorite was Heather from London. She knew and understood so much. She was with us until the Nazis sent all the aliens home."

Paul watched Franziska sit up on the dark rectangle of the Persian rug. She embraced her legs and rested her cheek on her knees. "I went to the *gymnasium* in Bremen, and then to the university there. Biology . . . until all this bombing started. Or have I told you all this before?"

He shook his head. "Only some of it. About your mother and the governesses."

"What about you, Paul?"

As he stood in his white cadet's uniform, the innocence of his undecorated chest and the rustling of the papers in his pocket made him feel like a child about to leave home. He murmured, "I spent my summers on an estate too. In Thuringia. The rest of the year we lived in Cologne . . ." He looked at the clock, and it was ten minutes after three. Around them the house was absolutely still.

Franziska saw his gaze, and rose. She walked towards him, naked through an errant shaft of moonlight.

He embraced her, and finally he murmured, "I have to go, Franzi."

Franziska kissed him, and at the touch of her lips on his cheek he became conscious of his own tears.

COLOGNE:
September 1985

1

That September, a breath-taking heatwave gripped most of the Rhineland. After the rainy summer, the heat raised billowing clouds of steam, and the humidity soared. The weather was the topic of conversation everywhere.

But by the time Paul Fontana arrived in Cologne on Wednesday, much of the humidity had gone and the air had become breathable again. Activity in the streets had picked up, and the old town in Cologne was as lively as ever.

When Fontana collected his rental car, the women at the Hertz counter said how glad they were to be able to wear the summer clothes they had not been able to wear all summer.

He rented a large Opel, and then spent the next two days desperately trying to reach Henry Wolff, in his capacity as the head of the West German section also known as Control. By Friday Fontana had still not succeeded.

Shortly before noon that day, Paul Fontana drove slowly along the left bank where the old town met the Rhine. His rental car had no air conditioning, but the windows were cranked down as far as they would go to admit the breeze from the river.

Paul Fontana was now fifty-nine. He had short-cropped hair, and his straight, trim body made him look younger than his years. Despite the dense traffic, he steered the big Opel with ease, always aware of the changing patterns, and never losing sight of the black Mercedes three cars behind him.

The car had been tailing him for two days now. It had picked him up yesterday in Cologne, tailed him to Bonn, then followed him from the U.S. embassy back to Cologne this morning. The driver was a clean-faced young man with sunglasses. The surveillance had all the markings of an Agency internal job: the dogged insistence, the absence of additional decoy cars, the indifference to whether or not the tail was spotted, as long as it was not shaken.

Fontana reviewed the possible connections; he could not make sense of the situation but his instinct warned him.

What could be wrong? For years he had considered himself Henry Wolff's key operative in West Germany. After all, Henry and he had known each other since day one. They had spent the last forty years together in this business. Almost side by side—almost like friends.

But the black Mercedes said that something was very wrong. And why had Henry refused Fontana's phone calls for the past two days?

And why was the tail armed? None of the men in the other cars or in the street wore jackets in this heat. But Fontana did, and so did the driver of the Mercedes. Fontana's reason was his shoulder holster; the tail's reason would certainly be the same.

On the stone benches by the river sat rows of secretaries and shopgirls eating their bag lunches. They chewed with eyes closed, faces and legs directed toward the sun. A breeze fanned the women's skin and ruffled their light summer clothes.

Between the benches and the river, young men paraded—their ties loosened, jackets dangling from one shoulder. They were looking at the women with appreciation, like buyers in an art gallery.

The sun had raised the sap of life—possibilities and anticipation were back in the air, as they should be.

Fontana coasted past the outdoor restaurant where he would meet Gaby. The table was booked for twelve o'clock, but it was unlikely that she would be on time. He found a parking spot not far away and dove into it.

Caught in traffic, like a log in a river, the Mercedes had to move on.

Fontana grinned at the passing driver. Two hundred yards away, the black Mercedes U-turned. It came back, slowly, then double-parked. From this angle, the reflection of the sky made the windshield impenetrable.

Fontana slipped out of his jacket and shrugged off the shoulder holster. He wrapped the straps around the Agency .38 and shoved the whole thing under the seat. He got out of the car, fed the meter, then walked toward the restaurant.

On the river, barges hooted and belched smoke. From the restaurant terrace came the sound of laughter and conversation; the smells of food and good coffee were in the air. Humanity at peace.

His jacket in the crook of his arm, Fontana pulled down his tie and rolled up his shirt cuffs to look like any other man.

Gaby was half an hour late, but finally she came running, loping in the awkward gait of an adolescent girl suddenly self-conscious about her blossoming body. She wore sandals, jeans, and a white blouse; her blond hair was pulled back into the usual ponytail.

Rising to welcome her, Fontana felt the paternal mixture of affection, pride, worry, and guilt to which—except for the latter—he had no clear right. Gaby was his *grand*daughter, not his daughter. But she was the only bright spot in a long litany of mistakes and losses; murky war-related things that to this very day nevertheless determined his life.

"I'm sorry I'm late, and I can't stay," said Gaby breathlessly. "I shouldn't even have left . . ."

"But I thought we were going to have lunch. What's the problem? They *do* let you out to eat, don't they?"

"Of course they do, but . . ." She stood, half leaning on the back of the chair, undecided. Around them no one paid

them any attention; people were busy eating, talking, ro-
mancing.

"Come on, Gaby," he laughed. "Just a few minutes.
Then I'll walk back with you to the shop." She worked in a
dry-cleaning establishment, a job she'd told him she hated.

"*No,* there's no need to walk back with me." She looked
over her shoulder, then scanned the sidewalk.

"Anything wrong?"

"No, nothing. Why?" She looked at him then sighed and
said, "All right. But I can't stay long." She slid onto her chair
like an exhausted runner. Fontana rarely saw her more than
three, four times a year. Each time he was taken aback by the
changes and new tensions.

He reached out to touch her hand on the table. "Hey, are
you sure everything's all right? You haven't been fighting
with your father again?"

"Oh, come on!" In her eyes was the familiar dreamy pet-
ulance, but this time there was something else too. Something like a hard, secret thrill. He watched her patiently,
giving her the space she had always demanded—the space
and forbearance Peter, her father, had finally run out of.
Without question Gaby was a difficult child. But, as his conscience told him, there were good reasons for that.

"You're staring!"

He smiled. "Forgive me, Gaby." It was typical that she
never called him *anything;* no name, no title such as Opa. As
though she refused to identify just what he meant to her or
how she saw him.

The waiter came, pad and pencil ready. Sweat plastered
his hair to his forehead.

Gaby said, "Just a Diet Coke for me."

"There's a minimum charge, folks. This is expensive real
estate."

Fontana nodded, then ordered the salad plate and a glass
of white wine.

When the waiter left, Fontana briefly put his hand on
hers. "I wanted to talk to you, Gaby . . ."

"What?" She sat up and in doing so shook off his hand.

"I'm repeating my offer to take you to Canada. McGill is

one of the best universities anywhere. I've researched this—it isn't just a whim. You'd have to do a supplementary year of high school, but I'm certain that your English is good enough. You'd catch on quickly."

She shook her head so that her ponytail flew. Something like panic flared in her eyes. "No, no. Damnit, don't!"

From the neighboring tables people looked at them, then made a civilized effort to ignore them.

"Shh . . ."

She moved to get up, but Fontana leaned forward and said urgently, "Please, Gaby. Please . . ."

She sat down again, unhappy and eager to return to her own world, whatever that was. Holding her head up high in a gesture of forced courage that tore at his heart, she said, "I can look after myself. I'm old enough. And I have a job. Perhaps not a great one, but it's a job. And also there is . . ." She broke off as though she'd almost said too much.

"What? What *is there?*"

"Nothing."

"If you aren't in touch with your father, are you at least keeping in touch with Uncle Helm? Don't cut yourself off altogether, Gaby. Sometimes one needs family."

"Family," she sneered. "We know how much *he* cared for mother. Doesn't that bother you sometimes? As for *Uncle Helm*—I don't know when I last saw him."

Fontana thought that one day, one day when she would be prepared to *listen,* when she was emotionally ready for it, he would tell her about her mother, and why she was born in a Nazi concentration camp. And he would tell her about Franziska. But not now, not while she was . . . like this.

The waiter came and put down their order. Gaby reached for the Diet Coke and gulped thirstily.

Fontana said patiently, "You know that your father had nothing to do with your mother's death. It's about time you stopped blaming him. Or Uncle Helm. You know what happened."

She let her gaze wander over the patio, then her eyes flickered to him and away again.

Fontana took a sip of wine, then said simply, "Your father loves you. Don't reject him altogether. Or any of us."

Looking at Gaby he found her staring at him, but then he realized that she was staring *through* him. She spoke in hardly more than a whisper, and he had to lean closer to hear her. "Uncle Helm is selfish. He is a worse, soulless fat cat than *he*, and you can all—. I don't want my family, it's not my family anyway. It's all bits and pieces. I'll live my own life, and there's someone who loves me for who I am. Not because he feels obligated . . ."

Fontana stared at her, shaken to the core. A blissful, dreamy expression had wiped Gaby's face clean of all anger, but then she focused her eyes on him. She shivered and put down the tall glass with a bang. "I shouldn't have come."

"Gaby, how can you say those things about Uncle Helm? Don't you realize . . . don't you——" He found himself speechless and Gaby noticed it, watched him with amusement.

Then her eyes shifted over his shoulder, and for a second she looked like a deer caught in the headlights of a car. Then she leaped up, said, "I've got to go!" and walked away, among the tables, down the steps and along the sidewalk. Fontana rose to follow her with his eyes.

But it wouldn't have been necessary to get up because long before she was gone from view, Gaby crossed the street and joined a dark-haired young man on the other side. He grabbed her arm roughly and pulled her away, talking to her with an angry expression. He wore slacks and a white shirt; though it was hard to be sure from this distance, he looked Latin or French rather than German. Then the thought came to Fontana that meddling with Gaby would be an effective way for Wolff to put pressure on an old friend and agent who was suddenly reluctant to toe the line.

Fontana stared after Gaby and the young man until they were swallowed up by the crowd. Then he got up, hurriedly put down enough money to cover the bill, and left.

The black Mercedes was gone, his rented Opel was parked at the meter the way he'd left it, windows down, doors unlocked. While talking with Gaby, he'd been distracted from the car, a mistake he might have to pay for.

He stood at the curb for a while, thinking. The absence of the Mercedes could mean several things. They could have booby-trapped his car, they could have switched tails, they could have called off the operation altogether, or—most likely—they could have slapped a beeper on the Opel.

Fontana walked around the car, visually inspecting the roof gutter and running his hand along the inner edges of bumpers and wheel wells: *nothing.* But beepers could be hard to find, and booby traps even more so.

His growing impatience drove him on. He risked opening the door, then sat on the seat and hurriedly slipped back into shoulder holster and jacket.

Seconds later he walked away from the car and the promenade, towards the car rental office on Neumarkt. He was perspiring freely by the time he got there, and the blast from the air conditioning made him shiver. He rented the fastest car they had—a big BMW—then tried again to reach Wolff. At the embassy in Bonn they said he was out of town, and at the safe house in Olpe they gave him the usual line about the wrong number.

The autobahn took him halfway there in minutes; he exited and continued on the regular road. In the surrounding fields, farmers worked with great wooden rakes to straighten the patches of wheat and oats that had been beaten flat by the rains of August.

At 1:15 he reached the turnoff to the gravel road, then the bridge across what had been a torrent in August but was now a dry river bed.

Then he saw the cloud of dust in the distance, coming his way and closing rapidly. Two minutes later, at the turn where one first glimpsed the estate building, he almost crashed into the truck that straddled the road. He braked and wrenched the wheel—the heavy BMW spun out and came to a stop sideways, only inches from the truck's gas tank.

By the side of the road stood Jack Teagarden and two young operatives with Uzis. Teagarden said, "Shit, Paul, don't you know better than to come here without calling first? Henry doesn't like surprises. Get out, now. Move it!"

Fontana pushed open the door; Teagarden was there in

three quick strides and pulled him out, nudged him backwards against the hood of the car.

"Easy, Jack. I came to see Henry."

"No kidding. He *said* you'd come. The boys and I, we've been waiting for you since last night."

Teagarden found the .38. He emptied the drum, threw the shells into the bush, and shoved the gun back under Fontana's arm. Actually, his name was Jacob C. Teagarden, but he liked it when people called him Jack. Except that, unlike the famous jazz musician, this Jack Teagarden was rough, humorless, and completely unimaginative. He had a hard face, pale eyes, and rough, horny hands. Wolff had brought him in from New York years ago, retrained him, and eventually made him the senior field operative with the Agency's Bonn section.

Now Teagarden told the two young men with Uzis to keep an eye on Fontana. They heard a car approaching fast. It stopped, spattering gravel. Then Henry Wolff appeared, dressed impeccably in a summer suit, white shirt, and beige tie. Minding his shiny shoes, he stepped gingerly through the dusty grass in front of the truck.

Henry surveyed the scene, then grinned. "Paul, my friend. You do get into some awkward situations. And on an empty stomach too. I understand you hardly touched your lunch today. And now you've got two rental cars on your credit card! What brings you here? You're not worried about the girl?"

Fontana said, "If that fellow was one of yours, Henry, then I'll . . ."

"You'll *what?*" Wolff came closer and sat casually on the fender of the BMW. "It's not us, Paul. But what did you want to see me about today?"

"You know. Just as you know that I've been trying to reach you for two days now." Fontana was aware of Teagarden and his Uzi boys watching, listening. Teagarden wiped his brow with his bare hand, then snapped away the sweat.

Wolff fussed with the perfect creases in his trouser legs and said musingly, "But you're not supposed to be in Germany. You know the rules, Paul. From Cyprus you were scheduled to return to your base in Montreal until you were reassigned."

"I know. Don't suddenly start pushing the rules with me, Henry. We go back too long for that."

Wolff shook his head. "Old times are old hat. If anything, they cut both ways. Liberties *and* obligations. You still owe me, Paul. I know what you want; the answer's no."

Fontana waved at Teagarden and the young operatives. They had lowered their machine pistols now, but posture and eyes were still alert. "Can we talk without them hanging around?"

Wolff said to Teagarden, "Run along, Jack. Take that truck with you." He reached into his jacket pocket and tossed him a key. "Here, move my car, but go easy on the shift."

They watched the maneuver in silence. Teagarden handled Wolff's vintage Mercedes like a raw egg.

Fontana looked at the back of Henry Wolff's head. His hair had gone much more gray than his own, but Henry Wolff was only two years older.

Old times and obligations: when they met in Cherbourg in June 1944 Fontana had been an American POW, and First Lieutenant Henry Wolff had been a green twenty-one-year-old American intelligence officer attached to General Omar Bradley's command. Officer Cadet Paul von Fontana had been his first sleeper, the first feather in his cap.

A different Wolff—a different Fontana: life had only apparently taken them on the same route. In real terms they had traveled in opposite directions.

When the truck with Teagarden and the operatives was gone, Fontana said, "Let's sit in my car, Henry. It has air conditioning."

Wolff smiled. "The heat bother you, Paul? Let's just stay here and get it over with. Gotta get back to the office. I know what you want. You want *out* . . . and you know that I can't let you go. Besides, you still owe us."

"That was a long time ago, Henry. Forty years, for Christ's sake. I can't do it anymore."

Wolff watched him coldly. Then he said, "The hell you can't. You're our most experienced operative this side of the Iron Curtain. Don't give me this crap. Take a rest. You're tired, and that happens to the best of us. Take a month or so. Look after your little business in Canada. Get laid, anything. But smarten up."

Fontana thought that there was only one approach left. He said, "Henry . . . if I ask you as an old friend; if I remind you of—"

"Shut up, Paul! Don't remind me of a single goddamn thing. You don't perform and you know what happens, right? Washington doesn't piss around, Paul. You know something? Every four or five years you get the bloody shakes. That Cyprus job—Washington simply changed its mind. The guy had to get iced and that's it, Paul."

"But you called me in to facilitate. Then you blew him away right under my nose."

Wolff shrugged. "Mid-East control; they've got their plate *filled* with spaghetti. They're not gonna piss around with one noodle."

"I want out, Henry."

"No way. You're much too valuable. And you know too damn much, Paul. Listen, I'll tell you something: the very things that make you unhappy are the things that make you a crack agent. Think about it. You got no country and you got no future. All you got is me and the Agency. I'm your brother. They're your family."

Fontana closed his eyes for a moment. Then he said slowly, almost with a sense of surprise, "*This* is my country. I have a granddaughter—"

Wolff laughed.

Fontana looked at him. In the steep angle of the sunlight a maze of small wrinkles showed over Wolff's face. Fontana said, "Don't laugh, Henry. Perhaps your judgment is no longer quite as acute."

"What's that supposed to mean?"

"It means, you touch Gaby Schott in any way at all and I'll turn kamikaze . . ."

Wolff's laughter froze, his mouth remained open for the

instant of his shock. Then he shrugged and slid off the fender. "You're crazy, Paul. And don't talk to me like that. Now, I want you to return to Canada and damn well stay there, okay? Don't set foot in Europe for at least two weeks."

"Oh? But what about my business—what if I get a consulting job here?"

"Tell me, and I'll have Financial Control check it out. If you're really losing money, they'll reimburse you." Wolff looked at his watch and added, "Christ, look at the time. Gotta go, Paul." He waved and walked to his car.

Fontana shouted, "You're wrong, you know. Just goddamn, pigheaded wrong, Henry."

Wolff took his time folding his tall, elegant figure into the 220SE. He started the engine and did a five-point turn. Then his arm came out the window and he beckoned.

Fontana walked over and bent down."Yes?"

"Paul . . . please use your head. More things than you imagine are out of control right now."

"Meaning . . .?"

"Look after your health."

"We're too old for threats, Henry."

"No, we're not. What I'm saying is, in time they'll let you off the hook. Until then, all I can do is give you lots of line. But you shake the hook and they'll dynamite you."

"Henry . . ."

"Gotta go! Once again, here's your current order: get out of Europe; be available at your base in Montreal. I'll call you before two weeks are up." The Mercedes swept away; silent, gleaming in the brilliant sunlight.

Fontana returned to Cologne. En route to his hotel, he made a detour that took him past the dry cleaners where Gaby worked. He parked the car and entered the establishment. Inside, the heat was like a furnace. At the steam presses, women with dark hair and Mediterranean faces worked like slaves in a forge.

A man with a worried face came to the counter, and
Fontana asked to speak to Gaby Schott. The man said she had
gone out for lunch but not returned. It was now almost
four. . . . The man said he was the proprietor and that the
young people today did not know what it meant to put in an
honest day's work. He made an angry, air-slapping motion
and muttered, "Eh, eh, eh. . . ."

Fontana left. He refused to allow himself to examine his
guilt all over again. Gaby was . . . how old was she? Eighteen?
Nineteen? At any rate, for better or worse, she had taken
charge of her own life.

Unless Wolff was lying.

From his hotel, Fontana called her father, Peter Schott.
Peter worked for the Green Party as aide-de-camp for Dietrich
Helm, the party's background strategist.

Peter and Herr Helm were in an urgent session, the secretary told him; it was expected to last well into the night.
Fontana left his name and said he'd call back.

Through Peter and Dietrich Helm he knew quite a bit
about the Green Party. Today it was no longer just a group of
rabble-rousing no-nukes. One of the smartest things this
party of young people in jeans and sneakers had done was to
take on the consulting services of Dietrich Helm. From his
small Cologne office Helm worked successfully behind the
scenes, away from the infighting and posturing in Bonn, to
increase the party's strategic edge. But visible or not, fame
had found Helm anyway.

In recent years, the Greens had advanced decisively in
the polls. They were now represented in the Bundestag, and
as a coalition partner had considerable clout. At the same
time, their politics brought its own problems, scaring capi-
talist industries and NATO alike. There was no doubt that the
Greens were controversial, but their success justified their
policy of confrontation. At least for the time being.

Minutes after Fontana hung up on the Green Party secretary, there was a knock on his door. He looked through the
spy and saw Teagarden's grinning mug distorted by the wide-
angle lens.

Teagarden wiggled his fingers and said like a barker,

"Hurry, hurry, hurry . . . open up, Paulie. Greetings from Henry. There's a plane to New York at six-thirty and he wants you on it. Connections to Montreal every two or three hours. Open up, shithead. Let's go. Uncle Jack will see ya off!"

2

When Gaby moved out of her father's apartment, she rented a small furnished room in an ancient apartment building on the east side, the industrial side of the Rhine. It was an odd room, taller than wide, more like the dead end of a hallway. The single window offered an uninspiring view of an industrial railway yard, the walls needed paint, the tap on the stone sink in the corner needed a new washer, and the door to the communal toilet in the hallway needed a new lock.

The place was depressing and horrid, but it was her own. It was her second stake in her claim on independence: the first had been leaving "home," the third had been Angelo Rossi's miraculous discovery of her, and the fourth were his plans for their shared future.

Now she lay on the lumpy daybed and watched him put his clothes back on.

She admired his body, its spare maleness, his strong arms and lean firm thighs. She wanted dearly to ask him again if he loved her, but she was afraid he might get impatient and tired of answering the same question. Or perhaps he might even take it as a sign that she was doubting him.

He finished zipping up his slacks, then padded barefoot over to the sink to wash his hands.

Next to the sink was a Formica table and two chairs. Above the table, a three-tiered kitchen shelf held the hot plate, some dishes, cutlery, and some canned goods.

The only other pieces of furniture in the room were a musty stuffed chair by the window, and next to it an orange crate covered by a napkin like a tablecloth. On the cloth lay her mother's framed photograph upside down. Gaby had turned it over just before undressing for Rossi earlier this afternoon.

"Get going, sweetie; there are some things we have to do," said Rossi. He was drying his hands on the kitchen towel that hung over the chair.

Gaby sat up, arms crossed to cover herself.

Rossi came over, pulled away her arms, looked at her breasts, then put a smacking kiss on each nipple.

"Do you like them, *caro?*" she whispered hopefully. "You don't think they're too big?"

He let go of her wrists, made a Latin gesture and grinned. "Too big? Of course not, they're wonderful. Now get dressed!" He slapped her playfully on her bare ass and she went to the sink to wash up as best she could.

Using the washcloth between her legs she said, "Don't look, please."

"I won't."

She looked over her shoulder and saw him standing by the window, pulling at his lower lip as though in thought. She said, "The only thing I'll miss about the dry cleaners is the shower at the back. Here I've only got this sink—how will I wash properly?"

"There are public baths. And you could also use your father's place when he is not in. Or even when he *is* in. When was the last time you saw your father?"

"I don't know. Who cares? A month ago. Why?"

"Just asking." He turned the photograph right-side up and asked, "Who is this? A friend?"

She squeezed the washcloth into the sink, then soaked it with water from the tap.

"Who is it, Gaby?"

She finished washing her chest and underarms before replying. "My mother. Years ago." She threw the cloth into the sink, then walked self-consciously over to the stuffed chair to get her clothes.

"Why do you put her upside down? Is she dead or something?"

"Yes." Gaby shrugged into her panties and jeans as quickly as she could.

The picture of her mother had been taken years ago in Leipzig, even before her mother was married. It showed her with her hair in braids coiled on top. She wore a white taffeta dress and smiled bravely into the lens of the studio photographer. On the back of the picture was stamped: *Leipziger Kunstfotostudio beim Brunnen*. Beneath that, someone had written in pencil: Vicky Fontana 1963.

Considering the fact that Gaby was already nine when her mother died, she knew very little about her. She knew that her mother had been born in some terrible place, a "camp" that was then liberated by the Russians. She knew that her mother had spoken German with a Russian accent. She knew that . . . there was little more that she knew with *certainty*. The rest was feelings and memorized impressions, like photos in an album: the old-fashioned flat in Leipzig, her mother's long hair when the braids were undone, then the new, more stylish haircut. . . .

There were of course many other memories, but those could never be allowed to surface. A shrink had once tried to pry, without success. Still, at times the memories came back—mostly at night, when she was alone. Then she *heard* again the harsh commands, the dogs, the shots—she *saw* the puffs of dirt around them, saw her mother stumble in the plowed strip of no-man's land—her father staring, panting, then running on, carrying the child . . .

"What?" asked Rossi, putting back the picture, facedown.

"Nothing." Gaby finished buttoning her blouse, then reached out and stood the photo upright. She went to Rossi, put her arms around him, and laid her head on his shoulder. In the railyard an engine puffed by, rattling the windows and the dishes on the shelf.

Rossi held her and stroked her hair with his free hand. He made low-throated calming sounds. "Shh, shh, come on now . . . there's a time when all of us have to live our own lives. Parents leave us, and often they hand over a bigger mess than they found. You look after me, I look after you; you'll join our family and you'll never be lonely again."

She raised her face and asked, "You mean that, *caro*?" *Caro* was the Italian term of endearment she'd learned. When she found out that he was Italian, she bought a dictionary and looked up and memorized a dozen key words to surprise him with. His command of German was excellent, and on top of that he impressed her with phrases in English, Japanese, French, and even Arabic.

Below the window, the engine continued its shunting work; because she'd never been in her room during the day, she had not known it would be so noisy. She wished she had a fancier place—he probably did, although she had never seen it.

Rossi said, "Look, sweetie, there are some things I want to talk to you about. Let's sit by the table. Are you hungry?"

She shrugged.

"I am." He looked at his watch, then said with a grin, "I'll be just a minute. You stay right here. I'll get us something to eat."

"Don't leave me alone!"

He gave her a quick curious glance, then said, "All right, come along."

They found a neighborhood supermarket where he bought a roasted chicken, ice cream, bread, and fruit. On the way back to the room, he picked up some takeout coffee.

Upstairs, Gaby surveyed their treasures. Excitedly she set the table while Rossi ripped apart the chicken. The ice cream container was put in the half-filled sink to slow down the melting. Gaby felt proud to be able to serve him like this, to have him eat at her table in her own room. Almost like a real family—she felt warmth and gratitude as she watched him enjoy his food.

The ice cream was melted, but she poured it into two cups and it was delicious.

Sipping his coffee, Rossi said, "You've known me now

for almost two months, right?" He watched her nod, then asked, "You trust me, Gaby?"

She stopped licking out the ice cream container and stared wide-eyed. "Of course I do. How can you even ask?"

He smiled. "I know . . . you remember some of the people I introduced you to? Madeleine, Theo, the Englishman, Banigan?"

She nodded, confused. "Yes, *caro*. I like Madeleine. She is very gracious. But I don't like that Theo. He is. . . ."

"I know. He seems a bit rough. But when you get to know him better, he's a good friend."

She sat up, suddenly apprehensive as though a third person had entered the room. "Why do you ask, *caro*?"

"Because I want you to like them. They are my family. What unites us is certain ideas and visions. More than visions; we have certain strong beliefs, and we are working to create a better future for all of us. We're part of a huge network."

She did not understand, but she sensed she was being tested, and she was afraid of losing his love. And so she resolved immediately to try to understand not just the meaning of his words, but *him*.

He smiled. "There is too much injustice in the world, sweetie, and not enough love, not enough sharing."

She nodded.

Rossi moved his chair closer and took her hand in his. He asked, "When was the last time you were in touch with your father?"

Her heart began to beat madly, and she tried to look away from Rossi's eyes, but could not. "I don't know. Why?" she murmured.

"If you called him and said you wanted to see him every now and then, would he be suspicious?"

She shrugged. "Suspicious of what?"

"Your motive."

She said with frank cynicism, "He'd be bowled over with joy. But why should I do that, *caro*? I wanted to get away from him, from this whole family business and from. . . ." She shrugged. Rossi let go of her hand and sat back in his chair.

"From what, Gaby? From his sort of world? The corrupt politicians like Helm, the political fat cats who sell us common folk down the river every time it suits them?"

He was not looking at her; he was fiddling with the styrofoam coffee cup, breaking it into tiny bits and pieces. His hands were slim and tanned, the fingers strong. Just looking at them, she remembered the first time she felt them caress her skin. . . .

"Is that it, Gaby?"

She realized that this was too important a moment to indulge in daydreams. She said, "Oh, I don't know. Uncle Helm's not as bad as some. He hired my father and helped us out when we first came to the West. But—yeah, I guess he must be corrupt because he's a politician, right? Is that what you mean? All these trade-offs and corruption have got to rub off."

Rossi leapt up from his chair. For a moment he stood before Gaby and a fire seemed to burn in his eyes. Then he began pacing up and down in front of her, always looking at her, fixing her. "Gaby, Gaby, don't you ever get tired of mediocrity? Aren't you bored out of your mind half the time? Your demeaning job, this demeaning room . . . how did you imagine your future? Did you ever dream of being someone else, of being rich and powerful and independent?"

She stared at him, followed him up and down with her whole face, not just her eyes. He seemed alive like no one else she'd ever met. His whole body, his voice, his eyes, his movements—everything radiated energy and purpose.

"Well, did you, Gaby?"

She giggled and made a helpless gesture.

"As a little girl or even lately did you ever invent another identity for yourself, a name?"

She giggled and said, *"Marion*—it has more fire and snap than Gabrielle, for crying out loud."

He clapped his hands. "Marion you shall be! Tomorrow you will have your new identity; passport, driver's license, birth certificate. Where do you want to be born? Berlin, Hamburg, New York? Our family has access to all the documents.

And you can open a new bank account for all your money."

"What money?" she laughed. "You don't want me to go back to the dry cleaners, so I don't even have a job."

"Job," he drawled. "Our team is self-employed. Just wait and see." He picked her up, let her straddle his biceps, lifted her clean off the ground, and gave her a few turns around the room before setting her down again.

"*Caro*, I don't know what you're talking about but it sounds wonderful. Will I be rich?"

"Very!"

"And famous?"

"Famous in your anonymity!"

"Oh la la!" She clapped her hands and did a little dance step.

He sat down and ran his fingers through his hair. As it revealed the top of his ear, she noticed again that a tiny piece of his ear was missing. Perhaps a work-related injury. The thought prompted her to ask, "Seriously now, what sort of work do you do?" She'd of course asked him that before, these past two months, but never received a clear answer. It was obvious that he had lots of money; his clothes were expensive, and his wallet when he took her out was always filled.

"What sort of work, sweetie?" He smiled at her and leaned back. "I'll tell you in time, over the next few days. And I'll show you exactly what I expect of you . . . just nod but don't interrupt."

She swallowed her apprehension, and nodded. "Okay."

"I'm never going to ask you to do anything you don't want to do, *that* I can promise you right now. Okay? First thing is, I want you to get to know my family better. And, in turn, I want them to get comfortable with you. They've got to accept you too because, well . . . there are lots of times when you need a whole team. The family—or at least *our* part of the family, because there's a whole lot more of us all over the world—the family is Madeleine, whom you've met and liked. Then there's Theo, and I'll want you to find a way to get along with him too. You remember Banigan, and there'll be another man who's not here yet. His name is Mahmoud, and he's from Beirut. In a way, he's really in charge of this very big, very rewarding operation we're about to do."

"And me? What can I do? I mean. . . ."

"Your contribution will be very important. I won't tell you the details just yet . . . but I really want you on board."

Excitement gripped her—a promise of mystery and adventure, a challenge where Rossi would make sure that the risks were manageable.

She looked at him with keen anticipation. In the stifling room she felt a thrill as though she were about to get on a rollercoaster.

She took a plunge and said, "Go on!"

"And I can trust you fully?"

She smiled and nodded.

In the dimming light from the single window, Rossi looked almost classically Roman: a strong chin, square forehead, straight prominent nose, and large dark eyes. He was watching her closely as he said, "We're planning the biggest snatch and squeeze this country has seen since Mathias Franke. . . ."

Her breath caught and she stuttered, "But he was killed."

Rossi made an impatient gesture. "A stupid mistake, I know. Our man will not be harmed, I can promise you that. And when it's over we'll all be far away, a lot richer, and a good number of our brothers and sisters will be free from prison."

"Who is the. . . . Is it a man? Would I have heard of him?" Apprehension and excitement made her tremble.

"You really want to know? You realize that once you know, once you're part of this, there's no way back."

In a flash she saw the essence of her life until she met Rossi—the nightmare of her arrival in the West, the prison of schools and her life with her father, the boredom of her existence, the squalor of her job and this room. Good riddance! She would embrace this man and his offer of a new life. Rossi was her future, her way out, and she would embrace him with both arms and with all her heart.

She said firmly, *"Si, caro*—I'm aware of that. Tell me."

"All right . . . yes, you know him. And this is where you come in. No rough stuff. Your role is passive. I'll tell you later. But the *target* is a big-shot politico. Big stuff right now. Which is why we chose him for the squeeze: public pressure will force the government to *do as we say.*"

"Who is he? What do I have to do?" whispered Gaby.

"Your role is standby insurance. In case we need your pull. Or in case there should be some surprise change in their routine. We may need you as bait for the squeeze"—Rossi saw her face and added very quickly—"but *I* need you regardless—and the family is always welcoming new members."

"Who is it, *caro?*"

"Ah! His name is Dietrich Helm, and he's as popular as Robin Hood right now. In exchange for his freedom we'll ask for a lot of money and the freedom of our brothers in jail here. And because Helm is so popular right now with his arms-limitation stance, the government will have to give us whatever we want."

Gaby had gone very pale.

3

All day Saturday, Henry Wolff could hear the snapping of the new assault rifles on single fire. Behind the Agency safe house, an old castle near the village of Olpe, there was a firing range. Today the small army of twenty-five operatives who had been flown in for the upcoming presidential visit were busy practicing with the new weapon.

Mercifully, Henry Wolff's window did not overlook the

firing range. Instead, it faced west, toward the urban and industrial cluster of Cologne, Bonn, and Dusseldorf on the far horizon. Stretching towards their distant haze and dazzle was a lovely landscape of verdant forests, ancient villages, wheat fields, and vineyards sloped to the sun.

Seated behind the big desk in his study on the second floor, Henry Wolff only had to raise his well-groomed head to see all this through the open window. But today he rarely did; instead he kept his eyes on the phones, and his ears were cocked for the sound of the Telex printer in the corner.

From the TV monitor came the murmur of the Yankee game. Toronto had just hit a home run. This was the second game in the series that decided the American League East championship. The thought that the Yankees might fall behind those upstart Canadians was hard to accept.

Wolff had not missed the Saturday ball games for as long as he could recall. Once, right after the war, when the OSS had been disbanded and he was awaiting word on his application to the new Central Intelligence Agency, Wolff had pitched for a triple A team in Texas. But his elbow began to give him trouble, and he returned to working for his father's chain of hardware stores.

The ball games gave him a sense of home. They counteracted the complex cross-currents of European culture that surrounded him. The ball games kept his American reflexes oiled and humming, and the ungainly dish on the turreted roof of the castle was a small price to pay for a clear NBC satellite signal.

But today Henry Wolff did not enjoy the game; not because the Yankees were down, but because he was too preoccupied with Equinox. This was zero-hour, and he sat tensely at the center of the painstakingly laid-out operation, waiting for the intelligence updates to come in from the field.

Because Equinox was so complex, it was laid out along strict need-to-know guidelines. Among Wolff's staff, people knew only the bits and pieces that were necessary for them to do their jobs.

For example, Paul Fontana, who had no need to know

anything about the project, had been ordered off the field while Jack Teagarden was only told what the Bonn government source was supposed to be doing but not why.

At four o'clock the black phone buzzed. It was Dr. Esser, the interior minister of the Bonn government. In a tone that clearly bespoke his disdain for Equinox he said, "An update please, Mr. Wolff."

Wolff said, "Nothing yet. Relax. We're on top of it."

"Mr. Wolff, if this targeting file is leaked to the media, all of NATO will know the next morning that the Bonn government has secretly allowed the Americans to deploy three times as many cruise missiles—"

"Not *three* times, Dr. Esser."

"Well—a *lot more* than anyone has known. Our opposition will crucify us. Nuclear is a very sensitive issue in Europe, and the West German electorate will be crying out for blood. Whose blood do you think?"

"Look, stop worrying. Trust us, okay? We do these things all the time. On the scale of things, Equinox is not the most difficult intelligence operation we've ever done."

"But this is yours and *ours*. I just want to make sure you understand that if this file falls into the wrong hands, it will be the end of my government. It will be the end of the NATO alliance as we know it. And Washington will once again be seen as—well, use your imagination. Equinox will be impossible to explain."

"True," agreed Wolff. "And if it goes the wrong way, I might lose my job. That prospect alone drives me to make sure things go the way we want them to."

"Your job!"

"It's a good job. *I* like it."

In the phone Esser sighed. To cheer him up, and to add a touch of lightness, Wolff said, "Listen, doctor—if need be, you can always put up a smoke screen. Throw the people another spy scandal. Complete with personal details and mistress's phone numbers. That's what people really care about. The nuclear threat just bores them. What they worry about is tonight's dinner or whether their bank is safe or whether that lump is cancer or if they're gonna get laid this weekend."

"Thank you, Mr. Wolff. Your black humor—or should I say, your *cynicism,* demonstrates our different points of view."

On the TV, some no-name Blue Jay pitcher wound up and delivered strike three. The curve ball sizzled past the Yankee hitter. The game took place in New York under a gloriously blue sky, and Wolff remembered the afternoons at the ballpark with nostalgia. And here he was in a goddamn German castle, massaging Esser.

On the red phone the button lit up and Wolff said, "The Bonn line just came on. If you'll hold for a moment—this might be for us."

The interior minister agreed and Wolff snapped up the red phone. It was Teagarden, out of breath.

Wolff listened to him, praised him, and told him to keep an eye on the source. Then he went back to the shielded black line where Dr. Esser was still waiting. He said, "I've just been informed that only minutes ago your man boarded a flight for East Berlin. He was carrying a briefcase."

Esser expelled air, then said, "I suppose that's good. I mean, in the scheme of things."

"Yes, sir, it's what we wanted him to do. Do I hear a note of chagrin?"

"No, of course not. I love sanctioning high treason. Especially when you Americans are twisting my government's arm. But enough of that. . . ."

"Thank you, Dr. Esser." Wolff grinned into the phone. "Equinox seems to be unrolling exactly as planned. My guess is that we will hear from the other side near the middle of next week."

"And Stolz—I mean, the source?"

"Yes, careful! We are keeping an eye on him. He'll be under full surveillance from now until the day he dies."

"A natural death, I hope."

Wolff made no promises.

The first indication that things had gone wrong with Equinox was that, by midweek, nothing, not even a word of acknowledgment, had been heard from either East Berlin or Moscow.

Wolff spent much time on the direct line to Washington Control justifying his faith in the courier, a sixty-year-old journalist by the unforgettable name of Attila Benn (aptly code-named "The Hun" in Agency files).

When by Friday noon the opposite side still had not acknowledged receiving the Equinox file, the West German chancellor called a crisis conference in his office. A scrambled satellite link with Washington was established, and Henry Wolff found himself in the hot seat.

The chancellor's crisis staff consisted of his senior ministers and their aides. They all sat around the long table and stared with incredulity at the speaker box as it snarled, "Henry assures me they're gonna play. Right, Henry, you've done your homework on this one? Let's give them the weekend, okay? Say, if they're not batting by Monday, we'll sink it."

"Batting?" asked Dr. Esser, the interior minister.

Wolff said, "American sports metaphors, sir. . . ." He grinned bravely, fighting the vivid impression that Equinox had turned from a gopher ball into a vicious ricochet about to flatten its very pitcher.

After the crisis session, Wolff drove back to Olpe, to wait by the phones once more. As the hours passed, his optimism waned. He checked and rechecked the layout of the operation. It seemed airtight.

Throughout the weekend Wolff kept faithful vigil near his phones, but when by Sunday night he had still not heard from East Berlin, his instinct told him that something had gone very wrong indeed. . . .

By that time Gaby Schott's integration into the "family" of Angelo Rossi was complete; her cooperation—albeit in ignorance of the eventual consequences—was assured.

And by Sunday evening, the first victim of the family's collision course with Equinox already lay cold and white on a marble slab in the Cologne police morgue.

4

Chief Inspector Gunter Stark of the Antiterrorist office in Cologne showed his pass to the unblinking eye of the TV camera. The gate to the morgue entrance of the huge police headquarters in Cologne slid open. Stark slipped past and took the elevator down to the basement.

It stopped with a knee-jarring bang, and Stark walked along the long corridor of institutional linoleum and sweating wall tiles. He stopped outside the door of what was colloquially known as the "butcher shop," took a deep breath of relatively normal air, and stepped inside.

They had laid out the old man on the marble table under the saws and drills and suction hoses. With the glaring sodium lights, the green gowns of the two doctors, and the matching green washable walls and floor, the room had an unreal, subaqueous feeling.

"Hail the chief," said Peter Mullen. He was the homicide coroner assigned to Cologne HQ.

"Hello, doc." Chief Inspector Stark nodded at Mullen and then shifted his gaze to include the night-duty assistant examiner. Doc Mullen was nearing sixty and had seen everything a hundred times. His assistant was a young man with glasses and very large hands.

At the moment those hands worked the cranium saw—a short-gripped, diamond-studded disk like an electric engraving bezel. It hummed at high speed, drawing a pink, bloodless line around the top of the corpse's head. The sharp smell of burning bone reached Stark's nose. They waited for the pink circle to close.

Above them, the building was busy; Sunday often brought a bumper crop of crime. Eventually Doc Mullen snapped on his latex gloves and said something about the unseasonable warmth. Stark nodded distractedly. His shirt stuck coldly to his back. He felt tired, but that feeling was at the very back of his consciousness. In the foreground were hard impatience, suspense, and just enough uncertainty to keep him from being hasty.

When the young assistant examiner applied the suction cup to pull off the battered cranial dome, Stark closed his eyes for the duration of a heartbeat. He opened them again when Mullen whistled through his teeth.

The coroner pulled down the microphone and kicked the recorder switch at the base of the table. He began to dictate. "Section of cranial dome reveals both hemispheres with massive damage. Bone splinters are embedded in the cortex. The centrum area shows contusions with absence of substantial clotting. The corpus callosum and the occipital lobe show evidence. . . ." Mullen continued describing the damage to the old man's head—damage without blood flow, meaning after death. When they were done, the young assistant reattached the cranial dome and skin with a handyman's stapling gun.

"You've sent his clothes and finger scrapings to Forensics?" asked Stark.

"Yes," said the coroner. He was selecting a narrow two-pronged bullet probe from a rack. "A thin jacket, drill pants, and work boots. He was shot point blank. Overall the same pattern as in the Amsterdam killing. Which is why I called you."

"I know. Thank you. It's all we need, doc—just weeks away from the summit." Stark looked at the tiny entry hole in the old man's chest. It looked like no more than a mole among the grizzled chest hair and the expanse of white skin. The arms were deeply tanned to the elbows, the hands big and calloused with broken fingernails. While the coroner guided the probe along the bullet path, Stark with difficulty uncurled the body's right hand and studied the palm. The skin was cracked and thick from years of manual work. A laborer somewhere; rolled-up shirt sleeves in the summer. What sort of tool? Shovel, ax, trowel? The old man's hand had a pale diagonal scrape that ran from the second joint of the forefinger all the way to the fleshy part of the heel. Stark walked around the table and looked at the left hand. It bore exactly the same mark.

They had trouble finding the bullet. Stark saw the coroner tracing a square on the chest, and then the assistant went to work with a two-handed rotary saw. They cut through the sternum and across, like a window.

Then the dictation continued: "Powder burns around the bullet entry through fourth rib. Excessive mushrooming through left lung lobe, and complete rupturing of lower right heart chamber. Bullet flattened and lodged . . ." Doc Mullen probed among the clotted, bruised organs. "Lodged against the spinal column some ten centimeters below entry point." He stopped the recorder, wiped the small object, and held it out for Stark to take. "This is what killed him."

The slug looked just like the one from Amsterdam: a soft-nosed .22 that had spread out crosswise almost to the size of a one-mark coin.

"Mahmoud?" asked the coroner, and then in the same breath: "I wonder, does he use this method only on Christians? How about Moslems or Buddhists?"

"Good question." Stark grimaced at the doctor. Then he dropped the bullet in his pocket and glanced at the face of the dead old man for the last time. A strong nose, square chin, stubble—a blue-collar worker? Why him?

Before leaving, Stark said, "Thanks for calling, Peter. If you're satisfied you can release him to the city morgue."

"Will do, chief. Good luck." The coroner pulled off his latex gloves and dropped them in a bucket. He turned to the sink.

The assistant had replaced the square of chest, but he had run out of staples. He was popping a new charge into the gun when Stark left the cutting room.

Cologne police HQ, known simply as "Blaubach," was a self-contained universe, much like the general hospitals of big cities or the huge aircraft carriers of World War Two. And like those, work at Blaubach went on during three shifts around the clock; the building was never silent, and people could work here for years and still have to ask their way around when something out of the ordinary led them off their trodden path.

As a younger, more romantic cop, Gunter Stark had often mused about the battleship analogy; to this very day, Blaubach represented for him the essence of law enforcement, the collective will of society to defend itself. As chief inspector for antiterrorism he had both great responsibility and great power. He was aware of the first and used the latter to the hilt.

On the third floor in Ballistics, a technician was preparing matching slugs for the microscope. Nodding "Hello," Stark pointed at the long water tank that dominated the room. "I want to try something. I'll need your tank and a .22 with a couple of shells."

While the technician went into the safe room, Stark took the slug from his pocket and laid it on the work bench. On his key ring he carried a small penknife, and he opened it now and tested the blade. It would do. From the safe room the technician called, "A revolver or an automatic?"

"Either is okay. And soft-nosed shells."

A minute later he sat at the vise under the bright lamp, carefully pressing the sharp edge of the blade into the lead nose, cutting the slug down to one-third of its length, but not opening the cut. Then he turned the shell in the vise and repeated the cut at a right angle to the other one. He removed the shell and squeezed the bullet gently with thumb and forefinger to make sure the cuts were well closed.

The technician handed him a Beretta, and Stark put the prepared round into the chamber and went to the tank. He inserted the muzzle into the port and fired. Discharging into the insulated water tank, the shot made very little noise.

The technician said, "I'll get it, chief." He rolled up his shirt sleeves and opened the lid of the tank.

"Got it!" Arm and hands dripping, the technician came over and placed the slug on the bench next to the other one.

It was a perfect cross. The speed of its travel through the evenly resistant mass of water had opened the knife cuts and spread the bullet until it resembled a Maltese cross—four arms of equal length. The one found in the old man's body looked similar, except that the uneven mass of bone and flesh had deformed and flattened the lead to a much greater extent.

He thanked the technician and went downstairs to the lobby. He showed his pass to the camera; the gate slid aside and Stark stepped into the sweltering evening.

Mobile Terminal—High-Speed AT-1, as his service Porsche was officially called, was a souped-up version of the regular 911 police Porsche. In addition to its top speed of 270 kilometers per hour, the car also offered state-of-the-art communication. There was a video slot with readout, and the VHF radio could be patched into the regular grid as well as the five other special channels available through the HQ operator. But most importantly, the system could be linked with the main police computer at the federal criminal office in Wiesbaden, known as *Bundeskriminal* among cops and crooks all over Europe.

The idea was to put Stark in touch with the federal and international antiterrorist world at the touch of a button; when the electronics in his car were not fired up, then any incoming message was rerouted to his belt unit, telling him to call HQ OP.

The evening breeze had mellowed the day's heat, and now the streets of the old town were packed with cars and pedestrians. The rest of Cologne might be quiet, but here the Sunday crowd partied: young, middle-aged, some elderly—but mostly young, from teenage to mid-twenties. Misha might be here with some friends, but then he remembered that she said she was going to a party in Muehlbach.

He double-parked on the Guerzenich and shouldered his way through the crowd in the street and outside the Jazzkeller. The sound of a saxophone came up the stone stairs. Around him kids laughed and shouted; they formed a circle with hands on shoulders and danced on the sidewalk, bumping cheerfully into people.

He pushed past a young woman with wild blond hair and she looked at him sideways and said, "Hello, my dear!"

He grinned at her in passing.

"Well wait, then," she laughed, but he waved over his shoulder and plunged on to the pub at the corner. High-ticket call girls cruised by on their night off in Mercedes and Alfa Romeo convertibles. Most of the cars on Sunday nights were expensive: BMWs, Lancias, Porsches, Jaguars, and the occasional Ferrari and Lamborghini. Common folk, those who worked for a living, did not go out on Sunday night. They might go to a movie, but they wouldn't go bar-hopping. That's what Friday nights were for. Seven o'clock on Monday morning came early.

Stark entered the pub, pushed his way to the counter, and held up two fingers. Karl saw him and promptly came down with a foaming mug of Koelsch and a Steinhaeger. He leaned close to establish a moment of privacy among the turmoil.

"Evening, Gunter."

"Cheers, Karl." They had gone to school together till grade eight. Then Karl had changed to a restaurant trade school and Stark had gone on to grade 13, then police academy. All good friendships were made early in life, Stark thought.

"How's Misha?"

Grinning, Stark said she was fine.

Karl gave him a clap on the shoulder, said, "See you," and went back to the tap.

Stark knew what those who knew about Misha thought. She was twenty-five, he was thirty-seven. Most people thought he was too old for Misha and too young for his job.

Around him, drink flowed and people were vibrantly alive and happy. Young people; tanned, healthy, dressed in designer casuals. Stark looked at a young woman with a gorgeous face and a wet-look T-shirt. She was in a bantering, laughing conversation with a single-minded Latin type. Looking halfway down the bar at her open face, lively eyes, and challenging smile, Stark thought that most of the folks in this part of town would probably get laid tonight.

He drained his glass and tossed back the chaser. When he caught Karl's eye he made a telephoning gesture with both hands, and Karl jerked his chin toward his office.

Stark made his way through the crowd and opened the door marked "private." He wanted more than the use of a phone, which would have been just as easy from the car; he wanted a moment of quiet to collect his thoughts.

Karl's private office was a masculine affair with leather club furniture, a fireplace, and a wildebeest head staring out from the wall. The double doors muffled the noise from the tap room to a background murmur.

Stark removed his suit jacket, sat down at the leather-topped desk, and pulled the phone towards him. At the apartment there was no answer, but then he hadn't really expected Misha to be home. Where was the party in Muehlbach supposed to be—at Guido's? Because he'd known he'd be busy, he had not listened too closely when she told him.

He put out beepers for Fritz and Georg, his two lieutenants. Then he placed a call for Superintendent Zander of Bundeskriminal in Wiesbaden.

Stark's area of responsibility covered all of the state of North Rhine Westphalia, the most populous and industrialized state in West Germany. Because Cologne was its biggest city, and because the autobahn offered such rapid access to the other parts of the state, the AT squad was based here. Stark liked Cologne, and he knew it well. He had grown up here, and as a young cop his first beat had been right here, in the old town.

Stark's immediate boss was Superintendent Zander, who in turn was answerable to the police commissioner in Bonn. The commissioner's name was Professor Dr. Voll, a disagreeable man with a politician's refined talent for covering his ass.

Waiting for the calls to come in, Stark leaned back for a moment and closed his eyes to recall . . . Mahmoud. And promptly the familiar dull, nagging pain returned to his stomach.

Stark told himself not to jump to conclusions. Scoring a .22 was a common way among professionals of giving the small projectile a deadly punch at close range. But the cruciform . . . a coincidence? Perhaps, perhaps not. At any rate, he could not take a chance. He would proceed on the likelihood that Mahmoud was operating in Cologne. With the recent splintering of the three dominant terrorist groups, there would be ample recruits to jump on his bandwagon.

Mahmoud . . . Stark saw the yellow eyes again and felt the incredible hatred and energy that had leapt from the man like radiation. Then the clear line of fire and Stark's shot; the big Walther slamming into his palm. Then the people screaming, the woman's white dress blooming red, a spreading bouquet of blood.

And Mahmoud gone in the confusion—his human shield discarded. Amsterdam, eight months ago, by the phone booth on Buitengracht where the trap had been set. Stark, whose help the Dutch police had accepted on recommendation of Interpol, returned to Cologne to face suspension. The subsequent top level inquiry unfortunately brought him to the police commissioner's attention:

"Chief inspector, why did you discharge your weapon when the target was not clear? Identified but not in a clear line of fire?" asked Professor Dr. Voll, a man who'd probably never seen a handgun up close, let alone fired one.

"But he was, sir. The target was clear."

"He was? What is your pistol rating, chief inspector?"

"Ninety-two, sir. Mahmoud is a . . . I don't think anyone realizes the man's strength and agility." Stark had looked to Zander at the end of the table for help. But his boss had not responded. It was up to Stark to clear his name.

"Your shot struck the woman in the center of her chest. How long does it take to raise a grown person—she weighed sixty-one kilos—how long does it take to raise such a considerable weight . . . how high? You were aiming at which portion of your target's body?"

"The head, sir. Always in these cases. It took him less time than it took me to squeeze the trigger."

"Right ... Chief inspector, the use of your personal weapon is strictly regulated." The police commissioner stared at Stark, then let his self-satisfied gaze wander briefly among the faces of the panel. He stabbed a finger at Stark and asked cynically, "Any reason, chief inspector, why you have not offered your resignation? If nothing else, your guilt feelings at this woman's death must weigh heavily on your conscience."

Stark turned his face sufficiently to see Superintendent Zander from the corner of his eye. And this time his boss broke the unwritten code and shook his head ever so slightly.

Stark took a deep breath and said, "Sir, if at the end of this investigation the panel finds me guilty of the charge of gross negligence, *then* I shall offer my resignation."

The hearing took three days. Stark's mental and physical health were examined. To gain a better understanding of his character, the panel looked at his service record, where they found only above-average performance and results. Remarkably enough, there was no hint of corruption, no abuse of police power, no conflict of interest.

Stark had come to the antiterrorism service following years of duty in uniform and plainclothes. His training included strike force action with GSG-9, the crack border guard unit, and apart from the debacle in Amsterdam his success with AT Cologne was undisputed.

In the end, the police commissioner gave the findings an ironic twist and asked the attending police psychiatrist, "Could it be that the chief inspector's outstanding results are rooted in some kind of identification with the criminal mind? He would have made a formidable terrorist himself, would he not? Does he like police work so much because it gives him an opportunity to exorcise some kind of . . . ah, well. You know what I mean."

Stark could not believe his ears, and it was then that Zander spoke up for him in a way that would earn him Stark's undying loyalty.

"With all due respect, sir," his boss said, "I don't think

we do know what you mean. Surely in your capacity as the head of the police force in this country you are not suggesting that every good law-enforcement officer is a criminal at heart?"

The police commissioner realized he had gone too far in justifying his job and enlarging its moral responsibilities. Stark could have sworn he saw him blush. The panel withdrew to deliberate, and Stark was cleared of all charges.

Back in harness, Stark made inquiries about the girl in the white dress. She'd been twenty-five, an exchange student from Wellington, New Zealand. She'd just come out of a bakery with a fellow student when Mahmoud grabbed her, twisted back her arms, and dragged her along, holding her up like a medieval shield.

The Dutch police rejected Stark's letter of condolence and apology to her parents. Red tape and politics. His guilt remained, but it lessened gradually.

Eventually Stark's psychic balance rebounded, and soon he was back hunting terrorists. His most recent cases were the Prendergast kidnapping, in which his team caught two of the remaining Baader-Meinhof members, and just two months ago, there was the shoot-out near Duesseldorf. That night the Action Group July was blown away by their own bombs—four men and two women specializing in American airline offices.

Stark pushed himself away from Karl's desk and got up. The wildebeest stared at him. In the light of the green-shaded desk lamp its eyes had an eerie cast.

The phone rang twice in quick succession. The first call was Fritz checking in from a noisy party, the other was Georg calling from a nightclub. Stark told them to meet him at police HQ as soon as possible. Both said they'd be there by ten.

It was now 9:45 P.M. Stark changed the call-back message for Zander to his mobile number. He grabbed his jacket and shouldered his way through the cheerful, randy crowd. At the bar he bought a frankfurter and a bun and ate them while walking. There was a ticket under his wiper—a democratically obligatory ticket because all the cars double-parked along the Guerzenich had been caught. His ticket, however, was not signed, meaning that the parking officer had recognized the AT mobile. Stark put the slip of paper in his pocket and drove off, carefully nosing around some kids who were dancing in the street.

Superintendent Zander's call reached him just at the exit to Langgasse. Stark pulled over to report his findings and put them in perspective.

With typical decisiveness Zander gave him top-priority clearance. He said, "I won't alert the regular police forces until you've got proof. No point crying wolf until we're sure." Behind Zander's voice, Stark could hear subdued conversation and the clinking of china and cutlery, the sounds of a restaurant.

"There's this economic summit in October."

"Let's be sure first. The regular security people are jumpy enough as it is. By the way, Esser will be calling you to set up a briefing with the Americans and the British."

Stark said this was all right with him. "On Mahmoud— for now I'll get along with just Fritz and Georg. But if I'm right we'll need a lot more personnel in a hurry."

"Of course. Now, Gunter . . . I don't have to tell you that there's this little black mark on your record now. So, Mahmoud or anybody else . . . this is just police work, right?"

Stark took his time responding, so that Zander felt the need to add, "Forget Amsterdam. You make a mistake and the commissioner will be delighted to nail you to his political cross. But I don't have to tell you that."

"I'm more concerned with stopping Mahmoud. I'm not really all that concerned with covering my ass."

"I know that. Which is why you're still chief of Cologne AT," said Zander factually. "Anyway, let's hope your hunch is wrong."

Stark disconnected, pushed away the gooseneck mike,

and switched back to the federal police hopper channel. Then he sped on, and minutes later he roared down the ramp at HQ to his parking stall. It was nearly ten o'clock.

They sat around the desk in Stark's office at Cologne HQ. Their ties were down, their shirt sleeves rolled up. Through the open window laughter and voices came up faintly from the sidewalk.

Fritz still had lipstick on his ear, and Georg pointed it out with glee.

Fritz produced a handkerchief.

"Facts," said Stark. "A murder done in Mahmoud's style." He filled them in on the autopsy findings. The old man's body had been discovered this morning by a jogger in a small park in North Cologne. No blood on the ground, no signs of struggle.

Georg said, "Obviously he was killed somewhere else and taken there."

"Why bother?" asked Stark rhetorically.

"Why hide the identity of a laborer?" added Fritz.

Stark, Georg, and Fritz made up the nucleus of Cologne AT—three men who, on Zander's authority, were empowered to mobilize an army of assistants and truckloads of electronic gear and weapons. AT could override all other jurisdictions and had done so in the past.

Fritz asked, "Why would they crack someone's head after they shot him in the heart with a spread .22? With a ruptured ventricle he was dead before he hit the ground."

Stark said, "Too quick a death. So they killed twice. For kicks, out of anger. To show off."

Georg agreed.

Stark, who had set up the Antiterrorism office in Cologne several years ago, had hand-picked Fritz and Georg as his personal seconds. Before joining the nucleus of AT Cologne, Fritz had been with the Vice squad. He was straw-blond with sharp features, and Stark had chosen him for his uncanny ability to reduce lists of *possibles* to two or three *probables*. Late-generation computers were a help here, but in the end it still boiled down to an excellent memory for detail, doggedness, legwork, and good hunches born of experience.

Georg looked just the opposite. He was tall and dark-haired, with a languid grace that hid the explosive energy that Stark had witnessed on dozens of occasions. Before joining Stark and Fritz, Georg had been a lieutenant with GSG-9, the federal paramilitary strike force.

Now Stark dug in his pocket for the mushroomed slugs. He said, "I'm aware that this could be just a fluke, but can we ignore it?"

The lieutenants leaned closer to look at the deadly lumps of lead on the table top.

Fritz said, "I see what you mean about Amsterdam."

Stark nodded. "But it *could* just be a coincidence."

Georg, who knew a lot about handguns, said, "It's an execution style. Probably one or two people were holding back the old man's arms. A third person shot him in the heart. A regular bullet would pass clean through the body and hit the guy behind. But a spread slug just tears the hell out of the organs, then stops."

On the floor above theirs, someone screamed. Then a woman yelled, "You dirty goddamn little pig. I wanna see my lawyer. I know my rights, you little fucker!"

"Is it still Vice that's up there?" Georg asked, and Fritz nodded.

There were some undefinable noises, then the woman yelled, "You touch me and I'll bite you again, you fucker! See those chompers?"

Stark said, "Let's begin by following the Amsterdam pattern—check out cars and rental accommodation. Let's also get in touch with Interpol and the Israelis. Mossad may have some unofficial things to add here."

On the wall the clock said 10:15 P.M. Some days in AT had sixty-two hours and more. Misha would still be at her party, maybe she'd be there all night. Misha . . . Stark wondered how much longer it could last.

Fritz and Georg grabbed their jackets and went out the door. Stark followed them to the elevator. The interdepartmental mail buggy came beeping down its electronic track. They stopped to see if it would turn into their AT department. But it beeped right past the door.

"No mail," said Fritz.

Georg grinned. "She had your ear tonight. She doesn't need to write to you."

Stark looked at his lieutenants, thinking that these two were his best friends, his closest and most reliable companions. There were one or two old school buddies like Karl, but they were history, whereas his lieutenants were the present. Stark, Fritz, and Georg had saved each other's lives several times.

In the elevator Stark saw the back of Georg's neck before him. He saw the patch of the skin graft that was a memento of the shoot-out in Weidenpesch two years ago when Stark had been trapped in a burning car and Georg had pulled him out.

They rode the elevator to the basement in silence, and Stark thought that for years now there had been little else but police work in his life.

He had been married once, briefly, soon after he was made a detective. The marriage had lasted only six months, only because a truck driver slammed across the median and caught Susanne's Fiat 650. The car and contents were so badly mangled that positive identification could be made only through Forensics.

She had been pretty and vivacious with an infectious laugh. It had taken a long time to get over her death, and in some ways he never really had.

In the basement, they walked through several security barriers to the computer room. Using priority code, Stark requested and received top-level access to the big computer in Wiesbaden 200 kilometers away.

"Mahmoud," Stark told the operator. "Also known as Ben Ahram, Pierre Benoit, Italo Gazzarra."

The operator nodded and his fingers danced over the keyboard.

The monitor came to life, not with a photo, but with a

colored identikit picture. After Amsterdam Stark had helped assemble it. The likeness was good: the slim dark face, the burning eyes, the thin mouth—lips pressed together. Dark hair, well cut.

"Go on," said Stark.

A printed bio rolled up. It had great gaps; gaps spanning some crucial years.

"Born 1949 in the small Lebanese village of Bir Bakeim. Village school education. Moved to Beirut . . . there was an aerial shot of a suburban house. *Father killed in sectarian violence.* Then the familiar story of resettlement after resettlement . . . *life in a string of refugee camps, ending up in Sabra. Mahmoud joins PLO militia, is trained by Russian experts in guerrilla warfare.* One of his sisters marries, moves to Alexandria. His mother and second sister die, it is not clear how . . . perhaps Israeli jets, perhaps Christian commandos. (This information courtesy of Mossad.)

By then Mahmoud has long left home. He is in Europe; a talent with languages helps him get along in French, Italian, German. International terrorism is like a cancer: cells break off and reform. Mahmoud is one of the main nuclei in Europe; he attracts members of the Red Brigades, the Baader Meinhof, the Commando Group Freedom. He lives well—his skill is delegation. Interpol and Mossad credit him with seventeen direct murders (usually by a machine pistol—he favors the German MP-5) and with twenty-five delegated murders (not counting innocent bystanders such as those at the Marseilles marina).

He likes Italian clothes, and he is a master of disguise. Preferred cars: big, fast Mercedes and BMWs.

Last action: Amsterdam, Holland: May 1985. Escaped with two million Dutch guilders ransom.

The screen went blank, then the words INPUT—UPDATE appeared.

The operator looked questioningly at Stark, who shook his head and said, "Not yet."

They signed out of the computer room and went back up to Stark's office. Over the next hour a battle plan evolved. It was based on what little they had to go on, and on their combined experience in antiterrorism.

Georg would handle baby carriages and stolen Mercedes and BMW sedans. Fritz would run a check on apartments that had been rented, then left empty for a protracted period of time.

Stark would look after the public distribution of the old man's picture and contact Interpol and Mossad about updating Mahmoud's file. In parting he said, "Remember, we're going out on a limb. All we have so far is an odd-shaped bullet and a good hunch. But we certainly can't ignore them. So . . . let's take a good run at it, and by tomorrow morning we should know a good deal more."

5

Gaby (or "Marion Bern," as her new driver's license and residence form declared) had already traveled far down the road of no return. It was shortly before midnight, and during these last few minutes of the Sunday of the killing she experienced for the first time what it meant to have done something that was both unspeakable and irreversible.

It was like a step away from herself, into a void. From now on she was in alien territory. She put her forehead on her arm and went back to sobbing.

Across from her, Rossi watched. He had seen this reaction many times before, and the noisy wet spectacle of first remorse no longer moved him. The next step, renewed obedience, was far more interesting.

From his corner Theo let fly a loud curse, then yelled, "Shut up!"

Rossi pointed a finger at Theo and warned him with his eyes.

Theo stared back, but his inner strength was far weaker than Rossi's. He looked away, then leaned his head against the wall and closed his eyes.

Marion raised her tear-stained face. Across the room, ignoring the others, she whispered, *"Caro."*

Rossi corrected her. "Rossi. *Mi chiamo Rossi!"* He smiled at her encouragingly. "Stop crying now, Marion. *Make* yourself stop, and it will pass. We all went through this. The first time——"

"But I didn't want to. I thought the gun was empty—I don't know *what* I thought. And you also squeezed my hand too hard."

"I'm sorry about that."

Theo cackled. "Fuck, man, I can't believe this!"

Ignoring the long-haired German, Marion pleaded, "Rossi, can I please leave? It's not too late . . . I won't breathe a word to anybody. Please?"

Rossi said, "Of course not. We talked about this, remember?"

"But why not? I promise I won't—"

"No, Marion. Too late for that."

Marion went back to her sobbing.

Now, with Marion among them, the family which Rossi had painstakingly assembled for the Helm squeeze consisted of five: there was Banigan from Ireland via England, Madeleine from Paris, Theo the cell resident in Cologne, and Rossi himself, from Milan. Mahmoud was expected later tonight.

The apartment was a one-bedroom affair on Kassemattstrasse in Cologne. The ceiling lights were on and the drapes were drawn in both rooms. (The drapes had to be opened and closed each morning and evening by the same female; those were Mahmoud's orders.)

The bathroom had the usual fixtures; so did the small kitchen, and both living room and bedroom had a night-current heating unit. The units were on despite the warm weather because they could be controlled only from a panel in the utility room. The five occupants were uncomfortably hot.

Except for the fixtures and a shaggy, spotted broadloom, there was not one stick of furniture in the apartment. They all sat on the floor against the wall, Marion hugging her knees, her face pressed into the crook of her elbow.

Eventually Banigan said, "Why can't we open the fuckin' window? Or why can't one of us go and ask the fuckin' super to turn off the juice?"

"Should've earlier," said Rossi. "You wake the super at midnight and he thinks, where have they been the past few days?"

Banigan agreed. Rossi was the advance man for this operation, and until Mahmoud's arrival he was in charge.

Theo said, "Tenants often go away for a weekend and return late on a Sunday."

"Maybe so, but you wake a man from his sleep to do you a favor and he's bound to resent you and remember you."

"The cunt shouldn't have lost the key." He meant Marion.

"Shut up, Theo," Rossi said wearily. "The heat'll break in a day or two. This is the third week of September." He half-raised himself on his fists, sidled along the wall to Marion and sat down next to her.

Theo muttered, "Goddamn kid's gonna drag us down, man." He got up abruptly and went into the bathroom. They heard him urinate loudly into the toilet bowl.

Madeleine, who'd been curled up, apparently sleeping until now, rolled over and got to her feet in a single fluid movement. She shut the bathroom door on Theo and went on into the kitchen. Moments later she was back, striding fluidly in Capezios, carrying five cold cans of Diet Coke. She put one on the floor where Theo had sat, threw one to Banigan who caught it deftly, then crossed the small room and sat down on Marion's other side.

She passed Rossi a can and held another one against Marion's clasped fingers. Feeling the cold, the girl sat up and accepted the drink. Theo returned, picked up his Coke, and went into the other room. They heard him stretch out on the floor, still muttering.

Speaking German with a French accent, Madeleine said,

"Ignore him, everybody. It's the usual thing with local cell contacts when out-of-towners take over."

Madeleine was dark-haired and slim with very fine pale skin. Her eyes were so dark they could in a certain light appear sightless. Her specialty was department stores and airline departure lounges; because of her elegance and refinement she could carry a Gucci handbag full of explosive and no one would think of searching her. Her other strength was a certain compassion and warmth; she was good glue for any strike team.

Gaby, or lately, Marion, had liked her since the first day she met her. She recognized in Madeleine the worldly cool arrogance mixed with the Parisian flair she had always admired in films and magazines.

Compared to the Frenchwoman, Marion felt childlike and immature. But she knew she was pretty: she had good skin and bone structure; her eyes were blue, her hands delicate, and her blond hair still smelled of Wella egg yolk shampoo from the time she'd washed it at her father's apartment while he was at the office. At the Green Party office with Uncle Helm.

Marion . . . sipping the Coke, she decided to concentrate on the positive side of things. The new name was a good thing, and so was the fact that she still had Rossi. He was making love to her several times each night—it was obvious that his desire and tenderness were no put-on. He'd said this whole thing would be a powerful experience for her, something for the better—a rite of passage that would snap her out of her bourgeois existence.

But the old man had looked so *shocked*. By the time she had understood what had happened it had been all over for him. And Rossi's hand had released hers, which in turn had dropped the gun . . . it fell slowly as in a dream, and Theo and Banigan had still held the old man's arms behind his back. Then Theo had picked up the rock. . . .

Her hands were damp and she wiped them on the thighs of her jeans. They were Sassoon designer jeans, tight and soft from many washes. On top she wore a white blouse that was getting grimier every day, and on her feet she had Adidas tennis shoes. What else was there to take stock of?

The old man's outraged face came back, his disbelief. Sipping the Coke, she again smelled the gunpowder on her hand. They clung to her—black grains like pepper still embedded in the skin. Soap and water had not been able to remove them, no matter how hard she'd rubbed.

Rossi caught her look and asked, "It's not hurting, is it?"

Marion shook her head, aware of the bobbing ponytail.

"The first time is always like this; you'll get used to it." Rossi added, "That's why I don't like revolvers. The gap between the drum and the frame always lets out gas. It marks your hand and wastes powder energy." He held up his own hand, the one that had forced hers, and showed her similar powder marks. Wide-eyed, she looked from his hand to his face.

Rossi asked, "Do you want to talk about it?"

She shook her head.

From the other side, Madeleine touched her knee and said, "It's all quite normal. You did well. Now forget it."

"Right," said Banigan. "And we needed that barge. Trick is to think of them as obstacles, not people. By now they'll have long found him, and because he's so far from home they won't know who the fuck he is or what hit him." He crushed his Coke can and said, "Why can't we open the window just a crack, man?"

"Rules," said Rossi. "A dozen tried and proven reasons I won't bother you with." He grinned coldly, showing his brilliant Italian teeth. His eyes, which could be liquid and soft with women, could at times such as now be hard and staring. The cartilage curl of his left ear had been sliced off by a bomb fragment at the Milan bus terminal in 1983. Rossi too wore expensive clothes—a cream-colored cotton shirt, tailored Paolo Vita slacks, silk socks, and hand-tooled Gucci loafers.

"Rules," gasped Banigan, not really objecting. In terms of clothes and all-round style, he and Theo looked like people dressed for a different party: ordinary scuffed jeans, T-shirts, running shoes. He was sweat-soaked and shiny-faced while

Rossi and Madeleine looked as though they'd just stepped out of an air-conditioned Maserati.

Suddenly Theo appeared in the door, finger to his lips, eyes alert. And then they heard it too, the eerie squeal of a German police siren. It had the rapid, slapping pulse that kept beat with the blue dome lights.

Rossi was already across the room and at the window, peering through the gap between drapes and wall without touching the material. Madeleine snapped off the light and bent down to unzip the traveling bag and take out her Beretta.

Marion sat, frozen.

Rossi watched the police skid the wrong way around the traffic circle and accelerate into Kassemattstrasse. The blue flashers painted the buildings with a speeding brush, then the search light behind the windshield came on, a brilliant beam casting for the house numbers. Right below them, the cruiser seemed to slow, then it spun around in a U-turn and stopped across the street. The siren was shut off.

Rossi forced himself to remain calm, but his mind raced, searching for possibilities.

Then there was a new siren, but a different sound, and an ambulance hurtled up from the underpass at the other end of the street. It pulled up behind the police cruiser.

The cops left their car, one of them casually hoisting up his pants, and then the ambulance attendants climbed out of the van and pulled a stretcher from the rear.

Rossi did not relax. He had seen tricks like these before, had even survived one of them.

There were three ambulance attendants and two police-men—Rossi kept counting them lest one of them slip away. But it all seemed genuine. The three medics entered the building. A couple of minutes later the party was back out-side; what looked like an old person with white hair lay on the stretcher. Then engines kicked into life. The cruiser led the way across the bridge, then they were gone and the night was quiet as before.

Rossi looked into the dark room and grinned at the anxious faces. "It's cool. Someone with a heart attack or something."

Madeleine put the gun back into her bag and flipped on the lights.

Rossi ordered, "Theo, you and Marion go down and check out the street and the building. Elevator, stairs, lobby."

Marion asked timidly, "Is that necessary?"

"Move it, sweetie," Rossi said unsmiling to her. "Let's make sure that none of those cops doubled back on us. First rule in this business is to make doubly sure of everything. You're not afraid, are you?"

It was a clear challenge and Marion felt herself blush. She was afraid—not so much of what was out there, but of getting more and more involved in this situation. In addition she had an intense dislike for Theo. The others were ruthless, but Theo was cruel and vicious, and he made no attempt to hide his hostility towards her.

Theo said, "Move it, kid. You and I are the midnight patrol."

She put down the Coke can and reached for her purse. But her hand was stopped by Madeleine, who smiled and said softy, *"Eh, ma petite . . . secoue-toi . . .* try to live without fear for just two days. You will learn a new life and never look back, *chérie. Crois-moi."*

Madeleine's hand felt cool on her own hot skin, but the touch was like a current of sisterhood, a special kind of humanity charged with a goal. Despite the hard light from the naked bulb in the ceiling, Madeleine looked like a Romantic portrait: elegance, vulnerability and secret strength. Madeleine squeezed her hand, then let her go. Marion rose. At the door she bumped into Rossi, who glared at her. "You must learn more quickly, Marion. *Your purse!"* He spoke with clear, cold enunciation as though to impress the words on her mind and her instincts forever. The purse contained *her* gun.

She said, "Yes, *caro."*

"Rossi," he corrected her.

She slung the purse over her shoulder, but he grabbed it, unzipped it and took out the gun. It had a very short barrel without a sight and the hammer had been filed down to avoid snagging on clothes. Rossi unhinged the drum: except for the spent shell it was empty.

"Load it, Marion." Rossi nodded at her purse.

She sat down cross-legged and fumbled in six shells from the speedloader. They plopped out of the little blue plastic drum into the steel one, and their scratched noses looked dull and harmless.

Rossi, Banigan, and Madeleine stood watching her, and Marion thought that this was another rite of passage.

From the door, Theo said, "Come on, let's move it!"

Marion got up and followed him, slipping the revolver into her purse which she then clutched, open, under her left arm.

The building was dark and silent as they sneaked down the old open staircase. Loose tiles clacked underfoot and the cast-iron railing felt cold and sticky.

Nothing moved throughout the building. It was nearly two o'clock in the morning and this was a working class neighborhood.

They crept through the lobby and paused at the massive wooden door. The street was quiet except for a passing truck.

They stood in the shadows, watching. Theo kept his hand in the side pocket of a dirty denim jacket. After a minute or two of silent vigil he put his arm around her waist. They walked down one side, then crossed the street and doubled back. Theo's hand crawled up to her breast and she held still for the sake of security. Opposite their own building they waited for a couple of workers in coveralls to pass on their bicycles, then they crossed the street again.

At the entrance she endured Theo's kiss only because she thought, with her back to the street, it gave him a last opportunity for a look around. His mouth tasted of rotten teeth and she closed her lips. When he tried to push past with his tongue she raised her right knee firmly.

"Little bitch," he gasped, and she walked away, leaving it to him to catch up. He did, at the elevator, and he was cursing her all the way to the third floor where the car stopped.

"Fuck," said Theo, "didn't you push fourth?"

And then the door was open and they stood face to face with a man in coveralls, work boots, and cap. Only the face didn't fit—the eyes in it were the hardest, most penetrating eyes Marion had ever felt on her.

"Quick," said the man. He reached in and somehow pulled them out with one hand, grabbing Marion's purse with the other. Then they felt themselves propelled up the last flight of stairs, literally whipped up, barely touching the stairs. It was as though a tornado had picked them up to drop them again after a dazzling dance of power.

At the end of the hall a door opened and they saw Madeleine in the ceiling light. Bending their arms behind their back, the man in coveralls raced them on tiptoes to the door, then pushed them inside.

Madeleine looked up. She was smiling.

Rossi came forward to greet the man, and Theo leaned pale-faced against a wall, holding his elbow, muttering to himself.

The man flung off his cap, then knelt and turned Marion's purse upside-down. Out fell the gun and her pills and hairbrush and her wallet. He went through the wallet, opened the pill compact and studied the brush. Then he shoved it all towards her across the rug and stood up. Marion noticed that in several places long splinters of wood stuck to his coverall.

Madeleine said, "She's clean, Mahmoud." She pronounced the name in the guttural Arabic way, "Machmood."

Mahmoud slipped out of his coverall and removed his boots. He wore white linen slacks, shirt, and jacket. From the pockets of his coverall he fished a pair of loafers and two cloth-wrapped bundles which he tossed to Rossi. He said, "Put it together."

Marion felt that with Mahmoud in the room it was not so much as though a man had entered, but rather as though a timebomb had rolled in through the door. He was tall and powerfully built, and the pupils of his eyes were a strange shade of brown. They looked like dancing yellow flames. But

the most unsettling thing about him was the numbing sense
of psychic energy, a power that had more to do with purpose
and will than with things physical.

Theo and Banigan were watching Mahmoud closely, and
only Rossi and Madeleine appeared more or less unaffected
by his entrance.

Rossi had nearly finished assembling a small, mean-
looking submachine gun. He clapped in the stick magazine,
pulled back the slide, and clicked up the safety.

He shoved the gun aside and said, "It's all set up, Mahmoud. The barge is standing by with provisions and the
snatch is laid on for tomorrow. Two o'clock. In the morning
we'll get a kid and a bicycle. She did the barge operator."
Rossi nodded proudly at Marion. "No hitches. She's coming
along fine." Mahmoud turned his eyes on Marion. She felt his
gaze like a blow. "And the target's her uncle, right, and she's
been briefed on what'll happen and why the fat cat is a good
lever?"

Rossi said, "Yes, she understands. She hasn't been close
to him in years. She knows that we picked him because popular opinion of him is very high, and the government won't be
able to ignore our demands for his freedom."

Still eyeing Marion, the Arab said to Rossi, "Sure she's
okay? Is she properly committed? You say she did the sailor,
so that's something anyway. What about her uncle—did she
help set up the time and the stop? Is she committed there
too? That was the idea, right?"

Marion was soaked in sweat. She felt like a mouse under
the stare of a snake. But she pulled herself together, swallowed, and managed to say, "The route to the office is usually
the same. With minor variations. We decided that right on
Hahnenstrasse—" Her voice failed her then, and she raised
her hand to her throat and looked at Rossi for help.

"We took her on board for two reasons, right, Mahmoud:
if there *had* been any trouble with logistics she'd have been
invaluable—and if there's hitch down the road she still will be
a great asset with the old guy. And we also found a good new
recruit. She's okay."

Mahmoud sat down on the floor and leaned against the wall. Tugging at his trouser legs he said casually, "You sound eager, Rossi. You covering something here? You two got a thing by any chance? You know the rules, right? Screwing's all right during recruitment and for emotional——"

"You tell the wop," snarled Theo. "He's been fuckin' her day and night. And none of us can even get a sniff of her!"

Mahmoud rolled over and rose before Theo. Then his arms seemed to fly out in two directions at once. A second later Theo's nose bled fiercely, and he was bent double, retching and clutching his stomach.

Above him Mahmoud said, "I don't tolerate disrespect, man. You don't perform and I'll take you out. You're warned."

Theo groaned and crawled across the floor to the bathroom. They heard him vomit but no one paid attention. Mahmoud was going over the plans for tomorrow.

There were no changes.

Afterwards Mahmoud asked, with an attempt at lightness, "Why's it so damn hot in here?"

Marion spoke up. She explained about the landlord/tenant act that stipulated heat as of September 1. Then she added, blushing, "And I'm sorry, I've lost the key to the utility room."

Mahmoud stared at her. Then he said, "It's all right, Marion. We'll be out of here by sunrise."

Later in the bathroom Rossi murmured, "Come on, baby, you need relaxing. Let me be good to you . . ."

The place still reeked of Theo's bile, and Theo himself was asleep next to the toilet bowl, but somehow none of that mattered. Marion felt vibrantly alive; daring, strong, and triumphant.

Rossi had undressed her, peeled her out of the hot sticky clothes, and she had helped him out of his. They'd gotten the shower temperature just right, lukewarm to be cooling but not cold, and now the water was streaming down, soaking them, cleansing them not only of sweat but of everything that had gone before; *everything*, thought Marion.

She clung to Rossi, and he kissed her streaming breasts, sucked her nipples with wild abandon, and all the while water knocked and thundered on the helmet of her wet hair. . . .

She rode a wave of fabulous frivolity—clutching life, bursting with power and courage. Rossi had asked her to take a leap of faith, and she had leaped, had linked arms with the family, and the window ledge of boredom and frustration was already far beyond reach.

Around them the shower curtain slid off the rail and they trampled it into the tub. Her new lifestyle left no room for bourgeois pettiness. They were immortal and their future was filled with adventure, wealth, and many other possibilities.

"Baby," he was saying when her mind cleared, "you're wonderful. You turn me on like no one else, ever." They were huddling in the tub, the wreck of the curtain around them, the water still coming down.

Beside the toilet bowl, Theo stirred. He was getting soaking wet, and he sat up staring at Rossi and Marion, who were laughing at him like playful children.

At that point Madeleine came in, unsurprised by the view. She turned the water off and, clapping her hands, said, "All right: get out, get out. We've got to wipe this floor before the water soaks through to the ceiling below. We want no irregularities, remember? Then get some rest. Do you know what time it is? Fucking in the shower, really!" But she smiled at them proudly; the team mother.

In the morning they ate stale doughnuts Madeleine had bought days ago and they finished the rest of the Diet Coke. Theo was first to be dispatched by Mahmoud.

"A van, Theo. A panel truck, like a white Ford. That's the

most common. I want you to go downtown, anywhere along the Ring. At nine o'clock there'll be all kinds of delivery vans, doors open, engines running, the fellows hopping in and out with merchandise. Grab one and meet us at the barge."

Madeleine got the bicycle job. "A woman's bike with a child seat. Something respectable with foot rests and all that, so that we don't get stopped by the police."

They laughed about that: imagine the squeeze blowing up because the bicycle had no foot rests for the bambino.

Banigan was assigned the second car. He was told to get it at Mendelssohn's, the collision place where the Cologne cell did all their car business.

"Isn't that too risky? I mean why can't I just take one downtown—in this heat there'll be all kinds of open sun roofs and win—" The ice in the Arab's eyes froze out his words. He looked away. "All right, all right. Forget it, man."

But apparently the challenge could not be forgotten so easily. While a dead silence echoed in the room, Mahmoud kept staring at Banigan. Then he whispered, "Don't do that again. It's the wrecker, man, okay?"

Banigan got up, shoved a gun down the small of his back under the dangling shirttail, and left.

Then it was just the three of them: Mahmoud, Rossi, and Marion. With fresh certainty and pride she asked, "So it's the kid for us?"

"Yes. You know where to go?"

"The day-care center on Deutzerstrasse. Rossi told me."

Mahmoud nodded slowly, his yellow eyes fixed on her face.

Rossi was stashing the submachine gun into the Air France bag. He said, "Let's go, Marion."

She followed him out of the apartment, making sure to carry her purse the way they'd taught her: unzipped but clutched tightly under her left arm. It was strange, but the thought of the gun was becoming a source of courage rather than fear.

The day-care center on Deutzerstrasse was only a fifteen-minute walk from the flat. When they reached it, they stood and observed the parents and nannies dropping off the children.

At five to nine the perfect situation arose. A big BMW 733 pulled up, and a young mother in expensive clothes and sunglasses hopped out while leaving the engine idling.

Rossi and Marion separated, moving quickly.

When the mother opened the curbside rear door to reach for the baby, Rossi gave her a hard shove that toppled her onto the floor in front of the backseats. She let out a scream. Rossi stepped on her and sat on the seat next to the baby. He put his hand firmly on the mother's mouth. Her sunglasses fell off. By then Marion was already in the driver seat. "Go!" yelled Rossi, and she yanked the lever into Drive and stepped on the gas. The big car leaped forward, slamming the rear door. Just then the baby began to yell. He considered hitting it but restrained himself for fear of rendering it unusable for the squeeze. It was a blond chubby little thing, boy or girl it was hard to say, with a great screaming mouth of gums and two teeth, eyes tightly shut to yell all the more loudly, thought Rossi.

He cursed passionately. He shouted at Marion to pull into a side street a few blocks away so that they could ditch the mother. The mother bit his hand and he yelled, *"Porca madonna!"* and stepped hard on her throat. He half raised himself in the car seat to add his weight to the pressure. The mother's eyes bulged, then he heard and felt the cracking of her larynx and neck. A spasm twisted her, then she went limp.

Minutes later they tossed her out of the slowing car in a tumble of limbs and sped away.

Rossi saw Marion's eyes in the rearview mirror. He felt flustered and irritated, and he grit his teeth, did what he could to restrain himself from smashing the baby to make it shut up.

He had been all for using a doll (the children's department at Kaufhof sold lifelike dolls that were at least as big as this kid), but Mahmoud had insisted on the real thing.

So be it. Mahmoud was in charge. They were speeding

along the southern embankment road already. In less than half an hour they'd be at the barge.

The baby was running out of breath. It began to sputter and cough, and he thought exhaustedly, that's right, choke you little bastard. As long as you shut up.

6

Despite the heavy Monday morning traffic, it had taken Stark less than half an hour to drive from Cologne HQ to Bonn. It was for these kinds of driving conditions that Germans built their cars: high-speed intercity travel.

His Porsche, and the blue-light privilege, enabled him to reach any part of his turf within an hour. And his turf was easily the busiest piece of real estate in Europe. Beyond Cologne, it contained cities such as Duesseldorf, Essen, Dortmund, and Bonn. It contained much of the country's heavy industry, much of the country's wealth, and much of its crime.

Money . . . Stark had realized long ago that money was the motive for just about everything. And yet, surely because he was raised this way, he'd never thought of money as a goal. His mother had been a courtroom illustrator, his father a documentary producer for the state TV channel. Whatever money came into the house came irregularly, but there always seemed to be enough for everyone to go on enjoying their lives.

As Stark swept into the ministerial parking lot, he remembered his parents' surprise at his career choice. But his promotions had come quickly enough for them to realize that the work suited his temperament. They were still alive and healthy, and Stark went to see them at the old flat in Lindenthal as often as he could. Which, according to them, was not nearly often enough.

Stark entered the building and ran up the stairs, two at a time, to the office of Dr. Karl Esser, the interior minister. Esser waved Stark to some chairs around the tiled coffee table in the corner and returned to his phone call.

Two men were already waiting there. One of them was Jack Teagarden, an "attaché" at the U.S. embassy in Bonn.

"Hey, Gunter," said Teagarden in a subdued holler. "I didn't know you were coming to this meeting. Say, this is Colonel Browning. The colonel just flew in from London about this economic conference hoopla—Chief Inspector Gunter Stark, Colonel. Antiterrorism . . . right, Gunter?" Teagarden grinned, and they sat down.

"So," said Teagarden in English, as always, "keepin' your nose clean, Gunter? Anything going down lately? Tell me, I'm starved for some excitement. Any new hardware on the market?"

Stark thought that Teagarden was a big tease and often a bore, but Stark had seen him in action twice, and both times the American had been impressive. His true function was that of a senior field operative for the CIA.

Stark grinned. "And how's the spying business, Jack? Not worried about your president's safety, are you?"

"With guys like you in charge of AT, who wouldn't be?"

Colonel Browning leaned forward, his eyes darting between them. Stark thought he looked like a young Spencer Tracy, all pockmarks and character.

Stark jerked a thumb at Teagarden. "The Americans are always very antsy, colonel. Never understood why. Statistically, their president is much safer abroad than at home. Is the British prime minister coming?"

"Yes," said the colonel. Stark waited for an elaboration, but none came. The economic summit was scheduled for the middle of October, and no one looked forward to the confusion and the logistical headaches it would bring. The federal police had been working on nothing else for the past two months, and Stark knew that the Americans had already flown in twenty-five field operatives to familiarize them with local conditions. Soon there would be Canadian Mounties, and French, Italian, and Japanese security police. Not to mention the hordes of media people.

All we needed was Mahmoud on the loose, thought Stark. But then he pushed the thought aside, at least for the time being.

Esser wound up his conversation and joined them. He was a slim, elegant man with graying hair and a hunted, overworked look. He said, "I see you've met. Gentlemen, this meeting is meant to assure our British friends that—"

At that moment, the slim red phone on the coffee table rang. Esser picked it up immediately. He said, "Yes . . ." and from then on he merely listened. But while he did so his face seemed to crumple slowly from within. Stark had the eerie impression of a spirit escaping from a shell at the same measure at which bad news flowed in.

His eyes met Teagarden's, then the commander's. They waited.

Stark had hardly slept last night. While waiting for the Interpol update and the final forensic data on the Damwald corpse, he had stretched out on the couch in the office, but his mind had been too full.

And Misha apparently never came home from that party. He'd phoned the apartment a half dozen times without reaching her.

Misha . . . he saw her before his mind's eye, and just as he thought he was on the threshold of a very important insight regarding her and him, regarding his passionate desire for her, Esser said, "No, no, wait! I have to think. I'll call you back. Don't do *anything.*" And he hung up.

For a moment there was only silence. Teagarden opened his mouth to say something, but Esser merely held out his hand, silencing him. Then he snatched up the red phone and punched one digit. It was answered immediately and they heard him say, "Esser, here. I must see the chancellor immediately." He paused, nodding in acknowledgment of an unheard-of question. Crisply he said, *"Equinox . . .* priority one."

He hung up the phone and rose. "Thank you, gentlemen. I'm sorry. Something just came up." Instead of shaking hands he merely waved them out of his office.

Most of the way back to Cologne he topped 220 kilometers per hour, and for a few minutes the Porsche reached 250. The blue light pulsed, and ahead of him cars moved over in a hurry.

Turning into the northern bridge across the Rhine, the car nearly spun out, but then it behaved and held traction. Along the inner ring, he switched on the siren and reached Cologne HQ at 10:35.

"Georg," he shouted down the corridor, "Fritz! My office! Progress report."

They appeared, dragging sheaves of computer print-out.

Stark said, "Something big's up and I don't know what. Esser just kicked us out like that! What's *Equinox?*"

They looked at him as though he'd gone crazy. Georg said, "You know . . . March and Septem—"

"Oh, Christ, man! I know *that* much. Never mind. Anything tie in with Mahmoud? Come on, shoot!"

"Yes," said Fritz. "A kidnapping this morning. Complete with assault and theft of his kind of vehicle."

Stark slumped in his chair and said, "Go on. Details."

Fritz reported the incident at the Deutzerstrasse daycare center. The mother had been found several blocks away—dead.

"Shot?" asked Stark.

"No. Looks more like strangulation. And broken bones when she was thrown from the car. They're doing an autopsy now. This report just came over the Telex."

"Stealing a kid and killing the mother? That's not kidnapping, that's . . . could that be?" Stark looked from Fritz to Georg. "We're still guessing," he cautioned them. "There may be no connection at all with the dead old man."

Georg said, "But the baby trick . . . remember Mathias Franke? That was Baader Meinhof. They used a baby carriage without a baby. But why would you steal a kid and waste the mother?"

Stark said, "Because you don't intend to ransom the baby—you plan on just *using* it. Perhaps wasting it too."

They looked at him. Fritz said, "Should I go and question the day-care staff?"

"Yes, and keep in close touch. And you and I, Georg— let's take a look at the print-outs. Empty flats, cars?"

They went down the columns. In the past twenty-four hours thirty-nine vans and cars had been reported stolen in North Rhine Westphalia. Stark said to Georg, "I'll go into details on the cars, you do apartments." Since the debacle at Munich, landlords and caretakers had standing orders to report any suspicious movements and vacancies.

Stark phoned Zander in Wiesbaden and asked for manpower, young detectives with good legs and no reputations to worry about, he specified. Zander said, "Will do."

He moved on to check for panel trucks, beginning with Ford Econolines and VW side-loaders.

Georg dug deeper for details. At 12:55 they got their first break: a tenant on Kassemattstrasse had reported water damage on his ceiling; the super had checked the apartment above and found it boiling with heat, the bathroom more or less clean except for vomit under the rim of the toilet bowl. Apart from that there were stains on the rug in one of the rooms that might or might not be blood.

"Let's go," shouted Stark. In the garage they leapt into the Porsche, screamed up the ramp, and tore along Blaubach. Georg called Forensics from the car phone. On the roof the light flashed and the siren whined; the city was choked with noon traffic but German drivers respect nothing more than a speeding Porsche with a blue light on top.

Georg reached behind and took two Ingram machine pistols from the "war chest" under the jump seat. He chambered the first rounds and flicked on the safety.

They parked directly in front of the building, raced into

the entrance and up the stairs, the guns half-hidden along-
side their legs. As they rushed along the hall to the designated
apartment, doors opened and housewives stuck out their
heads only to withdraw them quickly, seeing trouble.

But the place was as empty as the caretaker had reported
it to be. The stale, hot air smelled horrible. Two rooms,
kitchen, bathroom. They walked around carefully, prepared
for surprises. In some of the abandoned safe houses booby
traps had been found. In Hamburg a police photographer's
flash had triggered one via a hidden slave pulse. The entire forensic team blew up, together with the motel room.

Stark leveled his Ingram at the bedroom closet while
Georg ran a magnetic-field detector along the cracks: nothing
obvious. Still, they decided to leave it to the experts from the
forensic field team. Minutes later a threesome with young
faces and alert eyes like computer whiz kids arrived. They
were known by their specialties: fingerprints and blood, explosives, and electronics.

They set to work, unprompted, frowning at the machine
pistols. Large metallic objects might cue a magnet.

Electronics said softly, "I hope these have been treated
and cleared, chief inspector."

"Manganese," grinned Stark. "What do you think this
is—play school?"

But he and Georg put the Ingrams into their trouser
bands. They were small enough for that—not much bigger
than a .45 automatic, but they fired 380 ammo at better than
a thousand rounds a minute.

The team collected vomit to test for stomach contents—
clues for what might have been eaten where and when. Blood
was scraped off one of the rugs and fingerprints were lifted off
every conceivable surface. In some of the corners the shag
was still depressed by individual footprints; taped to the underside of the sink they found a Russian automatic: a Ma-
karov with wooden grip and crude, unpolished steel edges.

Using the new chemical sniffer that had replaced dogs,
Explosives searched every inch but came up cold.

They augered a hole into the closet door and inserted an

angle scope with ring lights: the closet was empty except for a pile of empty Coke cans.

"Diet Coke," smirked Georg. "Weight-conscious like the rest of us."

The cans yielded a treasure of clean individual fingerprints.

Stark's belt unit buzzed. He pressed the button and listened to Fritz announce his location. He told him to meet them downstairs at the car.

When they got there, Fritz already sat on the fender going over his notes. He reported that a teacher at the daycare center had witnessed the car racing away. A blue BMW 733; the parents' file produced Berger, Ingrid and Jochen, on Ziegelstrasse. Registration had them as K-JW705.

"Who drove?"

"Woman driver, young, blond with a ponytail. Blue jeans. The male was a dark type, he jumped into the backseat with the baby and the mother."

"Italian? Arab? Turkish?"

Fritz made a face. "Dark hair, light-colored shirt. The baby . . . here." He handed Stark a snapshot taken in a sandbox.

Stark stared at it, then passed it back to Fritz.

"Transmission to all units, fast, man! Code . . . wait, I'll do it." He snatched back the picture, slid into the Porsche and put the key into the ignition. The computer terminal was fitted into and under the dash. He powered it and entered the federal red light code. When the clear beep sounded he pushed the picture into the video slot. Because the video was meant for driver's licenses and other printed ID, the image would only be read in high-contrast black and white—still, it was better than no picture at all.

Fritz said, "Female infant, Sascha, blond, nine months old; dressed in play clothes."

Stark nodded, then pressed the "send" button. He repeated Fritz's description and, praying silently, sent out the red alert, warning all units to beware of possible terrorist action involving the Baby Trick. They all knew what that meant.

When the transmission was over, he got out of the car, momentarily helpless. Stark was aware of Fritz's and Georg's searching looks. He said tonelessly, "I have the awful feeling that something's going down right now. And we're just standing here."

The three-man site team came out of the building, lugging their gear. They piled the aluminum cases into an innocuous Bedford van. Fingerprints looked at Stark and said, "Give us an hour. Then we'll know a lot more."

Stark nodded and checked his watch: it was now just two minutes to one—lunchtime for most of Cologne.

After the emergency session in the chancellor's wing broke up, Karl Esser returned to his office, feeling sick with dread. Why had the government allowed itself to be railroaded into this risky Equinox business? NATO obligations were one thing, CIA pressure was quite another. And why was it suddenly *his* project, his problem?

Were they monitoring his phones? Wolff might, illegally of course, and he would not put it past the chancellor either. At any rate this was not the time to worry about that—it was the *big* leak, the one threatened by Dietrich Helm, that needed plugging *before* it became big enough to sink them all.

He picked up the phone and from memory tapped out Wolff's number, not at the embassy in Bonn, but at the country house in Olpe. The reason he knew the Olpe number by heart was that the CIA safe house was a sore point with him, much as it had been a sore point with all German governments since the end of World War Two.

At the other end, the phone was snatched up after the second ring, and the clipped American voice said, "Wolff."

"Esser."

"Yes?"

With an effort he prevented his voice from shaking when he said, "Problems with Equinox. What you ridiculed as my "doomsday scenario" has happened. Your courier did *not* go to East Berlin."

"No? What? Go on!"

"Instead, Mr. Wolff, he chose to leak it to the Green Party. Do I need to tell you what that means?"

"God damn him! God damn . . . I can't believe it."

"I do. We had a call from Dietrich Helm's office. He's coming to Bonn to talk about a deal."

"He's alone? He hasn't told that Green's boss—what's his name?"

"They're kids. Helm would want to explore his options before telling them. It's still contained."

"Driving? Did you say he is *driving* from Cologne to Bonn? Let me think for a moment."

"Don't bother, Mr. Wolff. We don't want a single-car accident! This is our problem now, and I expect you to take a backseat. But we'll keep you informed."

"The time for preventive action is now, before the thing gets out. We could take care of it for——"

"No! Out of the question. We shall listen to his proposal. We prefer negotiation to your radical solutions."

Wolff remained silent. Esser thought that probably he had no intention of leaving Equinox in the hands of Bonn, but until he had more information, he had no options. Carefully Wolff said, "Look, don't rush this now. Whatever you tell Helm, don't give the whole thing away."

"I'll call you later on in the afternoon," snapped Esser.

"After the meeting?"

"As soon as feasible."

"You do agree that our interests must not be—"

Angrily, Esser hung up. The clock on his desk said 1:15. Helm was not expected until 3:30; enough time perhaps to summon up the moral superiority necessary for a showdown with a blackmailer.

*   *   *

At the Agency castle in Olpe, Wolff stared at the tele-phone. He could wait for Esser to keep him informed to whichever degree suited Bonn . . . or he could take the initia-tive himself.

He paced for a while and then decided to take the initia-tive. The Equinox file had to be retrieved right away, before that manipulative Dietrich Helm had a chance to explore the many ways in which he could use it for the good of his party.

What Wolff needed was a neutral party, someone close enough to Helm to persuade him to return the documents . . . and then the solution stared in his face: what he needed was *Paul Fontana*. The strong emotion of wartime loyalties. . . .

Wolff sketched out his storyline, then reached for the phone. Already he felt much better.

7

Dietrich Helm was not far from his sixty-fifth birthday. He was a professorial-looking man with a shock of white hair. He wore rimless bifocals and had a preference for English tailor-ing. Somehow English tailors managed best to hide the arm prosthesis, and so Dietrich Helm always had his shirts, sports jackets, and suits made by a little tailor shop on Foster Street, off Savile Row in London.

The irony here was that, forty-three years ago, it had also been an Englishman, the pilot of a Spitfire, who had shot up Helm's arm with bursts from his wing guns.

At the time of the injury Major Dietrich von Helm still believed in the Wehrmacht, even if he, like most aristocrats, had never trusted the political leadership.

Major Dietrich von Helm was a born and bred Berliner.

He came from an engineering family where everyone seemed to have a knack for inventing things: an uncle had invented the wire recorder, his father an electric shaver, and Dietrich, who had a prewar engineering degree himself, had invented his own mechanical left arm, a revolutionary thing with double articulation.

Until the day he needed it, he had ranked second only to the famous Sepp Spiess in kills.

In France he had piloted a Junkers Ju-87 equipped with sound tubes—the kind of plane aptly called *Sturzkampfflugzeug,* or Stuka. He was shot down above Lille but was able to parachute out of the spiraling plane to land safely in a vineyard. During the Battle of Britain he flew a Messerschmitt.

After that, they gave him the new Focke Wulf 190A-5 to try. The plane was well-armed but von Helm found it handled poorly because the engine, a BMW 801, had low torque. He received leave to visit the BMW factory in Munich, and after looking at the blueprints for a while he made some suggestions that caused the engineers to shrug doubtfully. But they went to work anyway and five days later the new prototype BMW 801-A was tried out on the bench. It roared to life and even in its raw unpolished state the engine delivered 17,000 horsepower.

Albert Speer, by then already armaments minister, sent him a congratulatory letter. Then Speer came to see Dietrich von Helm in person with the request to help develop a new tank, bigger than the Leopard.

Von Helm said, "Why not?"

But there were no tanks in Dietrich von Helm's crystal ball. Three days after Speer's offer, the Spitfire shot his arm to pieces and he was barely able to limp back to Belgium where he belly-landed the Focke Wulf in a cornfield. He had called her "Ingrid," after his first girl.

He crawled out of the smoking, sputtering plane and had hardly gone thirty meters when she blew up.

It was the end of his flying career.

In fairness to Speer, the offer about the Royal Tiger tank was repeated—but by then Helm was convalescing in the therapy ward at Antwerp and busy inventing his articulated arm. Also by then Helm had lost all interest in the war. He had come to realize that Nazi victory would be far worse than defeat by the Allies.

The hammer blows to his psyche had come hard and swift. During a night raid the previous week his parents, both his sisters, and Uncle Max (of wire-recorder fame) had died in the fire storm. This personal loss was further aggravated by the rumors of mass exterminations by the Waffen SS on the eastern front, and by eyewitness reports from the elaborate network of German concentration camps and death camps all over Europe. But the personal coup de grace was the news that Helm's hero and World War One flying ace, General Udet, had committed suicide in disgust at what was happening to his country.

And so Helm said no to Speer. This might have been the end for him, but somehow it wasn't. A month after his convalescence and the installation of the prototype nickel-and-wood arm, Helm was reassigned to Colonel Claus von Stauffenberg in North Africa.

They became friends almost overnight. Sensing Stauffenberg's sympathetic viewpoint Helm confided his true feelings about the political leadership. Over the following weeks he learned of the anti-Hitler network among high-ranking officers.

Soon thereafter Stauffenberg and he were at the head of a scout column when a Hurricane roared out of the sun.

Stauffenberg took two .303 bullets while von Helm got away without a scratch.

Then came Cologne and his incongruous appointment as home-form instructor of *Sonderkadetten klasse K-1*. It took a while for him to realize that this was not the end of his being able to serve Germany, but the beginning, if in a very different way.

When the great allied bomb went through the roof of U-boat pen 18 at Bremerhaven, Major Dietrich von Helm was only twenty-four years old, but he was already an ardent member of the anti-Hitler movement known as *Schwarze Ka-*

pelle (Black Orchestra). Inspired by such men as Admiral Canaris and Count Stauffenberg, Dietrich had sworn to do what he could to help end the war.

That unseasonably hot Monday in September 1985 Dietrich Helm ate lunch as usual at home. He and his wife lived in a large comfortable house in an old residential neighborhood of Cologne. There was ample room for the three bodyguards to eat in the kitchen while he and Henrietta could be undisturbed in the dining room.

The reason he usually took Monday lunches at home was that weekends were invariably so crowded with house guests or social and business commitments that he and Henrietta had hardly one minute to themselves.

Helm was well aware of Henrietta's growing unhappiness about their busy schedule (and about the armed guards), and he had been married too long not to calm storms before the clouds could build too high. On the other hand, his wife was also very proud of him and pleased with his fame.

The recent polls had been most encouraging, and it was likely that after the coming elections the Greens might get a taste of *real* power—a coalition with the minority party, be they the Socialists or the Christian Democrats.

With all this going for him, Helm should have been a happy man. He had success, even fame, and he had a relatively patient (at times doting) wife. He had raised two daughters, and now the large house often rang with children's laughter again.

The voice of experience and maturity in a party of mostly young people, Dietrich Helm had prestige and an almost clear conscience. He knew that he would feel better this time tomorrow.

Through the open passage to the kitchen, Helm noticed with a certain irritation that the new man carried his pistol in the holster even while eating. Helm could not see the others from where he was sitting, but the chauffeur and the other guard were older and hence not so gun-proud.

He was about to remark on it to his wife, but then the maid came in to serve the consommé and he kept his mouth shut.

The by-product of success was visibility, and the drawback of both was conspicuousness. And not just in modern Germany. Ever since the murder of Matthias Franke and the abduction of his friend Hagge in Holland, Helm no longer resented the lack of privacy which bodyguards brought with them.

When the maid put the dish of consommé before him, Helm inquired in a low voice, "What's the name of the new man, Mitzi?"

She froze and said self-consciously, "Detective Sommer, sir. Karsten . . ."

He nodded, dismissing her, and began to eat hastily. It was already past one o'clock. His meeting with the chancellor was set for 3:30, but before that he had to meet with Peter Schott at the party office. Perhaps he ought to have invited Schott over for lunch. It would have saved time.

Then he thought of the documents in the wall safe in his study, and the mixed feelings of shame and triumph returned.

On the one hand he felt like a blackmailer, on the other like a successful politician who had finally been able to grab an important lever of power. He wondered about this targeting file. It listed so many more cruise missiles than he'd been aware of. And yet, the file certainly *looked* genuine.

Moved by her uncanny sixth sense, Henrietta inquired, "You seem tense, dear . . . and last night you were pacing. I heard you."

"Perhaps too much coffee too late, Hennie," he said. They had entertained the British and Japanese trade commissioners and their wives at dinner.

"Hm," agreed Henrietta. "Perhaps that is it. By the way, Carl Stolz has been trying to reach you, dear. He phoned just before you arrived."

Guilt stabbed him. "Oh? I'm supposed to meet with him tomorrow. Was there a message?"

She shook her head.

Helm wiped his mouth and stole a glance at his watch. From the kitchen came his chauffeur's good-natured laughter and Mitzi's squeal.

Now Mitzi came in juggling a tray; flushed, bright-eyed, and blowing wisps of curly hair out of her eyes. "Madame," she said, then with a half curtsy, "Sir!"

It was quiche, and he struggled with a few mouthfuls but then pushed away his plate and said, "Would you be angry with me, dear, if I rushed off? I must speak to Peter before driving down to Bonn." He flicked his cuff to check the time.

"Bonn? I didn't know you were going to Bonn this afternoon, dear."

He realized his slip too late, and so, not looking at her, said vaguely, "Yes. This upcoming economic summit, you see." He bent behind her chair to brush her cheek with his. She felt cool and smelled as well-groomed as she looked.

"Don't forget the concert tonight, dear. Suzanne is meeting us at Eugene's at seven-thirty. The Drechslers will be there too."

"Oh, yes," he said on his way out of the room. The men in the kitchen had picked up the signal: he heard the scraping of their chairs.

Upstairs in his study he flicked open the safe and took out the folder. The West German government long ago gave up the astonishing American practice of stamping Top Secret all over sensitive documents because it only guaranteed attention. Here any good spy would know that a document marked Top Secret was likely a plant. No, this file did look genuine.

Helm made certain the print-outs and maps were complete, then put the slim manila envelope into his briefcase. Carrying the case downstairs, he imagined that its weight had suddenly grown disproportionately.

Henrietta was nowhere to be seen, but the men stood

waiting in the anteroom. The new man, Karsten, reached for the briefcase but Helm shook his head. They left the house side by side to walk to the car in the driveway. After the air-conditioned cool and the subdued light in the house, the sun and heat struck Helm as unpleasant. But winter would come soon enough, and a Cologne winter meant gloom and dark-ness, ice-cold winds, and driven snow. One had better remem-ber that and not complain about sun and heat.

Manfred held open the curb-side rear door for him. Helm placed the briefcase on the seat between himself and young Karsten. The other guard, a federal agent named Hofmann, was in the passenger seat.

The engine purred to life and they backed out of the driveway.

Helm said, "I'm in a hurry, Manfred. The party office first, then Bonn. Government building."

Manfred pushed back his cap and said, "Very well, sir." He stepped on the gas and the big Mercedes raised its nose and swept away.

Karsten flicked away his lapel so that the butt of the au-tomatic became visible again.

Hofmann switched on the VHF radio and tuned in to the police band.

On the dash the digital clock said 13:42. Helm was just about to open his briefcase to go over some notes, when they received the red alert high-frequency beep that preceded all federal police communications on the priority band . . .

This is A.T. Chief Inspector Stark in Cologne . . . red alert—all units beware of possible terrorist action involving baby ploy—infant in question blond, female, nine months, mother likely blond also—red alert . . ."

In the front seat, Hofmann sat bolt upright, his right hand under his jacket.

Young Karsten said, "I know the Chief Inspector."

"Jesus Christ!" cursed Hofmann. "Baby trick, bastards. Get off the main route, Freddy, fast! Only side roads and back lanes if necessary." He looked back and said, "Sorry, sir. It may take a bit longer that way, but it's safer."

Over the roar of the engine, Hofmann shouted, "If a

woman with a baby carriage or something steps off the curb
don't stop, you hear, Freddy? Step on it and fly around her.
Ram past other cars, anything, but don't stop."

Helm picked up the briefcase and clutched it to his
chest. He was not afraid, only impatient. He said, "Don't
overdo it, fellows. I don't want any kind of accident, all right?"

Hofmann looked back and said, "But that's how they
took Mathias Franke. A woman with a baby carriage stepped
off the curb—"

"Hofmann," said Helm, "I *know.*"

They were entering Habsburg Ring, which was choked
with lunch traffic returning to the office. The time was exactly two o'clock. The sun streamed down in a golden dazzle
and the women on the sidewalks walked with bouncing happy
strides, showing off tanned legs and unrestrained breasts
under summer blouses.

Karsten said, "We're nearly there, sir."

Helm looked at him and it was almost as if he were really
seeing him for the first time. A young man with romantic no-
tions about his career, in a plum assignment. Karsten was assigned by the state, and they paid bodyguards well. A slim
young face, brown hair, clean fingernails, white shirt, and tie.

Hofmann ordered, "Get off this damn parking lot,
Manfred. Take Schaafenstrasse, then that little lane with the
pub. Swing around like that, okay?"

Harried, Manfred checked his mirrors, then nosed the
big car past a Ford panel truck. Behind them someone
honked in reprimand. "Shut up," muttered Manfred. The
turn into the side street was tight and the wheels of the big
car ran up the sidewalk.

"Move it, Fred," cursed Hofmann. A woman with a
stroller was trying to cross and they were blocking her way.
She stared incredulously at Hofmann's gun. The baby in the
stroller was blond.

Helm's heart suddenly beat so fiercely that he was afraid
he might be having an attack.

Then the car was off the curb and accelerating down the
side street. It was a one-way street and they were going the
wrong way. Cars swerved and drivers gave them the finger.

"Fuck," said Hofmann passionately while Manfred steered with skill and daring. "This is more dangerous than anything else." He looked back with a sheepish grin. His right hand with the gun was braced against the dash. To Karsten he said, "Safety on in the car, buddy."

Karsten took his finger out of the trigger guard of his Walther and flicked up the little lever on the slide. Then they swung off the one-way street back onto Neumarkt. Manfred said, "Here we are." The building that housed the offices of the Green Party was in view. It was 2:03 P.M.

Karsten put away the gun.

Manfred slowed to double-park. Just then a woman on a bicycle teetered out from between two cars. There was a baby seat on the bicycle with a baby in it.

Both the woman and the baby screamed when the big car was suddenly upon them. Manfred slammed on the brakes. They heard a bump, then the woman fell awkwardly off the bicycle and the baby toppled out, rolling out of view under the hood.

By then the car stood still. Someone said, "Christ, what happened?"

Helm's heart beat much too quickly.

Moved by guilt, Manfred, the driver, opened the door to get out and help, but Hofmann yelled, "Hold it, Freddy!"

On the sidewalk, people shouted. Time stood still.

Suddenly the rear doors of a panel truck in front of them flew open, and the bullet-resistant windshield of the Mercedes turned momentarily opaque before caving in. There was a rattle like hail on metal. From the dark of the truck small flames stabbed at them.

Then a dark-haired man in slacks and white shirt stepped up to the rear door on Helm's side. Pedestrians screamed and pushed back in panic. No one interfered when the man raised a gun and fired three shots. The first two blew in the window, the third shattered Karsten's white face.

"Out, fucker!" The gunman reached in and opened the door.

Another young man appeared, yelling something. Clutching the case with his good arm, Helm saw the "mother" drag herself to a nearby BMW. Her back was covered in blood.

Then the two young men pulled him out of his car and hustled him towards the van. From the corner of his eye, Helm saw the torn, bleeding forms of Hofmann and Manfred slumped in their seats.

The right front tire of the Mercedes rested on the blond baby. He saw only the twisted legs. Around him, people stood and gaped; they looked at him with terrified eyes. Then he felt himself lifted up by the seat of his pants and slammed into the van. In the process they yanked the prosthesis of his left arm from the stump. He felt the articulation strands tear loose from the muscles, and in his shocked, confused state he thought he was back in the cellar of the Gestapo house in Essen.

8

In Montreal, the buzz of the unlisted phone woke Paul Fontana. He sat up, counting the signals: three rings, then silence. It meant that Wolff would be calling back in thirty minutes via the shielded switchback line from Washington.

It was only just getting light outside his window. He turned on the bedside lamp and looked at his watch. Early morning in Montreal was lunchtime in Cologne.

He padded into the kitchen to start the coffee. He moved on into the bathroom and performed his morning toilet in a hurry.

Later he sprinkled fish food into the tank, then watched the fish while drinking coffee and eating a cold piece of last night's pizza.

Fontana's apartment was a spacious one-bedroom affair

in an old-fashioned building in Westmount. Now, with politics and rent control the building had retained only a shadow of its former character. As the beveled glass panes in the front doors were smashed, the landlord replaced them with cheap window glass, and the once-handsome gumwood wainscoting in the lobby had been spray-painted with a dazzle of Day-Glo idiocies against which the super's steel wool scrapers were helpless. Still, the tree-lined street itself was lovely, especially at this time of year when the maples became a sea of orange and red.

Watching the fish drift lazily after the morsels of food, Fontana wondered what Wolff wanted to tell him. In preparation for the call, he checked the date because, added to the date of his birth, it formed his agency code.

Then the phone buzzed and Fontana reached across the table. Wolff gave his code, and he countered with his own.

"Paul, you're familiar with the Greens, right?"

"Of course I am . . . Dietrich Helm and I have been close friends since the war. You'll remember that—"

"I do. Listen: Helm has gotten hold of a top secret defense document. You know their stance on nuclear, and so you can imagine the pressure he can bring to bear on Bonn. Not to mention the NATO alliance and Washington. We're talking about the nuclear defense plan for all of West Germany. The whole ball of wax, Paul. If he goes to the press with this thing, we're all going to have one hell of a lot of explaining to do. Heads of state will roll, Paulie. A real mess."

"If it's a top secret defense plan, why would Helm go to the media with it?"

There was a pause. "It's complicated, Paul. I'm going to brief you in detail when you get here. Basically, the documents prove that the Americans have a far greater military presence in Europe than the electorate has been led to believe."

"Is that true?"

"Paulie, wise up. Personally I don't think the average Joe gives a hoot about all this doomsday talk. Not as long as the breweries don't strike, and there's food on the table and the TV works—"

"Oh, shut up, Henry. What a bore you can be. Those documents you mention, how did Helm get a hold of them? And why the hell would he . . . something's fishy there. And why me?"

"Paulie—listen now: I want you to come and talk to Helm. From what I know of your past, you're the one guy that can get close enough to make him surrender the Equinox file."

"Is that what it's called?"

"Yes, now don't interrupt. I'll tell you more when you get here."

"What's Bonn's role in this, Henry?"

"Never mind, just—"

"I don't think I want to get involved in this one, Henry. I told you—I want *out;* not deeper *in.*"

For a moment there was silence on the line, and it was not merely the scrambler delay. Fontana could feel the changing of Wolff's tack, and the chill when the words finally came was unmistakable: "Paul, I'm not giving you a choice. Get it straight; you're going to do this assignment. Okay?"

Fontana closed his eyes to concentrate all the more on the receiver. "Henry, Dietrich's a friend. Why me?"

"Why you? Because you *are* his friend. Chances are he'll listen to you. Then it's also a chance for you to pay him back a debt. I have a long memory, Paul. Here's your chance to save the guy's life."

"I beg your pardon?" Fontana's scalp crawled with sudden insight. "You wouldn't, Henry! Not someone like Dietrich Helm? The media . . . public opinion would turn even more against the American presence in Europe."

"So? You know me, Paul. I'd decoy it real good . . . look, man—" Suddenly Wolff lost his patience, and he snapped, "Paul, get the fuck over here! If you hedge, we'll do Helm our way, okay? At this moment he's probably on his way to Bonn. The way I see it, we have tonight and tomorrow to let you try and sway him. Thereafter . . ."

Fontana said quickly, "Fine. I'll try. What's the plan?"

"Try and make the nine-fifteen Air Canada from Mon-

treal to New York. There, take the PanAm daytimer at eleven
to Frankfurt. It'll connect with the Lufthansa flight to Cologne. Got that? Your bookings are all confirmed, tickets at
the counter. The usual, Paul."

Paul Fontana ripped the strip of paper off the kitchen
pad and said, "All right. Who will give me ground support
over there?"

"Teagarden and Jackson. And I'll be there too. You keep
in touch via the Bonn embassy."

"All right, Henry."

"Paul . . ."

"Yes?"

"This is A-one. Double A—"

"You've made your point. I'll see what I can do. " He
hung up, then clicked into high-speed gear. Mlle. Patou, his
secretary, was still at home when he called. He told her he
had to leave for another few days. As usual when he went out
on Agency business he did not tell her where or why, and she
no longer asked.

Next he went into the bedroom to pack his suitcase: traveling clothes, fresh shirts, changes of underwear and shoes.
The special tools went into the toilet kit, gun and holster were
wrapped in lead foil and put into their nest in the modified
portable Olivetti, which still had the telephone digitizer
plugged in to look like any other electronic storage chip.

These items were the hardware of his trade, and even
though he was a facilitator and not an XPD operative, he carried gun, digitizer, and tool kit as a matter of course on all
Agency business.

Fontana finished packing. Thoughts of Henry Wolff and
Dietrich Helm kept intruding but he succeeded in pushing
them aside. He pocketed his traveling wallet with passport,
U.S. currency, and credit cards, then wrote a note to the
cleaning lady informing her that the fish had already been fed
today. At the door he took a last look around his apartment,
his "cave" as he thought of it, then left for the airport.

New York was less than an hour away. All went well
until he learned at the PanAm counter that his flight to

Frankfurt would be two hours late. He decided to take a Lufthansa flight that left in half an hour.

His ticket was rewritten, and at noon the Lufthansa day-timer lifted off from Kennedy.

Fontana looked out the window at the infinite sky and the fields of cotton clouds below. Now, with no activity to distract him, the memories rushed in. It was impossible not to think back to June 1944, the month Major Dietrich von Helm saved the life of Paul von Fontana, an act that would cause Helm's own name to appear on the Gestapo death list.

And later, in France, when Paul Fontana turned his back on Germany and signed up as Henry Wolff's first sleeper. . . .

9

The advance naval bombardment was already under way when Paul von Fontana reached the Cherbourg peninsula. Because Rommel was away, the cadet was assigned to the medical corps.

He began working as an orderly in the base hospital at Cherbourg. A trancelike numbness soon took hold of him.

If the first mutilated body and the first hundred grotesque injuries had filled him with dread and made him want to weep, these emotions were quickly cauterized by the very fact that there was no end to the conveyor belt of suffering that dumped its freight at the hospital door.

And all the time the shells kept roaring in from the sea, and the bombs kept raining from the sky.

The upper stories of the hospital were long gone, pulverized like the rest of Cherbourg, and the great vaulted two-level basement was filled to capacity.

The dead were piled up outside during pauses in the bombardment. There was a small mountain of them; rained on, bombed, decomposing.

Paul no longer thought of their wives and lovers who would never know.

There was talk of great tank battles raging to the east at St. Lô, but there was also talk about the Cherbourg peninsula being cut off from the mainland. The Allied invasion was now much more than a foothold—it was an inexorable force.

One morning Paul von Fontana was assigned to a detail of corpsmen and stretcher bearers at the embattled Fort du Roule. They had made no more than three trips between the hospital and the fort when Cherbourg was overrun by the Americans. Paul's stretcher detail was captured by an advance patrol under the command of a lanky captain with freckles on his arms and face. There was no thought of resistance.

It was noon on Paul's wrist watch, but he had no idea of the date. It seemed a hundred years since he had left Franziska. The gunner on his stretcher had taken a shell fragment in the belly. Stumbling over the rubble before their American guard, Paul held the rear handles, trying to jar the injured man as little as possible.

Swarms of large green flies buzzed around the bunch of intestine that had pushed past his hands until the coils lay blue and glistening beside him on the stretcher.

Paul thought, None of this is possible. It'll all go away.

The American marched them to a group of jeeps and six-by-sixes. A dozen Germans sat on the ground, hands on their heads. GIs stood around casually, pointing carbines. An American corpsman with a red-cross armband came up and pulled back an eyelid of the gut-shot gunner on Paul's stretcher. The American looked at Paul and said, "Shit, man. Put 'im down. He's gone. Dead . . . you understand?"

Paul put down the stretcher, stepped over it, and walked over to the other prisoners. He sat down, took off his helmet and put his hands on his head.

After a while the numbness left him to make room first

for a turmoil of emotion, then for a tremendous wave of such limb-loosening relief that he found it hard to keep his hands up.

It was over.

After a while a jeep pulled up and a young lieutenant with a sandy moustache jumped out. He exchanged a few words with the guard, then walked among the prisoners. He asked, *"Offiziere? Ist ein Offizier unter Euch?"*

Paul looked up and said in English, "Yes, here. I am an officer."

The American lieutenant came over and Paul stood up. The name strip above the right breast pocket on the khaki jacket said HENRY WOLFF.

"You speak English; how come?"

Paul shrugged and said, "I speak French, Greek, and Latin, too."

Henry Wolff laughed out loud. Then he looked at Paul's filthy white uniform and said, "Come along, scholar. The jeep."

Wolff took him to his tent, sat him down behind a folding table. He studied Paul's papers, then sent the guard for some soup.

While Paul ate ravenously, Wolff pointed out that in age they were only one year apart. He went on to say, "And you know something else? My grandfather came from Stuttgart. He was a tinker who immigrated to California and opened a hardware store. Now we have a chain of them. Wolff's Hardware. That's why I have some German, see?"

Paul nodded. His eyes kept appraising the American, looking for an opening, a chance to make his persuasive bid. As it happened, there was no need for him to offer anything; Wolff called a stenographer and the debriefing began. It was as natural as two interested parties cooperating towards the same goal.

And as he spoke, talking about everything but his friends among the cadets, Paul kept hearing Major von Helm's challenge: *your job is to help end the war, not prolong it.*

When he ran out of things to say, the silence was like a tombstone.

Then Wolff said, "Good stuff, Paul. You're smart. Are there lots of people like this Major von Helm?"

"Not nearly enough. There are thousands who think like him, but they won't have the courage to do anything about it."

"You mean, do things to end the war? Beyond what you've told us so far, would you be willing to *do* things, help us with a specific problem?"

"Such as what?"

"I'll tell you. You could save hundreds of lives—*your* soldiers' lives."

"Hundreds? How?"

Wolff sent a guard to fetch Colonel Verlinde. Verlinde was a tall, sharp-faced man, the head of military intelligence with General Omar Bradley's command. He sized up Cadet Fontana and came straight to the point.

He said, "The big fort, boy, Fort Roule. You have been inside. You know where the air shaft is?"

Fontana sat up. "What are you. . . . No, please don't ask me that."

Wolff jumped in: "Why not? We've got to silence those fifteen-inch guns. We can level the whole goddamn mountain, but think of all the lives *that* would cost. You were in there as a stretcher bearer, right? Tell us where the air shaft is."

Verlinde nodded at the stenographer and said, "You can go now, fella, but leave your pad."

When they were just three in the tent, Wolff followed up. "Anything else you've told us so far is good for insight into various things, Paul. But here's your chance to show your stuff. These guns are holding us up, Paul. The sooner we can move on, the sooner we get to Berlin."

"Or Cologne," added Verlinde.

* * *

An hour later they sat in an armored personnel carrier in an apple orchard on the south side of the mountain, at the lee side of Fort Roule's huge guns. In the half-track were Paul Fontana, Henry Wolff, Colonel Verlinde, and a radio spotter.

Above them circled a Liberator that had been called in from a bombing run on Caen. Liberators were precision bombers—the famous egg-down-a-smokestack machines.

Verlinde turned to Fontana and said, "All right, fella; tell the man exactly where the airshaft is."

Fontana murmured, "There—those rocks at half past twelve. One-third up the slope."

The radio operator whispered into his mike. Then the Liberator swung north on final target approach. They all watched through the inch-thick windows of the half-track. And they all saw how the bomb door swung open and the single huge bomb fell out, first level, then standing up. They could hear the rush of the wind through its stabilizers.

Wolff held his breath.

The plane was already veering off when the ground shook as though from an earthquake. There was muffled deep-down thunder. Then the entire mountain seemed to heave, and a moment later the whole south side collapsed and slid down in an avalanche of rocks and smoke.

Stones and blasted rock fragments rained on the roof of their half-track. Through the windows they could see into the underground fortifications of Fort Roule. It looked like a destroyed ant farm.

Then the men from the American assault battalion rose from their cover and stormed the breach. Wolff looked at Fontana and saw that his prisoner's eyes were on *him* in turn. Because there was really nothing to say, Wolff merely shrugged.

Later, Wolff made his first half-hearted sleeper proposition. But Fontana nearly panicked; he clamped his hands over his ears and refused to listen. Clearly, the afternoon had been too much too soon.

It was a stalemate. Wolff decided to let things rest for a while. The seed was planted in fertile ground. Now let it take root.

If a man had taken the first step already, it was not hard to make him take the next, the OSS man in Washington had assured the roomful of army intelligence officers over and over again. Never be too pushy. Instead, explain the options and put suggestions to your prospects. Then let them work it out for themselves. Good sleepers could not be won over by coercion.

Wolff let Fontana have a shower, then handed him over to the regular POW administration. For his safety, and to avoid any contact between him and German soldiers from Cherbourg who might possibly know him, he was assigned to a holding pen for prisoners from Bayeux.

By Friday, July 21, 1944, the Allies had more than a million men in France. A flexible pipeline floated on the English Channel to feed a constant flow of fuel to the invasion forces. Off the coast, harbors had been improvised with concrete blocks, and now shuttling supply vessels were being unloaded day and night. It was a scene like an enormous, well-oiled industrial enterprise: goal-oriented and invincible. At night, the beaches and loading docks were flood-lit to keep the work on schedule. German planes were not much of a concern because Goering's Luftwaffe had been decimated.

That day, July 21, the world learned that President Roosevelt, though ill and tired, had accepted his nomination for another term. His speech from a Pacific Coast naval base was broadcast to the nation; American staff officers in Europe heard of it during the morning briefing, and First Lieutenant Henry Wolff read excerpts of it in the *Information Pages*—known to army intelligence officers as BSP, or Bullshit Pages.

Wolff read about Roosevelt in his debriefing tent where

the desk was piled with Wehrmacht passes and other documents. When he heard his name being called, he looked up and saw Verlinde. The colonel was waving a piece of paper, and Wolff left the tent to meet him.

"Morning, fella. Making progress?" Verlinde was peering over Wolff's shoulder at the pile of papers on the desk.

"Some, sir."

"Good. Good. Say, remember that young cadet from Cherbourg—what was his name? Got this army intelligence thing——"

"Fontana, sir. What about him?"

"Here . . ." The colonel held up a piece of paper, and Wolff took it.

It was an AI brief, terse and somehow vague like all of them. Wolff had to read it twice before he understood the astonishing opportunity it offered. It virtually guaranteed him his first sleeper, his first intelligence coup.

FROM: Supreme Allied Command; Lieutenant
General Dwight D. Eisenhower
TO: All Staff; Commanders; Intelligence Sections
DISTRIBUTION: Open
MODE: Urgent
July 21, 1944 0400h

AN ASSASSINATION ATTEMPT ON ADOLF HITLER YESTER-
DAY REVEALS A DEEP RIFT BETWEEN THE WEHRMACHT
AND THE NAZI PARTY.

AT A MEETING IN RASTENBURG YESTERDAY, COLO-
NEL COUNT VON STAUFFENBERG DETONATED A BRIEF-
CASE BOMB THAT KILLED ONE AND INJURED MANY BUT
LEFT THE FUEHRER UNHARMED.

GESTAPO CHIEF HIMMLER HAS BEEN PUT IN
CHARGE OF THE INVESTIGATION, AND ALREADY THE
LIST OF SUSPECTED MEMBERS OF THE CONSPIRACY IS
MORE THAN A HUNDRED NAMES LONG.

BEFORE THE PURGE IS OVER, MORE THAN FIVE-
HUNDRED OFFICERS AND, IN MANY CASES, THEIR FAMI-
LIES TOO, WILL HAVE BEEN SHOT. THEY SPAN MUCH OF

THE WEHRMACHT: STAUFFENBERG, SPIESS, ROMMEL,
AND KLEBER ARE AMONG THE GENERALS—THE
LOWEST RANKING OFFICER IMPLICATED IS MAJOR VON
HELM, INVALIDED ACE FLIER.
    ALL OF THE ABOVE CONFIRMS LONG-SUSPECTED
WEAKNESSES WITHIN THE ENEMY CAMP . . . WEAK-
NESSES THAT AID OUR CAUSE.
S/A/C

Wolff looked up from the document.
    Verlinde grinned. "Well, what are you waiting for?"
    And Wolff dashed off. He made a phone call to the POW
pen in Bayeux, then called for his jeep and driver.

    By the time Wolff entered the interrogation room, Paul
von Fontana had been waiting, sitting still for three and half
hours. He was surrounded by a three-foot-square cage of
chicken wire in a corner of the room, and the chair he sat on
was a steel office type on casters that squealed every time he
moved.
    But far from being uneasy about the seemingly pointless
waiting period, Paul was grateful for the solitude. The dehu-
manizing aspect of being packed tightly with thousands of
angry and fearful men, the instant undercurrent of distrust
and unfounded hatred and jealousy (caused by petty things
like whole boots or a new razor blade), all those unexpected
things had perhaps been the hardest part of his captivity. It
was like being plunged into a surprise underworld of ugly
feelings instead of a sense of brotherhood.
    And so he sat quietly on his chair, searching patiently for
his lost identity. After a while a wonderful drowsiness over-
came him, and he nearly fell asleep. His mind had raced in
tight, blind circles for weeks, ever since he'd left Cologne, but
now it slowed down, like the mainspring of a clock nearing
the end of its tension. The thoughts that could have brought a
semblance of order to his inner world refused to take form.

Only a sense of respite came, and a dim hope for some kind of end, or a change.

Then the door was flung open and the American lieutenant walked in, brisk and youthful and smiling, his steel helmet under one arm, a folder under the other.

"Paul." He beamed like a student bumping into a close buddy in a Rathskeller. "Good to see you again. I brought you something. Wait till you read this!" Wolff indicated the folder, then stopped dead and looked around the room. He yelled, "Guard! Let him out of this dumb wire thing and get us a table."

The guard poked his head in the door and said, "Regulations, 'tenant."

"Fuck the regs, corporal. This is special. Now move it."

The guard frowned, then withdrew his head, leaving the door open. A moment later he was back with a folding metal table. He set it up in the middle of the room and went into the corner to unlock the cage.

Wolff said, "Come and bring your chair, Paul. I'd like to show you something."

Paul rose obediently and pushed his chair toward the American. He wondered what victory over Nazi Germany would feel like. Clear, untroubled conscience, morality on one's side. He looked at Henry Wolff, about his own age but optimistic, and he felt only shame.

Before opening the folder, Wolff looked at him and asked, "Can I get you anything? Food? Coffee?"

Paul shook his head; then he said, "A cigarette, perhaps."

"Ah, you're smoking now?" Wolff pushed his pack of Camels across the table, and Paul shook one out, lit it.

Blowing the smoke out self-consciously he said, "Something to do. Plus it helps cut the hunger."

"The food all right?"

Paul shrugged. "Bread and beet soup, mostly. Adequate."

"There are so many of you. Several hundred thousand, by now. And more prisoners every day."

Paul grinned. "You don't have to apologize for the food."

Wolff said, "Damn right I don't." He opened the folder
and tossed the first blown-up photograph in front of Paul.
"Take a look, buddy. This is what *your* soldiers are doing to
their POW's. Mass shootings, Paul. No bread and beet soup
for those poor fuckers. These pictures are courtesy of the So-
viet army. And there's more."

Paul stared in horror at the pictures as the American
flipped them in front of him, like playing cards, describing
them: mutilated partisan girls strung up in an apple orchard;
a whole Ukrainian village leveled in retalliation; a concentration camp full of walking skeletons. . . .

"Enough!" Paul raised his hands. "That's not the Wehrmacht, you know. That's all SS!" As if that made a difference.

"Maybe, Paul," said Wolff. He scooped up the pictures,
then took the elastic band off the second batch in his folder.
"But we don't know that. And that's *your* problem—not ours.
to us it's all one enemy. Anyway, principled guys like you and
your Major von Helm are definitely in the minority. And
they're *losing*, Paul; they're going nowhere fast. Let me show
you something."

He watched the American put down the pictures and
pick up a sheet of paper with typing on it instead. He reached
for it, held it with both hands. And as Paul read, his horror
grew into an enormous bottomless dread, and by the time he
got to the last line his vision was so blurred that he had to read
it again. And again: *lowest ranking officer implicated is Major
von Helm, invalided ace flier.*

Wolff pulled the paper deftly from his fingers and said,
"So you see, Paul. It isn't really *us* who are your enemies.
That man was right: your job is not to prolong the war—it's to
help end it. The sooner the better, so that this sort of thing
can stop. . . ." Like a cardsharp Wolff fanned out his follow-
up: pictures of the grisly battleground at Falaise; aerial shots
of devastated Hamburg, Berlin. And Cologne, where only the
cathedral stood, like a tombstone in a landscape of rubble.

Paul tried not to weep, but he couldn't help it.

Across the table, the American said gently, "It's the
Nazis who are doing this to Germany, Paul. Help us *prevent*

anything like this from happening ever again, and we'll help you make a fresh start. You could be out of here and on your way by tomorrow morning."

The American lit two cigarettes and, like a comrade in the field, offered one to Paul, who took it. Then Wolff reached into his folder once more and almost casually laid his ultimate trump card next to the photo of devastated Cologne: it was a full view of Dietrich von Helm when he was still an active flier. He was just climbing into the cockpit of a Focke Wulf, his *Ingrid,* and he had paused to grin squarely at the camera. He looked invincible, as though death would never find him, treachery never touch him.

Wolff said, "Are you going at least to try and continue where he had to leave off? Sign up, Paul. We're the good guys. America stands for all the things that he stood for as well. Sign up and we'll give you the chance to carry his ball. You'll never look back."

Paul looked up from the photograph in time to see Wolff expel a lungful of smoke and to hear him ask, "So what do you say, Paul?"

The Lufthansa captain announced that they were just passing over Gander, Newfoundland. Then the stewardesses rolled lunch trolleys down the aisles.

Fontana unwrapped the cutlery, and from the surface of the spoon his face stared back at him: distorted and much older than in his memory, but as confused about the truly important things as ever.

He had spent decades trying to retrace his steps, trying to make up for past mistakes. As though by understanding the random turmoil of those years he could somehow negate them: negate the bomb that fell on his parents' house; negate the fact that Franziska had been doomed the day her father had betrothed her in Junker fashion to the fair-haired hero of the day; negate the fact that Germany had condemned itself by the choices of its own people—not by the times, and not by force of circumstance.

The losses were incalculable. Personally, he had lost his country, his first and only love, and his daughter to the bullets of East German border guards.

The only gain had been the continued close friendship among the former cadets and Dietrich Helm; by some miracle they all had survived the war.

The Gestapo had already become suspicious of Helm following the timely escape of Fontana into the invasion area, and following the Stauffenberg bomb Helm was taken away. His entire class of special cadets was disbanded, demoted to common soldiers, and sent to the front. Among Fontana's friends Attila Benn was sent to Russia, Herbert Dornier to the Ardennes, and Carl Stolz to Italy.

In addition Justus von Ribnitz, Franziska's father, was shot dead during a search of the villa, and Franziska was thrown into the Stettin concentration camp. Himmler's purge was thorough.

Sitting in his window seat on the Lufthansa flight, Fontana thought that he could still remember every detail of his ceaseless search for Franziska. Finally in 1955, with Agency help, he received permission to look into the records of the Stettin concentration camp . . . and found these words on the list of infants liberated by the Russians: *Vicky Fontana; mother; Franziska Ribnitz.*

"Unusual," said the young East German guard who was watching Fontana in the reading room of the East Berlin People's Archives. "Usually it's just the mother's name. She must have insisted on. . . ." The prim and proper young man broke off, then took a second look at the visitor's badge on Fontana's lapel.

Additional documents indicated that Franziska had died shortly after childbirth. Vicky owed her survival merely to the fact that Stettin had been a holding camp, and the Russians arrived sooner than the Germans had expected.

And his own dreams of adventure in America had of course remained just that: dreams. "America" had been the

OSS training camp in Vermont, then a new undercover identity in Canada; work for the Agency against enemies of NATO
(which in his mind meant chiefly Germany), and a lifetime
on the run from his own past. A past that had grown each day,
and that would continue to grow as long as Henry Wolff refused to let him off the hook.

*"I'll give you lots of line, but if you shake the hook they'll
dynamite you."*

So be it.

The food was good, and he ordered a bottle of Rhine wine
and ate and drank, and a sense of balance returned as though
the intake of food were tipping his psychic scale away from
doom. He would be practical and do exactly as Wolff had said:
talk to Dietrich and get him to hand over the documents. That
accomplished, he would again go to Wolff. . . .

And he would once more try to talk sense into Gaby. Perhaps one day, if the mood was right and she was not as snap-
pish and distracted as usual, he could tell her why her mother
had been *born* in a concentration camp . . . why no one
wanted to talk about her grandmother Franziska . . . and why
her uncle Helm fought so determinedly against any more nuclear deployment in Western Europe.

And while he was at it, he might also tell Gaby just why
her family was, in her words, "all in weird bits and pieces."
Perhaps, once she had a better perspective on who she was,
she might stop despising Dietrich Helm and hating her father. She might even learn to accept the truth that she owed
her life and freedom to the very fact that her father kept on
running with her in his arms—kept on running away from
the dogs and the border guards, away from the slumped form
of her fallen mother.

Fontana had seen Vicky only twice. Once at the orphanage when she was fourteen, the second time when she married Peter Schott. Thereafter he was refused entry into East
Germany, and they would never see each other again. . . .

The stewardess removed his empty tray, and Fontana
pulled down the blind and tilted back his seat. He forced himself to stop thinking about all the ifs and buts of the past and

instead turned his mind to the upcoming negotiation with Dietrich Helm. Here was his chance to return the favor of June 1944; if he failed, Wolff's only option would be an XPD. Those were the rules, and he had long ago accepted them.

10

Chief Inspector Gunter Stark was examining photos of the scrape marks on the old man's corpse with the police physiotherapist when his belt unit went off. He picked up the phone to the HQ operator three floors below him and was told of an apparent terrorist action on Neumarkt. A squad car was already on the scene.

"Rope burns," said the physiotherapist. "They sure look like rope burns to me."

Stark stared at him. Then he turned and, already running, shouted, "I'll get back to you. Keep the pix for me." He raced down the stairs, three at a time, and leaped into his car. He switched on the squad band for more details. All the while he was speeding to the scene, flying down the wrong side of the street, dodging in and out of traffic, horn and blue light pulsing.

He arrived at 2:24 P.M. and quickly took in what had happened. The sergeant of the response unit circled the car with him; meanwhile other units arrived: crowd control, ambulance, traffic control, photography, and his own AT site team. Barriers were erected to push back the crowd, and a man-high canvas fence was put up to form a controlled space around the car and bicycle. Then they went to work, recording the site and interviewing witnesses. Stark put out a call for Fritz and Georg.

His lieutenants arrived and he told them to coordinate the witness interviews while he worked with Photography and Forensics. The medics, having pronounced all three men as well as the baby dead, were released and told to send morgue vehicles at five. Stark ordered a news blackout, then went to work.

The faces of the driver Manfred Raabe and Detective Karsten Sommer were virtually unrecognizable: the driver because, judging from the state of the seat and headrest behind him, he had taken a full burst of automatic fire, the detective on the rear seat because a single point-blank shot from a large-caliber weapon had shattered the entire bone structure of his face.

The older bodyguard on the passenger seat, a plainclothes federal, had been shot in the chest and abdomen. He had a gun in his right hand, a large Walther police model that had been discharged, and the ejected nine-millimeter shell was found in his bloody lap.

The baby matched the description by the day-care staff on Deutzerstrasse: a little blond girl in play clothes. The front right tire of the heavy car had rolled over her chest.

The blood-and-fingerprints man said, "I would guess that Helm is not injured. There is no blood and no bullet entries on his side of the seat, and the front seats and headrests are bullet-absorbing."

"How come the windows didn't hold?" Stark asked rhetorically. "Teflon shells?"

The men shrugged.

"We'll know more when Ballistics digs up the slugs," said Fritz. He had entered the perimeter with an attractive woman in her thirties whom he introduced as Dr. Angela Frisch. "Our best witness, chief; saw everything from the word go."

Stark showed her his ID. "Will you come to the office and make a statement, doctor?"

She gaped at the butchery, and he saw her horror. In the heat the blood was beginning to smell. Swarms of flies had appeared from nowhere. He took her elbow and moved her aside and out of the way of the field team. "Is your doctorate a medical degree or an academic one?"

"I am a psychiatrist. Industrial. . . ." She looked at him, and controlling her emotions with a great effort she launched into her narrative.

She had been at the curb, waiting for a gap in traffic. Next to her was a young mother with a yelling baby on the bicycle seat. Then there was a violent movement and a young man pushed the bicycle into the path of a car.

Stark asked, "What did he look like?"

She described a man whom he remembered from the picture file. Theo Brandstaetter was a remnant of the splintered Action Group September.

Angela Frisch continued. She fought bravely to remain precise and factual. In the end Stark asked a few follow-up questions.

"The mother was injured? How—gunshot or car?"

"Gunshot, I think. She was bleeding and the blond one helped her into the van. By then, the kidnapped man was already thrown in."

The photographer waved at Stark to say he was finished, and another team member came up to report the shell count. It was surprisingly low: only eight. Stark said, "That's because the automatic weapon was in the van."

"Yes. Two calibers, chief. Mostly nine mils but there are also three forty-fives."

Stark nodded. The nine millimeters came likely from an MP5, copper jackets interspersed with Teflon: the European terrorists' favorite weapon. Up close, Teflon slugs could penetrate an engine block or a bullet-proof vest. Or, as here, bullet-proof glass.

Stark asked Dr. Frisch to accompany him to the office where her statement would be taken down and where she would be asked to go through the picture file. She agreed, averting her eyes from the shot-up car.

Stark knew that Fritz and Georg would look after the site. The bodies would be transferred to the morgue and a furniture van would take Helm's car to the police warehouse.

By five, the street would belong again to endless, anonymous traffic.

In Olpe, Wolff was on the phone to Jack Teagarden at the U.S. embassy in Bonn. The man's denseness irritated Wolff so much that he came close to yelling at him. "I can't reach him any more, do you understand? I phoned him in Montreal an hour ago and now there's no answer at his number. Which means he's already on his way. There's a connecting flight in New York but that place is such a madhouse I'll never be able to head him off from there."

"And what do you want from me? I mean—"

"I told you already. Take some muscle and go to the Bonn/Cologne airport. He'll arrive on the daytime PanAm. I want you to give Paul a good scare. Tell him he's off the case and I want him to go back to Canada."

"Don't you want him to talk to Helm anymore?"

"Good morning, Jack—tell me where Helm is!"

"Yeah. I get you. But why *scare* him—"

"For one, I want to put Paul under pressure. Don't worry, he won't leave. He'll get away from you, but he won't leave Cologne. He and Helm are good friends. Paul wouldn't leave now for anything."

"So you don't want us putting him on a plane."

"Do you actually ever *listen* to me, Jack? Christ! Another thing: make sure he sees the newspapers."

"What? You want him to get the Helm news, is that it? He can't miss it—it's all over the place. But do you want him to stay here or not?"

"*Yes*, I want him here. Then you and Metzger keep an eye on him. Day and night, you hear?"

"Yeah, yeah. Anything else?"

"Get a tap on all the phone lines into that Green Party office."

"Okay," said Teagarden.

*   *   *

The computer of the Federal Criminal Office in Wiesbaden was a fourth-generation mainframe system with an international data base. It could be accessed via local security operators from control points all over West Germany.

Driving to Cologne HQ that Monday, Stark was able to prime Wiesbaden from his mobile terminal for an upcoming character and motivation selection, and he was able to enrich the computer's terrorist file with a number of new details on the latest snatch, such as the mix of calibers used.

All the while the Porsche cut through the traffic, dodging, slowing, then speeding up. The gooseneck mike on the dash enabled Stark to speak without taking his eyes off the road, and for the occasional channel switch the buttons were large and easily distinguishable.

Stark finished with the computer and switched over to the AT section band. He dictated a preliminary report to the superintendent, then phoned his own office to say he was coming in with a prime witness. The desk sergeant relayed a priority request from Bonn: the chancellor was requesting regular updates on the kidnapping, and Stark's orders were to report several times per day to the interior minister directly.

All this time he was aware of his passenger, of her pale-faced self-control and unflagging courage. But the ride from the site to Cologne HQ did not take long, and between steering, shifting, and radio operation there was no time to do more than look at her once or twice.

They roared down the ramp and he swung into his bay by the elevator. Stark helped Angela Frisch out of the low car, then led the way. He showed his pass to the video camera and when the steel doors had slid aside took her into the control room.

The operator had already accessed the terrorism file, and now she stood by, waiting for Stark's requests.

"Brandstaetter, Theo," said Stark.

The operator's fingers tapped out the name, and seconds later, they saw the first images—slowed down and computer-enhanced, taped by a security camera during a bank holdup in Hamburg two years ago.

Stark watched Angela Frisch go rigid, transfixed by the monitor.

"That's him," she said.

"Are you sure?"

The operator selected the best frontal shot, then narrowed the field, enlarging the face. A grimace of bared teeth, hanging hair, wild eyes.

"Yes, I'm absolutely certain," said Angela Frisch. "He was the one who pushed that bicycle in front of the car." She kept her eyes on the screen as the list of criminal acts and associations rolled by like movie credits.

Because Stark was familiar with Theo's file, he took time out to watch Angela Frisch from the side. She was a striking sight. About his own age, and tanned as though she had just come back from a vacation in a better climate. The white cotton outfit complemented her coloring and its cut and fit hinted at more tanned shapeliness underneath. She had prominent cheekbones and a generous mouth. Her eyes were that shade of light brown that edges on green, and her auburn hair was done in that casual carefully negligent way that made some women look like wayward mops. But in Angela's case it somehow rounded out the overall impression of style and restrained sensuality.

She caught him staring, and for a moment their eyes met. He saw the flash of surprise and quickly returned to the topic of terrorism.

He said, "Well, that's one of them. You see, they don't even bother wearing masks."

"Masks would get in the way. Terrorists have to blend into the society they want to terrorize."

Stark nodded. Already he was searching for plausible ways to keep Angela Frisch in his orbit. The only woman in his life at the moment was Misha, and comparing the two would be like comparing . . . well, there was no comparison.

The operator snapped him out of his incongruous romantic reverie. "What next? Is there anything else, inspector?" She wore a sergeant's uniform complete with the clumpy shoes and bobby pins to keep her hair in regulation harness. Probably she resented Angela Frisch for the breeze of outdoor sensuality she had brought into the dull computer room.

Stark asked for the file on Mahmoud. It contained tape supplied by various secret services such as Mossad, the CIA, Interpol, and the Italian and Spanish police.

Angela Frisch shook her hand. "I don't think so. I would have remembered his face."

Stark said, "Chances are he was in the van operating the automatic weapon. He wouldn't want to risk one of his men killing Helm."

They moved on to the dark-haired "mother" on the bicycle. On the fourth try they hit on Françoise Muton, also known as Madeleine. Specialty: bombing department stores.

Rossi took a bit longer because dark-haired Latin types abound in international terrorism; also, Cologne was an unusual place for him. Rossi operated infrequently outside Italy. But in the end the electronic brain came up with three selections. The third one was correct: *Angelo Giacomo Rossi*— twice caught and twice escaped; cell liaison with the Milan Red Brigades and Red Army Faction; wanted in Italy for the bombing of the Milan bus terminal as well as for the murder of State Attorney Francopo Poldi, also shot point blank in the face with a .45-caliber handgun.

He laughed at them in slow motion from the screen. The tape had been made in a Milan courtroom before his second escape. Sleek, cool, and very good-looking, he typified the new breed of career terrorist who was in the business because it was glamorous, never dull, and a very good living.

"Anyone else?" asked Stark. "Even at the fringe, lending what you now might recognize as support?"

"The driver of the other car, a blond woman." Angela Frisch had mentioned the support vehicle before.

"Yes, the stolen BMW. Can you describe the driver to the sergeant?"

Angela Frisch tried, but she did not get very far. The computer added up the known facts: a blond female in her early twenties, driver of a support car, assisting in a kidnapping and armed assault.

A dozen files came up; Germans, Americans, Austrians, Dutch, French; all possibilities, none definite.

"Could be a wig, of course," said Stark. "Or simply bleached hair tied in a ponytail."

After the computer session, Stark had Angela Frisch sign the Restricted Information Consent form. He asked, "Is this your home address?"

She nodded, watching him.

"And if we catch one or more of them, will it be all right if I ask you to identify them?" He handed her his card.

"Of course. Any time. This other phone number is the office."

The desk clerk gave her a cab slip, then Stark walked her to the main entrance. She put on sunglasses, shook his hand and strode away, upright and gorgeous.

From his office, Stark called Esser. The minister listened to his report, then snapped, "Good—back to work, chief inspector," and hung up.

Zander called from Wiesbaden. "Your command status is confirmed. They are very keen to solve this one, chief inspector. And you're getting everything else you asked for too."

"Manpower and communication equipment? We need—"

"Listen and I'll tell you what you're getting. Three hundred detectives and uniformed cops from all over the country, four listening vans, a thermographic van, as much electronic gear as you need, and the clerical staff to run it. Talk to the chief of police and tell him how much additional office space you need in Cologne HQ. They're also giving you additional computer banks for lead processing."

Stark was impressed. He called the chief of police and within two hours an entire floor was cleared of staff who were moved to secondary locations.

Communications arrived with truckloads of gear and installation equipment. Intercoms were strung together, and two hundred lines and a temporary switchboard were set up in the office across the hall from Stark's.

As the additional manpower arrived, Fritz and Georg helped with briefing them. Soon the walls were papered with large-scale maps of Cologne and surroundings. All known terrorist contacts were hauled in, all addresses and meeting points staked out. The laser vans began their eavesdropping work.

By six o'clock that Monday evening the taut web was waiting for the slightest tug on the line.

Everyone waited for a word from the kidnappers.

Since now there was nothing left to do but wait, Stark finally drove out to the Helm house. By then the residence as well as Helm's Green Party consulting office were under close surveillance. All phone lines were tapped and monitored live, people coming and going were being videotaped, and technicians inside the listening vans bounced laser beams off windows to record conversations within.

On the way, Stark began to think about Angela Frisch. She was probably not married; at any rate, he had seen no rings on her fingers. He thought of the green eyes, the lips, her quizzical gaze.

The route to the Helm residence took him within a block of Misha's apartment, and prompted by an odd emotion that was almost like guilt he made the short detour.

Looking up at her window, he saw that the drawing light was already on. He clicked the line switch and tapped out her number. It rang for what seemed like a depressingly long time. But sometimes when she worked she ignored the phone.

When he disconnected, the Porsche shot past her building and out onto the main route again.

They were finished before 9:00. Every possible question had been asked, and even though he would later methodically once more go over the detective's notes, Stark knew that nothing Mrs. Helm had said was of help.

He drove back into town and ended up outside Misha's apartment building. For several months now he had been spending the domestic part of his nights there; his own place on Grafenplatz had become a joyless desert.

He parked the Porsche so that he would be able to see it from the window, then took the elevator up and knocked on her door.

As he had taught her to do, she observed him through the spy hole.

"All right. All right. It *is* me, Misha."

At length she snapped aside the latch and bolt. Stark slipped in sideways, and by the time he shut the door Misha was already back across the room at the easel.

"Well, well," she said melodiously. "Off duty so soon?"

He went to embrace her but she tried to avoid him. "My brush," she protested. "Be careful. This illustration has to be finished by tomorrow evening."

"Sure." He let go of her and pulled up a chair.

"A drink?"

He shook his head, and she caught on right away. "You're just dropping in, right, Gunter? Back to the grindstone after a little chat, or a quick screw perhaps?"

"Come on, Misha . . ." He looked at her helplessly.

Was it ridiculous that he was still chivalrously careful not to hurt her? Her own weapons were so much sharper, and she wielded them with lusty abandon. A cut and a slash — then a Band-Aid.

Her eyes intent on her brush, she purred, "I'm sorry darling, but it's true. It's often true, isn't it? You drop in for a good fuck. Like a little boy after school for a cookie and milk before he bops off again to play cowboys and Indians."

It was true; he had to concede that there might be a perspective from which it was true. He went into the little kitchen, poured himself a beer, and returned to the chair. The belt unit and the shoulder holster dug into his sides.

He took a long, deep swallow. Cheered, he said, "I'm sorry, Misha. There's a crisis on right now."

"But there *always* is, isn't there, darling?"

"Well. . . ."

Misha had made allowances for the heat. Her wonderful young breasts poked against the sun and a palm tree on a faded T-shirt that said *"Cap d'Antibes,"* and her slim thighs and ass were lost in a pair of white linen culottes.

As for her long dark hair, it was pulled up into a high ponytail that left a riot of soft fuzzy curls all along her hairline. In a certain light and in a more romantic mood he had thought of her as wearing a crown.

And in a different mood again, he had reflected on the notion that Misha had for him the same attraction a candle has for a moth. And with similar results.

"Have you been working all day?"

"Pretty well. I got this assignment over the weekend. A cover illustration."

"Who's it for?"

She named a glossy magazine aimed at women professionals.

"How was the party?"

"Terrific. Guido has made a new recording and Marianne's agency got the contract for Nina Ricci. They asked about you."

He looked sharply at her, trying to decide if she was fibbing. But they just might have asked about him. From their perspective, he was a star in his own right. He drained the beer and went up to Misha. When the brush was not touching the board, he grabbed her from behind and nuzzled her neck. She held still for a moment then reached back and grabbed him through the pants. "And what is this?"

Happily and seductively he said, "A friend. An enthusiastic admirer."

With something like a sigh, Misha put down the brush and turned around. She slipped the T-shirt over her head, dropped the culottes, and stood facing him like a slim wistful child. She could make the largest, most innocent eyes; the contrast with her sensuous mouth and knowing hands was devastating. She unzipped him and he popped out of his fly with an eagerness that was almost embarrassing.

Licking his ear, she smacked, "Take off this damn gun and things." Misha helped him with the holster, shirt, and pants, then steered him backwards to the rug in the middle of the room.

He prayed silently that the belt unit would not go off for at least half an hour, then he forgot all about it.

Afterwards, Misha said, "You know, Gunter, this may well have been the last time. We've got some serious talking to do."

He groaned, stretching luxuriously, and said, "Oh no. Not again."

"This time for real. I'm considering moving in with Guido."

Stark sat up like a shot. Misha padded into the bathroom and shut the door. "Guido wants to marry me. Did you know that?" she shouted.

Muttering to himself Stark climbed back into his clothes. He would have liked to have a shower or at least a wash, but not with Misha holding the bathroom like a fort. And anyway it was already nearly midnight. Time to go to the office; he could wash there and get a few hours of sleep on the couch.

From habit he said, "But *I* want to marry you, Misha. What is this nonsense you're talking now? Guido, for crying out loud! Guido and his fucking piano playing."

"*Harpsichord,* you moron. Guido is probably the best Bach interpreter in Europe. We could live in Rome or Paris. Not in beer-guzzling, boring Cologne. Double-keyboard harpsichord, dear."

Her culottes and T-shirt lay in a forlorn pile by the easel. He picked them up and put them on the stool. The painting was of a woman dressed to kill, looking at the as-yet-undeveloped outline of a man.

Stark went to the bathroom door and leaned against the frame. He tried to think of something new to say in his defense, but nothing came to mind. Then he heard the shower go on. Humming happily, Misha stepped into the glass booth and slid shut the door.

He ripped a piece of paper off her sketch pad and wrote on it, "Please don't do a damn thing before we've had a good long talk. Gunter." He let himself out and made sure the door was properly latched.

The age difference was only one of several problems between them. Racing down the stairs as had become his habit, he thought in self-defense that he honestly *did* want to marry her, and the day would come yet when there would be the time and the leisure to talk about it. Time and leisure—that was of course the root of the problem. Time *for* Misha and leisure *with* her. Or was it?

On the last flight of stairs he thought that the day would come when he would make himself face the strange coincidence that the three women who'd played a major role in his life so far had all been the same age. Susanne, his wife; the New Zealand girl who had died from his bullet; and now Misha. The girl was dead eight months—just six weeks longer than he had known Misha. Stark sometimes wondered if there was any connection between the dead stranger and his crazy, blinding love and desire for Misha. A shrink would build it up and decorate it like a Christmas tree. Guilt, loss, revenge . . .

For the first few months with Misha he had sometimes awakened, bathed in sweat, the spreading bouquet of blood on the white dress still close enough to touch. The guilt was still there—it always would be. But at least it no longer handicapped him. It only made him more aware, not hesitant.

And it made him hate terrorists so bad he could taste it, feel his hatred in his very bones and muscles. But the hatred had to be controlled and channeled into lawful police practices.

He stepped into the street, his eyes on the Porsche. He felt his muscles tense, his step lighten. The car had attracted two kids in their early teens—they were trying to break in, perhaps to go for a quickie joy ride, or perhaps to rip off the electronics inside.

Stark clapped his hands together with a smack that echoed down the dark street and yelled, "Police, stop!" They dropped their screwdriver and took off in a flurry of jean legs and running shoes. Stark laughed out loud. They had scratched the paint a bit, but not much, and he got in and followed them for a while in low gear, the engine roaring in the night. Then the kids turned into a side street, and he let them go.

Shortly after midnight, Stark was back in the office. Fritz and Georg were still there; the place was a madhouse of coming and going, phones ringing, printers clacking. A report had just come in from Forensics: the bullet team over at the police garage had dug a total of 115 slugs out of the car frame and upholstery; also, powder burns on Inspector Hofmann's hand proved that he had fired his weapon during the attack.

"Perhaps this was the shot that hit Madeleine, the fake mother. She was seen dragging herself to a BMW."

Georg looked up from the report and asked, "Why would he shoot her rather than try and stop the machine gun?"

"Maybe she was the only target around. Maybe she came up from under the hood of the car pointing a gun." Stark looked at them and asked, "How long would an attack like this take?" The eyewitness reports had varied wildly.

"Fifteen, twenty seconds. One hundred and fifteen slugs is something like two bursts of three seconds each," Georg said.

"Not a lot of thinking time. . . ." For a moment the vision of Françoise Muton being hit by a nine-millimeter police bullet slowed him. It was too close to his own ghost. Then he said, "Fritz, run a thorough check on all the quacks we know around here. You can delegate, but stay on top. Don't bother with legal doctors."

While Fritz went to the phone, one of the buttons on the other phones on Stark's desk lit up and from next door the operator shouted, "Chief inspector, for you. The minister."

It was Karl Esser wanting to know what progress had been made. Stark told him.

Esser said, "Good work, chief inspector. You've got all

their identities and details of the attack. Now all you've got to do is find them. You realize the urgency, don't you?"

"Yes, sir." Stark rolled his eyes at Fritz who was just getting off the phone. "I'll keep you posted."

Then it was 2:15 A.M., and no word yet from the kidnappers.

Make your move, make your demands, thought Stark. Out loud he asked, "Any news on that last set of prints?"

Fritz shook his head. Stark thought the prints would likely belong to the blond driver with the ponytail. All the others on the Coke cans in the apartment had been identified. They were Mahmoud, Rossi, Theo Brandstaetter, Madeleine, and an Englishman called Eric Banigan. The blond was not on anyone's file; she had no record, and her prints were small and delicate, her hands no larger than a child's.

Stark pushed aside the blowup and said to Georg, "I hope you guys are on top of the taps in the Green Party offices here in Cologne and in Bonn. Any leads from within the party?"

Fritz said there were none. The Greens were unable to help.

The windows were open to the cooling night air. Somewhere an Italian compressor horn blared, but otherwise life was slowing in the city.

From a room down the corridor, they heard one of the desk sergeants brief another batch of temporary transferees on the Cologne squad code and on the layout of the city. Housekeeping. Meanwhile the computers kept sorting info, the printers kept clacking, the tape operators kept listening, and a hundred detectives ran around doing legwork, bringing back bits of information. It was a tight net, getting tighter all the time. Stark hoped that Dietrich Helm would hold out.

He looked at the clock: 3 A.M.—half a day after the kidnapping.

11

Because headwinds delayed the Lufthansa flight's arrival, Fontana missed the connecting flight at Frankfurt, and as a consequence did not arrive in Cologne until 3:25 Tuesday morning. Despite the ungodly hour, the airport was crowded (as his own flight had been) with countless priests, nuns, and ministers in a multitude of robes to attend a world ecumenical conference.

He went first in search of his bag, then in search of Jack Teagarden. First he looked, then he had him paged, but there was no sign of him anywhere. Fontana stepped over tiers of bald monks in saffron robes sleeping on the floor and phoned the Bonn number. Teagarden answered almost immediately. "Paul, man; where you been? We were looking all over for you. Henry wants you to turn around and go back to Montreal. But before you leave, we've got to talk to you."

"I beg your pardon? Go back—why?"

"Langley orders, Paul. And why are you late?"

"What? Now just a minute, Jack; what's going on? I came on Lufthansa—couldn't you guys figure that out for yourself? That PanAm I was booked on was delayed with mechanical problems."

"Yeah, sure. We've been cooling our heels for hours waiting for you. Harris and I just came back from meeting the Frankfurt flight, man."

"All right. Whatever. . . ." Fontana rubbed his face wearily. "What's this about turning around? Has the problem been resolved?"

"Never mind. Change of plans: Henry wants you to return to Canada."

Despite his confusion, warning bells began to ring at the back of Fontana's mind. Suspicion, the first, most basic instinct.

"But I don't understand, Jack. Henry was in such a hurry for me to come over here. . . ." He looked up in alarm and saw a woman in white with enormous starched wings on her coif. She was smiling and rapping on the glass with a five-mark piece. Perhaps she wanted change, or perhaps she was telling him to hurry. He turned his back on her and hunched closer to the phone.

"Paul! Hear this, Paul," Jack was saying, "Stay right where you are. I'll meet you and fill you in. Where will I find you?"

Fontona looked around and saw an all-night café at the end of the first level. He told Teagarden.

When he left the phone booth, the woman in white had vanished. Fontana threaded his way through the Buddhists and walked towards the café. The PA system was announcing the arrival of a flight from Singapore.

Fontana bought himself a tall cold glass of beer and took it to the only free chair in the restaurant. Two men were sitting at the same table, one reading a paper, the other staring morosely into his coffee. Fontana's eyes flicked back to the paper, and then he read the headline and saw the picture of the shot-up car.

He got up abruptly and went to the counter where he bought all the late editions he could get his hands on. The Helm kidnapping was on the front page of every one.

He held the papers indecisively for a moment, then put them under his arm, picked up his suitcase, and left the café. He checked his watch: 4:15. He had perhaps another fifteen minutes before Teagarden would show.

Hertz was out of cars, but Avis rented him a midsize Opel. He used his real driver's license and credit card because the two phony ones were only too well known to the Agency.

He found the car on the crowded lot and swung it around so that he could watch the main entrance in the mirror. Four-thirty, and the sky was still pitch-black.

Predictably, the tabloids had made the most of the story. The blood everywhere, the bodies of the chauffeur, two guards, and a baby under the tire. Helm abducted in broad daylight on Neumarkt, one of the busiest streets in the world. It was clear to Fontana that Dietrich's abduction was the reason Wolff was calling him off. *But why?*

The papers said it happened around two in the afternoon—allowing for the difference in time zones, that was soon after this morning's phone call. Which could mean one of two things: Wolff had not yet known of the abduction, and had nothing to do with it . . . or Wolff had simply changed his mind after the telephone conversation and found a way to seize Helm. In which case Wolff would not want Fontana around now. One of the reasons the Agency booked transportation and hotels was to be able to intercept a traveling field man at any time—they knew Fontana's time of arrival and could always head him off.

Sitting in the dark car, one among hundreds in the lot, Fontana thought he'd know a lot more in just a few minutes. A parallel came to mind: only a month ago in Cyprus the Mideast section sent him to talk to one of the local politicians, a man whom Fontana knew well, and who was very outspoken against American installations on the island. Fontana flew into Nicosia, and by the time he arrived, the politician had already been blown away by a car bomb.

Fontana investigated quietly and soon found the telltale fish hook, still attached to a shred of nylon line, in a rear tire: the fishhook bomb was the pet method with the Agency's XPD ops these days. It was cheap and almost fail-safe since it was triggered by tension when the car moved off, not when the driver (often a mere chauffeur) started the engine.

Yes, Helm's abduction could very well be Agency work. Even the level of brutality did not exclude the possibility: decoy actions had to look like the real thing, and lives meant absolutely nothing to terrorists. And if Wolff's boys were behind it, they would want to get rid of him, Fontana, as swiftly as possible.

Then he saw the car in the mirror: a dark Mercedes

without lights, cruising, then stopping right in front of the main entrance. His inner alarm bell jangled.

Three men in the car—the driver remaining in his seat while the other two got out and strode into the pool of light. They walked briskly, with purpose.

The one on the right was Teagarden: tall, angular, the big hands now in the pockets of his suit jacket. The other one was the man they called "Metzger" because he'd worked for years as a butcher at the Rhine/Main base.

Fontana slid further down in his seat. He lowered the chair back so that he could control his angle of view without tilting the mirror and without raising his head.

While Teagarden and Metzger were gone, the driver rolled down the window and lit a cigarette. When the match flared, Fontana recognized Jackson Harris, the Agency's dirty tricks man in the Bonn section.

Several things went through Fontana's mind, but the most prominent thought was that he could under no circumstances abandon Dietrich Helm.

At 4:50 Teagarden and Metzger returned to the Mercedes. Teagarden took his hands out of his pockets. Something glinted in the light: the standard issue .38. Teagarden put it in the shoulder holster, then climbed into the backseat. He slammed the door in exasperation, and on the other side Metzger followed suit. Teagarden's pale face turned slowly, taking in the sea of parked cars. The mouth moved, lips curled, then the Mercedes sped away.

Fontana gave them another half hour before he made a move. Then he sat up slowly, stretching his stiff back. In front of the main entrance a charter bus was taking on the saffron-robed monks, and the first light was creeping into the sky. Cars were starting up here and there on the parking lot, and their headlights came on. He would be inconspicuous, and he *had* to disappear before daylight—now they might still be cruising, later, when they could see into cars, they would be stationary near the parking lot exit.

Fontana started the motor and switched on the low beams. Before driving off, he removed the gun from the typewriter and strapped it on. Then he backed out of the slot and rolled away.

There was no sign of Teagarden's Mercedes as Fontana slipped through the exit and headed toward downtown Cologne. A plan of attack was forming in his mind. He would stay at the Pension Dornier, a place Wolff knew nothing of. As for his first contact, Peter Schott, as Dietrich Helm's second, was probably the best bet.

On the passenger seat the newspapers lay like a demand note. A forty-year interest-free loan had matured, an IOU sealed with no more than a look, an understanding.

A feeling of anticipation, almost of joy rose in Fontana. He gripped the wheel harder and stepped on the gas.

The darkness was complete. Marion sat tailor-fashion, her back to the sloping bulkhead, her palms open on her thighs. The only light came from the open hatch above the companionway to the castle. It spilled through the door and into the wretched cabin like the pale light in a dream. It leached out all color and rendered the scene in black and white, thereby eliminating some of the horror. Madeleine's blood-soaked blouse now looked merely velvety, and the cut above Helm's eyes from the smashed bifocals made him look less like a victim and more like a clown with funny dark makeup.

What the fairytale light could not mitigate was the grotesqueness of his artificial arm. It lay across his lap, and the metal parts and the silvery threads that had come out of his stump glinted eerily. She had always hated his arm; the mere sight of his leather hand, let alone its touch, had given her the creeps as long as she could remember. It was one reason for her hatred of him—but the biggest reason, or muddle of reasons, was that in many ways he was responsible for the tragedy that had befallen her family. If Peter had abandoned her mother where she fell, Helm had been the catalyst of the whole horrid escapade. The defection was his idea, the result of his endless prompting, the result of his promise to Peter that he would give him a job and look after them in the West.

Sitting completely immobile, Marion imagined leaving her body behind so that her spirit could soar and be free. For a while she did not even blink. Because she could not see Helm's eyes, she knew that he could not see hers either. Of course he had recognized her, but the only way to deal with that was to remember that in the end no real harm would come to him and that she would live far away from here, far from Germany and her past. She imagined a warm climate, white buildings in the sun, palm trees against a blue sky. She would live like an exotic flower, fed by Rossi's love.

The cabin was in the bow of the barge; it was shaped like a sloppy triangle and had a wooden floor and steel walls. Except for Madeleine, who was lying on the bunk, and Mahmoud, who was upstairs in the castle, they all sat on the floor, slumped over in positions of tense sleep or exhaustion.

Right across from her was Theo; because of his dark clothes and hairy face, he was the hardest to make out. Banigan was half under the instrument board, Rossi sat next to the door, and Helm leaned against the partition that separated the filthy little toilet from the living space.

Marion promised herself once again that this stage in the operation was merely transitional and that soon things would improve. She reached for her purse, put it in her lap, and held on to it like to a talisman.

Then Madeleine began to pant and toss on the cot. Marion stared at her, then without a thought inched closer until she could touch the cot.

Madeleine was breathing like a person with a terrible cold, labored and snortling with a liquid sound.

Across the room, Theo stirred, then stood. He said, "Keep her quiet, man. She's gonna wake the neighborhood." He slouched like a dark ghost across the cabin and went into the washroom.

Marion moved closer still and took Madeleine's right hand in hers. She leaned forward to see the Frenchwoman's face. What had been slim elegance had now become a frightening translucency. Madeleine was still talking and whispering, dry-lipped clucking sounds, a gurgling French. She was clutching Marion's hand with desperate strength, raised it to her face, covered her eyes and nose with it.

Marion began to cry; she was terrified but she did not dare pull away her hand.

Then Mahmoud came down the companionway. He stood suddenly in the cabin and said to Theo, "Your turn. Keep your eyes peeled."

Marion grabbed his shirt with her free hand and said, "Please, can't we help her? Mahmoud, we can't—"

Mahmoud pried her fingers off his shirt and stepped back. "Shh! No. And no unnecessary talk." He walked across the cabin, stopped momentarily in front of Helm, then sat down next to Rossi.

Madeleine was kissing Marion's hand and clutching it with desperation. Between kisses she gurgled, *"Maman, cher maman . . . j'ai peur, terriblement peur. . . reste avec moi."*

Mahmoud said, "Shh!"

Paul Fontana cautiously circled the block of buildings around the Pension Dornier. The sky had the deep iridescence of black mother-of-pearl, forecasting another hot day. Pigeons crisscrossed Bahnhofplatz on their early-morning sorties away from the nooks and crannies of the cathedral. Traffic was still light and concentrated on the area around the railroad station.

Fontana parked on nearby Gereonstrasse, then took a diversionary route through the side streets, past reflecting store windows. When he was certain that the coast was clear, he slipped into the hotel entrance.

Fontana's Bremerhaven friends were among the few cadets in Major von Helm's class who had survived the war. They were Herbert Dornier, Carl Stolz, and Attila Benn. They had kept in touch with each other and with Helm. On most of his frequent trips to West Germany, Fontana managed a

meeting with at least one of them. They knew about his consulting business in Canada and accepted it as the reason for
his traveling.

Helm's political career had grown out of his postwar role
of industrial adviser under Adenauer. Attila Benn had become
a newspaper journalist. Carl Stolz had also become a politician: he was the deputy defense minister in the present government, and Herbert Dornier ran a hotel.

After the war his friends, like most German aristocrats,
dropped the "von" in their names. In the new Germany
money was far more important than titles. Fontana knew that
Helm had had to sell the Ribnitz estate in Stralsund for taxes,
just as Carl Stolz had to sell his family's holdings in Bavaria.
On the other hand, Attila Benn, who had originally been from
Berlin Koepenick, which was now in East Berlin, was now
benefitting from the connections he had kept up. In recent
years he had become a widely syndicated East Berlin corre-
spondent for a Cologne daily.

Herbert Dornier appeared to have done least well. When
Fontana entered the hotel, he found Dornier slumped over
like an aging student, peacefully asleep at the reception desk.
His balding, pink-domed head rested on his elbow.

The lobby looked much the same as it had for fifteen,
twenty years, except it seemed even more shabby. Herbert's
hotel was like a rock in the swift current of time. It eroded
more and more, and pretty soon it would be washed away.
Nothing could ever stand still; it was against the law of nature. But Herbert refused to face that fact; he was a romantic
youth in an old body with a crippled leg. His view of the world
had foundered in 1944 when the Nazis had defeated their
common hero Major von Helm, and the American machine
gun bullets in the Ardennes had damaged more than his leg:
they had damaged some central will to go on trying to infuse
life with purpose. Dornier, who before the war had had plans
to go to the Duesseldorf seminary and pursue the priesthood,
simply gave up. Released from the American POW camp, he
married his rehabilitation social worker. Anna inherited the
hotel, but it was bomb-damaged. They received an interest-
free Marshall Plan loan to rebuild it, then furnished it with

whatever they could get their hands on. Over the years, the junk was replaced with furniture ranging from Biedermeier to Black Forest curlicue.

Around them children popped up everywhere like the grass in June, but Herbert and Anna remained childless. Then, in the late sixties, she came down with some mysterious disease that Herbert refused to discuss. At any rate, it made her bedridden and totally dependent.

Since then, Herbert had looked after her and run the hotel with minimum help, and from all appearances with minimum success.

The lobby reeked of failure: the carpets and stuffed chairs were threadbare, the coffee table had cigarette burns. Still, for Fontana's purpose, the place was perfect.

He leaned over and whispered into Dornier's ear, "Good morning, sir. I need a room."

Dornier sat up so abruptly that his glasses slipped. He adjusted them, then said with touching pleasure, "Paul, what a surprise. How are you?"

"Fine, Herbert." He smiled.

Dornier frowned for a moment, then looked down at the newspaper, folded it and pointed at the headlines. Then, with a mixture of disbelief and hope in his voice, he asked, "Have you seen this?"

"It's why I'm here. I was in Munich on some business when it happened."

Herbert nodded. "Terrible," he said. "But I'm not surprised."

"What do you mean?"

"Well, the way things are going. The media had made him out like some kind of folk hero or something. If those bastards ask for money for him, I don't see how the government can say no and hope to be in power next time round."

Fontana said, "I thought that maybe we should try to help him."

Dornier's eyes opened wide. "We? What are you talking about? There are special antiterrorist units now."

Fontana looked into his old friend's fading eyes, the bushy eyebrows cocked like an owl's. Just as Wolff knew nothing about *them*, his friends knew nothing about Fontana's work for the Agency. He had wondered at times if they would understand. It would be hard to explain because his original reasons lay so far in the past that they had become murky even to himself.

He said, "I don't know yet, Herbert. But I'm going to find out. There are certain people I know, certain connections. I need a room and a phone."

"That's all?" Dornier reached behind him and took a key off the board. The board was practically filled with keys. It meant that business was bad. Dornier came around the desk and led the way. "What kind of connections, Paul?"

Following behind his friend, Fontana could not help but notice with a mixture of impatience and pity the slow, hobbling walk and the deteriorating posture. He asked, "How's the leg, Herbert? Bother you much?"

Dornier waved him off. "Connections from your consulting?"

Fontana lied briskly: "Without going too much into details, Herbert, I was marginally involved in the latest computer deal between Wiesbaden and IBM. I did market research for the Americans on it. So I got to know quite a few of the security people, and I know the system."

Dornier seemed to accept the explanation; in itself a bad sign, thought Fontana, of how far his friend had allowed himself to slip away from reality.

The room was small and musty. Fontana went to the window and threw it open. It was nearly daylight now, and the traffic volume and noise had increased. Looking out, he could just see the main portal of the cathedral less than one block away.

He turned back into the room and said, "Shut the door, Herbert. Let's sit down for a minute."

Dornier came in, obedient and trusting. He peered into the bathroom and looked once around the room. "There should be towels and soap, Paul. If you need anything. . . ."

"I know, Herbert." Fontana sat on the stuffed and tassled chair that had once been a thing of great beauty. He watched Dornier stiffly lower himself onto the bed. He could still see his friend in the white uniform, blood from the head wound dripping on his chest. Some memories never went away. He asked, "Will you help, Herbert? Shh—wait. All you have to do is keep me here, let me use the phone, take messages if need be, and above all don't say a word to *anyone*— hear that, Herbert? Not to anyone. Not even Anna. How is she, by the way?"

Dornier shrugged. "No change. You can't imagine the . . . oh, well. She should have full-time nursing help, but do you know how much that would cost?"

"How much, Herbert?"

Dornier was looking out the window. "Four thousand five hundred marks a month, Paul. Can you imagine? Plus food and lodging."

"Yes, that is expensive." A crazy thought came to Fontana about creating a new bridge for himself back into Europe, but it was premature and he put it out of his mind.

Dornier said, "Of course I'll do what I can. But in all honesty I don't see how there could be much you and I could do."

"Not just the two of us."

Dornier looked at him with a sudden gleam of boyish interest. "You mean all of us? Attila, Carl . . . the cadets?" He watched Fontana nod, then his expression became less hopeful. "But that's all so long ago, Paul. You know what they've become? Carl's a big-shot politician, and Attila is a widely syndicated columnist. Hard-nosed guys, Paul. Not starry-eyed romantics like us."

Fontana said, "I'm not a starry-eyed romantic, Herbert." He reached for the phone and swiftly unscrewed the mouth piece. It was clean, as expected. He went on to check the bottom of the machine, then moved to the light plugs and switches, took off the cover plates, then replaced the screws.

Dornier looked on in confusion. Finally he said, "You must be watching too much TV, Paul. What's with you? Don't you think the police are much better equipped?"

"Maybe, Herbert. But equipment is not everything. There are a couple of insights I have that the cops don't have." He was thinking about the political connections:

Wolff, the Green Party, Peter Schott, and Gaby . . . *Gaby*? He remembered the young man, her scorn for Helm. Distractedly he took off his jacket.

Dornier's eyes became round and almost as big as his glasses. He swallowed visibly, then asked, "Paul, what . . . what kind of work is it you do? You're not a gun runner, are you?"

"No." He tossed the .38 on the bed and went up to his friend. He put his hands on his shoulders and said calmly and with a deliberate edge in his voice, "Trust me, Herbert. I have experience and I am well-connected. I'm not going to say more; just believe me when I tell you that I know what I'm doing."

Dornier looked at him; his pale eyes were confused yet trusting like a child's. On the spur of the moment Fontana embraced him, then clapped his back and said, "Go now, and send me up some breakfast and the phone book."

Dornier walked away, mumbling.

After Fontana had showered, changed his clothes, and eaten breakfast, he phoned Attila Benn's home number. A woman, presumably Attila's wife, told him to go to hell. It was now just past six o'clock. He dialed Benn's number again and this time the woman told him Attila was in Berlin on assignment for his paper.

"East or West Berlin?"

"Who knows? He'd never tell me a thing. Try the paper; maybe they'll tell you where you can reach him. What do you want from him anyway?"

He hung up gently. He'd never met Attila Benn's wife.

Carl Stolz's number was a government extension, and at the paper no one would be in before nine either. Fontana decided to get some sleep, but before that there was one more call he could make.

He went to the suitcase and gently unwrapped the digitizer. With the Exact-o knife from his kit he made an incision in the insulation of the telephone cable, then pinpointed the right leads. He clipped the alligator needles into incoming and dialed Teagarden's Bonn number. As soon as the clicks in his receiver had stopped, he connected the second alligator. The digitizer was no more than a small cluster of the right kinds of chips, but it worked like a charm bouncing back any tracer signals from the main relay station.

"Yeah?" A man's voice that he did not recognize.

"Jack Teagarden, please."

Pause. Then: "Who's that?"

"Paul Fontana," he enunciated slowly, with relish.

"Hold it!" There was clatter and some voices, then Jack came on. "Where the fuck are you, Fontana? We've been looking all over for you."

"I know. I saw you. You and those two bully boys. I was glad to be out of the way."

"Wolff wants to talk to you. What the fuck do you think you're doing? He told you to come in!"

"Where is he? I tried the Olpe line from the airport but—"

"Never mind. He's got his hands full at the moment."

Fontana laughed. "Jack, you really are an asshole. Tell Henry I'll call back tonight." He hung up, then lay down on the bed, pulling a blanket up to his knees.

He woke at 9:30: the sun stood above the rooftops and traffic below his window was bedlam. He knew that by now his rented car would have been taken care of: he had purposely parked it in a tow-away zone. Wolff's men might look all over North Rhine Westphalia, but they'd never check the Cologne car pound.

Fontana returned to the phone, working the digitizer just to be sure, and called Benn's newspaper. They informed him that they were not allowed to release their correspondents' addresses or telephone numbers even while on assignment. But if he left a number. . . .

He hung up and dialed Carl Stolz's government extension. A male secretary told him that the Honorable Mr. Stolz was currently at his home in Wiesbaden. He was given the number, and rang it, but there was no answer.

Fontana considered phoning Helm's house but decided not to; instead he phoned the party office and asked for Peter Schott.

Schott came on, and when Fontana mentioned his name, he audibly drew in his breath. Fontana heard him say "Thank God," and he was touched.

Fontana asked, "Can we meet?"

"Yes, but where? Not here."

"Perhaps a restaurant. And bring Helm's appointment book. What—"

"Listen, Paul," said Schott quickly, "I have a better idea. The *Lorelei*, the Rhine steamer. It leaves the downtown dock at noon."

"I don't want to spend a lot of time cruising, Peter."

"A one-hour round trip in privacy. All right?"

Fontana agreed, hung up, and rolled the digitizer into a nest of socks.

He drew up a list of knowns and unknowns, studied it, then burned it. At eleven he left his room, walked past the front desk into the street and flagged a cab. Traffic was fast and impatient.

When they reached the intersection nearest the Green Party office he had the driver position the car so that they had a clear but distant view of the entrance to the building. Then they waited. One-mark increments ticked by like pennies.

At 11:35 Peter Schott came bustling out, flagging a taxi. Seconds after he was gone, an ancient Ford Taurus pulled away from the curb. Fontana backed a hunch and told his own driver to follow them at a distance. The cabby gave him a funny look, but a fifty-mark note persuaded him. Halfway to the dock, Fontana told him to speed up and pass them.

Then he watched them arrive, first Schott's cab, then the old Ford.

A man with a blond brush cut got out of the Ford, locked it and checked in with the parking attendant. Tourists waiting to board clustered at the barrier. Fontana went to shake Peter Schott's hand and between the pauses of a normal greeting asked, "Ever seen that blond young man before?"

Schott looked from the corner of his eye and shook his head.

"He followed you here from the office. When we go on board never leave him out of your sight, but always keep your distance."

Schott nodded. "What's going on, Paul? He's probably police."

"Maybe."

They bought their tickets and boarded. The fact that the young man waited until the last moment to cross the gangplank gave him away as a pro.

12

The barge was moored some twenty kilometers south of Cologne proper, at an industrial embankment commonly called the "scrap yard docks" in the great Rhine loop near Porz. There were another two dozen barges just like it, all docked for reasons like changes of ownership, loss of license, even abandonment. Most of the barges were lived on, either by their captains' families or by illegitimate squatters; scruffy dogs and cats abounded, and laundry lines displayed every conceivable human garment. Few of the people knew one another, and those who did avoided each other for that very reason.

The barge Rossi had pinpointed was called *Nijmegen*, probably because it had once hauled steel and coal for a

Dutch owner. She was a rusted, neglected hulk with foul-smelling bilges, and her fore and aft decks were buried under layers of seagull droppings and coal dust.

The *Nijmegen*'s primitive living quarters were below the forecastle, where the old man had lived until Rossi had decreed that their need was greater than his. And not only greater, Rossi had judged; their need was nobler too: theirs was revolutionary while the old man's had been merely vegative.

By Tuesday noon a certain housekeeping routine was established on Mahmoud's insistence; he clearly understood the value of routine, especially in marginal situations. To his visible annoyance, however, tensions and problems continued to mount. Rossi sensed the undercurrents and was uneasy.

The biggest and most immediate problem was Madeleine. The bodyguard's bullet had penetrated the right side of her chest. That she was still alive twenty-four hours later was both a miracle and a nuisance, thought Rossi.

Specifically, it was the sound of her breathing that got to everyone. Madeleine was slowly drowning in her own blood, and each liquid rattle was a further assault on group morale. Rossi caught Mahmoud's look, and he nodded in mute agreement. If Madeleine did not die soon on her own, they would have to help her with it.

From his corner where he was chained to a vent pipe, Helm said, "I feel sorry for you all. This is the most senseless and stupid thing you could have done. You'll get nothing for me, and how many lives will this exercise in futility have cost?"

Without looking up from the faded knees of his jeans, Theo said, "If you don't shut up now, I'll personally cut out your fuckin' fascist tongue. Then we can send it along with our communiqué."

Banigan laughed his weird, yapping laugh. "I wonder, do they take tongue prints? How'd they know it was his?"

"Quiet," demanded Mahmoud. Unlike the rest, who had to sit on the damp wooden floor, he sat on the only chair, and he sat curiously straight-backed, with his hands folded in his lap, a distant, peaceful expression on his face.

Any time now, the Milan note would reach the German government. Rossi had arranged it weeks ago with the Italian cell. They were reliable.

Rossi looked at Marion. He worried about her. She was still sitting by Madeleine's bed, and now, catching his eye, she cried, "Why can't we get a doctor for her? Look at her!"

Theo laughed, but Mahmoud silenced him with a raised hand and a snakelike hiss. "Tzzzzz . . . quiet." Then, turning his yellow eyes on Marion he said calmly, "Two reasons, sister. First, because all life is no more than a movement towards death. Death is what gives us dignity; the way in which we die is our most significant statement. Death comes naturally at its proper time, and it must not be feared. Instead, it must be embraced." He paused for effect, and into the pause Helm's laugh cut them like a knife.

Rossi saw Mahmoud's face whip around. Then the Arab looked from Helm to him, narrowing his eyes.

Rossi stood up, brushing down the trousers where they had hiked up on his legs. He walked calmly over to Helm, picked up the prosthesis, and swung it like a flail down on Helm's chest. He struck him three times, then dropped the arm with a clatter, and playfully kicked Helm's head before returning to his place.

Helm lay still. Marion saw blood filling his ear, then he turned his face sideways to the bulkhead and vomited.

"As I was saying," continued Mahmoud. "Our sister's dignity is one reason why we can't get a doctor. The other is, of course, security. Marion, I'm surprised at you." He looked away from her, and it felt like a spotlight moving on and leaving her in the dark.

Marion tried hard to stave off a repeat of last night's panic. Rossi had told her to be brave—she would get used to it soon enough. But the brutality and the squalor were impossible to bear. She reached deep within her, dragged up every morsel of contempt for society, but still she was afraid.

From where Marion sat, she saw Madeleine's sharpened profile; the sweat pouring off cheekbones and forehead, red bubbles popping between open lips, the blood-soaked, filthy mattress on the old sailor's bunk.

"Agenda," said Mahmoud firmly. They all sat up and looked at him. "At thirteen hundred hours our communiqué will reach the West German embassy in Milan, and within minutes Bonn will know all they need to know. The deadline is midnight tonight. As soon as we hear from our brothers on the radio that all conditions have been met, our return to our home cells will begin in stages."

Banigan asked, "And if they stall?"

"We give them new deadlines in shortening increments. Each accompanied by a token. He has two ears, five fingers, one prick . . ."; at that even Mahmoud had to grin. "And so on. The longer they wait, the less of him they'll get in the end."

Theo said, "We agreed that he had to be iced no matter what."

Rossi interjected, "All in good time. Tokens have to be cut off while the body is alive. Any pathologist can tell if the blood was still flowing at the moment of the cut."

Marion blurted, "I didn't know that. I mean, not that you'd kill him!"

Mahmoud gave her a sharp look, than asked Rossi, "Who was supposed to brief her on that change?"

Rossi nodded at Madeleine, and in her corner Marion shouted in sudden terror, "No, no, you can't! You said you wouldn't!"

"Shh!" hissed Rossi and Banigan. Theo gave her a scornful look and said, "Fuckin' cunt; see what I meant all along?" He turned to Mahmoud for support.

But the Arab ignored him, gazing thoughtfully and calmly at Marion for a long time. Eventually he said, "Sister, one must swim *with* the current. We are the current."

Marion lowered her head on her knees and began to sob. She fell over and curled up like a baby.

"The heat," said Rossi. "She'll be all right. Leave Marion to me. She did a good job yesterday. This is her first action."

Theo muttered another curse.

For a moment all they heard were Madeleine's gurgling, Marion's sobbing, and some distant voices and music on another barge. A moment of fears and ominous pauses, when Marion's mother used to say that an angel had just passed. Marion tried not to think of her mother.

She sat up again and wiped her eyes.

Suddenly Mahmoud put a finger to his lips—voices were near, and they heard the dull sound of approaching footsteps on the concrete wharf. A man's loud voice said, "Half of these will go for no more than scrap. At least the owners aren't sinking them in the river. The channels are shallow enough as it is. . . ."

As though moved by final panic Madeleine began to cry and cough and whine all at once. Mahmoud moved to the bunk with lightning speed and put a pillow on her face.

Up above, the voices went on: ". . . but if you're lookin' for some good diesel engines or even just parts, I'm sure something could be arranged. Take this old bomb for instance, the *Nijmegen*—" the voice was right on top of them now "—want to check her out? It'll just take a minute."

"Tzzz!" Mahmoud waved Marion over to the bunk to take his place at the pillow. She obeyed. At the same time Rossi produced a length of rope, and the others suddenly held long knives in their hands, crouching by the door, ready to leap.

Under Marion's hands Madeleine tossed her head, struggling for breath. She raised the pillow slightly, but Madeleine's frightful gasp made her quickly press down even harder. The clothes she had once admired were soaked in blood, and Marion leaned back to avoid the flailing white hands.

They heard footsteps above their heads, then the clanking of the engine hatch. The men's voices rang hollow in the steel belly of the barge. One said, "Not bad, you see? Two Volvo diesels still in pretty good shape."

Marion fought hard against Madeleine's surprising strength.

"Tzzzz!" hissed Mahmoud.

In desperation Marion pressed down even harder and half lay on the pillow. Madeleine's fingernails raked her face and arms, then the thin legs kicked a quick, feeble tattoo on the mattress.

Before Marion's eyes, the bullet wound made grotesque sucking and gurgling noises, then a great pink bubble rose followed by a final rush of blood. Madeleine lay still.

The next thing Marion knew was that the men were un-clenching her fingers and Rossi was supporting her. The pillow slipped off Madeleine's face uncovering the sharp features of a face she had never seen before.

Banigan said, "Fuck, man that was a close one. A bloody scrap buyer, who'd have known?"

Marion crawled away on all fours, back into her corner. She knew that she was close to madness. She tried to hide behind her hands, but smelling, then seeing the blood, she lowered them again. Her whole body seemed rank and foul as never before.

The men were watching her like a time bomb. She embraced her legs, lowered her head and slid down an endless slope of whispering dread.

The excursion steamer *Lorelei* cast off the Porz dock. Above her stern the German inland marine flag and that of the Rhenish Steamship Company fluttered in the breeze. Gulls wheeled, and tourists along the railings could be heard commenting on the sights.

Fontana and his son-in-law Peter Schott sat at a table on the restaurant deck. They had finished a light meal and were now drinking espresso. A few tables away the blond tail was pretending to read a newspaper.

Fontana was going over the last few days in Helm's day planner again. Appointment after appointment, often no more than fifteen minutes apart.

Peter said, "This is my desk copy for him. He carries another in his briefcase that does not have so much detail." He ran a nervous hand through his hair, but the breeze only pushed the strands back onto his forehead. He was in his early forties, dark-haired and good-looking. His temples were just beginning to go gray. Peter and Vicky had been raised by the same war orphanage behind the Iron Curtain, and the first time Fontana had seen him was at Vicky's wedding. Which was also the last time he saw Vicky.

"Peter, I'm looking for a motive for his kidnapping other than pure ransom. Let's for a moment consider the possibility that Dieter was carrying something valuable or secret."

Peter looked up in surprise. "But why complicate things? Any hour now there'll be something on the radio or a letter delivered, and they'll ask for money."

Fontana nodded. "Possibly. But if we discovered that over the last few days someone gave him something, or met him several times. . . ." The fact that he was unable to tell Peter about his work for the Agency or the missing top-secret military documents complicated things. Fontana moved his chair sideways so that they could both look at the appointment book. "Thursday—you say all these are appointments to do with a Japanese delegation. Friday, labor unions and newspaper people, again about the Japanese thing. But this one, tell me about this again." He tapped his finger on a entry made by a different hand.

Peter leaned closer. "Dieter wrote this in himself so that I would keep the time free. Friday lunch with Attila Benn, you know him. The columnist."

"Of course I do. Did they meet often?"

"About once a month, maybe less. Sometimes Carl Stolz would join them over lunch. Old times, I think."

"Stolz, but not Dornier?"

Peter shook his head. "His wife is very sick. Dieter tried to send him business, but the hotel is a dump." Fontana looked up. The blond tail was still busy with his newspaper. Despite the warmth his jacket was buttoned up. Fontana was almost certain he was a local detective doing the logical thing: shadowing Helm's secretary. Very likely this was still a strictly compartmentalized search and manhunt. For fear of leaks to the media, the chancellor's people and Wolff surely had kept the fact about the missing file to themselves. The local police were chasing only the kidnappers, and both Wolff and Bonn were hoping that a speedy solution of the kidnap case would also solve the other problem.

Fontana turned the pages to Monday. "And this appointment in Bonn—why isn't it written down? And why would he stop off at the office before driving to Bonn?"

"He told me just before lunch that he was going to see Esser at three. Mondays he always eats lunch at home. Maybe he needed something else, so they detoured via the office."

"Could be," said Fontana. The police, Bonn, Wolff, Peter, he himself—each had different pieces of the puzzle. The case reminded him of the parable of the blind men describing an elephant by touch alone. Colossal legs, snaky trunk, thin hairy tail—but who could put it all together?

Fontana closed the appointment book. "Have the police seen this?"

"They copied every page in it."

"They would have to. Now, Peter—could we just talk about Gaby for a moment? I saw her a little more than a week ago. We had lunch, and a strange thing happened. . . ." He described the situation, watching the chagrin in Peter's face.

"What can I say?" Peter asked helplessly. "I no longer have—Paul, forgive me, but I have no control over her. This is—I realize this must sound bad to your ears, coming from your son-in-law, but Gaby has pretty well burned all the bridges she ever had. She moved out, I hate to think how long ago, and neither Dietrich nor I have seen her or heard from her since."

"But, for God's sake, Peter, she's still a minor. You are still legally responsible for her. Not to mention. . . ."

"Morally? No lectures, Paul; please. She's not twenty-one but she's eighteen—so 'minor' depends on your definition. There comes a point when parents—a single parent, a single father, just can't . . ."

"Sorry. I didn't mean it that way. When's the last time you had any contact with her?"

"Contact? I told you . . . well, wait. I know that she was

at the apartment last Thursday while I was at the office. I could tell from the things in the bathroom. She must have washed her hair. The shampoo was left open and the blow dryer was out. That kid used to wash her hair every day of the week."

"Was that the first time she came when you were out?"

Peter nodded. "I think so."

"She left her job at the dry cleaners. What does she do for money? Where is she staying? Who with? I told you about that Latin type. You should have seen the panic on her face. And yet she ran to him. Why? *Who is he?* What does he—" Fontana broke off when he saw the sudden change in Peter's face. "What? What is it?"

"Nothing, never mind."

"You look as though you'd suddenly thought of something that scared you." Fontana eyed Peter suspiciously.

Peter shook his head. But then he spoke, haltingly, almost despite himself. "When she left the apartment . . . I went through her things. You understand I wasn't prying—I merely wanted to find out where she'd gone. . . ."

"Of course, I understand. Go on! What did you find?"

"I found—*oh, God*—" Peter ran his hand over his face. Despite the breeze, beads of perspiration had popped up on his forehead and upper lip.

Fontana leaned forward and asked, "You found *what*?"

"I found a scrapbook full of pictures and magazine articles on the Baader-Meinhof group. Full-page color pictures of all those characters and write-ups on them. Things cut out painstakingly and pasted in. Like a . . . like a family album."

They stared at each other. Then Fontana asked, "And where is it now?"

"I didn't think too much of it at the time. I—"

"Peter—where is it now?"

"She must have picked it up when I was not there. She took everything personal out of her room. Clothes, pictures . . ."

Fontana waited for the unspoken terrible thoughts between them to run their course. He was good at waiting; the hours and days he had waited in his life would add up to years.

Peter made a small gesture and said hopefully, "I'm sure it's quite meaningless. Lots of young people have passing sympathies with terrorists. With 'revolutionaries.' Remember when they all walked around with Che Guevara T-shirts and red bandannas."

Fontana said, "Number one, Gaby despises Dietrich Helm. Two, she has a history of emotional instability. Three, she romanticizes about terrorism. And four, she is closely involved with at least one unsavory character. I'm guessing, but if he is the one who in her words 'loves her for what she is'. . ." He let his words trail away, not wanting to express his fear in words.

"You think she's being used, don't you?"

"It hadn't occurred to me until you mentioned the scrapbook. I'm just thinking out loud, Peter. I've been reading about their method of recruitment. They get a lead—they could have pinpointed her months ago, a year ago, even. Before their choice of victims was narrowed down to Dietrich Helm. They might have won her over to their side *just in case* they needed her contacts. Let's face it: to a group like that, Gaby would be like a dollar bill lying on the sidewalk. You pick it up."

"Impossible. She bore a grudge against Dietrich—but this. No!"

"Let's hope not. Let's hope we are completely wrong."

"When did she stop seeing the psychiatrist, Peter?"

"Two, three years ago."

"Will you get in touch with him, please? We should see him as soon as possible. Leave a message at Dornier's hotel. Now another thing: last Thursday she washed her hair at your place?"

Peter nodded, puzzled.

"You say she used a hair dryer? A brush too? What kind of handle on the brush?"

"Plastic, why?"

"Leave the hair on the brush—or did you clean it already?"

"Paul, what are you getting at? Yes, I combed out the brush and put the hair into the wastebasket in the bathroom. It's bound to be still there."

"Good. Put it in a separate envelope and wrap the brush securely without touching the handle more than necessary. Send them to Dornier's hotel too." He held up his hand. "Shh. Don't ask me questions, just do it." Fontana got out his wallet and removed the American Express card. He wiped it thoroughly with the napkin, then held it out to Peter. "Don't be too obvious about it, but carefully put down your fingerprints. Right hand, thumb and all fingers in a row. Just do it! The lab has to be able to tell yours from hers on the brush." He watched Peter fumble on the table, his hand hidden from the blond tail. Musingly Fontana said, "She's blaming both you and Dietrich for what happened to Vicky. Even to this day."

"It's not as simple as that, Paul. She's blaming the whole world for everything. She has an enormous undefined grudge against her own life and her inability to make sense of it. With his last invoice the psychiatrist sent me a note that put it in those layman's terms. He said it was not unusual with teenagers, but in her case the childhood trauma made the situation more complicated. But, look, enough of that. I think you're completely wrong. I think it's much more likely that Dietrich's abduction was a German police operation." He passed back the credit card and Fontana put it back into his wallet.

"I've thought of that too, Peter. But would they be quite so brutal? You've seen the pictures. Remember Tiedge? Bonn hasn't even got the guts to fire a spy from the civil service. No, I don't think so." On the other hand, thinking of Wolff, Cyprus, and the Agency in general, he knew that this savagery was right out of the field operators' manual.

Which meant that there were two possibilities he had to pursue; one, unfortunately, was his own grandchild, the other Henry Wolff. And he needed to get in touch with Carl Stolz to explore the possible origin of the leak.

Fontana stood up and stepped to the railing.

To their right, a string of barges struggled upstream, and

the *Lorelei* tooted her horn in greeting. On the barges, dogs barked and ragged children played. Laundry flapped in the breeze, and women stood with their hands on their padded hips.

The air was warm and fragrant, alive with the coppery dazzle of a perfect Indian summer day.

Fontana's heart ached, and he gripped the railing, closed his eyes, and raised his face into the breeze. He registered the foreign voices around him with gratitude. A woman exclaimed, *"Regarde-là, mon chou! C'est grande, n'est-pas?"*

Then the ship's bell clanged, and her engines slowed in preparation for docking. The blond tail put away his newspaper and followed Fontana and Schott at a distance of two or three people. The gaggle of tourists crowded the exit, waiting for the gangplank to be lowered.

In the commotion Fontana scanned the crowd and caught an exchange of glances between the blond tail and another single traveler, tall and angular with short-cropped brown hair. He had a crooked nose and a thin mouth, and the way he tilted his head ever so slightly towards Peter Schott would have meant nothing to anyone other than a man with as many Agency miles on the clock as Fontana. When hunters hunted hunters, it was hard to think of new tricks.

On the jetty Fontana and Peter shook hands, then Peter flagged a taxi and Fontana said he'd walk for a while. A minute later he saw the blond tail take off after Peter's taxi. Fontana stood before a store window scanning the reflection.

The tall man with the crooked nose had disappeared in the crowd and was nowhere to be seen. Fontana stepped into a phone booth and called the hotel. Dornier said there was no message.

Fontana phoned Carl Stolz's Wiesbaden number and was greatly relieved to reach him.

*   *   *

In Bonn, the secretary of the minister for external affairs put the call from Italy on hold and rang through to the inner office.

"What?" said the minister. He was drafting a speech and had asked not to be interrupted.

"I'm sorry, sir," said the secretary. "This is urgent. A call from our consul in Milan. It's on the private line."

Minutes later the minister for external affairs had relayed the content of the terrorist communiqué to the chancellor, who in turn had called Dr. Karl Esser. A videograph was on its way.

Esser tried to reach Chief Inspector Stark, and when he was unsuccessful, he succumbed to a rare fit of temper. "Try! Keep bloody well trying," he yelled at the switchboard operator at Cologne HQ. "And put him through the second you reach him."

13

Stark was among the last passengers to get off the *Lorelei*. While Fritz continued his role as decoy tail on Schott, Stark melted away to check out Schott's contact. He was an older man, in his late fifties, who walked with great self-assurance and agility. He had a full head of graying hair, a lean face with quick eyes, and a trim figure. He wore an impeccable yet innocuous brown lightweight suit and an open-necked shirt.

Stark saw him move to the phone booth at the entrance to the parking lot. He slipped into the Porsche and punched in HQ Op. He said, "The booth down by the main dock. There's a connection in progress. Give me the number he's calling."

While he waited he clicked his belt unit back on. It beeped instantly. Mercifully, the operator was back within seconds, and he scribbled down the Wiesbaden number she gave him. He told her to keep monitoring that booth until he cancelled. She said, "Will do," and he flicked over to the unit band.

"Stark here."

"Where the hell have you been, chief inspector? I've been trying to reach you for nearly half an hour." Esser's anger was unmistakable.

"Sorry, sir. I was in a tight situation and had to turn off the belt unit. You could have left a message with HQ. They would have . . ."

"Never mind. We heard from the terrorists. A note was delivered in Milan."

"Milan? They must want to impress us with their international network." Stark kept his eyes on the contact in the phone booth. "What are the demands?"

"The release of the two we're holding in Frankfurt, as well as six members of the Red Brigades in Milan. Transportation to Beirut, and one hundred thousand marks each. Deadline is midnight tonight."

The contact hung up the phone and left the booth. Stark said quickly, "I have to go, sir. Please have Milan fly the original communiqué to Wiesbaden Forensics. I shall call you back as soon as possible, sir. I apologize."

Stark followed the contact at a safe distance to the Hertz car rental office at the end of Paradiesgasse. He backed up the Porsche until he could watch both the exit to the parking lot and the main entrance. The place was hopping with tourists, and after a while the contact exited, holding a key and looking around.

There was a momentary commotion as a man bumped into him, almost knocking him over. The man apologized profusely, touching the contact's arm and looking him up and down, probably asking if he was sure he was all right.

The contact was annoyed. He turned his back and walked towards a light-blue BMW of the six hundred line. A

few minutes later, the car had turned south along the em-
ent road.

Stark allowed five cars to get between them before following. At the same time he put a call out for Georg, then
asked Cologne OP to get immediate clearance for a tap on the
Wiesbaden number.

The blue BMW drove along Militaerring towards the autobahn. Georg checked in and Stark told him to arrange for
five additional tail cars in a rotating pattern. It was a wild
guess, but there had been no other contacts worth following.

Why Wiesbaden? Minutes later he had part of the answer: HQ called back to say that there was a problem with
getting clearance on the Wiesbaden tap.

"What problem?"

"That number belongs to Mr. Carl Stolz, the deputy
minister of defense, and we aren't allowed to tap without. . . ."

"I know. Go through Esser's office. No, wait!" This was
the sort of ticklish decision for which a policeman could be
hailed or crucified. He said, "Correction, operator. I'll get
back to you on that."

The blue BMW was speeding up the ramp to the A555 as
the first two of the additional tail cars fell in behind the
he. Stark switched on the common band and asked, "Stark
here. Who else is coming?"

Georg said, "Krumm, Thile, and Fuchs, sir."

"All right. That blue BMW five cars ahead is the target.
He's probably going to Wiesbaden. Georg, you take over. Lose
him, guys, and I'll have your balls. Go on; start passing me; I'll
fall back."

He changed lanes and slowed. Traffic swallowed him immediately.

Stark phoned Zander and explained the problem with
Carl Stolz.

"You're in charge, chief inspector."

"I know. What would you do?"

"Get permission from Esser."

"Thank you, sir." He disconnected and called the interior minister.

Esser interrupted halfway, shouting, "No! Not without proper procedure. It seems to me you're following a very wild hunch here, chief inspector."

"Perhaps, but all other leads are being processed simultaneously. Schott is Helm's number two. Do we have any more details on the communiqué?"

"There's a videograph just in from Milan. As I told you, the deadline is midnight tonight and they want to hear our agreement over all Cologne radio stations. You understand that our no-deal policy precludes negotiation with terrorists."

"Especially over public airwaves. But we don't want them panicking either. Let's acknowledge and say the government is considering its response. Let's buy some time."

"Agreed. Meanwhile, freeing Helm is your priority—never mind Carl Stolz. Stay away from Stolz. No tap on his phone."

"May I ask why not, minister? I have proof that Schott's contact has called Carl Stolz. I want to know why."

There was a pause, then Esser shouted, "No tap, all right?"

"Understood, sir." Stark disconnected. At the Siegburg autobahn junction he caught sight of Krumm and Fuchs, both in unmarked cars with souped-up V-6 engines under the hood. He identified the target car several kilometers ahead and watched them take off. The Porsche stayed in the slow lane, but even that moved at 130.

South of the Koblenz turnoff, Georg came on to say that rotation was proceeding smoothly and all was well. A few minutes later, Stark was checking his mirrors when he saw Jack Teagarden's grinning mug in a black Mercedes right on his tail. He found him on the regular police channel.

"What the hell are you doing following me, Teagarden?"

The CIA man laughed. "A great day for a little drive, chief inspector, don't you think?"

Stark suppressed his anger and said, "If you mess around with this operation in any way at all, Teagarden, I'll make sure you get shipped back home. And I can do it."

When Teagarden next pushed his send button, Stark heard only thunderous music and Teagarden singing along. In the mirror Stark saw that the fellow on the passenger seat was waving his arms like a drunken sailor. Teagarden yelled, "Sorry, Gunter, can't hear a damn word you're saying."

By midafternoon Fontana was reasonably certain that he was being tailed. There were at least three cars, maybe more. The multicar pursuit was one of the oldest tricks in the book, and if the staggering was done well with long enough pauses between passing and switching, only a suspicious pro would ever catch on.

Fontana thought they ought to have filtered in the cars more gradually, and that on a long stretch like this the first vehicle should have dropped out altogether.

The one behind him now was the green Volvo with the red-haired kid hanging on for dear life. Fontana decided to make sure, and when he reached the Limburg rest station he signaled and turned off.

Sure enough, the Volvo went on, but ten cars later the Ford barreled down the exit looking for him. By then Fontana was at the pumps, getting gas. The Ford slowed when he saw him, then stopped, pretending to wait for a parking slot by the restaurant. The driver looked no older than twenty-five.

Fontana wandered over to him and casually leaned against the door. The man rolled down the window. He was clearly puzzled and embarrassed. He pushed against the door but Fontana's weight kept it shut.

Pretending not to notice that the young man was trying to get out, he smiled his most benign smile and said in rapid English, "Sorry, but I seem to be lost. Can you tell me where the hell I am?"

"What?" the young man asked in German. And then a bit less nervous, "Sorry, uh, not good English."

Which, Fontana thought, lessened the chance of his working for the Agency: because, after all these years in Germany, Teagarden still spoke no German, all his ops spoke English.

Fontana stood back with an apologetic smile. "Sorry." Across the lane, the attendant was yelling for him to move his car.

He had seen the two-way radio clipped to the underside of the dash. The facts that the car looked like an indifferent low-budget model on the outside, yet could move near the top speed of the BMW, and that the antenna was the uncommon four-channel ceramic type, gave the driver away as an agent.

He moved his car, then went into the restaurant where he bought a map of Wiesbaden and a cup of coffee. Then he did some studying.

"You stupid dolts," Stark yelled at his team over the radio. "He spotted you a mile away. Krumm and Fuchs, get off this case. Go home. In fact all of you buzz off back to Cologne. Except you, Georg. Get your ass down to kilometer two forty-five." He shoved away the curved gooseneck mike and stared into the rear-view mirror. Teagarden's Mercedes was pulling off onto the parking site and coming up behind him.

Stark got out and wandered back. "Teagarden, I hope you know what you're doing. I don't have to explain about jurisdictions, do I?"

"No, you don't." Teagarden and his passenger grinned at him like choirboys. They simply sat, not bothering to explain or pretend, but Stark knew he had no case. He returned to the Porsche just in time to see the contact's BMW whip along the passing lane in a dazzle of spoke wheels and chrome.

He flung himself after him, fishtailing out of the parking strip on hot rubber. All three lanes were pretty crowded and he knew it would be hard to keep up with the BMW without being seen.

At four o'clock they neared the Wiesbaden exit. Georg had checked in from somewhere behind him, and Stark himself was some twelve or fifteen cars behind the contact. All three lanes were moving at the usual clip when the blue exit signs popped up left and right. The Wiesbaden/Frankfurt autobahn junction was a headache at the best of times, but Stark knew it by heart. Which was why he was doubly surprised, then ready to explode, when by the time he had reached the airport exit the blue BMW had simply dropped out of sight.

The worst thing was that he had to keep going for another ten kilometers before he could get off. By then he was practically in Mainz.

Behind him Teagarden blew his fucking horn, and Georg was a voice in the wilderness asking where the hell everybody was.

He exited onto the regular highway and pulled over on the curb in a cloud of dust. He was out of his car by the time Teagarden came up behind him, and his gun was out even before the Mercedes had come to a full stop. Stark put three slugs into the fancy radiator grill, climbed back into his car, and drove off.

In his mirror he still caught sight of Teagarden and his partner getting out like shellshocked men. Then he wheeled off into the feeder lane, doubling back towards the Wiesbaden address that HQ Op had radioed him earlier.

Carl Stolz once lived in a fine old house on the Graben, but two years previously, when his wife died, he moved into a condominium on Rundelstrasse. It was an elegant street with ancient linden trees and the kind of chestnut trees that reminded grown men of their childhood.

Fontana reached the politician's house at 5:15 and was promptly let in by Stolz himself. They took the elevator up to the apartment.

Fontana had been here once before, less than a year ago when he needed information regarding a major shipment of West German tanks to Israel. The Americans hated seeing

U.S. dollars being spent on anything other than U.S. hardware, but the Leopard II outperformed its competition on the desert tank range, and the deal went through.

Now they walked from the elevator to the apartment, and Stolz opened up with a key. Stolz was fifty-nine, like himself, but he looked older, and there was a nervous, distracted air about him. Fontana decided to proceed with caution.

Once the door was closed behind them, however, Stolz came right out with it: "I can guess why you're here, Paul. It's about Deitrich, right?"

Fontana nodded and sat down on the couch in the living room. "There must be something we can do for him. I happen to know that there's more to this abduction than meets the eye, Carl. There are certain highly sensitive documents involved—I'm not sure what kind."

In the kitchen Stolz uncorked the obligatory bottle of Rhine wine. Fontana could see him from where he sat; shirtsleeves and tie, gold-rimmed spectacles, gray, thinning hair. He wiped the dust from two glasses, then set them on the coffee table.

The apartment was a typical well-heeled bachelor's affair: good modern furniture of leather, corduroy, and wood, an Afghan rug on blond parquet flooring; bedroom, bathroom, living room, kitchenette, and a deep balcony looking out on green treetops. Open French doors admitted the evening air. In the distance the Wiesbaden rush-hour traffic roared with a clamor of horns and streetcar bells.

On the wall, framed in gold, hung the stunning Dürer drawing *The Four Horsemen of the Apocalypse*. Carl had once said that today Dürer would have drawn five men. The fifth horseman would be Uncle Sam with a Minuteman or a Pershing missile rather than a mere scythe.

Once, on a visit during their cadet days, Fontana had seen the Dürer in the Stolz family house in Heidelberg. Carl was the last of the line; there were no sisters or brothers, and there were no children—at least no more. There had been a son, but he died several years ago at a well-publicized fluke accident during a NATO maneuver.

Carl poured, and they toasted each other.

"How do you know about the documents, Paul?"

"From Peter Schott," Fontana lied easily.

Stolz searched his face for a moment, then said, "You don't think it's just a regular kidnapping—terrorists asking for the release of some of their own? Money, free departure . . ."

"There's nothing in the papers and nothing on the radio about those terms. In fact, there's no news at all."

"There's a news blackout, of course. Standard procedure, Paul. The police would have imposed that first off."

"When was the last time you saw him, Carl?"

Stolz stood up abruptly, went to the open balcony door, and looked out for a moment. Then he turned and sat down again. "Look, Paul—let's not play games. I know your little secret. You work for the Americans, don't you? Did the CIA send you to sound me out?"

Fontana stared at him. From years of practice his mind tried to shift into the gears of duplicity, but he fought the impulse. Closely watching his friend's face he said, "I sometimes do work for the Americans, and not just on government contracts as I told you the last time . . . but, *no*, the CIA knows nothing of my coming to see you."

Stolz leaned forward. He rested his elbows on his knees and pushed his glasses back into the red notch in the bridge of his nose. His eyes grew larger. "Peter Schott couldn't have told you about the documents. Who did?"

Fontana leaned back. On the wall behind him were shelves with books interspersed with the elements of a hi-fi. He looked for the right button, then turned on the radio. Voices filled the room. He leaned forward again until his face was close to Stolz's.

"All right, Carl: before the kidnapping happened, I was assigned the job of talking to Dietrich and convincing him to surrender those papers. I was to be briefed fully on arrival in Cologne, but by the time I got there the terrorists had taken Helm. My section head called me off, and I'm sure right now they're trying to find me."

"Dangerous, Paul. It's a safe bet that your people are behind the abduction."

"Why do you say that?"

"Because it's imperative that they get the file back. We are talking about American top-priority interests."

Fontana watched his friend's face. "I'm told that the documents give evidence of a much greater American nuclear presence in West Germany than the public knows."

Stolz frowned at him. Then he said drily, "The documents in question, my friend, are what's commonly called the Nuclear Targeting File. They contain every silo, every cruise position in West Germany, and they also contain the targeting code, in other words, what the missiles are aimed at. In great detail, I might add: the code tells which part of Leningrad or Moscow is covered by which missile, how the multiple war heads will separate. And yes, there are *far* more than there ought to be."

Fontana caught another glimpse of the truth. He considered the implications, then asked with a sense of disbelief, "Carl, did *you* leak them to the Greens?"

"No!"

"But you know who did?"

"No!"

"So how do you know the Americans are behind the abduction?"

"I can put two and two together. The Americans always have more than one motive. The plan is to use West Germany as the buffer zone in case of a nuclear war. They've got more missiles here than anyone can imagine. We are still the vanquished, Paul. The occupation after World War Two continues, don't you know? We are the pawns in the front line of attack."

"If the Americans staged the abduction to retrieve the file, who leaked them in the first place? You must have an idea. You're high up in the Ministry of Defense. Who has access to the file?"

Stolz leaned back and held up his hands. From the loudspeaker came a mixture of men's and women's voices; it was a panel discussion on the West German film industry. Behind the wall of sound, Stolz's lips moved with the words, "Don't,

Paul, I cannot tell you. I mean, I don't know." He was barely audible, and Fontana leaned as far over the table as he could.

With an urgency close to anger he demanded, "You must tell me everything you can—we've *got* to help Dietrich. Don't you remember all the things we believed in?"

Stolz almost smiled. "Dear Paul. Just look at us. We're not knights in shining armor. None of us. Not even Dietrich Helm. But anyway, I've told you all I can. They're your people . . . search your heart. And your files."

Fontana got up. A feeling close to panic gripped him, as though parts of his past were rising to cloud his perception of reality. He went around the table and wordlessly gripped his friend's shoulder. Close to Stolz's ear he then said, "It's never too late. The truly important things never change. Please help by making sure that I can always reach you over the next few days."

Stolz turned his face and looked up. Moving across the room, almost running to the door, Fontana felt his eyes on his back; he was aware of Stolz's presence all the way down to the car. Then it faded, making room for a greater urgency.

He had to get to the digitizer as soon as possible—he had to reach Wolff or at least Teagarden. A plan was shaping in his mind. He now had a working hypothesis and was eager to test it.

Before leaving Wiesbaden he briefly stopped at a gas station to use the washroom. From the mirror, a gray-faced, harried man stared back at him. He threw cold water on his face, then dried himself and, back in front of the mirror, combed his hair.

And raising his hand with the comb, he saw the bug. He froze for a second, then rushed into one of the toilet cubicles to take off his jacket.

It looked like no more than several layers of clear tape stuck to outer material of his sleeve. Peeling it off, he remembered the incident at the car rental place, the man who'd bumped into him, then gripped his arm as though for support.

Fontana cursed himself. It was a bug commonly called a

"bouncer" or "superchip" because not only did it emit a homing beam but it also transmitted sound, conversations. While his fingers flew over the rest of his clothes, his mind raced for reasons and answers. A bouncer like this, no bigger than a fingernail but jammed with circuitry and platinum transponders, was a high-ticket item. Only the top layers of the CIA, GRU, and Mossad to his knowledge had them—they were complicated devices because each bouncer had to be tuned with infinite precision to its mother unit.

He wrapped the bouncer in toilet paper and dropped it into the bowl. When it was soaked he flushed it down. Then he threw his suit jacket back on and buttoned it up to cover the holster. Minutes later he hammered the BMW back the way he'd come, leaning on the horn through red lights, then slowing and switching off his lights when he reached Rundel-strasse.

He ran across the lawn and rang Stolz's bell. There was no answer, so he put his hand flat on the row of bells and pushed them all. The buzzer rang and he raced up the stairs as fast as his heart allowed.

Carl's door was locked, and Fontana pounded with his fist while fear and dread climbed up inside him. Down the hall people poked their heads out, and one brave soul called, "Hey, what's with the noise?"

Fontana pounded once more, then took a few steps back. Because the door was very solid and his bones no longer young, he saw no alternative. He took the .38 from his holster, leaned against the opposite wall, and fired twice at the lock.

Down the hall the heads were gone, but the door swung open and he ran inside.

Carl lay by the stereo: under his shattered head the pool of blood was still spreading, and the gun in his limp hand was still warm.

Fontana leaned against the wall, gasping for breath, then his mind clicked into gear again, and he raced out on the balcony. But it was already too dark and the trees were too dense to see anything.

He went back to Carl's body and was hopelessly feeling for a pulse when he heard the high-pitched scream of a police siren, still far away but coming closer.

The instinct honed over thirty years of field work kicked, and Fontana walked out of the apartment, then ran down the stairs and was in his car well before the response unit arrived. Driving off he saw them in his mirror: two green Fords with flashing lights and a white Porsche.

When he was out of sight, he headed for the autobahn. He floored the pedal and pushed the big car to its limit all the way back to Cologne.

Dornier was asleep again at the desk, and Fontana decided not to wake him. He had a lot of thinking to do before he could do any explaining. In his pigeonhole were two envelopes and a message: the envelopes contained a tangle of fine blond hair and a plastic brush.

The message said, "Call Carl Stolz."

He went upstairs, unwrapped the digitizer, and called Teagarden's number at the U.S. embassy in Bonn. A recording told him about the business hours. There was no answer at Henry Wolff's number at the Olpe safe house. After some ten rings he decided to wait until the morning. He looked in bewilderment at the brush and the hair.

It was 2:35 A.M. on Wednesday morning when he sat down in the tasseled chair to collect his thoughts. Eventually sleep overwhelmed him despite his ragged nerves. But it was not an easy sleep. It was haunted by the face of Carl as a young man, by boys in white uniforms, by the distorted echo of Major von Helm's pledge. But the joy and enthusiasm of 1944 was already overshadowed by foreknowledge.

Later, his dream shifted and Franziska appeared. She was so close that he could almost touch her. She whispered to him and pointed at two children behind a barbed-wire fence.

Franziska's words were unintelligible and the children stood, completely immobile. Only their eyes grew and grew until they swallowed him up like dark caves.

The blood under Stolz's head was still warm, and what had been hurriedly contrived to look like a suicide looked immediately to Stark's eye like murder. The broken teeth gave it away.

Stark had picked up the squad call about a shooting at Stolz's address. For the last few blocks he had tailed the green police Fords with a feeling of great apprehension. By then Georg had caught up with him. Outside Stolz's building, Stark had identified himself to the Wiesbaden response team and taken charge. While Georg stayed in the car to establish contact with Zander, Stark ran up the stairs.

Now he ordered an electronic sweep, then extensive photography. Only then could Fingerprints and Blood begin their work.

Stark said, "I want a special report on those two glasses. Content, saliva test, and prints. Then the sofa—an isolated vacuuming for clothes fibers. And a detailed coroner's report on the gunshot. Everything."

He went down to the Porsche and sent Georg back upstairs while he reported to his boss. "The guy we chased down here was Schott's contact from the *Lorelei*," he told Zander over the car phone. "If the minister had given us permission to tap the Stolz phone, this could have been avoided."

"You're guessing. Your man shook you off, that's all. You're sure it's not a suicide?"

"When people shoot themselves in the mouth, they don't smash three front teeth in the process. Whoever did this slammed the barrel in hard, then fired and put the gun back into Stolz's hand."

"Christ, Gunter, that's all we need. The media are going to love it. As for you, let me quickly whisper this warning in your ear: watch your step with the minister and the police commissioner. And don't cross the lines as *they* see them. They're really hot on the Helm abduction, so you'd better have some progress to show.''

Proceeding on his own initiative, Georg had ordered a "scrub" on Carl Stolz's telephone line, and within minutes Wiesbaden HQ called back reporting a secondary drain on the line. "Secondary drain" could mean an improperly installed extension phone, but most often it was a tap, a voice-activated recorder somewhere along the line.

Georg checked on the extension in the bedroom. When that seemed all right, he hurried back downstairs to tell Stark.

Georg was just pushing open the inner glass door when he saw a pair of legs swing from the lower branches of the chestnut tree. Then a man leapt down, flexing his knees like a gymnast, and coming up right behind the Porsche, gun in hand.

Stark must have seen movement in the mirror, but the car door was not even open when Georg started firing. His shot shattered the man's gun hand and ricocheted into his face. Before he was down Georg was beside him. Stark was still getting out of the car.

The man had been spun around and he slid down the trunk of the chestnut tree, his face painting the bark like a grotesque brush. Georg kicked away the revolver, then grabbed the man's arm and pulled him over on his back.

There were shouts on the balcony above, but leaves and branches were in the way; moments later members of the response team were down, staring at the body.

Unfairly, Stark yelled at Georg, "Why shoot to kill, damnit?" He was pale with anger at the close call.

Photography had finished with the body under the tree, and they were stuffing him into a body bag when the first TV van pulled up—a minute later, reporters from all media came

down like the usual flock of vultures. In the midst of the confusion, Stark's belt unit summoned him to the car phone.
Predictably, it was the minister of the interior.

Esser was in a rage. "What the hell are you doing down
in Wiesbaden chasing secondary contacts? That is work for
your bloody support people of which you've ordered hundreds
at the cost of millions to the taxpayer. You've got an army out
there doing legwork for you and what do you do? You personally tail, then lose, a low-grade lead."

"Low grade? Carl Stolz low-grade? If you'd given me
permission to tap his phone—"

"Enough, chief inspector. I want you in my office by
nine o'clock tomorrow. Secondly, I want you to hand the Stolz
case back to the investigating lieutenant in Wiesbaden. It is
not, I repeat, *not* your case. Thirdly, I want some goddamn
results on the Helm abduction!"

"Sir! There are some late developments here about
which the superintendent could not have informed you yet."

"What?" snapped Esser.

And with a certain relish, Stark said, "Another body."
Into the stunned silence, he elaborated about the man whom
Georg had shot, but to his astonishment this far from ap-
peased Esser.

"Enough, chief inspector! I order you to hand over to the
lieutenant this minute. Your case is the *Helm* case, and I
want you in my office with some very good explanations for
your strange conduct. Now let me to speak to the lieutenant!"

Stark did as he was told. Watching the proceedings
around him while fending off the bloody media, he could
not stop wondering why Esser was so determinedly denying
the possibility of a connection between the Stolz and Helm
cases.

The more he wondered, the more curious he grew. Why
was Esser more concerned about the kidnapping of a func-
tionary of an opposition party than the murder of a senior
member of his own government? What about that phone tap
on Stolz's line that Georg had discovered? What was the
CIA's interest in all of this?

14

"They are stalling," said Mahmoud with a thin-lipped smile. "That's what they're doing. Stringing us along." He looked at Rossi. "Right?"

Rossi nodded.

It was two minutes after midnight; a day and a half since the snatch. The deadline specified in the Milan communiqué had just passed and instead of some sort of counter offer, the final newscast on the radio had merely said that the government had received a ransom note in the Helm kidnapping case and was studying the situation.

In his corner Helm said, "I told you so. There is a firm, unshakable no-deal policy. When will you people ever understand that civilized societies find you so detestable that—"

"Shut your fuckin' mouth!" said Theo. "You bloody Nazi fascist. It's you and your kind that are detestable."

"Shhh," hissed Mahmoud. He clicked off the small transistor radio, stepped over Marion's and Banigan's outstretched legs on the floor, and sat tailor fashion by Helm's side.

Rossi watched with fascination. He had been in similar situations with Mahmoud twice before. Both had had to be abandoned, but in each case they had at least gotten publicity once the bodies had been found. A snatch could work on many levels; even if the ransom conditions were not met, the snatch itself was an exercise in the revolutionary struggle, and the more coldbloodedness displayed, the more it furthered the image of the brotherhood and improved the chances of private snatches for money.

In hardly more than a whisper, Mahmoud asked Helm, "So what do you know? What do you suggest?"

"If you let me go now, you have a chance to return underground. Take it while you can. You can bet there's a huge police operation out there. Hundreds of phones tapped, all your known hiding spots raided, your colleagues in jail being questioned by experts. During every minute that passes, our antiterrorism squads make progress and you fall behind." Helm spoke firmly, yet with astonishing indifference.

In the heat, the steel belly of the barge was like an oven. Because the head was now full, they had hacked a hole through the floor boards and were relieving themselves into the bilges. The smell of that, along with the smell of Madeleine's body from the bottom of the cargo access well, was rapidly becoming unbearable.

Mahmoud leaned closer to Helm and said lightly, "So you think we should just walk away. Leave you alive and walk away?"

With a visible show of willpower, Helm sat up as best he could. His feet still chained to the vent pipe, he leaned against the wall. Blood showed on his shirt where Theo had flailed him with his prosthesis, and his crotch was soaked in urine. But despite all that, his face maintained that expression of incomprehensible indifference. Rossi watched him, wondering about the strength of the man.

Helm said, "Yes, it would be better for you if you left me alive. There is a certain unwritten code. If you kill me, our police will have to hunt you until they catch you and can hold up your heads to the crowd."

"But you've seen our faces," said Banigan from across the room. "Some of us can't afford that."

Helm actually chuckled at that. It was a strange sound under the circumstances and it seemed that no one had heard such evidence of lightheartedness in a long time. They stared at him; their faces shone palely in the dim light of the hurricane lamp.

Helm said, "By now they'll know exactly who every one of you is. They'll know your faces, your fingerprints, the chemical composition of your hair, the guns you use; they'll even have an accurate computerized prediction of your behavior." Helm leaned back his head and closed his eyes. Then he opened them again and looked straight at Marion. "They'll even know who among you is not really part of your pathetic organization. Who was coerced into your preposterous fold."

Mahmoud kept watching Helm closely, and Rossi said, "She wasn't coerced, you idiot. She came along gladly."

Helm said to Mahmoud, "Unchain me. What possible threat can I be to you?"

"True. An old man like you. I'll give you fifteen minutes off the leash. Make a move to the door, or so much as open your mouth to scream, and I'll cut your throat." Mahmoud showed him the curved knife, then unlocked and unwound the thin bicycle chain. Mahmoud said, "Let's spoil him. Pass him a Coke!"

Rossi, who was closest to the stack of cases, tossed one over. There were cans of luncheon meat too, and bread, but since arriving at the barge no one had eaten a bite.

Wedging the can between his knees, Helm pulled the tab and the hot Coke gushed like a fountain. He drank with loud gulps, then set the empty can on the floor next to his briefcase. Mahmoud looked at it as if seeing it consciously for the first time. He held out a hand and said, "Pass me that. Pass me that case."

Helm lifted it with his one hand and pushed it across his legs.

Mahmoud undid the catch and emptied it on the floor. A few papers fluttered out; a Mont Blanc pen, a phone book, a small leather-bound diary, and a manila envelope. No weapon, nothing electronic.

Rossi crawled over and leafed through the papers to see if they could be used to their advantage. Mahmoud looked too. Like all top-echelon corporate gibberish, they were incomprehensible. The diary was neatly blocked out with appointment after appointment for weeks ahead.

Rossi laughed. "They'll miss you, won't they? There, first thing tomorrow morning: breakfast meeting with C.S.,

question mark. Who the fuck is C.S., old man?" Rossi
laughed.

Helm said with dignity, "Carl Stolz, a friend of mine."

Behind them Theo sneered, "That old papist shit of a politico. A Nazi brother from your past, right?"

"The Nazis were hardly papist," said Helm, and everyone looked at him for a second of astonishment.

"Well, whatever the fuck they were," said Theo impatiently, "you were one of them, everybody knows that."

Helm looked at them in turn with infuriating bemuse-
ment, then pointed at Marion. "When I was just a few years
older than Gaby, the Nazis imprisoned me in a cellar for eight
months and beat me almost every day. Compared to them
you're naive little hamsters. Aimless, angry little rats. Which
is why nothing you can do or say will affect me beneath the
surface. I know this must be hard to understand for emotional
children like you."

"Fuck," said Theo. He leaped up to beat Helm, but
Mahmoud barred his way and lightly waved him away.

Rossi looked first at Marion's pale, shocked face and said,
"Funny guy, your uncle." Then he added with a sneer, "Why
don't I cut the first piece off him so's we can send it?"

"Wait. Never rush things," said Mahmoud. He opened
the manila envelope and pulled out the contents: a bunch of
accordion-folded computer print-outs with nothing but numbers. He looked at the pages with disgust, then scooped up
the lot and shoved it back into the briefcase. "If you want to
piss do it now. I'll be chaining you up again in a minute."

Helm rose stiffly and stepped to the hole in the floorboards. He did his business, then buttoned up his fly.

When he returned to his place, Mahmoud relashed the
bicycle chain. Then he went to the small folding table to turn
the radio on low again. It played a program of late-night jazz.
Mahmoud opened a Coke and drank greedily. Sweat streamed
off him, soaking into his wet clothes. Then the radio crackled
and the announcer came on: "We interrupt this program with
a news flash: Carl Stolz, assistant to the deputy minister for
national defense, has been found shot dead in his apartment
in Wiesbaden. Police refuse to say whether it is a case of sui-

cide or murder. They also refuse to speculate on whether Stolz's death has anything at all to do with the abduction of Green Party strategist Dietrich Helm . . . further information will be broadcast as it becomes available . . ." Jazz sounded again.

Mahmoud stared at the radio and when Theo opened his mouth to make a comment, Rossi said, "Shush."

Then Mahmoud snapped his fingers. "The briefcase again." Rossi brought it, and the Arab dumped the contents on the table. "Line by line, brother. Look for any military context."

"What's on your mind, brother?"

"Do it."

They went through the papers and booklets again. The phone book might have a multitude of secondary or tertiary meanings, as could the diary.

While Rossi continued the search, Mahmoud went over to Helm. Leaning close, he said, "Tell me. Better tell me now, old man."

"I don't know what you're talking about," Helm murmured.

"You had an *appointment* with Carl Stolz. Why?"

"He's an old colleague. We were to have breakfast together."

Mahmoud read behind the eyes and the forehead of Helm and was infuriated by the absence of fear. He was about to strike him, then changed his mind. He turned to Banigan and Theo and hissed, "Take off his shoes."

They did, not missing the chance to make fun of the smell. When the feet were bare, Mahmoud tightened the bicycle chain, then ripped a piece of wire out from under the circuit board. He quickly stripped the insulation with his knife, then began whipping Helm's soles. Each smack of the bare, four-stranded copper raised thin purple welts. After the tenth stroke the soles erupted and began to bleed. Counting out softly, Mahmoud struck twenty more times.

Panting, he put away the wire. He said, "We still do this where I come from. *La bastonnade*—the French taught us."

Helm was leaning against the wall. His eyes were closed

and his lips were pressed together. Mahmoud brought his face close, and hissed, "What's your connection with Stolz?"

Helm said nothing; he did not even move.

Banigan said with contempt, "Old codger's fainted again."

Mahmoud found an oily rag and stuffed it into Helm's mouth. Then he pointed at a flashlight and snapped his fingers. Banigan handed it to him. The Arab shook the batteries onto the floor, then stepped on them hard with the heels of his shoes. Acid oozed out like honey. He scooped it up with the blade of his knife and spread it methodically on Helm's soles.

Thin acrid smoke began to curl away lazily like the fumes of dry ice. Helm's eyes snapped wide open and they could hear his muffled scream right through the rag.

On his soles, the blood turned yellow, then white. The air in the already filthy cabin became unbreathable.

Helm fainted. He slid along the steel wall until he lay slumped on his side.

Mahmoud took a step back and looked at him. Out loud he said, "What is going on, brothers? Use your heads. What is going on? How is our fat cat here tied in with this dead Stolz? And who did the icing? It is stealing our thunder. Who cares about an abduction when they've got a murder to talk about?" His voice had been rising from its normal hiss to a subdued shout. He spun on his heels and ordered, "Back to the fucker's briefcase. Search, search, brothers!"

Once again they went over the diary and the phone book; they unscrewed the fountain pen and squeezed out the ink. Meanwhile Mahmoud looked into the manila envelope. He pulled out the entire fan-folded computer print-out. One end fell to the floor and he stood up to extend the whole length. Something that looked like a map fell out.

Mahmoud picked it up and said, *"Allah akbar."*

The others watched him now, sensing a fresh electricity in the room. Only Marion still squatted in her place, her eyes unfocused, cheek resting on her denim knees.

Mahmoud looked from the map to Rossi and spoke an

entire sentence in Arabic. No one understood, but his excitement transmitted to them, and they stood up, crowded around him.

Rossi smiled and said, "Come again, brother."

Mahmoud held the map out to Theo. "What are these places, Theo? Those place names, man—am I dreaming?"

Theo looked at the map, then swallowed hard. "Shit," he said softly. "Shit, man; those're missile sites. The goddamn silos. I remember those names from the newspaper and from all those no-nuke demonstrations. Take a look!" He passed it around.

Rossi stared at it and said in awe, "This is . . . hey, this together with the computer print-out is probably the nuclear defense plan for the whole goddamn country." He bent down to the fan-folded paper and was soon able to match the numbers printed next to the various place names.

Theo said, "There's a lot of place names I've never heard of. Like these two here, KB-78 and KB-79 right here in Cologne. I didn't know we had missile sites right in our fuckin' backyard, man."

"You didn't?" asked Mahmoud.

"No. But a good half of them have been in the news." Theo bit a grimy fingernail, then tapped the map in several places. "These here are the cruise missiles that there was so much noise about."

Mahmoud said, "Let's see, brothers—Theo is from Cologne, and he's been taking part in most of the no-nuke demonstrations. And yet there's rockets right here in Cologne, and he didn't know about them."

"Right," said Theo.

Mahmoud continued, "So, what does that mean? Could it mean that there's a lot more missiles around than the public and the media know?"

Rossi looked at Mahmoud and a triumphant smile spread on his face. "I see what you're after, brother. You're saying, why don't we call some of the radio stations and tell them what we found in Helm's briefcase? Give them some of the reference numbers here as an appetizer, and see what the government does then."

"Exactly," said Mahmoud. "This information is a much better bargaining tool than the fat cat's life."

Rossi beamed and embraced Mahmoud. Soon they all stood in a circle, hands on each other's shoulders.

Rossi shouted, "Hey, Marion, come here. Come, baby." He made room, and with new hope in her eyes Marion came to join in.

To celebrate their find, they opened a few cans of luncheon meat, ate some moldy bread, and drank more Diet Coke. Mahmoud established a system of watches, two hours each, so that they could finally get some sleep.

The hatch was opened to the small castle on top, and a riverside window was cranked open to let some of the stink escape.

Helm was still unconscious, or perhaps just pretended to be, and Mahmoud assigned Marion to look after him. She took the rag out of his mouth and washed his feet thoroughly with several cans of Coke. Then she put his socks and shoes back on.

Mahmoud took the first watch, then Rossi, Banigan, and Theo.

When Mahmoud was on duty, Rossi crawled over and screwed Marion. But he did it quickly and impatiently, and she took no comfort in it. Again she felt a dual identity, as if she had escaped her body and was now able to watch and judge without getting involved.

At some point she fell asleep, but woke when a slight wind came up and tiny waves lapped against the outside of the hull. Looking up, she came face to face with Helm's gaze.

He beckoned slowly with his single hand and obediently she crept closer. Her heart was pounding so loudly that she was afraid it might wake everybody up. She could see them in the faint moonglow that spilled down the hatch: Mahmoud on the turned-over mattress on which Madeleine had died, Banigan slumped over the table, and Theo on the floor, his long dirty hair streaked over his face. Rossi would be upstairs.

Marion reached Helm and, still on hands and knees, looked up into his face, like a submissive dog. He beckoned her even closer, and she brought her ear near his mouth.

"Gaby, what on earth are you doing among these people? What is happening to you? What did they do to make you join?"

She heard herself whisper stubbornly, "I wanted to join." She almost added, 'Uncle Dietrich,' but stopped herself in time.

"But why? *Why?*"

"It's the first important step I've taken all my life. There is no other way to make society understand."

"Understand what? The Russian Revolution is long over; these fellows are murderers, bored fools. They're not *revolutionaries*—they're terrorists and they're in the business for kicks and for the comfortable living."

"Comfort?" she hissed. "You call living like this comfortable?" She waved her hand around the bare cabin, the sleeping men, the foul mess.

"That's the kick part. The comfort is in the money." He stared at her, trying to see her face in the dark, and she wanted to back off, crawl back to her place on the floor. "Gaby . . . Gaby, what did you imagine would become of you among these people?"

With angry defiance, she said, "They're no different from me and I'm no different from them. We're the lost generation, betrayed by our parents."

"What? Why?"

"Because there is no goddamn future for us. It's all used up, coming to an end. Any time now some fat-cat moron will push the button with the big N on it. How decent and sensible is that?" Her words suddenly struck her as shopworn and hollow, and she became angry.

"Come now; you're too young to talk like that. Too young to—"

She clamped her hands over her ears and backed away

from him, inch by inch in the dark until she was back home on her square foot of floorboards by the wall.

She began to hum to herself, hands still clamped over her ears, gently rocking back and forth: a private world of sounds and comforts right inside her head.

After a while Rossi came down the hatch and woke Banigan, and much later still the soothing night was defeated by the day, and a gray merciless light spread through the open hatch. A light that seemed to point out nothing but squalor and defeat. A hopeless light, full of shadows, as in a tomb.

Marion embraced her legs and pressed her face into her knees. She tried to think of happy things—her clean childhood bed in Leipzig, her mother . . .

Theo, who'd had the last watch this morning, came down the hatchway and through the door. He had his fingers to his lips and Mahmoud moved like lightning to stuff the rag back into Helm's mouth.

Theo whispered, "I think it's those same guys, the salvage dealer."

Within seconds they were in position again: Banigan ready to leap, but with an eye on their prisoner lest he rip the rag out of his mouth; Rossi, Mahmoud, and Theo, knives in hand by the now-closed door.

They could hear the voices and footsteps now—they came closer . . . stopped . . . went on, then came back.

"Electronics, I don't know; most of these barges don't have much in the way of that stuff. A river is a river."

The other voice said, "Except in fog. Then—"

"Yeah, the odd one has sounders and VHF. Wanna check?"

Footsteps on the steel deck above, then the screeching of the castle door, then the hatch and steps coming down the stairs.

"Jeez Almighty, what's this awful smell? Gawd."

Marion was afraid she might lose control and begin to scream. Theo and Mahmoud shifted their knives, ready to pull the men into the cabin.

Marion thought, They'll cut their throats. It'll be quick

and the blood can go down the piss hole. They can drag them over there quickly before it's all over the floor.

But her mind was slipping and she put her fist into her mouth and bit on it hard.

"Wasn't this the tub with the diesels? Shit, man, that smell, don't open that door, who knows . . . don't think there's anything I want in there."

"Wanna take another look at the diesels? You can have them for two thousand each. Gotta haul them out yourself, though."

Footsteps back up the stairs and along the wooden boards to the engine hatch. Then the voices again, further away.

"That's better. Gimme the clean stink of diesel any day. But that reek up front—some of these people live like rats, you know. Worse."

"Maybe. What about it—two thousand each?"

"I dunno. Gotta have someone check them out. If they're okay, fine. I'll send my man tomorrow."

The footsteps came back along the planks, then into the castle, over the steel, and off the barge.

Then the different sound on the wharf, and the voices grew fainter.

"Tzzzz," hissed Mahmoud. "We've got to move."

Rossi was watching Marion. She saw his concern and pulled herself together.

"Agenda," said Mahmoud. "Theo and Marion will leave almost immediately to get us a car. Go to the wrecking place and get one that's been painted over. Maybe our old van. Can't take chances with stealing a new one now. While they're gone, Rossi will get off another note. About our find. Then, off to the other hole."

"Where?" asked Theo.

"The Kalk hole. It's a good one."

"You lead the way," said Theo. "We don't even know where it is."

"I will. Let's move." Mahmoud then pointed at Helm. "Banigan, put the papers back in the fucker's case. He can carry it." The Arab grinned. "And ease off on that gag before we lose him."

Theo and Marion cleaned up as best they could, then very cautiously went up on deck. It was just after nine o'clock in the morning and except for a few scruffy dogs nothing stirred on the other barges. An oppressive haze lay heavily on the dead harbor and on the sluggish river beyond. In the east, the sun had just cleared the tin shacks and the factories, but already heat waves shimmered above the low roofs.

The bicycles were still there, a tumble of rusting steel leaning against the embankment railing. They climbed on without a word and pedaled off toward Ensen, a few kilometers closer to Cologne proper.

The landscape around them was one of industry and indifference; gravel pits, abandoned cars, small factories with piles of waste at the back door. The people who lived and worked around here looked much like Marion and Theo: neglected and resentful.

The closer they came to Fabrikstrasse, the closer they also came to the roaring eight-lane madness of the autobahn system around Cologne. The air was filled with the warlike noise of countless high-revving engines and with the hiss and slap of steel-belted tires measuring off the spacer gaps between the concrete slabs.

"Fuckin' shit world!" yelled Theo over the noise. "Serves this whole damn society right to get blown up. Deserves nothin' better."

Marion bumped along behind him. Her rear tire was badly in need of air, and each pothole in the road jarred her tailbone. In skirting around them, she almost fell twice; she gave up trying to avoid them, and merely trailed Theo, gritting her teeth.

Further along, a huge black junkyard dog with chewed ears bolted out of a gate. He trailed a chain and an uprooted peg; rattling like Cerberus, he made straight for Theo.

Theo got off his bike and let it keel over. He crouched low and picked up some rocks; he bared his teeth and growled just like a dog himself—a hairy creature in filthy clothes.

Marion stopped and stared at the two in wonder, man and beast facing off. Then the animal recognized the superior ferocity; it froze stiff-legged, then slunk off, chain and all.

The incident cheered Theo, and he yelled over his shoulder at Marion, "Fuckin' dog, showed him. Dog eat dog, man, that's our world." He banged at his front wheel to straighten the handlebar, and they continued.

The wrecking yard was an acre of stacked car bodies surrounded by a tall wooden fence which the local teenagers had adorned with slogans and symbols that expressed their states of mind and soul. The fence brimmed with four-letter words and genitalia; with telephone numbers offering a good time, and with names inside spray-painted hearts.

For some reason which she did not at the moment have the peace of mind to examine, the crushing sadness of the fence was for Marion the final assault. For a moment, she reverted to the person she hadn't been in years.

Later, even while Mahmoud was beating her until she bled out of mouth and nose, she would not be able to recollect exactly what she had done; but on this Wednesday morning shortly after ten, she simply let her bicycle fall over, and while Theo rapped with Aaron Mendelssohn, Marion became little Gaby. She stepped into the phone booth by the junkyard gate and phoned her father.

Because she did not have the necessary one-mark piece, she dialed "O" and placed the call collect. The receptionist at the Green Party office chirped, "Oh, Gaby, it's been a long time; your father is on the other line, can you hold?"

At this point Gaby began to cry, and the receptionist asked, "Gaby, are you all right? Wait, just one moment . . ."

Around her the phone booth was a psychedelic circus of spray-painted loves and hates, of "fucks" and "sucks"; of nature's push to procreate gone berserk, turned murderous.

Then she heard her father's voice: "Gaby, Gaby! Where are you?"

Crying, Gaby said, "I didn't mean to do it. Uncle Helm

and I are with these horrible people—'' Then Theo's grimace appeared in her vision. Yelling "Fuckin' cunt, who're you phonin', don't you know the rules, you little shit?" he ripped the receiver out of her hands and banged it down on the cradle. From the corner of her eye she saw Mendelssohn watching them, but her mind chose to linger with the image of her father staring at the phone, wondering about her.

She came to her senses when Theo grabbed her throat; then he wrestled her out of the booth and hit her twice in the face so hard that she fell down. He was about to kick her too when Aaron Mendelssohn yelled, "Hey, Theo, you wanna kill her or what? Cut it out, man!" The wrecker came over and pushed Theo back. He was a huge man with a grime-blackened face and hands like frying pans. "Get off her, man! Not on my lot, you little turd. Take your van and beat it."

Theo picked her up, threw her into the van, threw the bicycles in after her, and took off like a lunatic.

15

It was at three o'clock in the morning, during the dreary drive back from Wiesbaden, that Gunter Stark made one of his better intuitive leaps.

To his left, the Rhine harbors were brightly lit and bustling with loading activity. Some of the freighters looked as big as oceangoing vessels. On a pleasure yacht, a deck party was still in full swing. Stark heard the music and watched some couples dance up a storm—then he saw something else that made him slow and pull over the Porsche in the middle of the Severins bridge. He stared at the yacht. His gaze moved on to the freighters and the barges.

Ropes everywhere: coiled, limp, or taut; mooring lines, fastening lines, hauling lines. *Rope burns,* the physiotherapist had said about the marks on the dead laborer's hands.

A harbor with all this activity and confusion would be a perfect place to hide someone.

Stark sped on to the office; Misha and sleep would have to wait once more. He put calls out to Georg and Fritz and ordered them in. Next he roused the harbor commissioner from sleep, and when the man was fully awake Stark asked for permission to order all approaches to all four river harbors sealed.

"By road *and* water?" asked the commissioner incredulously. "Are you aware of the extent of your request, chief inspector?"

Stark said he was. By that time he had parked outside HQ, and the first of his two lieutenants had already rolled in.

"But now, in the middle of the night, chief inspector; there's no time to organize things."

"Leave that to us. Just give me your approval in principle."

The commissioner hemmed and hawed for a while longer until Stark told him to consider it quickly, then hung up.

Upstairs, he and his lieutenants used the phones in an organized frenzy of activity, pulling in everyone they could lay their hands on and coordinating a dragnet for all harbors. Stark requested and received GSG-9 assistance and at 4:35, while the city if not the harbor was still fast asleep, the operation began.

Each basin was blocked by police vessels at the water entrance, and by cruisers on land. Police helicopters with search lights hovered over the area, sweeping it with brilliant beams, like giant, probing fingers.

On the ground eight task forces consisting of twenty men each advanced methodically from the end of the wharfs to the center. The men wore wide-angle tungsten helmets and combat suits; they were armed with flash grenades, flare pistols, and the new GSG automatic pancake guns that could blow a hole like a shotgun at three meters but would not penetrate an airliner's fuselage or the side of a vessel at more than ten meters.

They searched buildings, ships, and cars with thoroughness and maximum speed. In a luxury yacht they found the results of a lovers' murder/suicide in one of the plush bathrooms; on a freighter down from Holland they discovered fifteen kilos of cocaine in crates of tulip bulbs precleared for the USA, and in a powerful Bellini motor launch registered in Vienna they found four crates of Stinger antiaircraft missiles.

But they found not a trace of Helm and his kidnappers.

At 7:15 Stark called off the operation, and an hour later he was already en route to the meeting in Bonn. For the first time since he'd been issued the Porsche, he sat in the passenger seat; young Koppel, a pool driver with excellent reflexes, was behind the wheel. Stark was simply too tired to trust himself with the aggressive machine—also he needed both hands on radio and phone to run reassignments.

"A hundred and sixty men, four harbor police launches, four choppers, and a truckload of GSG-9 equipment!" Esser spoke as crisply as a lawyer in court, listing his grievances. "You shut down all Cologne harbors for two and a half hours—without the proper clearances, needless to say—and you find not a trace of what you're looking for."

"Sir," Superintendent Zander came to Stark's assistance, "the search teams *did* find the cache of illegal weapons and a couple million dollars' worth of drugs. Not to mention the homicide—"

Esser turned acidly to the police commissioner and said, "Has it been made clear to these people what the job is? I mean, do they understand that nothing, *nothing*, has a higher priority than the Helm abduction?"

The commissioner, an elderly, self-protective politician with a blue schnapps nose, looked accusingly first at Zander, then at Stark. Everyone remembered his role at the inquiry into the Amsterdam shooting.

Stark, who was greatly tempted to stretch out on the minister's Berber rug and nap, said tiredly, "Can we get down to business now? It's *because* I understood the priority that I insisted on using all men and facilities I could get my hands on. And if the harbor commissioner was upset, then I expected my superiors would straighten things out." Lack of sleep and his clear conscience gave him an edge this morning. He added, "Will someone tell me what's going on?"

The police commissioner squinted at him, then transferred his gaze to the fifth man in the room. There was an unusual degree of submission in the commissioner's eyes.

The fifth man at the meeting wore a dark pinstripe suit despite the weather, and he looked both dignified and devious, like deputy foreign ministers everywhere. Now he wiped the croissant crumbs off his lips and asked with false innocence, "The *documents*—Dr. Esser, your man does understand what to do about that part of the Helm case?"

"Well—" Esser broke off because one of the girls in his front office (young Ellie who, Stark thought, always smelled of lilacs) offered more coffee all around. Stark used the occasion to sneak another croissant and another dollop of cherry jam. It was the first civilized meal he'd had in days.

When Ellie was gone, Stark swallowed hastily and asked, "What documents? Is there something I should know?" He looked at the superintendent, but Zander was watching Esser.

The interior minister looked up from his pad and pushed up his glasses. Everyone was watching him now, but only the deputy foreign minister had the confidence to cut through Esser's embarrassment. "Well, what? The State Department and the CIA are hounding me to death on this thing. Why are you waffling? It's the damn papers we want, isn't it? The rest is just another abduction, right?"

Esser took a run at it and said, "No, the police know nothing about Equinox. I thought that first things should come first."

"I think you've got your priorities a little. . . . May I have a word with you in private, Dr. Esser?"

Esser looked around unhappily, then stood up and led the deputy foreign minister out of the room.

The police commissioner stirred his coffee busily, and Stark and Zander looked at each other.

Stark said, "This is no time to screw around, sir. We're forty hours into a major abduction. What the hell are they doing jerking me around?"

Zander, a wise old survivor, who had once been a special assignment street cop too, held out a calming hand, then put a forefinger to his lips.

Across from them the police commissioner saw the gesture but pretended that he had not. He merely cleared his throat, then took a sip of coffee and smacked his lips.

In the outer office, the typewriters and word processors clacked and rattled away and the phones rang constantly. Ellie came and cleared away the dishes, and a moment later Esser and the deputy foreign minister were back.

Esser had clearly taken the lead again. Sitting down he said, "The papers we're referring to pertain to a highly sensitive affair, and by the chancellor's orders I am not at liberty to discuss it. If the slightest hint of Equinox were to reach the media, the consequences for this government and for broader military alliances could be disastrous." Esser focused his gaze on Stark and said, "The priorities are number one: find Dietrich Helm; two: secure any and all documents in his or his abductors' possession, and three: report to me in person."

Before Stark could blurt out something undiplomatic, Superintendent Zander said, "Right, sir; understood."

A tenuous equilibrium returned to the room, then Esser said, "And now, chief inspector, if we could have an update?"

Stark gave them a report, brisk but with an impressive command of facts, details, and leads.

He told them about the extensive network his boosted communications team had set up—the phone taps within Germany and the cooperation from antiterrorist units in neighboring countries. Then there were the various electronic surveillance systems keeping an eye on all points of contact in Helm's private and professional life. The operation was in high gear.

Impatiently the deputy foreign minister said, "But what it boils down to is that you're still waiting for them to make a move. All this manpower, and we're sitting, waiting."

"Not true," said Stark. "We're not passive. We are getting closer all the time. We know all their identities, and from past patterns we are virtually certain that they are holed up right here in Cologne. It's a matter of detailed and thorough police work. Unfortunately that takes time."

"Time," echoed the deputy foreign minister. "You have all this manpower and equipment. Chief inspector, I can't remember a police operation when the man in charge was given so much freedom."

"Not all that much, sir. If we'd been able to tap Carl Stolz's phone—"

"Never mind," said Esser. "I told you why. Remember your priorities."

Stark caught the quick exchange of glances between the deputy foreign minister and Esser.

Stark said, "There'll be communication from a local source any time now. The Milan message was arranged before the kidnapping. Now they are in place and can't move freely—the next communication will come from Cologne."

The police commissioner cleared his throat and croaked, "What about the Milan message?" He had not spoke for a long time and probably felt ignored.

Stark said, "No useful clues. A third-generation photocopy on a poor machine. Standard procedure in these cases, sir."

"The father of the dead baby has threatened to launch a lawsuit against the day-care center. For neglect of duty."

Everyone looked at the police commissioner, wondering what that had to do with anything, and Stark said politely, "Well, sir. What can I say?"

"What about medical doctors? That fake mother was shot."

"We've thought of that, sir. There's the gunshot law, but there're also a thousand quacks. We're checking."

The police commissioner asked, desperately, "Rope burns, you were saying you searched the harbors because of the rope burns on the corpse—there are other vessels up and down the Rhine. Have you given up? And what about other trades where ropes are used?"

"We've checked all construction sites within a ten-kilometer radius, and, yes, we are continuing the boat search. I have four teams working their way up and down both sides of the Rhine."

After the meeting, down in the open parking lot surrounded by black government limos like so many hearses, Stark said to Zander, "Sir, just one thing: What the hell is going on; what is Equinox? This is the second time I've heard of it. The first time was in Esser's office too. Could the government be . . ."

The superintendent looked him in the eye and said, "Frankly, Gunter, I don't know. But then our job is only to enforce the law, not to run the country, thank God." He took off his suit jacket and climbed into his Mercedes. "Carry on, chief inspector. And remember, you're a cop, not Don Quixote."

On the A555 north to Cologne Stark lowered his seat back and closed his eyes. Young Koppel said, "I'll keep an eye on the radio, chief."

"Do that! And don't get us killed."

He was so exhausted that he actually did doze off for fifteen minutes. Sergeant Koppel's voice reached him on the bottom of the ocean, and he sat up with a jolt and took the phone.

"Stark here."

"Sir." It was Fritz. "We just picked up a very strange phone call to Peter Schott. It seems to have come from his daughter—did you know he had a daughter? Anyway, one 'Gaby' phoned and said she was with 'Uncle Helm' and some—"

"Play me the tape, Fritz; you're mumbling."

Sitting bolt upright in the speeding Porsche, Stark listened to the call tone, the secretary, then Peter Schott himself. He heard Gaby's pathetic sentence and a half, and finally the vicious cursing . . .

Fritz came back on, and Stark said, "You locked in on it, I hope."

"Of course. The new automatic—"

"Fritz. Where?"

"Public phone booth eighty-nine-A in Ensen. It's on Fabrikstrasse, coordinates M/N eighty-six-two on the map. Outside a scrapyard or wrecker."

"Wait." Stark unfolded the map, studied it for a moment, then said, "Fritz, I'm going to call in a GSG-9 strike team. Meet us there. I'm going to have them chopper in, and rappel. Let's go!" He disconnected, then straightened his seat-back and said to Koppel, "Step on it, sergeant. You know where we're going."

Koppel turned on the siren and lights and floored the accelerator. The speedometer needle leapt up and within seconds trembled at 250 kmh. In the passing lane, cars could not move over fast enough.

Meanwhile Stark called the army barracks and got his GSG-9 paramilitary strike team and helicopters.

"What weapons, chief inspector?" asked the major.

"MP5s with two-hundred-round drums. Teflon shells— we're going into a wrecking place. Flak jackets, stun grenades, but no fragmentation grenades." He gave the map coordinates and disconnected. A wild feeling of excitement surged inside him, and all fatigue was gone. He took out his service Walther, chambered a round, and flicked on the safety. Beside him Koppel heard the metallic noises but kept his eyes on the road. Stark said, "You'll stay in the car, sergeant. There'll be enough soldiers. Watch the radio."

They had reached the Porz turnoff by the time they heard the heavy slapping of the twin-rotor Chinook. Stark called the chopper on the special alternating squad band, "Major, as soon as our car is on Fabrikstrasse, I want you to hover above that wrecking place. No one leaves—no one. I'll be coming through the gate on foot. Please have your men rappel at assault speed. Good luck."

They plunged down the ramp and thundered over the potholes. At the gate, Stark leaped out of the Porsche, gun in hand.

The noise from the Chinook was deafening. The rotors kicked up a sandstorm, and the soldiers dropped like stones down their rappel ropes. They fanned out, then stood awaiting further orders.

On the entire graveyard of cars not a soul stirred. Near Stark, the dented hood of an old Opel Rekord flapped in the downdraft like a toothless mouth. The major ran up to Stark and offered him a spare set of ski goggles against the grit.

Stark yelled into his ear, "Have your men search everywhere. Comb this place from corner to corner!"

There was only one building on the lot, apparently a combination spray booth, workshop, and office. It had two entrances, and Stark motioned over two soldiers; they gave cover while he and the major stormed the doors.

Stark's had only been leaned to, and he fell in, headlong. Sliding over the greasy floor, he saw the man above him. The major crashed through the rear door, and together they stood then, staring at the man in coveralls . . .

He was huge, taller even than Stark and half again as heavy, and the fact that he had been hoisted on a beam and tackle until his oily boots were a meter off the ground made him seem even taller.

What they could see of his face was black with soot, and his huge hands were black also. The neck was broken, and through the point of the lower jaw a heavy iron hook had penetrated far enough to exit again between the teeth.

From the hook a thick iron chain went up to the beam and tackle of the kind used to hoist engine blocks from or into car bodies.

Stark stepped outside and leaned against the wood siding, then he pounded his fist on the boards until the pain made him stop.

The soldiers had completed their search but found no

human trace. The major came out of the building and yelled, "He's been shot, too, Gunter. An entry wound in the chest with point-blank powder burns."

Stark went back inside and then, squinting up in the dim light, he saw it too: a small scorched entry in the front but no exit wound. He knew that the bullet that had burst the man's heart would be shaped like a small cross.

An hour and a half later Stark knew everything there was to know about the shack, the phone booth, and the way Aaron Mendelssohn died.

One of the key clues had been the fresh tracks of two bicycles in the dust by the scrapyard gate.

Back in the office, while organizing the new sweep, he briefed Georg. "It looks like they came in the morning on bikes from the hiding place to pick up their car. Tire tracks and paint on the nozzle indicate that the last car painted was a van, blue. Schott's daughter must have panicked—by the way, shouldn't Fritz be here by now with Schott?"

Georg nodded and said, "Soon, I'm sure."

"So, Gaby made the call from the booth and the terrorist with her overheard, and shut her up. Mendelssohn probably witnessed that, and Mahmoud, thinking that we would somehow trace the call, took no chances and killed Mendelssohn. Same as the corpse on Sunday: a .22 scored to mushroom all the way."

The phone rang on Stark's desk, but it was not Fritz and the security team bringing in Schott; it was Misha. "Well, well," she said. "Finally. Is this the number of the phone on your desk?"

"Yes. Misha, I'm in the middle of something. But it's good to hear from you. What . . ?"

"Just wanted to know if you're still alive. They never put me through to your car or anything. And I haven't seen you or heard from you for a whole day and a night."

"It's pretty busy just now, Misha. Can I call you later? I have to go."

"When will you call?"

He sighed involuntarily. "This evening. Then I'll explain."

"I won't sit around here waiting, Gunter. Call me at Guido's. Bye." She hung up with a bang in his ear.

Stark rubbed his face and looked at Georg. "Where was I? Bicycle tracks; they tell us that the hiding place is nearby. Too far to walk, though."

"Four, five kilometers?"

"About that. And the rope burns are still a fact. Let's call off the other three teams and concentrate on the Porz side of the Rhine. Check all barges and wharf buildings five kilometers up and down from Mendelssohn's. And keep an eye out for blue vans. I'm afraid they're planning a move. They usually move after a communiqué."

The phone rang again and Stark snatched it up.

It was Fritz, panting. "Can't find Schott anywhere, chief!"

"His office or his home?"

"No. After his daughter phoned, he just disappeared. But we did hook into the rental-car contact. They might get back together."

"Stay with it. We need him. We've got to have Schott, Fritz."

Then he and Georg organized two strike teams and two helicopters for a search of the barges within cycling distance of Mendelssohn's. The soldiers were to be equipped with flak jackets, stun grenades, and pancake guns.

At 1:25 P.M. the two choppers landed on the roof of Blaubach and Georg and Stark climbed aboard.

That morning Paul Fontana had awakened at first light, still in the tasseled chair where he had fallen asleep after returning from Wiesbaden.

In his sleep his subconscious must have been working on the puzzle because on his way to the shower the key pieces suddenly stared at him so boldly that he stopped in mid-stride: Stolz's anti-American feelings must have prompted him to leak the file to Dietrich Helm, who as Green strategist could use the military secrets in a way that must have appealed to Carl's notion of right and wrong. It was the amber glow of cadet romance, and its sadness and futility gripped Fontana's heart.

If Carl's leaking of the file to the Greens was the first piece of the puzzle, the inevitable counteraction by Wolff's people was the companion piece: the Agency obviously knew as early as Monday morning and moved with typical swiftness and thoroughness to retrieve the papers and plug the leak.

Fontana showered, then shaved and dressed. His guilt regarding Stolz's death lessened because he understood now that Carl had acted from free choice. He had been no fool; he must have known the risks he took.

When he was dressed, Fontana went downstairs to get some breakfast. Dornier stared at him strangely from behind the desk. Fontana saw that his friend's consternation was caused by the newspaper story on Carl Stolz's death.

Dornier asked, "Did you see this? What is going on, Paul?"

Fontana looked at the story, then said to Dornier, "Come along, Herbert. Let's talk." He led the way to the dining room and chose a table in the far corner. Across from them sat Dornier's only other hotel guests, a group of five monks in brown robes. They all had cheerful round faces and fringes of white hair around tonsures like pink pancakes. They talked loudly in a galloping language Fontana could not place.

"Finland," whispered Dornier. "They carry their money folded in tiny squares in their string purses. But they eat like horses, and at breakfast they take every one of the jam pots and buns in the basket."

Fontana nodded, then said without transition, "Herbert, I think that Carl leaked some top-secret military documents to the Greens. The documents deal with NATO strategy and with the American nuclear presence in West Germany. You know how Carl felt about the nuclear threat, and I wouldn't be surprised if he felt he was doing his own government a favor by having the opposition expose the extent to which, in his view, the Americans were pushing Bonn to allow more deployment. But he was asking for it, Herbert."

With his big round eyes and his bushy eyebrows rising above the old spectacles, Dornier looked more like an owl than ever before. "But why did they kill him? And who?" he whispered, leaning over the table.

Fontana said, "How about the CIA?"

"But why didn't they just tell the government so they could deal with him legally? Did they have to take a man's life just because he believes in something?"

At this, Fontana could not help but smile. He quickly reached out and patted his old friend's hand. "Herbert," he said, "you're so right. But this is an age of expedience. Jets have replaced ocean liners because they get you from A to B more quickly. Exposing Carl to the Bonn government would bring on a scandal. Too much publicity. So . . ."

Dornier took off his glasses and wiped them on the dangling corner of the tablecloth. He looked vulnerable and sad and old.

"Herbert, he did what he believed in, and he certainly knew the risks he was taking. You don't rise to the top in the Ministry of Defense by being naive. Carl knew the game and the rules, and if he decided to play the final card close to his heart because he *believed*—well, he went as a hero. Philosophers call it 'significant action,' Herbert."

Dornier finished wiping his glasses. He put them back on and his eyes became magnified again. "Did he suffer, Paul?"

Fontana wondered about the question. Did it imply that he was there, or at least for some secret reason knew more about Carl's death than he had admitted? He decided the question was simply an expression of Dornier's need to be reassured. He said, "Not at all. I'm sure he didn't, Herbert."

"Good. Perhaps it was more like absolution, pay the debt and be done with it. I know that after his son's accident and then his wife's death, Carl was no longer quite the same."

Dornier took a deep breath. "The paper says the police shot his killer. It was meant to look like an armed robbery or something, I guess." Dornier paused, frowning. "But tell me, Paul, what's your role in all this? First Dietrich Helm, now Carl Stolz, and you mysteriously in the middle—none of this makes any sense to me."

"Herbert . . . I could tell you I have nothing to do with it, but that would be a lie. *I do*—and have for years been on the fringe of this sort of life. But you must believe me when I tell you that I have nothing to do with Carl or Helm. I'm here to help rescue him because I owe him and love him like all of us did. You must believe that, Herbert. I promise when all this is over, I'll tell you in detail how I got involved."

Dornier looked at him; the big eyes swam behind the glasses, searching his face. Then he nodded slowly and looked away.

Across the room, the Finnish monks rose noisily, banging chairs, talking all at once. Their hobnailed boots raked the old carpet. Dornier asked, "See what I mean? All the buns, all the jam—*tabula rasa*. Not one sparrow could survive on the crumbs they leave behind."

Then they were alone in the dining room and Fontana asked, "Herbert, do you trust me?"

Dornier nodded.

"Good. I now think I know where Helm is being kept. It's either in Bonn or in Olpe. Can you help me get a new car? They know about the BMW I used yesterday. I need it picked up and exchanged for another one. Call Hertz for me, then get me another car. They don't know your face." He took keys and papers out of his pocket and pushed them across the table.

Dornier looked troubled. "I wish I could do more, Paul. But with Anna upstairs I really can't leave the hotel for more than an hour at a time."

"I understand. Which reminds me: would Anna not be better off in full-time care? They've got some fabulous convalescent places these days. I've heard of one in the Taunus—"

"So have we. Do you know how much these places cost—a fortune, that's what. I told you the cost of even just in-house help, well, a place like the one in Taunus is two, three times as much. You are talking fifty thousand marks a year, Paul. Do you know how much this hotel makes a year?"

"I can guess. That is something else I want to talk to you about—business. I was thinking of buying into it. I've saved up quite a little nest egg, and I wouldn't at all mind having a foothold in Europe again. And Cologne makes more sense than any other place."

Dornier stared at him open-mouthed. Then a blush of excitement rose from his neck right up to his forehead. "You mean that, Paul? By God, we could renovate, we could . . ."

"Advertise a bit in the right places, hire more help. Herbert, this is a great location, and the building has lots of character."

"Paul! Oh, I don't know what to say."

"All right, all in good time. Let's get Helm back first. And how about a bit of breakfast? The rental places won't be open for another half hour at least."

Dornier waved to the only serving help, a dark-haired girl who was just clearing the Finns' table, and told her to bring two *cafés complets*.

Afterwards, Fontana went up to his room, connected the digitizer, and attempted once more to track down Attila Benn. This time the paper relented and they gave him the number of their bureau in East Berlin. Fontana placed his call, then waited.

While he waited, the phone rang twice in quick succession. The first time it was Herbert Dornier calling up from the desk to say that key and papers for the new rental car were in Fontana's pigeonhole; the gray Opel Admiral was on the railroad station lot just two streets away.

The second call was from a panic-stricken Peter Schott: "Paul—thank heavens you're there. I had a call from Gaby!"

Fontana listened to Schott retelling the conversation, narrating the event right to the abrupt ending.

Fontana said, "Peter . . . we were afraid of something like that—"

"Wait! And now the police are looking for me. They came to the office."

"Where are you now?"

Peter mentioned a gas station on Duerenerstrasse in Cologne.

"Let me think, Peter." Fontana sat on the bed, still clutching the receiver. On the dresser lay the envelopes with Gaby's hair and the brush. He knew now that he'd been wrong about Henry Wolff's role in Helm's abduction. Perhaps it was a regular extortion case after all. At any rate, his earlier hunch about Gaby's role in it was correct. Whether they were after the targeting file or after Helm himself was now immaterial. Only two things mattered: Helm's life and the fact that Gaby wanted out. Once she was away from the terrorists, surely she would cooperate.

He said, "Peter, listen, police or not—you've got to keep yourself available for her phone calls. If she was cut off, she may call back."

"Paul, I'm so confused. I've *got* to see you. You have to help me!"

Fontana said quickly, "All right, where exactly is this gas station?"

Schott told him, the relief audible in his voice.

On his way out of the hotel, Fontana asked Dornier to take a message from Benn, if he called.

He found the new rental car and sped off to meet Peter Schott.

16

Mahmoud said to Gaby, "All right, I believe you. Maybe you didn't tell your father that you were with us and the fat cat."

"It's true, I swear," sobbed Gaby. "I just said I wanted to come home." Her nose had stopped bleeding, but her face was a mess of blood and tears and snot. She rubbed her eyes, and looked at her hands in disgust.

"You want to go home," mused Mahmoud. "Well, let's see what we can do for you."

Gaby looked up. "You'd let me go? I promise I won't say a word to anyone."

Mahmoud laughed.

"I mean it," said Gaby eagerly.

"We'll see what we can do for you. But first you have to do something. You have to call your father again and tell him that you didn't really mean it. Say you were just feeling low, or something. Or, no—tell him you *ran away*. That'll do it. Convince him that everything's all right with you! And . . . listen to me, cunt! Sit up and listen. Make sure to arrange a meeting. You want to come home, but you want to talk to him alone. He can't bring a soul with him."

"Why can't I just go to the apartment? Or the office?"

"Fuck, no! We need a public place with a crowd. A big crowd, and it has to be outdoors. Theo, you're the local— think of a place."

"Yes," said Rossi. "A crowded outdoor place. And the sooner the better. Before your father starts putting two and two together and brings in the cops."

"Wait," said Mahmoud. "I bet you the pigs have taps on the office phones. Is there any other place where you can call him? Like someplace he goes regularly. Or someone that can get a message to him?"

Gaby said, "He always eats lunch at the same two restaurants. I mean, there's two restaurants nearby and he sort of alternates. I know what they're called. We can look them up in the phone book."

"Good," said Rossi. "And Theo, you think of a good place where they can meet."

"I got the perfect fuckin' place for the job," said Theo. He was picking a little pill out of an aspirin tin and now he popped it in his mouth. Then he ripped open a Diet Coke. It gushed over his shirt and face, but some of it went into his mouth, and he swallowed. Furtively he pushed the little tin back into his jeans pocket. He closed his eyes, waiting for the hit, and said dreamily, "There's this outdoor dancing place in the park. That's always jumping with people. Perfect spot, man." He smiled, closing his eyes.

Mahmoud looked at Rossi, then took a lightning step to Theo, and feinted a blow to his face while pulling out the aspirin tin with two fingers of his left hand.

"Hey, gimme back . . ." Theo lunged for the Arab, who took a dancing step backwards and raised a leg. Theo went flying across the cabin.

Banigan watched idly; Helm was gagged and blindfolded, and Marion still cowered by the door, numb to anything other than her pain and fear.

Mahmoud opened the little tin, took out one of the pills, and touched it to his pointed tongue. "Bennies," he said to Rossi. "Did you know that? I told you *no junkies*. I don't tolerate junkies in the family, man!"

Rossi said, "I was not aware he was popping. I can't know everything."

"You should. That's what I expect when I put you in charge. Junkies, dopers, shit!" He looked with contempt at Theo, who was getting up, pretending to brush dust off his jeans. He was calmer now, and a new hard edge had come into his eyes. Moving towards Gaby on the mattress, he said, "I'll need those back, Mahmoud. Just so you know."

Theo reached for Marion's ponytail and yanked her up, propped her against the wall. Harshly he said, "You're gonna do it, you cunt. You're gonna phone your papa again, or you'll have a real problem."

Rossi said, "Let go of her. I'll look after her. I'll talk to her in the van. I think we should get out of here now."

Mahmoud nodded and said to Theo, "Rossi is right. You and Banigan get him up and into the van." He jerked his chin at Helm.

They had just returned from Mendelssohn's, and Mahmoud knew that they had no more than an hour to find new transportation, get rid of the van, and go underground at the Kalk hole. He put the transistor radio into Helm's briefcase and said, "Rossi, you go up and check that everything's clear. I bring her, and those two will bring *him*."

The repainted van was a rear- and side-loading model, and on their return from Mendelssohn's execution Mahmoud had told Theo to park it right next to the barge, with the panel door slid back.

Now, on Rossi's signal, they pushed up Helm and Marion and shoved them into the van. Theo took the wheel and Banigan the passenger seat. As they drove off, a fat man on the neighboring barge stared after them, and a half dozen scruffy dogs yapped.

A change of location ought to be done at night, but this time they had no choice, thought Mahmoud.

There were no helicopters in the air yet, but he knew they would be here before long. He clutched the briefcase firmly in his hands and braced his back against the steel frame. The Cologne/Bonn airport was just fifteen minutes away, and its parking lot would be filled with cars whose owners would not miss them for many hours, maybe days.

The van was the closed-box type, and except for the light coming through the rear cabin window it was dark in the loading area. At first the corrugated floor jolted over the pot-holed wharf area, then they turned onto the main road and the ride became smooth.

Rossi reached out and took Marion's hand; at first she wanted to pull it away, then she relented. Soothingly he said, "They're right; you've got to call your father back and arrange a meeting. If only to show him that you are okay."

Marion whispered, "I'm so afraid, please, *caro*, I want out. Please tell them to let me go."

Rossi looked across and saw Mahmoud's contemptuous gaze. He knew that Marion was doomed, that as soon as she had lured her father to a rendezvous, she would only be a handicap to the group. In a way, this made things easier. Marion was dead already. He said, "All will be well, trust me. We're going to get two new cars, then we phone your father. You must get him to meet you right away."

"And then?" She looked at him, her tear-stained, child-ish face raised.

"They'll let you go. That's a fact. You've done well."

As if to warn Marion, Helm began kicking up a deafening noise on the floor panel. Marion gave a start and Mahmoud moved quickly to tighten the bicycle chain that went around Helm's ankles and through the rope that looped his hand to his belt. Completely trussed up, he fell over, then lay sideways on the steel floor.

Mahmoud pulled his knife from his sleeve, leaned over Helm, and hissed something in his ear that neither Rossi nor Marion could understand.

To distract her, Rossi squeezed her hand and whispered, "By this evening you'll be free. Did Theo give you back the revolver?"

She nodded, then leaned her head on his shoulder. He felt her tremble all over, and he thought, Theo was right, damnit; Theo was right after all. She's pulled us down. And the irony is, we didn't even need her.

It was something to remember for future operations; there was a lesson in this one—in the entire role she'd played, and in the testing of her—that needed to be examined. But first things first.

Without her noticing it, Rossi looked down at Marion's face—the tear stains along her thin cheeks, the dark bruises from Mahmoud's beating after Theo had told them about her phone call, the pink little tongue that licked the swollen, snotty upper lip. Rossi realized for the first time that she was little more than a resentful child gone woefully wrong, and for the first time in years he felt a stab of doubt.

But it left as quickly as it had come because in this business there was no room for doubt.

At the autobahn cross a police siren came closer with tremendous speed, and Theo pulled over to make room for a white Porsche flying past. A minute later they heard the unmistakable clatter of a troop-carrying helicopter.

"Chinook," said Mahmoud grimly. "For your sake I *do* hope your father's not gone to the cops yet. But we gotta hurry!"

The helicopter noise diminished rapidly and they sped down the cloverleaf ramp to the airport. There the parking lot would be filled with cars. They would drop the van and pick up two other vehicles. After that Rossi knew just how to handle Marion and her father.

"There," said Fritz, "see him?" The gray Opel Admiral was parked by the gas station and Schott and the contact from the *Lorelei* were inside. Despite the weather the windows were rolled up, which was good.

Fritz pulled the Volkswagen beetle onto the parking strip so that the technicians on the backseat had a clear line of reception. He reached behind and said, "Give me some ears."

"Just a minute, lieutenant. We're not quite ready."

Fritz looked around and watched impatiently as they fiddled with the connection, then cranked the gallium laser antenna into alignment with the windows of the Opel.

They had followed the car all the way from the railroad station parking lot. The beeper on the car had made it a cinch to tail; up to a dozen cars between them all the way, with no danger of losing it.

This part of the operation had been a textbook chapter without a hitch: they'd tapped the Hertz lines and watched the office. This morning a call came through asking for the BMW 633 to be picked up and a new car to be readied. They'd tailed the old fellow from the hotel, and when he'd left the Opel the technician had slapped a magnetized beeper onto the rear bumper.

And now the car had led them to Schott! Fritz was pleased.

One of the technicians on the backseat said, "Got it," and passed him headphones. At the same time he clicked on the little cassette recorder.

Fritz recognized Peter Schott's voice: "I . . . I have no idea! My God, Paul. What can I do? If you'd heard the panic in the poor girl's voice, and then that other fellow, the viciousness . . ."

"Peter . . . please. Pull yourself together. Now we know that Gaby is involved in Helm's kidnapping. We don't know in what way, but we *do* know that she wants out. That's our chance."

A truck went by, and in the vibration of the windows Schott's words were inaudible. Duerenerstrasse was lined with dying trees, small industrial workshops, storefronts, and office buildings. Noontime traffic was unceasing.

Impatiently Fritz asked, "Can't you adjust that damn thing a bit better?"

The technician without earphones said, "With this sort of equipment you're reading the vibrations from the speech pattern off the window. That's tough in this noise. Later on we can filter the tape, lieutenant. We can filter the extraneous hash . . ."

"Hope you're right," said Fritz, concentrating again on the phones.

"You got the things I sent you? What are you going to do with them?"

"I had a plan . . . but now that she's contacted you the picture is changed. That's our best opportunity."

"What do you mean?"

"If she's desperate enough she'll try to call you again. You must try to find out where she is. I think there's no question now that she's in with the gang that took Dietrich."

"Are you suggesting that . . ."

Interference thundered in Fritz's earphones. He held them away from his ears, grimacing.

Looking into the mirror he saw a Mercedes parked on the other side of the street. The car seemed vaguely familiar, and he stared at it for a moment, trying to decide what it reminded him of. Then the signal in the earphones cleared and he returned his attention to Fontana's Opel.

" . . . success with the psychiatrist?"

"Not yet. I left my name and number. He's supposed to call me back."

"So that's one more reason for you to go back to the office right away. Don't you see? If she'll call you anywhere, it'll be there."

"Gaby's not a *terrorist*. She's not a . . . I know her better than you, Paul."

"Maybe. If anything, she got lined up and sucked into something and is now desperate to get out."

"The police are watching the office. For all I know, they're tapping the phones too."

"Of course . . . let me think. Well—there's nothing we can do about that. At any rate, be available for her call. Don't change the regular pattern of your day."

"Jesus, Paul. I'm so . . . what's going to become of us? Why does there have to be so much tragedy in our family? Why can't we be like other people and just . . . live?"

There was silence for a moment, then Fontana said, "Well, let's at least see what we can do for Helm. Is that your car over there? Why don't you get back now?"

"But what if the police—"

"Get your ass to the office before I kick it out of here."

Fritz watched Schott get out of the Opel and walk to a blue Fiat. The situation called for a snap judgment: tail Schott or stay with the contact? Then he realized that Schott would at any rate run into the surveillance net at the office building and would be taken care of. He reached for the microphone on the dash and alerted the department car on Neumarkt to watch out for a blue Fiat 1600. He said, "Your bird is returning to the nest. Stay with him now."

Fritz put back the mike knowing that Stark would be pleased with him today. But when he looked across to the Opel, his momentary sense of accomplishment vanished. He remembered where he had seen the Mercedes. Presently it pulled up next to the Opel. Jack Teagarden and "Metzger" got out. They moved quickly. Teagarden had his left hand in his jacket pocket.

Teagarden slipped into the passenger seat, and Metzger planted his square, muscular body against the driver's side door of the Opel. The window came down and Fritz saw Fontana's surprise turn not into fear but anger.

Fritz leaped out of the Volkswagen and raced towards the Opel. He shouted, "Stop! Police!"

Metzger turned to watch him approach. In the Opel Teagarden snarled, "Up, Paul! Crank up the window, and start this fucking car. I'll tell you where we're going."

Metzger stepped sideways to prevent Fritz from reaching the door handle.

Fritz said, "I'm warning you. This man is under our surveillance, in our jurisdiction. What you are doing is illegal."

Metzger said, "No kidding." He had a brawler's grin complete with two chipped teeth. His neck and shoulders were massive, and his hands were curled as if he were still holding the meat cleaver he'd wielded for years as a butcher on the U.S. Rhine Main base. He stood, watching Fritz closely.

Then the Opel started up, and as it pulled away, Fritz caught a glimpse of the .38 in Teagarden's fist pointing sideways at Fontana's stomach.

Fritz controlled the foolish impulse to take a swing at Metzger. He said, "Christ! What the hell do you think you're doing?"

Metzger moved backwards to the Mercedes, keeping his eyes on Fritz. He opened the door and said, "Easy come, easy go. See ya, buddy."

Trying to reach Stark from the Volkswagen Fritz had to go through Cologne HQ. The operator said the chief inspector was on board a helicopter and she would set up a patch. At 11:30 Stark came through. His voice was nearly drowned out by the whine of the turbine and the slap of the rotor.

Fritz told him the good news first. They had reconnected with Peter Schott and recorded what might turn out to be a useful conversation. Schott was on his way back to his office where he was expecting a second call from his daughter.

"Good work," shouted Stark.

"But unfortunately we've lost his contact to Teagarden." He described what had happened.

"Damnit," said Stark. "But as long as we stay on top of Schott and Gaby, we're all right."

Fritz said, "We've still got a beeper on that Opel. Do you want us to find out where they're taking the contact?"

"Yes. And keep me posted. Georg and I are on our way to check all those barges around Mendelssohn's."

"Will do. Over and out."

Stark put the mike back on the hook and looked out the open door. They had reached Mendelssohn's lot; Georg's chopper was about to put down but Stark waved his own pilot on, further upstream to the cluster of barges in the Rhine loop. The barges were moored with heavy docking lines. Rope burns, Stark thought grimly . . .

They landed on the Urbach soccer field, then swept east through the shacks and wharf buildings and charged across the potholed dirt road. The string of disused barges sat in the lazy backflow, and the heat rose in great shimmering waves off the rusted steel decks. A few dogs barked halfheartedly, and here and there stout women in grubby dusters paused in their chores and watched. Not far away some barefoot kids played soccer on the road, and somewhere a transistor radio blared out tinny pop music.

The kids stopped playing and sidled closer to check out the soldiers. Stark held out an imperious hand, and they froze, gaping. From the fourth-last barge a fat man in a T-shirt waved and shouted, "There! That one. Strange hippies in that one. They left a couple of hours ago."

Stark said over his shoulder, "Fan out and keep your eyes open." Then he jogged over to the fat man to be told with neighborly malice that a group of very suspicious-looking characters had bundled into a blue van and taken off.

Stark looked at the *Nijmegen;* the tangle of bicycles by the wharf railing was the only clue. On the barge nothing moved. Cocking his head and tapping his nose, the fat man said, "The way some of those people live is enough to make you sick."

Stark picked three soldiers and posted the other six along the wharf. Then he took an Ingram and ran his hand over the front of the bulletproof vest to make sure it was closed.

They opened the hatch and went below. The smell was unbearable not only for olfactory reasons but also because it fed his basic fear that the worst had already happened.

The ripped-off arm prosthesis lying in a corner made him shiver with dread.

The flies led them to the cargo access door, and they checked for the wires or fishing lines of booby traps, then pulled on the handle. The body was not Dietrich Helm's.

Françoise Muton, alias Madeleine, had already passed rigor mortis and entered the second stage of decay. Green bottle flies had laid eggs inside her mouth and nose, and maggots swarmed in the pulpy hole of her chest wound. The skin of her face had fallen back to the bone, baring the teeth in a thin-lipped grin.

He looked around quickly for the briefcase but could not find it. Stark went upstairs and summoned the radio operator. The fat man on the other barge was watching. While Stark waited for HQ to come on, the fat man shouted, "Well, what did you find? A body?"

Stark ignored him. His feeling of nausea left, and even the brackish, stale heat of the wharf now seemed like an elixir.

He ordered a full AT site team and put out calls to Georg and Fritz. Then he walked over to the man on the other barge to ask the routine questions.

Jack Teagarden said, "Shut up and drive, Paul. How are we for gas?"

"That's another thing. This is not a company car. It's on my personal credit card."

"I'm glad to see your sense of humor is returning, Paul. This is your exit coming: Overath. We're getting off the turnpike and taking a state highway."

"No kidding. Let me guess: Olpe?" In the mirror, the Mercedes was still there, with Metzger's chunky outline like a boulder behind the wheel. He signaled, then slowed for the exit. The regulation .38 was still in Teagarden's hand on his knee; it had not moved much since Duerenerstrasse a good half hour ago.

Fontana said, "When will you ever get your semantics right, Jack? This isn't a turnpike, it's the autobahn. Do you get your Wendy's hamburgers flown in, and your Frooty Frootloops for breakfast?"

"Shut up, Paul. Just drive."

Fontana wheeled around to follow the sign to Overath and Olpe. He said, "How long've you been posted in Germany now, Jack. Fifteen years? How much longer before you develop a feel for the country?"

"The day I go native here will be a snowy day in August, Paul. Krauts . . . can't trust them worth a damn. Look at you, for example: devious to the last." Teagarden laughed, showing his expense account crowns and fillings. For a moment, Fontana was tempted to smash him sideways in the gut, but it was hard to fight a man who had a gun and steer a car at the same time.

Around them traffic was thinning as they entered deeper into the countryside. Harvesting was now in full swing, and flocks of crows and starlings swooped from field to field, sampling the swaths made by the combines like so many buffet tables. And the sun streamed down, painting it all a glorious gold.

Teagarden said, "See that turn down there? Take it."

"I seem to have been here before, Jack. It all seems vaguely familiar."

"Drive. What were you meeting with that Schott feller for, Paul? I bet you know a lot we don't know. But you'll tell us, I'm sure. You know that Jackson took a medical course, Paul?"

"Jackson Harris, your dirty tricks guy—what kind of medical course? First aid?" While his mouth talked, his brain worked overtime. What was on their mind? Were they planning to kill him?

"First aid—shit!" guffawed Teagarden. "No, stuff we learned in Latin America, Paul. Interesting stuff. Jackson really caught on."

"Are you trying to scare me, Teagarden? Jackson Harris with a dentist's drill and a syringe? What a joke, man."

"Let's wait and see." Teagarden turned his face and looked fully at Fontana. Grinning he said, "The drill's more like a Black and Decker model, Paul."

Fontana drove on. The road became a winding gravel path, climbing, dropping, then climbing again. They drove through a stand of evergreens; the product of good reforestation, tall and straight, spaced equidistantly, the underbrush removed.

In the distance, Fontana saw the building that always reminded him so painfully of his youth: a four-story building very much like the main structure on the Fontana estate in Thuringia. Local granite, snow-shedding copper roofs, turrets, leaded windows; a large thoroughfare for the old-time caleches and six-in-hands.

Only Thuringia was in East Germany now, behind barbed-wire fences and minefields, and the Fontana estate according to his research had been turned into a potato-farming holiday commune for young people who had distinguished themselves through hard political work for the party.

Teagarden's voice woke Paul from his memory flash. "Did you know those SWAT guys bugged you, Paul? The equipment those Krauts've got puts us to shame, man. A gallium-arsenide laser with a battery that's half as heavy as our gear. And half as big, too. The whole thing can apparently be hooked into just about anything."

Fontana gave him a sideways glance, then turned back to the road. Behind them, the Mercedes was bumping along. He asked, "You mean, that blond guy bugged us, Schott and me?"

"Clever Paul. You're catching on. They followed you and we followed them. Piece of cake."

They had almost reached the estate building now, and Teagarden said, "Blow your horn, Paul; then go slow through the gate."

He did as told, then watched with amazement the appearance of a small army. Some of the faces he knew, most he did not. Young men in their early thirties, clean slim faces, short hair parted on the side, white shirts with button-down collars, ties, suit trousers, and polished brogues. Most had the regulation shoulder holster under their left arm, some had Uzi machine pistols.

Fontana counted eleven agents—then twelve, thirteen, and still they kept appearing from doorways and looking out of windows, then pulling back. Getting out of the car, he said to Teagarden, "What's with all the operatives, Jack? You must be really worried about that economic summit."

But then Metzger grabbed his wrist and pulled him along. Jack shouted, "See ya, Paul! Keep your eyes on the drill." And he laughed his inane cackle.

Metzger led Fontana down a flagstoned hall, past a huge kitchen where women in white aprons and serving hats were working at tables and stoves. Then Metzger kicked open a door and pulled Fontana into a great cavernous room with only a desk and a lamp and two chairs. An iron grille was set into the windowsill, and the window itself was opened, giving a view of the undulating countryside and the haze and smog in the distance that might be Cologne.

"Sit down," ordered Metzger. He pushed Fontana into the chair in front of the desk, then reached for two gleaming ring shackles and snapped Fontana's wrists to the arms of the chair.

"Listen, you ape, what kind of a game is this? Can I know the rules, or is this some sort of hide and seek?"

Metzger strolled over to the window, leaned against the wall and looked out.

Precious time passed. Time in which Gaby might be calling Peter again—time in which she might be giving a clue as to where she was—where Helm was being kept.

Then the door opened and Henry Wolff strolled in, followed by Jack Teagarden. Wolff walked to the chair behind the desk. He sat down and smiled at Fontana. When he smiled, he looked amazingly young, like that American film actor whose name Fontana always forgot. In a way Wolff was perhaps the most successful actor of all—certainly enduring, and always rehearsed and ready for his part.

Now, as if he were delivering a cue, he said, "Paul, my friend. I hadn't expected to see you again so soon. Why can't you follow orders like everyone else?"

Fontana sat still, waiting.

Wolff leaned forward and said with casual charm, "All right, Paul . . . if you're wondering why you're here—it's because I have something to tell you. *Two things* . . . the one's a present, a kind of parting gift. The other is a piece of long-awaited good news for you. Curious?"

17

Fontana sat still. Of course he was curious. But Henry was tricky—you rarely had a clear sense of where he was coming from and what he had in mind. He rattled his handcuffs and said, "Tell those clowns to take them off, will you?"

"Oh, sure. Sometimes the boys get a little overeager. They like to scare people, flex their muscles. You know the kind. When I told them, 'bring in Paul, I've great news and a little gift for him,' I should have added, 'but be nice to Paul. He's a friend.' Oh well. Forgive the inconvenience." Wolff beckoned Metzger, who pushed his bulk off the window frame and unlocked Fontana.

When the shackles lay on the desk, Wolff said, "Why don't you run along, boys? Paul and I will have a little chat now. I'm sure he won't attack me. Will you, Paul?"

Fontana rubbed his wrists.

Wolff was still grinning, waiting in silence for Teagarden

and Metzger to leave. The grin showed the wrinkles around the eyes, and it showed Henry's perfect teeth; a great lab job, not too even and not too white. Fontana thought that he still looked a bit like the young first lieutenant of those days. Even the freckles were still there, except that they had gathered into large clusters that in another few years would be age spots. The only thing different about Wolff today was that behind the aura of American boyishness one very quickly got a chilling sense of steel. Some of that had already been perceptible even then, but over the years it had grown, focused, and refined itself. Today, Henry Wolff was like a top-class fencer and chess player rolled in one, still nimble on his feet, always with several tactical moves lined up in his mind, all well-planned and preemptive.

Fontana said, "So, what's this all about?"

"Paul . . . after the last time we spoke and you made your noises again about wanting to get out, I had a long talk with Washington. I told them, 'Look, the man has done his share for us and he wants out.' 'But he knows too much,' they said. Well, who doesn't? Which agent after . . . how many years is it now, Paul?"

"Cut the bull, Henry. What did they say?"

Wolff leaned back and paused, timing his answer. "The reason I called you off was because they agreed to *let you go*. As of last week you're no longer under any obligation to us. How's that?"

The first emotion was one of tremendous relief. But it was quickly followed by suspicion. The news was wonderful, but the timing told him it was one of Wolff's moves. He said, "Good. Finally. They should have let me go thirty years ago."

"Hey, Paul! I expected more enthusiasm. You've been badgering me for years. Now I get them to cut you loose and all you can say is, '*Good. Finally*'? I went out on a limb for you."

"Thank you, Henry. Do I get a golden handshake too? A ballpoint pen or an engraved ashtray or something?"

"Paul . . . you're going to get something better than that. Much better. You're going to get the present of your life. I don't mean, your *life* as a present, but the best piece of information you've had in forty years—but wait." Wolff reached into his jacket and took out a folded manila envelope. He looked at it for a moment, undecided whether to open it. He put it on the desk.

The sight of the envelope made Fontana's heart beat faster.

"Paul," said Wolff. "This is special. I know that over the years you and I have had the occasional disagreement. And I know that sometimes you are suspicious of my motives. I never lied to you, but sometimes I told you only parts of the truth. And only in one instance did I withhold personal information that I felt might get in the way of your work for the Agency."

Fontana looked from Wolff's face to the envelope. He saw Wolff's familiar hands pick it up and open it . . . reach into it, and return with a black-and-white photograph. Wolff tilted it so that Fontana could not see its front.

Wolff said, "Paul, this is my going-away present for you. The result of Agency work and my initiative. I could have told you sooner, but you'll understand that under the circumstances. . . . Here." He stood up and reached across the desk, handed Fontana the photograph.

When he looked at the picture, his hands trembled so badly that he had to rest them on the edge of the desk.

It was a photo of Vicky. She wore some kind of smock and rubber boots, and she was straddling a row of vegetables. In her hands was a hoe, and she was cleaning dirt from its head. In the background other women were bent over similar rows of vegetables.

Vicky's hair was cut short in a careless way, like the other women's too, and on one of the distant backs Fontana could make out what looked like a six-digit number. He looked again at his daughter's face in the foreground; it was a sharp, clear photo, and he had no doubt about her identity.

Wolff said, "You okay, Paul? Can I get you a drink or something?"

Fontana looked up. He managed to control his emotions. "Where and when was this taken?"

"Two days ago in the kitchen garden of Pankow jail, East

Berlin. It was taken by one of our people with some very fancy equipment."

"And how long have you known that she is alive?"

"Ah, well . . . " Wolff allowed his embarrassment to show for a brief moment. "That's what I mean, Paul. I've known for some time, but obviously I couldn't tell you."

"Why not?"

"Because it would be too tempting for you to make deals with the Russians for her release. You've been working on high-level operations all this time. Who in your circumstances would have had the moral strength *not* to buy the freedom of his daughter with a bit of information? Think of the operations that went through your hands these past three years. Stuff that was really hot at the time—"

"Three years? You've known for three years, you bastard, and you never told me?"

"Easy, Paul. I'm taking a chance telling you even now. Don't give me a hard time. I'm just trying to do a job, okay?"

Through the open window they heard the whine and slap of an approaching jet-copter. It thundered over the building, then the pitch changed as it landed.

"Who the hell—?" said Wolff. He pressed a button on the desk and immediately Teagarden stuck his head in the door. "Go check," said Wolff, and Teagarden withdrew.

Fontana was looking at the photo. He knew he should still be furious with Wolff, but knew too that to do so was pointless. Besides, the argument about risk factors and trade opportunities made sense.

Wolff said, "I can imagine how you must feel, Paul. It's all a bit sudden. But listen . . . let me tell you whatever I know about your daughter. She was badly wounded by those border guards but not killed—obviously. In all fairness Peter Schott could not have known that. And if he had turned . . . well. You can guess for yourself what they would have done to the three of them. As far as we know, Vicky has been in the Pankow prison ever since she came out of the hospital eight years ago."

"And the sentence?"

"Don't know for certain, but the usual term is fourteen years in jail followed by ten years of social work on a collective farm."

"Do you think there's any chance of getting her out?"

"See how your mind immediately turns to that? It's natural," Wolff said. "But I don't know, Paul. At least you can visit, I guess. It's a medium-security place—"

From the hall came rapid footsteps, then the door was flung open. Followed by Teagarden, a tall angular man strode into the room. He looked familiar to Fontana.

"Gunter!" exclaimed Wolff. "What a rare honor. Do you know Paul Fontana? This is Chief Inspector Gunter Stark of Antiterrorism, Paul."

Stark nodded at Fontana, then turned to Wolff. "Have you got a minute?"

Wolff rose. He glanced at Fontana and said, "I won't be long, okay? Have a little chat with Jack."

As Stark and Wolff left the room, Fontana remembered where he had seen the chief inspector before: he and the blond young man from this morning had been Peter Schott's tandem tail on the *Lorelei*.

When they were alone, Teagarden said, "I heard the good news, Paulie. You're goin' out to pasture in Canada. How's the grass over there? Nice and juicy?"

Fontana ignored the taunts. He picked up the photo of Vicky and put it in his inner jacket pocket. He leaned back and stared blindly out the window.

"Well, what?" demanded Teagarden.

"Shut up, Jack. I have to think."

Was there something wrong about the chain of events today? At the back of his mind, along with the joy about Vicky's being alive and about being a private citizen again, he felt a nagging doubt. Was the chronology too much of a coincidence? Was Henry, the master string-puller, timing things this way on purpose? Was Fontana expected to respond in a certain way?

The thoughts bothered him. Then he realized that Henry's gifts had turned his priorities inside out.

There was nothing he could do for Vicky at the moment. The immediate crisis demanding his full attention was that of Helm and Gaby. When that was resolved, *then* he would see about Vicky.

Had Gaby tried again to reach her father? She had said, "Uncle Helm and I are with these horrible people . . . " At least that suggested that he was still alive.

His thoughts were interrupted by Wolff's return. At the same time the jet-copter thundered over the castle, back towards Cologne.

"Noisy bastard," said Wolff, smiling at Fontana. "Sorry to keep you, Paul. Anyway . . . " he waved his hands. "Something came up and I have to run. You're free to go, Paul. Your car is where you left it. Lie low for a few days. Relax. Think about things. Do some sight-seeing in Cologne. I'll talk to you soon."

"What did Stark want?"

"What? Oh, he was bitching about jurisdictions. The usual crap. Says you were under their surveillance and we had no right to interfere."

"What about Helm and the papers? Do they have a lead?"

"Yeah." A probing glance. "He says they're very close. Not to worry. Maybe the government will make a deal with the kidnappers."

"Can I help you, Henry? Maybe I—"

"Shit, no. What's with you? You're out of this for good. Now leave it alone. Go!"

"Henry, together we could—"

"Goodbye, Paul. I really have to run. Jack, see him to his car." Wolff raised his hand and wiggled his fingers.

In the courtyard the Opel was covered in dust from the chopper blades. Fontana turned the car around under the watchful eyes of Wolff's army. Then he stepped on the gas and raced all the way back to Cologne.

Fontana knew that he no longer understood Wolff's thinking. In time he would figure it out. For now, he would concentrate on Helm and Gaby and on Peter Schott.

It was impossible to drive up to the hotel. A huge interdenominational service was taking place at the cathedral and the crowds spilled over, well beyond the pedestrian zone, as far as Stolkgasse and St. Andreas. Loudspeakers had been strung to lampposts and trees, but clearly the crowd far exceeded expectations.

On the fringes were the demonstrators; an orderly line of placards demanding the admission of women to the priesthood and the removal of all sexism in the church.

Fontana parked half on the sidewalk on Ursulastrasse, then walked, pushing his way through the crowd. It was hard even to move on foot, and outside the hotel the crowd of worshippers stood shoulder to shoulder. From a nearby loudspeaker sounded the rhythmic altar bells of what Fontana thought might have been the Eucharist. Then came the words in a number of languages. Before they had reached either English or German, Fontana had entered the lobby.

Dornier was behind the desk, and for the first time as long as Fontana remembered, there was a happy smile on his face.

Fontana frowned at him, and Dornier quickly supplied the answer: "The hotel is *full*! For the first time since the anticruise demonstrations, when they all wanted cheap accommodations, this place is full."

"The mass?" Fontana saw the slip of paper in his pigeonhole and reached for it.

Dornier said, "All they really needed was windows, but windows come only with rooms, and the rooms—" he leaned closer, whispering, "—the rooms today are twice as much as yesterday."

"Make hay while the sun shines, Herbert. Any good Catholic knows that." Fontana waved, then hurried across the lobby and up the stairs. The call was from Peter, and it was marked "urgent."

In his room he connected the digitizer and dialed. Below, the crowd chanted — a thousand-voiced, unintelligible mumble.

Peter came to the phone. His excitement communicated

easily over the wire. "Gaby called again! She ran away from them, Paul. She wants to meet with me. She says she can explain everything."

"What about Helm?"

"She'll tell us about it. She says he's fine."

"Jesus . . . now what? How did she sound?"

"Still terrified, but relieved. We only spoke for a very short time."

"Will you meet her? When and where?"

"The open-air restaurant at the Rhine Park. At eight o'clock."

"Eight o'clock at the park restaurant? It'll be *very* crowded."

"She says she'll feel more secure in a crowd because she can watch me. And she wants to meet only with me. She says if there's anyone else with me, she'll not come forward." There was a pause as Peter thought about that. Is that strange? No, it's not, he told himself.

"It could be a trap," said Fontana.

"What kind of trap?" Peter shouted impatiently. "Trap for whom? She ran away from them, don't you understand? She says they were on a boat or something and she escaped while they were moving to another hiding spot."

Fontana put a finger into his left ear to shut out the noise of the religious crowd below his window. "Where's she now?" he asked.

"For heaven's sake, Paul! She didn't say."

"Calm down. I want to come with you, just in case."

"No! I shouldn't have told you. The police don't even know. She called me at that restaurant where I often go for lunch. You were right when you said not to change my routine."

"You mean this time she didn't call you on your office phone?"

"That's what I'm telling you. The cops don't know about this meeting. She guessed right, but then she's been to that restaurant several times with me in the past."

"Well, good. But let me come with you tonight."

"No! I shouldn't have told you—"

"Wait! Wait, Peter. Don't hang up. Let's not make a mistake now. Okay, so maybe it's true and she ran away. Why can't I come and sit far away from you? Or hide in the crowd or in the bushes, just in case you need help?"

Peter argued for a while longer, but eventually he agreed. "But she mustn't see you. If she runs away because she recognizes you . . . "

Fontana promised. Then he said, "Now, about getting to the park. It's a safe bet that the police are keeping an eye on both you and me. I have a plan, Peter. Meet me outside your office building at six-thirty, in half an hour. We'll drive together in my car."

Fontana hung up and put away the digitizer. In his head, the alarm bells rang insistently. He sat on the bed and cleaned his gun. The .38 was an Agency special. It was a powerful weapon with a snub-nosed barrel. Wolff had given it to him, a personalized sort of badge and reminder of his debt. It had come in a fancy leather case lined with red velvet. In the bottom left corner a small brass plate said, *To Paul from Henry: France 1944.*

Years of carrying it had worn the gunblue off the edges and corners. He had rarely needed to use it because, as he had reminded himself often enough over the years, he was first of all a facilitator. The path to becoming that sort of person was hard to reconstruct. But forty years was a long time. Especially if one never stopped to look back, one could travel a long distance in forty years.

He plopped out the shells, wiped the chambers, then reloaded them, leaving one empty for the hammer. The bullets were flat-fronted wad cutters to give the weapon maximum impact at close range.

While he worked, he thought. How had they traced him to the gas station where he met Schott, and how had Chief Inspector Stark found him at the CIA safe house?

He checked his clothes thoroughly: he was clean. The car, perhaps. He would check it too.

Below his window, the loudspeakers vibrated with the choral responses to the *agnus dei* sung in German.

Eventually Fontana left the hotel and went straight to

his car. Halfway to Schott's office, he suspected that he was being tailed again. This time it was a green late-model Ford that kept disappearing and reappearing more than ten cars behind him.

Fontana stopped at a self-serve gas station and busied himself with filling up, checking the oil and tire pressure. Crouching, he spotted the beeper inside the rear bumper. He could see it clearly—a magnetized silvery disk, no bigger than a camera battery. He left it there for the time being and continued on to Schott's.

Peter was already waiting in the entrance to the building. Fontana stopped and got out of the car. The green Ford cruised past, crossed an intersection then pulled over, out of sight. Because of the beeper the driver did not need to maintain eye contact.

While Peter Schott climbed into the Opel, Fontana removed the beeper. Pretending to be a tourist, he flagged a passing car, a Citroën, and asked directions to a street which he knew was just around the corner. While the driver explained, Fontana leaned close and stuck the beeper to the Citroën's roof.

Fritz sat in the tail car, his eye on the beeper readout. This was an instrument much like a compass: attracted to the beeper, the needle indicated the relative position of the target car.

While Fritz waited for Fontana, the needle pointed to the rear. Fritz picked up his radio and called the team that was covering Schott. "Can you see your man?"

"He's getting into a black Opel driven by an older guy."

"That's Fontana. He's a real fox. We have a beeper on his car, so I'll take over. Stay here and keep an eye on the office. Over and out."

The needle swung sharply to the right. Fritz sat up with a jolt, started the engine, and did a slow right turn to catch up with the Opel once it had passed.

He went as far as the intersection to wait for Fontana, but already the needle sent him left again, and he sped off as soon as the light allowed, chasing after the elusive Opel. He crossed the Ring and was speeding as much as he dared, when, passing a white Citroën, the needle did a sharp right, then pointed backwards.

To make sure, he slowed and let the Citroën pass again; the needle spun with the French car, and Fritz knew he had been tricked by Fontana. Cursing, Fritz pulled over and called Georg, who was stationed in the laser van near Fontana's hotel.

"I lost him," said Fritz. "The guy knows all the tricks inside out." He described what had happened, then asked, "Did you get any conversation that might give us a clue where they've gone?"

"There was a lengthy telephone conversation, but we couldn't tune out the exterior noise. There's this huge service going on, and the street is full of chanting and praying. All that noise vibrates the window more than the talk behind it. This operation is jinxed, you know. We should have tapped his phone, but it's complicated with a hotel switchboard. And usually a window tap is much better anyway. You can get telephone and room conversations."

"I know. But did you record, anyway?"

"Sure. Perhaps they can—"

"Get the tape to the lab, fast. A technician told me they can filter out most extraneous noises. I'll call Gunter and we'll meet you there."

He reached Stark at HQ in the computer room, and twenty minutes later they were assembled in the electronics lab. A technician converted the tape that contained the telephone conversation mixed with the religious ceremony into digital information. A part that contained only sounds of the ceremony was rerecorded over and over for length, and digitized as well. Now the slow process of computerized detraction began.

Stark sat on a stool, listening tensely as Fontana's side of the conversation emerged from the noise. Slowly, much too slowly, syllables took shape, words emerged . . .

*   *   *

In order not to add pressure to the moment, Fontana did not tell his son-in-law that Vicky was still alive. There would be time for that after tonight's crisis was over.

At the moment his eyes did not leave Peter, who sat at a table close to the corner between flower beds and dance floor. They had chosen the table with care, well before the restaurant had become as crowded as it was now; Peter was shielded sufficiently by dancers and other diners, and no one could take a shot at him without coming up close.

Fontana sat two tables away, so that it would be impossible for anyone to approach Peter without being seen.

The open-air dance floor was clearly a great attraction for locals and tourists of all ages. The orchestra specialized in flamboyance and fun rather than precision, and the tiled dance floor by the lit fountain was crowded with cheerful, flushed faces. Presently, tango time having concluded for the moment, it was the turn of the younger generation, and they bobbed, jumped, and tumbled around to Italian, German, and American pop tunes.

Peter turned quickly to reassure himself that Fontana was still there.

A short distance away, two clowns set off a string of firecrackers, and Fontana's pulse raced. A couple approached Peter Schott, indicating the three empty chairs at his table. But he did well, going through the planned routine of pointing at the dance floor and shrugging his regrets that the chairs were taken. As if this had been the cue, a sequence of events began that, even though it lasted only seconds, seemed like an eternal nightmare.

From somewhere they heard the sound of a helicopter, then a young woman in jeans and a dirty blouse appeared by the side of the fountain. She was looking for someone, and Peter Schott did the very thing Fontana had told him not to do. He got up, waved excitedly, and called "Gaby, Gaby!"

The young woman saw and recognized him; she walked towards the restaurant, and Peter Schott rushed to meet her.

By the time he had leapt over the flower bed, Fontana was already standing, gun in hand but not yet taken from the holster.

Just then a dark-haired young man appeared at the edge of the dance floor. In the blink of an eye he brought up a .45 automatic in a two-fisted grip, leveled it, and fired.

Peter's head snapped forward as though he'd been hit with a club from behind. He fell in his stride, face down, and the gunman's .45 shifted towards Gaby. Fontana saw her only from the corner of his eye, because he had already reached the gunman and now he swung his own weapon like a stone and clubbed the man behind the ear.

Then the helicopter swooped down, and its noise and the first shrieks from the crowd silenced the orchestra. The helicopter hovered low; its brilliant lights glared and its jets and rotor whined and beat the air. The awning collapsed and striped tablecloths were ripped away. People cowered, screaming, covering their heads against the tornadolike downdraft.

Gaby still stood, her hand to her mouth, her eyes open in terror. She was backing away from the corpse of her father when Chief Inspector Stark rushed into the circle of light and wrestled her to the ground. She kicked and struggled, but he held her firmly. Fontana saw it only in a flash because his own prisoner suddenly lunged for his legs, and he jumped back to avoid a tackle and raised his .38. He tried to kick away the .45 but could not reach it. He yelled, "One move and you're dead!"

The first soldiers had rappelled and reached the ground, when Gaby somehow escaped Stark while he was clamping handcuffs on her wrists, and she cowered screaming by her father under whose shattered head the blood looked black like ink.

Fontana still fixed the killer waiting for someone to come and help, when the man suddenly let out a high-pitched, furious scream, then swung around.

214 /   Kurt Maxwell

He had rolled away with the agility of desperation, and he was on one knee, his gun now rising in his hand, when Fontana nudged the trigger of his .38 and shot him in the forehead.

18

Stark sent back the chopper but kept the soldiers for crowd control. The site team arrived within half an hour; apart from their usual paraphernalia they came with two ambulances and one paddy wagon. The ambulances left very quickly again with one shrouded stretcher each.

That makes three, thought Stark grimly. Rossi, Madeleine, and Gaby. He wondered how Mahmoud, Banigan, and Theo would react to tonight's events. He worried about Helm's safety now more than ever before.

Back at HQ, Stark immediately prepared to interrogate Gaby and Paul Fontana. He told Georg to keep in the background. Fritz was sent to inform Esser and Zander of the latest developments.

After fingerprinting and photography, two guards led Fontana and Gaby into the room.

"Fucking pig," yelled Gaby at Stark. "I'll bite my tongue off before I talk to you. And that shit—" she tried to kick Fontana but her guard restrained her "—take the handcuffs off me and I scratch his fucking eyes out. I saw what he did. He's a killer, a *killer*. Fucking family, bastards, all of them."

Gaby was dragged to a chair. Fontana sat down at the opposite end of the table. Gaby pounded her cuffed hands on the table and began to howl.

With so much riding on every minute now, Stark was

afraid he might lose his temper and hit her. He yelled, "Shut up!"

Gaby stopped howling, surprised. She slumped forward on the table, crying hysterically.

Stark sat next to Fontana. He had to raise his voice. "What is your CIA connection, and what is your role in all this? Who the hell *are you?*"

"I am one of their agents . . . but this is not agency business. I'm her grandfather."

"Her *grandfather* . . . and?"

"It's a long story. But basically, the agency took me off the case, but I stayed on it. I want to save Helm's life. He is a very old friend of mine."

"What does the CIA have to do with his abduction?"

"I'm not sure. Ask Henry Wolff."

"All right—what *do* you know? Speak quickly if you really want to help your friend. He may not have a lot of time left." Stark looked at the clock above the door. It was 10:30 P.M., the evening of the second day after the kidnapping.

Fontana said, "This afternoon Gaby called her father and said she had escaped. She said she wanted to come home."

"We know that."

"You do? How—"

"Never mind. Do you have any idea where Helm's being kept?"

"No. I'm hoping that Gaby will tell us."

Across the table, Gaby yelled, "Hell no, you bastards. Let him rot in hell. Let them all rot in hell. You too."

"Gaby," said Fontana. "Listen, Gaby—"

But she began to shriek. She clamped her hands over her ears and shrieked until Stark motioned to the two guards to take her out of the room. Stark cupped his hands and shouted, "Take her to medexam, then put her in a holding room."

Then he was alone with Fontana and Georg. He said to Georg, "You and Fritz go spell each other. Take a nap. Get something to eat. This'll be a long night."

Fingerprints sent in the reports. Stark scanned Fontana's, then moved on to Gaby's. Her prints matched the missing set on the Diet Coke cans that had been found in the closet of the apartment and on board the old barge. Her prints were also on the little .22 that had been found in her purse. Ballistics was firing a test now.

Stark looked up and said to Fontana. "She's been in the midst of this all along."

"Not *all along*," said Fontana. "Don't prejudge her. I think she was coerced and set up."

"Do you?" Stark grinned without humor. "Ballistics will tell us shortly if her gun fired the shots that killed the old sailor whose barge they confiscated. And Mendelssohn—but you wouldn't know about him. Two counts of homicide to begin with. Later I'll bring in an eyewitness of the kidnapping to identify Gaby. I think your granddaughter was the driver of the backup car. A stolen BMW."

"All very circumstantial and you know it. You won't get her to open up by hanging all kinds of charges on her."

Stark took a deep breath. "All right. How? Tell me."

"Let *me* talk to her in private. But before that, I have to make a deal with you."

"What kind of deal? But—hold it! I can't let you talk to her alone anyway . . . you're a suspect too. I have to hold you as well. You were at the scene of the Stolz murder. We found your prints on the hi-fi and on that wine glass." Stark tapped on the fingerprint report on Fontana.

Fontana made an impatient gesture.

"Well, let's see—what kind of deal?" asked Stark.

Fontana told him.

Stark listened in disbelief. "No way. We don't bargain like that. Maybe in America—"

Fontana said, "Bullshit—but try it your way for a while. Just don't take too long. See how far you can get with Gaby. Then come back to me. Listen . . . I *do* want to help."

Stark looked at Fontana with mixed feelings but with renewed respect.

Fontana said, "And by the way—she has a history of psychiatric problems. She was in treatment."

"Are you serious? Which shrink?"

Fontana raised his hands. "Peter Schott would have known."

"Great! Just great," said Stark. He stood up. "Stay here." He went to the phone on the sergeant's desk outside the interrogation room.

Five minutes later, he hung up in disgust. The police psychiatrist at HQ could not be reached. "Try again in an hour, chief inspector," the nurse had trilled in his ear.

Stark said to Fontana, "I'll have to have them lock you up. Sorry. Talk to you later."

"I don't have to tell you to hurry," said Fontana.

Stark's next step was to get a positive identification of Gaby at the scene of the kidnapping. He went upstairs to his office and searched his desk until he found Angela Frisch's number.

It took her only three rings to answer.

Stark said, "I'm sorry to be calling so late, Dr. Frisch. This is Gunter Stark . . . we met Monday."

"I remember. Please call me Angela."

"I hope I didn't wake you."

She actually laughed at that. "It's not only policemen who work late. I was going over some papers."

"I wondered if you would help us out by identifying someone in connection with the Helm kidnapping."

"Identify which one?"

"Well—you'll understand. I can't really influence you in—"

"Of course. Yes, I'd be glad to. When—now?"

"If that's not asking too much."

She said she'd be ready in ten minutes.

Angela Frisch lived in Klettenberg, a residential district that had once been a separate village. Because there was hardly any traffic and he was not constrained by speed limits, he reached her address in thirteen minutes.

She was already waiting in the entrance to the apartment building. He saw her as he turned into the drive: auburn hair, white summer jacket and skirt, purse slung over her shoulder. Her face was shadowed in the angle of the light from the overhead bulb. She recognized the Porsche and had the passenger door open before he could get out to assist her.

"Good evening." She slid into the leather seat, careful not to scrape her shins in the narrow tunnel left by the electronics.

"Good evening, Angela. I really appreciate this." The car swept out of the drive and back onto Luxemburgerstrasse. He said, "Rossi was killed last evening."

"At the dance floor in the park? There was something on the radio. Who was the other body?"

"A man called Peter Schott. The personal secretary to Helm. We caught a young female. We think we know who she is, but we need an identification for the scene of the kidnapping."

He stole a sideways glance at her. Considering the time of day—11:30 P.M.—she seemed wide-awake. Alert, and very desirable.

At HQ, Stark checked Angela in with the guard, then led her to the observation window to Gaby's holding room. Gaby was back from the medexam but the bed was empty. Then they heard the toilet flush, and Gaby padded barefoot across the room. Her blond hair came down to her shoulders. Climbing into bed, she reached up with both hands to pull back her hair, and at that moment Angela said, "There's no doubt— she was the driver of the BMW. Same profile, hair in a ponytail. I'm sure of it."

Stark took Angela's elbow and led her away. Upstairs in his office he scanned the ballistics and medexam reports while Angela read the identification form and signed it.

Because Gaby's involvement with the Helm kidnapping was now clearly established, he felt free to show the reports to Angela. He watched her read them, noticed again with relief that the slim hands that held the document were ringless.

Ballistics confirmed that the .22 found in her handbag was the murder weapon used on the old sailor and on Mendelssohn. And the powder burns on Gaby's right hand matched the gas exhaust of the little gun. Finally, a semen smear taken from her vagina matched sperm samples taken in the cutting room from Rossi's testicles.

Angela looked up. "You killed her lover."

"Or rapist. We can't be sure. Rossi shot her father in the back of the head and was about to shoot her too. So what was her exact role in all this? Was she coerced—if so to what degree? But the main question is: how can I make her cooperate with us? She must know the hiding place. If she tells us in time, we can save Dietrich Helm."

"And eliminate Mahmoud," added Angela.

Stark nodded, adding, "And Theo and Banigan."

"Have you spoken to her yet?"

"No. I wanted positive identification first. And also . . . which reminds me—excuse me." He looked at his watch, then reached for the phone to try the police psychiatrist once more.

This time yet another nurse told him the doctor had just returned from Frankfurt and was off-duty until 9 A.M.

Stark groaned. "It's only midnight," he pleaded with the nurse. "Can't we make an exception? Nurse . . . are you there, nurse?" He thought he could hear her yawn.

"Absolutely not. He's been going full tilt for the past three days. He'll kill me if we wake him."

"I have a top-priority case here—are you telling me that I have to sit on my hands for another nine hours—"

"Chief inspector," the nurse said tiredly, "I'm not telling you anything. What *can* I tell you? Psychiatry is a very demanding field. Give the man some sleep. What's a few more hours to you?"

"Thanks, nurse. Good night." He hung up cursing under his breath.

"I couldn't help but overhear," said Angela. "Can I help?"

He brightened. "Help with what? You've done your share."

"Well . . . I wrote my doctoral thesis on young offenders. I could help you talk to her. I mean, *help* unofficially of course. I'm aware of the red tape in cases like these. But I feel somehow involved."

Stark said, "I have to try and make her cooperate. I am in

charge and I am fully responsible for the outcome. The red tape never begins until *after* things have gone wrong. Then I would have to justify my actions."

"You understand, I'm not guaranteeing that I'll be able to get through to her. But at least I can help you get an idea of the nature of her resistance."

"I understand. Thanks—I appreciate your offer. Every minute counts, and I'm grateful for any qualified help I can get."

They rode the elelvator down and checked in with the guard. Stark turned in his gun, and Angela left her purse on the chair outside the door. They entered the room. Gaby was asleep now. Her hair was mussed up, her cherry lips parted.

Angela said, "Every daddy's little princess." She sat on a chair opposite, looking at the girl with curiosity and apprehension. "Children can sleep no matter what."

Stark cleared his throat, then called her name.

Gaby woke with a start and sat up. She blinked and looked around, disoriented. She said, "Not you again." But she spoke almost with resignation. Her demeanor now was in sharp contrast with that of less than two hours ago.

Stark said, "Could we please talk to you?"

Gaby swung her legs off the bed. They had taken her clothes and issued her with standard garb: gray cotton skirt and pale blue blouse. Her hair fell forward, and she reached up with one hand to hold it back while with the other snapping an elastic around a simple ponytail.

Then she sat, her hands demurely on her thighs, whispering through snow-white childish teeth, "Yes?" She looked from him to Angela. Her eyes clouded over and truculence swept into her face like an ominous cloud.

Stark said, "They killed your father. Did you want that to happen? Did you set him up? Were you supposed to lure him into the open so that Rossi could kill him?"

"No! No!" She stood up, then collapsed again onto the edge of the bed. "No! I had no idea they would do that! If I'd known . . . " She put her face in her hands and cried.

"You must hate them. Look what they did to you. I believe you never expected these things to happen."

Gaby kept on wailing, rocking up and down. Angela walked over and sat on the bed beside her. She put an arm around Gaby's shoulder but the girl leaped up, half stumbling over the low table. "Get away!" she screamed. "Get away, don't touch me. Don't anyone ever touch me again!" She let herself fall to the floor and curled up like a baby, her face pressed to her knees.

The door opened and the woman constable looked in. She looked questioningly at Stark but he shook his head and waved her away.

Firmly he said to Gaby, "Stop this and get up."

She ignored him and so he sat down on the floor and leaned close to her. "Too many have died already. At least let's try to save your uncle. He is still alive, isn't he?"

When she did not respond, he ordered firmly but calmly, "Get up. Enough of this."

From the bed, Angela said, "Gaby, we know that you loved your father. We know that—"

"Love, love!" the girl screamed. She rolled over, got to her hands and knees, and crawled away into the farthest corner. There she cowered like a threatened animal. "Love, love. What do any of you know about love? Your whole generation, what do you know about love? All you know is threat and confrontation and indifference. Look what you've done to the world. Look what you've done to our country, our cities, our nature. Look at the future you're building for us. For us, your children. What is there for us to look forward to?"

They stared at her, numbed momentarily by her innocent fury and passion, by the new chasm that had sprung up between them.

Angela made a helpless gesture. "The state of the world in the late twentieth century is not anyone's *fault*, Gaby. And terrorism and murder won't exactly improve things. I never understood just how you people could reconcile the two."

Gaby sneered. "Of course you don't. Your generation is merely straddling the present with one foot in the fascism of the past and the other in the big final bang. You've never understood anything. Understanding takes feeling, but all you've got is cold brains like your computers and the force of your fucking self-serving laws. You have no heart, none of you. Germany has become like America. A monstrous staring match—back down, or else!" She sat down, leaning into the corner, her arms hugging her knees. Tears sprang from her eyes and she brought up her hands to stem them.

Stark took a deep breath and said, "Gaby, we can talk about all this later. You have said some very true things, but for now we *must* know where they've taken Dietrich Helm. You must tell us!"

"I *must*," she sneered, "must I? You self-assured little pig. Henchman of your fat-cat society. I am my own person, I am *me*. I am *Marion*." She leaned back her head and closed her eyes. Tears streamed down her young pale cheeks, and she began to roll her head sideways, from wall to wall, humming.

Angela motioned to Stark. She got up and went to the door. Stark followed her.

In the car, she finally said, "I won't bore you with psychiatric terms, and I'd only be guessing anyway. But the child needs help badly. Of course physically she's no longer a child, but emotionally she is."

On the dash, the clock said 1:15.

Stark asked, "So what do I do? How do I make her cooperate? I mean, helping her is one thing, but there isn't time for that now. I'm talking minutes, hours. How long would it take for a psychiatrist to figure her out and turn her around so that she becomes ready to cooperate?"

"Impossible to say. Several sessions. A few days—a week. One would have to get to the root cause of her behavior. The human mind—"

"Angela! I've got a major abduction case on my hands. Three highly dangerous terrorists on the loose, a month before an international economic summit in Bonn. I can't spend a lot of time worrying about the devious subtleties of Gaby Schott's mind!"

"But you have to, Gunter. If you want to get anywhere with her, you have to do precisely that."

"All right. *Parallel* to psychiatric work, what can I try now? It's after one o'clock in the morning, and let's assume the police psychiatrist is ready to begin work in six hours. Until then, what can I try? Do you understand my dilemma?"

"Of course. Let me think."

Except for a few garbage trucks, the streets were virtually empty. At intersections Stark merely took his foot off the gas, then sped on. By the time Angela answered, the Porsche was entering her driveway.

She said, "*Immediately*, you might try to have another woman her own age talk to Gaby. It's a long shot. Have her pretend to be curious about Gaby, really interested in her. Perhaps you can make Gaby want to impress her."

Stark thought of Misha. It was worth a try. "And if that doesn't work?"

She opened the car door and carefully extricated her bare, tanned legs from the instrument tunnel. "If that doesn't work—I'm reluctant to say this, but what might work is a strong emotional shock, emotional blackmail. An instant chance to relieve guilt. You see, what you really need to offer her is a way out of her dilemma. I hope that's not too unprofessional for me to—"

"It's not," he interrupted her. "I understand, but this is an emergency."

"Well, good luck then." Angela offered her hand, and Stark shook it.

He asked, "When this is over, may I see you again?"

She shot him a glance, then smiled. "Yes. I'd like that."

He turned out of the driveway and sped along Luxemburgerstrasse while establishing contact with the office. Georg came to the phone, saying that Fritz was out cold on the cot.

"Wake him," said Stark. "One of you go to the morgue, get the slug that killed Peter Schott and take it up to Ballistics."

"All right."

"Wait. Lean on Forensics to speed up the evaluation of the vacuuming on Rossi's and Gaby's clothes. And while you're at Forensics, bring back the prosthesis. Put it on my desk. I'll be needing it shortly."

"No kidding! Same arm?"

"Very funny . . . one more thing. Have them move Gaby down to the basement cells. No more comfort. Make her shiver a bit. You can reach me the usual way."

HQ Op patched him through to Misha's home number, but against his feeble hope, she was not there. They patched him through to the Muehlheim number and he let it ring.

Eventually Guido answered, drugged with sleep.

"Wake up, Guido, this is Gunter. Tell Misha to get dressed. I'm coming round to pick her up."

"Wha . . . whassamadder? You crazy, Gunter? Do you know what time it is?"

"Two o'clock in the morning. Sorry about that."

"Sorry . . . don't you have—"

"Move it, Guido. This is an emergency. I'll be there in a few minutes." He pushed the button to cut the connection, then put a message on the superintendent's tape. Speeding across Muehleimer bridge, he put an update on the interior minister's tape also. Minutes later he pulled up at Guido's, then leaned on the buzzer. There was no answer, and so he pushed again, yelling, "Guido, if you don't open this goddamn door this minute I'll wake everybody in the building."

In the intercom, Guido said, "Go away, Gunter. Misha doesn't want to come with you. She's had enough of you."

Stark put his flat hand against the row of buttons, triggering buzzers in every apartment. Then he said calmly, "Guido, in two-oh-three, if you don't open up now I'll smash this door and then I'll come up to break every one of your delicate little double-keyboard harpischord fingers."

The lock clicked and he ran up the two flights of stairs.

"You brute," said Misha breathlessly. "How can you do the things you do?" She wore a nightie he'd never seen on her.

Behind her Guido stared at him pale-faced. He wore white silk pajamas and his hair had a cowlick smack on top of his head. Down the corridor doors opened, then quickly shut again.

Stark said to Misha, "Please. I've never asked you anything like this before—I need your help. Come along. With any luck you'll be back in less than two hours."

"What do you want from her?" asked Guido.

Stark ignored him. "Do we really have to talk halfway out in the hall? Misha, I want you to come with me to HQ and talk to a suspect for me."

"Are you crazy, Gunter? You ignore me for months and now you barge in here in the middle of the night asking me to come talk to one of your criminals."

"Misha!" he shouted. "I've never asked you a favor before."

"Shh," said Guido. "Don't shout so much."

"Get dressed, Misha. For Christ's sake."

"Don't, Misha," said Guido.

Stark glared at Guido. Then his belt unit buzzed and he pushed past the two, walked across Guido's ankle-deep white shag. Guido's phone was a replica of Mickey Mouse. One spoke into one ear and listened to the other.

HQ switched the call: it was the interior minister. His voice was like an ice pick. "Chief inspector, how do you think the two or three surviving terrorists will react now? You are forcing their hand."

"Sir?" From across the room, Guido was staring at him with timid fury, while Misha kept clutching the nightie to her neck.

"Damnit, man—" Esser gulped audibly for air. "Chief inspector, I want you in my office at seven o'clock this morning. I hope your unemployment insurance is paid up. Goodbye."

Stark replaced Mickey Mouse's head. "*Jesus . . .* " he said. "Where were we?"

"You were just about to leave," said Misha.

Stark's belt unit buzzed again.

Guido said, "Busy man. Why doesn't he just bring his desk in here and set up shop?"

This time it was Fritz. He said that dust and oil samples

on Rossi's clothes and shoes matched samples taken at the barge and at Mendelssohn's.

"So that's no help. We know they're not there anymore. Anything else?"

"I brought the prosthesis, and Paul Fontana wants to know how much more time you're going to waste. Those were his words."

Stark took a deep breath. He said, "Tell him I accept. I'll be there shortly."

He hung up, and with no more than a smile for Misha he walked out of the apartment.

Running down the stairs to the Porsche it occurred to him that this was the end of their relationship. But really she had left him, or he had left her, months ago. They had coasted on, drifting further apart while waiting for some event to separate them.

When he reached HQ he roared down the one-way ramp, parked in his stall, then rushed upstairs to get the prosthesis. Shortly after 3 A.M. he entered Fontana's holding room. He went to the table, put the artificial arm down gently, and sat on the chair.

Fontana offered his hand, and Stark shook it.

The older man said with just a shade of a smile, "And we will not betray each other's trust. After all, we both want the same thing. Right?"

Stark said, "Yes." He looked at Fontana and found himself wishing that he would age into a man like this.

19

Because of the strike in the lumber industry there was not a soul around who could hear or see them. It was the best hole imaginable. Even so, Theo was scared. Fear with him always crystallized into violence.

"I say, ice the fucker and let's get out of this snatch, man. They killed Rossi and got the cunt. She'll finger us!"

Mahmoud looked at him, searched his face inch by inch with those snail eyes Theo hated. When the snails had crept up to Theo's eyes, the Arab whispered, "Easy, Theo. Easy. Time's on our side. Time and the fact that we've still got him *and* the documents. What if we ice him now, and then they ask for some proof that he's still alive? See? So cool it, okay? We've come this far, and we'll go the rest. You, Banigan, and I."

They had strapped Helm to the chain conveyor under the band saw, and if things went wrong, a push on the big red button on the wall would start the whole thing and send him through the blade, crotch first. A ritual execution to write home about.

The publicity of that stunt alone would be worth abandoning this snatch, thought Theo. A fat-cat politico neatly sliced lengthwise like a side of beef. The media could be relied upon to lap it up. Banigan agreed. But for now at least, Mahmoud had persuaded them to hold off.

They returned to the immediate future. Mahmoud said, "It'll be light soon, Theo; you should be off before seven. Go over there and I'll pump up some water so's you can wash up a bit. Comb your hair too. They might pick you up for something stupid like vagrancy."

They went to the old-fashioned flail pump and the Arab worked it rhythmically. Theo splashed his face, then scrubbed with an industrial cleanser. Meanwhile Banigan hunted in the closets and found a newly pressed coverall that hid Theo's filthy clothes nicely.

Mahmoud stood back and looked at him critically. "Not bad. Now, tell me what you're going to do."

Obediently, Theo recited his mission, and Mahmoud gave him a benny as a reward. Theo popped it and welcomed the hit with closed eyes.

When he stepped out of the hut, the sky was pearl-white on the eastern horizon. Among the stacks of lumber yesterday's heat still trembled, cracking the wood, drying it out, perfuming the air with the clean smell of resin. Birds everywhere greeted the new day with enthusiasm.

Theo rushed from stack to stack, then walked naturally across the open stretch to the hanging gate. From the river came the hooting of a tug, then a steamer bell answered.

It was 7:00 on Thursday morning.

In Bonn, Stark walked down the carpeted corridor to Esser's office. The door to the anteroom was open and he stepped inside, with a tentative knock.

The police commissioner and his own boss Zander sat on the leather furniture, both looking like penitents about to meet the wrath of God.

Zander looked at his wrist watch.

"I know," said Stark. "But I could not come sooner. There's an emergency on. If he doesn't know that, I'll tell him."

The commissioner cleared his throat and Zander said to Stark, "You'll calm down first, chief inspector."

The gilded French carriage clock between the two Breughels chimed with Renaissance clarity. It was 7:30.

Stark asked, "Has he been on the phone all this time? And you've been waiting all this time?"

Zander nodded.

Stark sat down and Zander turned to him. "Anything new?"

"Fontana is cooperating. He told me to ask you what the CIA has to do with the Helm abduction."

"How do I know? Keep your nose clean and your priorities straight."

From the inner office, through the open door, came Esser's voice. He was speaking English, *shouting* English. Stark picked up the words, *Mr. Wolff will have to be satisfied with that . . . I know . . . I know . . . tell him, in half an hour.*"

Zander said, "No good eavesdropping. Just confuses a man."

They heard Esser slam down the phone and pound the desk. Then he shouted from the inner office, "Come in!"

The police commissioner was first, then Zander, then Stark. They threaded their way past the empty secretarial desks and past a clacking Telex machine. Through the window they had a passing view of the governmental parking lot. It was still empty, like a football field at dawn.

Esser came straight to the point. Without getting up from behind his desk, he pointed a trembling forefinger at Stark and, looking from Zander to the police commissioner said, "I want this man suspended as of this minute, gentlemen. Until you find a suitable replacement, the superintendent will be in charge of the Helm case. Understood?"

"Well, sir," said Zander. He wrinkled his craggy old brow and puffed out his cheeks.

"Well, what? What?" The minister stared at them and a vein rose on his forehead. It reminded Stark of a party trick.

Zander said bravely, "Perhaps that's not such a good idea, sir. The chief inspector is the one . . . I mean, there has been some progress. This case is only two and a half days old. Why do you want to replace him? I mean—"

"Sit down all of you," sighed the minister. On his desk the phone rang and he glared at it as though it were his personal enemy. Looking at the open door to the anteroom, he shouted, "Isn't there anybody in yet?"

But there was only silence and, rolling his eyes wearily,

Esser picked it up. For a moment Stark actually felt sorry for the man.

Then the momentary slackness was gone and tension again quivered in the room. The minister stuck a finger into his free ear and yelled, "Once again; who are you, sir?"

They all stared at him, felt the bad news transfer from the black receiver into Esser's ear, into his whole body.

"When? Just now? Very well, thank you. Please give me your name and number. Your address too. And you must hold yourself available for the police, chaplain."

The minister put down the phone, then hammered his fist on the desk that the pencils jumped.

Zander cleared his throat and asked soothingly, "Anything we can do to help, sir?"

Esser stared at them in turn, then bored his eyes into Stark. "The documents I told you about—our worst fears have just come true. The terrorists are threatening to pass them to the media. We have until noon to meet their conditions. Then they are going to telephone the first set of data to a radio station."

Stark made a face. "Noon today? How was the message sent?"

"The chaplain of St. Monica's in Weidenpesch received it over the phone."

Zander asked Stark, "Are you covering—"

"No, sir," Stark interrupted. "Weidenpesch is beyond the radius. We haven't the manpower to register every single phone call in the state."

Someone entered the outer office, humming a tune. Then Ellie stuck her head in the door and chirped, "Good morning, all. Coffee?"

"No!" snapped Esser, and Ellie muttered, "Oh dear," and pulled back her head. Today she wore braids, piled up like Gretel.

"Superintendent, tell me your plan," said Esser. "But before you begin—" He paused, then continued with a firmness meant to make up for his embarrassment. "The *documents are more important than the kidnapping itself.* We must plug the leak first—and if in the process we can—let me rephrase that: the first priority is to recapture the documents that are now in the possession of the terrorists."

Stark said, "Sir, I'm confident that we'll be able to get the documents *and* save Helm in the process."

"Are you, chief inspector?" Esser looked at him now with new gratitude. "What's on your mind?"

"Media taps, sir. We *want* them to call. It'll take a lot of manpower, but we can actually tap all the telephone lines into and out of all the newspapers, radio stations, and TV stations in greater Cologne. The threat said radio specifically, but I think we should play it safe."

"Can that be done?" asked Esser.

"Anything can be done, minister," said the commissioner, but everyone ignored him.

"Go on," said Esser to Stark.

Stark told the minister about the insta-lock system whereby operators could intercept and block phone calls without the caller becoming aware of it immediately. At the same time the computer at Telephone Central could pinpoint the location of the outgoing call. The system had performed well on similar occasions, said Stark.

"Good, good," said Esser. "So what next?"

"We'll make contact with that priest and see what we can learn from that. I expect not much. But we are proceeding on another front too. I'm confident that the young woman we caught last night will cooperate with us."

Good," Esser said again. Then he added, "Well, carry on, chief inspector."

Stark asked, "Do I assume I'm still on the case?"

"Yes," said Zander. "Isn't he?" Esser nodded and the commissioner looked down at his folded hands.

"I have just one question, minister," said Stark. "What does the CIA have to do with this case? Are they interested in Helm or in the papers? Are they aware of—"

"You don't need to know that, chief inspector," snapped Esser. "Just get them both before it's too late." He handed Stark the note with the priest's name and number.

Standing up, Stark said to Zander, "I'll proceed with the media taps immediately, sir. What about the additional personnel?"

Zander looked at the police commissioner and asked, "Do we have your clearance to pull them in from Rhineland HQ, sir?"

"What'll it cost?"

"For heaven's sake, commissioner," shouted Esser.

"All right, all right. Go ahead, superintendent."

Stark turned and strode off. In the anteroom two more typists were at their desks. Ellie was on the phone; she grinned and wiggled her fingers at him. A stack of morning papers had just been brought up, and Stark glanced at them in passing. The Rhine Park incident was on every front page: big headlines and a picture taken by a visitor with a snapshot camera. It looked like a war scene, and in the foreground stood Fontana aiming his gun at Rossi on the ground.

Stark left quickly before the minister could ask one of his classic questions, such as why a man had been shot after he was already on the ground.

On the parking lot there were just a handful of additional cars. One of them was a metallic silver Mercedes, the sleek, classic 220 with the rounded, low hood and yellow fog lamps. The Mercedes was parked next to Stark's car and on its front fender leaned the slim, American, forever-young figure of Henry Wolff. Today he wore a pearl-gray summer suit of what looked like and probably was Italian silk; to the pale blue shirt was matched a slightly darker blue tie, and Mr. Wolff's feet were snug in black, hand-stitched Milan loafers. Living on a dollar expense account in Europe clearly helped a man express his taste for the finer things.

"Gunter." Wolff grinned. "What a coincidence meeting you here at this hour. Most of Bonn's still asleep. But then it usually is. How're you keeping?"

"Fine, Henry. What are you and Esser cooking up?"

Wolff was toying with a car key ring in the form of a silver dollar. His hands were tanned and manicured; they suggested nimbleness and speed. He said, "Quite a shoot-out last night. This place is getting as bad as back home. Worse, I'd say."

Stark got into the Porsche and rolled down the window. He put in the key and started the engine.

"Wait, Gunter," said Wolff. He pushed himself off the fender and came closer. The Porsche engine murmured, then accepted the slight nudge on the gas pedal with a rasping growl. "Hang on," said Wolff. "How are you doing with Paul?"

"How do you know we've got him? Listen, if you guys don't hold back a bit there could be some trouble. This is not your home turf."

"Gunter, my boy." Wolff grinned. "We know everything, and we've got to. How else could we keep the forces of evil out of Western Europe?"

"I have to go."

"Just one thing; when you make your move on Helm, we've got to come along. You know why, don't you?"

Stark leaned his head out the window and waved Wolff closer. "Henry, if it turns out you people are behind the Stolz killing, I'll personally make sure they'll nail your elegant old scalp to the wall."

Wolff straightened and shrugged.

"I'm getting a make on the killer. Prints and mug, Henry."

"You are? I thought you were told to hand over to Wiesbaden."

"Did you think so, Henry? Now why would you think that? And what do you know about the recording?"

Wolff gave him a sharp look. "You had the place covered? Where is the recording?"

Stark grinned, shifted into first, and fishtailed away from Wolff, across the empty lot and out the gate. Traffic was heavy, but most of it went the other way as civil servants rolled into town from the surrounding suburbs. The air was filled with the hum and electricity of industriousness and anticipation. Most cars had only one passenger, and a good half of those were women. A new breed of professional, political, and driven women; slim, impeccably groomed, early thirties, sharp as a new Solingen blade. The cars were mid-sized European makes, turbocharged, air-conditioned, hi-fi-equipped, upper-range models.

Tailing a red Lancia that was clipping along near two hundred, Stark buzzed the office. Fritz was called to the phone, and Stark told him to initiate the wiretaps on all media lines in greater Cologne. There were a dozen radio stations, including the shortwave service of Deutsche Welle, a half dozen TV stations apart from the big WDR, and countless newspapers, magazines, and periodicals.

"A massive operation," said Fritz. "I'll get on it right away."

"Good, I'll be there shortly, Fritz."

He clicked on the blue flasher and the Lancia moved over. Passing it, Stark caught a glimpse of the woman driver: auburn hair like Angela but nowhere nearly as attractive. The thought of Angela gave him a lift.

The stone-faced guard unlocked Gaby's cell, stepped aside for Fontana to pass, then locked it again behind him.

Gaby sat on the floor in the corner, her cheek on her knees. The cell was bare except for a cot; three walls were gray concrete, the front was steel bars. On this side of the floor were four more cells like it, all empty. Not a sound could be heard except for the creaking of the wooden chair on which the guard sat, out of sight.

Fontana walked over to Gaby. He placed the arm prosthesis on the linoleum floor and sat down next to it.

Gaby did not look up.

He thought he had been running away for forty years only to reach this spot on the floor—this was where the maze had ended; in a police cell, face to face with his granddaughter.

She began to raise her head. The movement spread to

her whole body. When she saw the prosthesis she inched away until her back was against the wall. A shadow of fear passed over her face, then the eyes glazed over.

She said, "What the fuck did you bring that thing for?"

"Because I want to tell you about it. Today we are going to talk about your family. I'm going to tell you about the people. About yourself."

"Don't bother—"

He interrupted her, gently but firmly. "Be quiet. Listen, please."

"Why the hell would I want to listen to you? To *you*? You're the one who killed Angelo. I saw it." Tears sprang to her eyes and rolled down her cheeks. She wiped them away angrily, staring at him.

"*Angelo* means angel. Thirty-odd years ago his proud papa and mama had him christened in that hopeful name. The only other 'Angelo' that quickly comes to mind is Archangelo Corelli. You may not have heard of him. He wrote great music."

"Crap! They both expressed how they felt about life and humanity in the best way they could. Both were dissatisfied."

"Maybe, Gaby. Yours was about to shoot *you* when I hit him."

"What do you want?" Her eyes flickered to the mechanical arm.

"I want to talk to you about Uncle Dietrich — shh, hear me out. You must!"

She leaned her head back against the concrete, closed her eyes, and pressed her lips together.

He paused, suddenly realizing that he had no idea where to begin.

Gaby snapped open her eyes and said, "Are you a cop?"

He shook his head. "I'm just a very old friend of Dietrich's."

"Oh, no kidding," she moaned. "Tell me about it."

He nodded numbly, then pulled himself together, shut out his own emotions, and concentrated on hers. "I've known him since the war."

"The war? Which war—there's wars everywhere now."

"World War Two. Long time ago."

"He was a Nazi. Were you one too?"

"He was not—he was *Wehrmacht,* and personally, secretly, he was opposed to everything the politicians stood for. He was a flying ace until he lost his arm." He touched the prosthesis. "He invented this himself. Double articulation, it was revolutionary in its day. Then the anti-Hitler—are you interested?"

"No." She smirked. "Who really cares? Fact is, they murdered millions, right?"

"Does the date of July twentieth mean anything to you, or the name Stauffenberg? Or Rommel, or Dollfuss? What about Himmler or Goering? What do they teach you in school today?"

"Don't bother me. Goering was a drug addict. What did you come here for?"

"To plead for Dietrich Helm. I want you to help me free him. Gaby, please. It is never too late to change. This is the time!"

She stared at him, emotions alternating in her eyes like sunshine flashing through fast-moving clouds. Breathing quickly she asked, "And then what? He's free, then what?" She hid her face in her hands and began to sob explosively, deep gasps that shook her whole body.

Fontana said, "You mean he's seen you and recognized you. If he lives he'll be a living reminder of your betrayal. So you really don't mind if he dies, if the whole gang dies and everyone who knows about it. What about you, would you like to die too?"

Sobbing and hiccuping she said, "I don't care anymore. I never wanted things to go this far."

"And how did they? I don't think it was *your* fault."

She shrugged. "They just did. I couldn't help it."

"But how did you get involved with them in the first place? What attracted you to them?"

"Nothing. I was approached. They knew about my connection to the Greens. No one was supposed to get killed. It was a—" she broke off, sobbing, stumbling for the right word—"it was harmless. A bit of excitement. It *seemed* harmless until they said I had to pass a test . . . "

"Was the test to set up your father? To see if you were committed enough to betray him?"

"No, no! I never did. They tricked me into that. I . . . Oh, shut up and go away! Who asked you to come here anyway?" She raised her hand angrily as though to hit him, but Fontana did not flinch. She stared at him, then tried to back away even further, pressing herself into the corner. "What do you want from me?"

Lightly he said, "I told you already. I've told you what I want, now let me tell you *why*: I want to save Dietrich's life because many years ago he saved mine. I was in love with a woman and times were such that, because of it, I was hunted and they would have shot me if Dietrich had not helped me get away. He saved my life, you see, Gaby?"

He looked at her, smiling, and for a moment she believed him. Then defiance flared up again and she laughed cynically, "They were going to kill you because you loved some woman? Come on, come on."

"It's true. I know it seems strange by the relaxed rules of today's society. Her name was Franziska. Your grandmother."

For a moment Gaby perked up. "So that's how it all hangs together. Was she sent to that camp because of you?"

"It was more complicated than that. We can talk about it in a minute. Perhaps all of this should have come into the open much sooner, but you never made it very easy for *anyone* to talk to you. But look, Gaby . . . " He hesitated for a moment to reassess his strategy: he would keep the news of her mother's survival for his final trump card. First he would try and show her a way out of her self-imposed isolation.

Calmly he asked, "Can we examine your alternatives together? Can we look at your choices and their consequences?"

She narrowed her eyes and drew a deep breath but did not disagree.

He said, "The police have offered to release you in my custody if you help me find the hideout. They'll free you now, and afterwards they'll make a deal . . . " He hesitated, then plunged on: " . . . pleading coercion, and pending a psychiatric evaluation of—" He broke off, then said, "You should get off very lightly."

She closed her eyes and in the harsh light from the naked bulb he saw the tears well between the lashes, then roll freely down her cheeks. A runaway child, lost and afraid of the dark. A darkness so complete, nothing would ever dispel it. No matter what, her life would never be good again. At this moment they both knew it. So as to speed her decision, Fontana coaxed, "Avoiding jail is not the only reason, Gaby. Do you feel the other one? It's you . . . if you help me rescue Dietrich, it means you've turned around. The mistakes can't be unmade, but it's never too late to change."

She was rocking back and forth, eyes closed, palms on her thighs. When Fontana was afraid he might lose her, he reached into his pocket and took out the recent photograph of Vicky. He held it out and said, "Open your eyes. This is your mother. I want to tell you a bit about your family."

She took the picture, and the transformation in her face tore at his heart.

Quickly he said, "She's alive. In jail in Pankow, but alive, Gaby. Please don't cry now. I need your help. I have a sure-fire plan to ger her out of jail and bring her here . . . please trust me now. This has to be a secret between you and me. A secret until she's safe here with us . . . "

"You've let her go? And Fontana?" Zander stared at Stark in utter astonishment. "What on earth — all right, you better tell me. What's on your mind?"

"Well, first of all, he's wearing a bouncer. That's part of the deal. We've got three communicating teams on their tail and we're monitoring them live. So they can't get away, if that's what you're worrying about. Secondly, after an hour or so of peace she may just remember fragments of conversations that lead us to the latest hideout. Already she's told him about the latest car switch at the airport yesterday. We've found the van, and my people are working on it now. They stole two cars, an Audi 5000 and a Volvo. She says they took the speakers out of the rear panel for breathing holes and transported Helm in the trunk.''

"Where to?''

Stark shook his head. "She doesn't know. Rossi drove her to the Rhine Park restaurant; Theo, Banigan and Mahmoud took the Volvo with Helm in the trunk to the other place.''

"I see. I'm not happy about you making deals, by the way. I mean her getting away with this, and both Fontana and Gaby being kept out of the story.''

Stark said, "Not *getting away*—charges haven't even been formulated yet. But I promised special consideration in exchange for her information. It was the only way to get him to make her cooperate. And it seems to be working.''

"Where are Fontana and Gaby now?''

"At the police garage. We're giving them a car, and from there they are going to drive straight to Fontana's hotel. The three teams will track them from now until this whole thing is over. In addition we still have the laser tap on the window, so that we can record whatever Gaby tells him. Fontana has been instructed to repeat the key information with his face close to the windowpane. Just in case.''

"And you are going to supervise all of this from the laser van?''

"Yes. The van is parked two blocks away from the hotel, and the laser unit is strapped to a utility pole right outside his window. The outdoor church services at the cathedral are finished so we won't have any problems with the sound.''

Zander still appeared worried.

Stark continued: "So that's one approach—Fontana and Gaby. Him debriefing her and us listening in. The second approach is the phone taps on the media lines. In their message to the priest the terrorists gave us until noon today. Then they will phone a radio station and expose part of those documents. Whatever the hell they are.''

"National security,'' said Zander. "Let's leave it at that.''

"Well . . . all right, it's just eleven o'clock now—one hour until the deadline. Telephone Central has hooked into all the media lines in greater Cologne, and I told them to be prepared to stand by for twenty-four hours if necessary."

"And if the call comes?"

"It'll take five seconds to identify and block it. At the same time they'll get a fix on the caller's location. Georg will be manning a hot line that's been patched from Telephone Central into the office here. As soon as the call pops up, he'll call me at the laser van and dispatch the strike team that's standing by on the helipad." Stark took Zander's arm and led him out of the way of the catering truck. The air on the whole floor began to smell of roast chicken and coffee. Around them phones rang and people came and went.

The operator called, "The lieutenant for you, chief inspector."

Stark excused himself and picked up his phone. It was Georg reporting from Telephone Central. All the media lines had now been branched off into the insta-lock system, he said. Two hundred officers had been pulled in from police forces all over the state. Each operator was monitoring three media lines with headsets, keyboards, and VDTs—should more than one line be in use at the same time, the operator had to rock three thumb keys back and forth to keep track of the conversations.

When the terrorist call came in, the operator would push the red lock-and-search key.

Stark said, "And right after that you'll know the location and you'll dispatch the chopper and call me?"

"That's it," said Georg.

A half hour before the noon deadline Stark was in the laser van. His Porsche was parked right next to it, ready to race to the location of the terrorist call.

He felt strung out. This was it: by tonight Helm should be a free man.

Today the area around the cathedral was far less congested: the religious crowd had moved on to St. Severin's in Silvanstrasse, a church in pure Romanesque style.

Stark wondered whether for a connoisseur of churches a week in Cologne might parallel the enjoyment of a gourmet and wine connoisseur in the Loire Valley. It was an incongruous thought: he was neither religious nor gourmet.

Nerves, he told himself. Relax, but not too much.

Over a live two-way radio line he was linked to Georg at HQ. The other monitoring controls included live patches into the three teams tailing Fontana and Gaby, and a decoding readout for the laser tap off Fontana's hotel window. Apart from that, the bouncer they had taped to Fontana's back with surgical tape transmitted its own steady beacon pulse from which the decoder would isolate all speech once they came into range.

Three technicians were in the back of the van with him, electronics wizards all of them. On the inside, the van looked much like a mobile electronics shop: stacked cabinets with supplies, wires neatly coiled on racks, and a narrow U-shaped counter to which the controls were bolted. The men sat on typing chairs, listening and fine-tuning constantly.

On the outside too the laser van was no more than the battered, obviously much-used panel truck of a TV repair firm. The logos and phone numbers painted on the side were made almost unreadable by scratches and dirt, and the numerous receiving antennae on the roof were camouflaged with aluminum ladders and lengths of conduit pipe.

All seemed to be going well until 11:50, when Fritz called from the police garage, where Fontana and Gaby had been given a clean Peugeot 505 and were about to set off for the hotel.

Fritz said, "The Americans are on top of us. Teagarden and Jackson are watching from the corner."

"How the hell? Are they perhaps picking up his bouncer? I thought those things are keyed only into their own mother units."

The chief technician made a face and, when Stark nodded at him, said, "We're all using the same technology. If they fish for the signal long enough they can find it. We could do it to them, too."

Stark turned back to the patch with Fritz. "Try the blind alley trick on the Americans. You know how to do that, don't you?" He was referring to the way Fontana had shaken Fritz on Wednesday afternoon.

Seven minutes later, Fritz called back. "They took the bait. We peeled the bouncer off Paul Fontana's back, put it in a closed van, and sent it off to HQ. The Americans went after it. I recognized Teagarden and your friend Henry Wolff."

"Are you sure there was just that one team?"

"Pretty sure."

"Fritz, listen. Put Fontana and Gaby into another closed car, pull out, and watch very closely. I don't want Wolff to be on our tail when we make our move. This is not their turf. When you're sure Gaby and Fontana aren't being followed, bring them to the hotel. That's the one place the Americans don't know about. Have a driver deliver the Peugeot separately and leave the keys under the mat."

"Got it," said Fritz and disconnected.

The technician on the window tap held up a finger and pointed at the small peephole lens set into the side wall of the truck.

Stark leaned to it and saw a Cologne Hydro vehicle. In the bucket at the end of the boom a maintenance man was replacing street lights. The boom was now at the lamppost to which they'd fixed the galium laser transmitter and in the tiny image it was hard to tell if the maintenance man was fiddling with it. With a curse Stark dashed out of the van and down the street.

Sure enough, the man was just about to clip the steel straps that secured the transmitter. "Hey," called Stark, "hold it!"

The man looked down from the bucket and cupped his hand around his ear. A few pedestrians gave the scene a second look but moved on. Stark stepped on the running board and showed his AT pass to the man behind the wheel.

"Your man is just about to fuck up a sensitive operation.

If he moves that transmitter at all we'll have to realign it, and that'll take too long. Stop him now!"

The driver spoke into his walkie-talkie, and Stark stepped down into the street. The bucket man listened to his set, gave Stark a curious glance, and with a shrug let go of the strap.

"Ask him if he's moved it at all," Stark ordered the driver.

The bucket man shook his head, then proceeded to replace the light globe—hand over hand exchanging the old one with a new one from a rack around the bucket.

Cars honked at Stark to get out of the way, and a speeding cab nearly ran over his feet. He returned to the van and took the earphones. The laser technician said, "A man just entered the room, chief. He made a telephone call and asked for the foreign desk. He's still talking to someone on the phone."

Stark clamped the phones over his ears. He heard a deep male voice: " . . . tell him to call me back here at the Pension Dornier. I'm in Fontana's room, three-oh-four . . . "Yes—no—*Benn*. Attila Benn." The phone was slammed down, and the man said "idiots."

Stark leaned to the microphone with Georg. "Have someone get me the dope on a guy called Attila Benn. Hurry."

Fritz buzzed to say that Fontana and Gaby were now on their way. The hotel entrance was covered by four plain-clothes detectives.

In the earphones there was now nothing. "Come on, come on, say something," Stark muttered.

An ambulance came wailing down Komoedienstrasse, obliterating all other sounds. Traffic was dense, and it seemed minutes before the interference was gone.

In Fontana's room the phone rang and Benn picked it up. A choppy monologue: "Yes" . . . "I'm not sure when I can be there" . . . "You could call it that" . . . "The copy from East Berlin should run soonest for obvious reasons" . . . "Yes, keep me informed. I'll call you periodically." Then silence again.

At 12:18 came Fritz's clipped words, "Rounding your corner now, chief—ready at the entrance."

Down the street the detectives, who had tiny speakers like hearing aids behind their ears, paired off: two by the entrance, two on the sidewalk. Then the undercover van with the label of a bakery came down Komoedienstrasse and turned right. Seconds later, Stark watched Fontana and Gaby climb out through the side door and disappear into the hotel.

Stark decided not to replace the bouncer on Fontana. Wolff would get in the way again. With the laser tap and the three teams, Stark was so close on Fontana and Gaby that surely nothing could go wrong.

Then his earphones came to life. First there were some indistinct noises, then Fontana's voice muffled by the distance from the door to the window.

"Attila, I'm so glad to see you. Your timing couldn't be better."

"Paul, good to see you again. Who's this?"

"This is Gaby . . . my granddaughter."

"Is she helping you?"

"Let's sit down, my friend. Let me bring you up to date. I don't suppose in East Berlin—"

"I've seen today's Cologne papers, Paul. What on earth is going on?"

The scene at Telephone Central would have impressed even the futuristic architects of Walt Disney's EPCOT.

Dimly lit only by the indirect ceiling lights and their greenish VDTs, the 209 operators sat like an army of human spiders spinning electronic nets.

Except for the nervous clacking of the thumb toggles there was little sound; all the operators wore large leather-padded Grundig earphones; their eyes were glued to their screens in the vacuous gaze of someone closed off in a private world of concentration and eavesdropping.

Four supervisors in soundless tennis shoes on the soundless felt broadloom cruised the aisles between the terminals. A climate control system kept temperature and humidity to within one degree Celsius and a correspondingly steady level of humidity, and at ten-minute intervals ozone and negative ions were disseminated through slits in the baseboards.

The tension level and nervous atmosphere were those of a war room at full alert. But by 1:30, one and a half hours after the deadline, there had still not been any attempt by the terrorists to make good their threat of publicity.

On the conveyor track in the saw room, Dietrich Helm began to struggle against the deadening, suffocating daze that had made the pain, the humiliation, and the hopelessness bearable until now.

It was like a fog rolling back slowly to reveal once more the various features of a familiar landscape. Except that what came clear first was the distant horizon, the past, and the way it related to his present reality. The astonishing truth was that the time he had spent in the basement of the Gestapo house in Essen had been far more terrible than this ordeal.

What had made it more terrible was the fact that the brutality had been organized, a well-oiled routine of torture and pain administered without passion but with scientific calm. By comparison these terrorists had been mere children, naive, undisciplined, random waifs blundering through unexplored territory.

What made these young people cruel was their lack of self-respect and self-knowledge—what had made the Gestapo cruel had been their sense of lordship over life and death.

About Gaby Schott—what was he to make of Gaby Schott's betrayal of him? She was a nuclear-age Judas, surrendering him in exchange for a sense of belonging to her chosen family.

But he was only mildly curious about Gaby. Her motivation was like a garbled computer print-out; human error lay behind it, and the result was unintelligible and uninteresting.

He looked around, began to explore with rising interest his current reality. He was in a work shed of sorts, a lumber shed near the river. Frequently he could hear the tooting of ships, and the changing pitch of jet engines told him he was near the airport also. Rodenkirchen, Kalk, or Porz, he guessed.

He lay on his back on a steel-link conveyor track. The blade of a high-speed band saw rose between his legs. It continued upwards to a large flywheel, then down again to the big drive pulley and the electric motor housing. On the upright steel column by his side there was a large red on/off button, a kind of dead-man switch that was likely wired in a three-line circuit to override the auxiliary starter that would be more conveniently placed close to the panel near the door.

They had tied his hand with bailing cord to the track behind his head, and his feet were fixed the same way. The pain in the stump of his right arm, where they had ripped the articulation strands from the muscles, no longer bothered him.

He rolled over onto his left side as much as possible. Looking at his watch, he suddenly felt irrationally hungry. Two o'clock on Thursday, the third day of his kidnapping. Mathias had had to put up with this sort of treatment for close to three weeks. Then they'd killed him.

Suddenly Helm knew that he would fight; a man who had already lived through so much had a right to go on living until his natural death. The thought buoyed him tremendously, and it gave him an even greater sense of exhilaration to realize that he had nothing to lose.

Hunger—he became aware of it again. He tried to move his left hand and found that the bailing cord possessed a certain degree of stretch. It was really no more than thickly twisted sisal, and if he worked his wrist for an hour or two, the cord would be worn through by the steel links of the conveyor.

He lay back, gritted his teeth, and worked his fist and arm methodically.

Beyond the door he could hear the transistor radio. It

had been on for hours. It was tuned to the all-news station, and he guessed the terrorists were waiting for a message of some kind.

Then they began to argue again. He did not know what had become of Gaby and Rossi; since they had moved to the new location there was only Banigan, the Arab, and the dirty German, Theo. Theo was the most vicious and angry of them all.

The radio was turned too low for him to understand, but he could hear their argument very easily.

Theo was all for killing him and bailing out, but the Arab prevailed. The Arab had tremendous power over Theo and Banigan. Leadership, willpower, physical strength, and the drug Theo needed to feed his habit. Helm guessed it was Benzedrine; bennies, the poor man's wings, they called them.

Continuing to work his hand, he listened:

"Now, Theo, time to go, man. We make a threat, we have to follow up. Go call the station. Banigan and I will wait here."

"Fuck, man, fuck, fuck, fuck. This is bad, bad. They're ignoring us like so much shit. I tell you, Mahmoud, let's cool the old asshole and be done with it."

"Theo—go! You want one for the road, man?"

"Shit—you're killing me, man. Let's—"

"Do you?"

"Yeah, yeah. Right. I'll go. But if they blow me, man, promise you'll do him before getting out."

"Promise. Here."

"How many are left in the tin?"

"Plenty, Theo. Come on, you strong, virile, dangerous terrorist, get on with it. Feeling better?"

"Yeah, man. Better. Before I go, I wanna check on the old shit in there . . . " Footsteps, then the door crashed open.

Helm lay still, submitting, defeated; his eyes half open.

Theo's hairy face appeared against the wooden ceiling. Grinning at him: "Fucker!" hissed Theo, and slapped his cheeks with fingertips and fingernails four times, fast as a snake strikes.

Helm saw the dilated pupils, the white scum in the corners of Theo's eyes. He groaned, pretending pain, when all he felt was hatred and impatience.

Theo walked away into the corner of the shed and pissed interminably on the floor. Then the door slammed, and Helm was alone once more.

He went back to working his wrist rhythmically in sharp twists and pulls. The cord was getting looser already.

Helm's heart filled with anticipation.

20

Stark sat in the van, listening intently to the conversation in Fontana's hotel room. He had both phones clamped on his ears now, and a tape was being made as well.

He heard Fontana's urgent voice: "They must have mentioned the last location at some time. Think Gaby, think . . ."

Then the other voice, that of Attila Benn, asked calmly, in an obvious attempt to lessen the tension while still retaining control, "Are you finished with your food, Gaby? If so, I'll put the tray outside the door."

"Yeah, yeah. Take it."

There were some indistinct noises, then Benn came back and said, "Think back to anything that was said prior to your leaving that barge. Who was in charge?"

"Mahmoud. But Rossi had already staked it out. It was his job to secure the holes and to stock them with food and Coke. Except the last one."

"Coca-Cola—not cocaine?"

There was a hesitation, then she said, "Diet Coke—but Theo did take drugs. Some kind of pills."

"What color?"

"Not sure. Small. Bennies, I think."

Over the live speaker the red light came on and Stark slipped off one earphone. Georg asked, "Can you hear me, chief?"

"Shoot."

"They've put Attila Benn into the computer and the stuff just arrived. Where do you want it?"

"How much is it?" He looked at the tape to make sure the laser tap was still being recorded.

"Not much. There's a picture too."

"Go ahead, but be quick."

"Age fifty-nine; syndicated columnist with the Springer press, specializing on East-West stories, good contacts in East Berlin; married but no children, his wife is fifteen years younger than he; excellent professional reputation; good credit rating; no record either traffic or otherwise. Now, under war- and postwar history it becomes more interesting: Benn was a cadet in Helm's class until June 1944, then he was demoted and shipped to the eastern front. POW by the Russians, and released in 1951."

"So we have Stolz, Dornier, Fontana, and now Benn," said Stark.

"Right. Description: one hundred seventy-five centi-meters, sixty-eight kilos, gray hair, glasses, a preference for three-piece suits. Eyes, gray; small horizontal scar on his right cheek from minor shrapnel wound. That's it."

"Thanks, Georg."

He slipped both earphones back on in time to hear Gaby's crying. Then Benn said, "But you've got to. You must understand that this is the bottom line. There must have been some kind of reference to the new location."

Fontana interjected, "After they left the van at the air-port and took off with the two new cars, where did you go?"

"Rossi and I waited until seven-thirty in the parking lots at various shopping plazas. Wherever there were crowds. Mahmoud, Banigan, and Theo left."

"Where to? Any reference about the rendezvous after the Rhine Park?"

"Yes, earlier on the barge, *that's it;* Kalk!"

"What?"

"Kalk, that's——"

"I know. Across the river. Where? Any details?"

Silence in his earphones, and Stark found himself urging her on to think and remember.

Fontana asked, "Were you aware of *any* other hiding places?"

"Just the flat in Deutz."

"How did they refer to the place in Kalk? There are various terms, aren't there?"

"Pad, cube, hole, slide . . . Mahmoud called Kalk a hole."

"What do the words mean?"

"Deutz, they called a pad, the barge was a hole, a cube is a high rise, slides are trains and subways, planes are kites . . ."

"And they called it the Kalk *hole*?" Benn's voice, urgently. Stark held his breath. "What else could be called a *hole*? Barges, boats—what else?"

Silence . . . then Fontana urged, "Come, Gaby. Be creative. What else could be a hole? Could it be a generic term?"

Stark snapped his fingers and said urgently to the chief technician, "Get us a scale map of Kalk fast. When you've got it, tape it up."

Gaby was saying, "I don't know."

Silence . . . and Stark was close to biting his fingernails.

"All right," Fontana said. "Let's back up. Rossi was prepping the hiding places, and yet only Mahmoud knew where the Kalk hole was. Why?"

"How should I know? I was on the fringe half the time. How often do I have to tell you that?" Gaby began to cry. She added a sentence, sobbing, which Stark could not understand.

Fontana said, "All right. All right. Perhaps you should rest a bit. Lie back on the bed. Sometimes when one relaxes, answers pop up from nowhere."

*   *   *

By three o'clock the tension at Telephone Central had peaked, and the first tiny lapses of attention began to occur. They were no more than a slightly less careful listening, and a slower rocking of the thumb toggle when more than one line was active. The operators began to listen to longer stretches of any one conversation. The supervisors caught all these things and pointed them out to the operators. Still, the fact that three hours had passed and the kidnappers had not made good their threat somehow made it seem less likely by the minute that they ever would.

The all-news radio station had a total of thirty-six lines, monitored by twelve operators. One of those was Officer Olga Schimmelpfennig. Olga was a native of Cologne. She was a recent graduate of the police college, dark-haired, good-looking in a youthful healthy way, and very bright. At college they had nicknamed her *"Stiefelchen,"* or Boots because of the story about Olga from the Volga who loved her new boots so much she never took them off, not even in bed. But at college everyone had a nickname, and Olga did not mind hers at all. She lived with a roommate in a small flat in Lindenthal, and she enjoyed police work. It was exciting and challenging, and since the new law had been passed a woman could go far in this career.

By three o'clock "Boots" Schimmelpfennig guessed she had gotten to know pretty well everybody at All-News radio, at least all the reporters, assignment editors, and news editors. Much of the chatter on the phone was monosyllabic news lingo, jaded, and indicative of the professional shallowness that soon possesses any reporter dealing only with headlines and snippets of stories.

Because of this terseness of tone and up-front, crux-of-the-matter language, it took her nearly five seconds to recognize the target call when it popped up on her third line. Until that moment, when her mind clicked and she slammed down the red L/S key, she had mistaken the communication for yet another speculative update on the terrorist story.

The lock-and-search function fixed the outgoing line. Boots felt cold sweat break out all over her body; the additional five seconds until the number came up on her screen seemed like an eternity. The moment it appeared, she pressed INTERRUPT. The digitized location references crawled up from bottom screen and the automatic patch with Cologne HQ kicked in.

Boots leapt up and shouted, "Here! here! I got it!"

Her aisle supervisor came running, and the one from the next aisle came too. In Boots' headphones, the reporter still kept calling, "Hello, hello, can't you hear me, what the hell's going on?"

Her supervisor stared at the screen, then pushed the playback button for the tape that had begun recording the call as soon as L/S had been pushed. Over the small control speaker they heard "...*gonna tell you just once so you listen up and don't ask any questions. Fact is we found some top secret stuff in the fat cat's case—*"

In the bottom right corner of Boots' screen, the digital clock that measured the call from the first connection to interruption stood at 09.

"Nine seconds!" said the supervisor. She gave Boots an exuberant hug and a smacking kiss on the cheek. "You caught it and stopped it. Sounds like he was just going to rattle out his message and then hang up. So he'll never even know his call was cut off. Good work, Olga. Congratulations!"

At that moment, even though the weather forecast was negative, the chopper pilot changed rotor pitch and lifted off. The machine, a Saab Jetcommander, was full with GSG-9 men and equipment.

And on the ground, Stark was already in the Porsche, roaring under siren and flasher down the blocked-off pedestrian zone on Frankenwerft and under the Deutzer bridge. Because this was a regular weekday, there were not too many people around. The few who were there had ample warning to get out of the way. They pressed against the embankment wall and stared after the maniac Porsche until it was gone.

Fritz was in the passenger seat, directing him and readying the two Ingrams from the war chest.

The laser van was now in Georg's command, and a live patch via HQ Op kept them in touch. The girl was now asleep, and probably so as not to disturb her, Fontana and Benn were whispering so quietly as to be unintelligible.

"Right on Bendernstrasse," said Fritz, looking up from the map long enough to point.

The call had come from a booth behind the Buchheim freight terminal at the corner of Marktstrasse. The area was as good as any in which to hide.

As they went under the railroad bridge, Stark turned off siren and lights. Around the next turn they could see the booth, and instantly assessing the situation Stark radioed the chopper to lay back and circle the target point but not get closer than ten kilometers. Then they pulled over to the curb and watched.

Because of the strike in the lumber industry, this end of the freight terminal was virtually deserted. On the side rails stood boxcar after boxcar filled with sawed lumber for export. The cars were already bonded and sealed with steel straps. At the end of the track was a wooden building, a sort of combined stationmaster's house and repair shed. Stark watched the only human being in sight; he wore a workman's coverall, and his boots looked even older than his bicycle, which was very old. He bumped into a side street, then was gone.

"Now what?" asked Fritz, both Ingrams in his lap.

"Let's take a walk and see," answered Stark. He took one of the machine pistols, put it inside his jacket, and clamped it against his body with his arm.

But their walk showed them little they had not already seen from the car. The wooden building was the only likely hiding place around here, except for each and every boxcar.

Fritz counted them. "Sixty-seven. How will we ever check them all without—"

Stark interrupted him. "You listen for Georg, I'll talk to the superintendent."

Zander was still at HQ. "I'm just off the line to the minister. Did you know that it *was* on the radio? The all-news station at first, but now they're all mouthing it."

"But we've heard the tape. And there's nothing conclusive on it."

"That's never stopped the news media from speculating."

Stark cursed, then he said, "Whatever, sir, this is much more important now. I need a cordon around the Buchheim freight terminal. I've got a chopper up there watching, but still we need a hundred soldiers right away."

"Done," said Zander simply. "What else?"

"The thermographic camera van. There's just one building here, and sixty-odd boxcars. I don't want to make a move until I know who's in that shack."

"Why not wait till dark?"

"Would you? Are you telling me to—"

"No, I'm not."

"All right. Speaking of dark; it's getting pretty dark now." Stark bent to look out the windshield. Clouds were piling up in the east, and a sharp gust of wind filled the air with sawdust and grit. "The sooner I get the cordon, sir, the better. I don't know how long I can keep that chopper up there."

When Zander was off the air, Stark called the police weatherman and was told to expect thunderstorms by the end of the day. A wide low-pressure area was heading for North Rhine Westphalia from the Baltic Sea and heavy rainfall and thunderstorms were predicted.

"Shit," said Stark in a fit of sudden temper. "Couldn't that come tomorrow, or on the weekend as usual?"

"At least the heat's breaking, chief."

A newspaper came down the street like a bat and plastered itself temporarily against the windshield. Then it took off again, and the car trembled in the wind.

"Air mobile to ground mobile!"

"Yes, Jetcommander, what is it?"

"It's getting very blustery up here, chief inspector. Can't guarantee that we can hold our pattern much longer."

"Yes, I expected that. Stay as long as you possibly can.

Then have the men rappel at M/K three and wait in formation."

"M/K three, understood."

Fifteen minutes later the first six-by-sixes arrived full of soldiers, and Stark spread them out in a line with visual contact and within calling distance. At 4:15 P.M. the cordon was complete and he ordered the Jetcommander to unload and the men to proceed to the phone booth.

The thermographic team arrived in their odd-looking Volkswagen camper. Stark pointed out the wooden building, then climbed on board. The van rolled down the street; behind them, around the corner, the GSG-9 men were out of sight.

Stark cranked up the passenger window to keep out the flying grit and dust. The sky was virtually black now, and an ominous, almost purple light gave everything an eerie quality. Suddenly the wind stopped and a great bolt of lightning split the sky in the northeast. The rolling, crashing thunderclap came within a few seconds, and as if on cue, the first fat raindrops splattered on the ground.

Then it began to pour, and among the drops, hail fell with a deafening din on the roof of the van.

Stark shouted, "Will the camera work in this?"

The operator nodded, making final adjustments to some of the countless controls on camera and monitor. The equipment looked much like a television news camera, only bigger and with a lens as thick as a stovepipe. Mounted on a shockproof support was a monitor with a bright pink screen.

The first image of the building showed only the negative outline and great clouds of heat rising from the metal flashing around windowsills and chimney. The operator adjusted the sensitivity until the clouds of heat became black billowing holes in the image, then narrowed the field and began to scan the house in a level grid pattern along the horizontal.

"There!" he nudged Stark with his elbow and pointed at the screen.

Stark saw elongated clusters of red squares. Two moved, one was still, perhaps lying down. Stark's pulse began to speed up. He said, "I'll be damned. Let's hit them."

He murmured into the walkie-talkie, then checked his Ingram and got out of the van. Down the street, the GSG-9 assault team moved his way: dark, rushing shadows crouching low, pausing, then rushing on.

The noise of the rain and hail obliterated every other sound. Fritz appeared by his side, with a toothy, nervous, pre-assault grin. Stark cupped his hands around his ear and asked, "Did you inform Zander of the attack?"

Fritz nodded.

The GSG-9 commander, a young captain with a crescent-shaped knife scar from eye to mouth, pointed with both index fingers at the single draped window and the door of the shack. He held up one of the new multiflash stun grenades and gave the two-handed sign to advance.

The rain and hail came down like a collapsing ceiling, but the good thing about it was that the noise on the roof of the shack would easily cover their approach until the very end, thought Stark.

He made a final round to assure himself that there was really only one window. Then the soldiers piled up at the door, their MP5s ready.

The captain looked at them, nodded, primed the grenade, and lobbed it through the windowpane. A brilliant light flared up as though the shack had been struck by lightning and five rapid concussions blew out the rest of the glass.

The first three men threw themselves against the door. It splintered and fell in, and the rest of the GSG-9 men poured in, among them Stark and Fritz.

"Police! Hands up! Don't move!"

"What the fuck?" said a woman's voice. "Walter, who the hell are these bozos? Did you do this?"

Stark pushed past the soldiers, who had stopped in their tracks, and then he too saw the mind-boggling scene. Except that, unlike some of the men, it would take him weeks to find it at all funny.

The woman lay stark naked on a cot; her stomach, breasts, and shaven crotch glistening with petroleum jelly.

The jelly had come out of the two jars in the trembling hands of the two young men in tight rubber shorts. The rubber shorts had holes cut out for their now collapsed equipment.

Fritz laughed, and then some of the other soldiers laughed too.

Stark backed out of the cabin in a hurry. But he still heard the young captain say, "Sorry, folks. Wrong number. Proceed."

The woman began to shriek with laughter, and the GSG-9 tripped out of the shack struggling to regain a soldierly composure.

"The boxcars!" Stark ordered. "One after the other." He waved to the VW camper, then turned to Fritz with more anger than necessary. "Wipe that stupid grin off your face, lieutenant! Go get the Porsche, then take care of the radio. I want to talk to Zander and Georg."

Fritz ran off in a hurry. Water splashed underfoot as at a river crossing. Everyone was soaked to their skin, and the rain now came down worse than ever, but the hail at least had stopped. The black sky and the rain made it as dark as nightfall, even though it was only 4:35.

An hour later, when they had finished with the last boxcar without finding a trace of Helm or the kidnappers, Stark glumly returned to the radio to file his report with the superintendent. He was told Zander was in an urgent meeting. Minutes later Stark received a call back. "A very bad situation, chief inspector," Zander barked.

"Don't tell me. What do you mean?"

"I have to suspend you. Orders from the commissioner who in turn got his from the minister."

"But not now, in the middle of a breakthrough!"

"Don't argue, Gunter. You're off the case. Go back to the office and give me your situation summary. All tie-ins, the lot. I'm bringing someone else into Cologne tomorrow."

"Tomorrow? What the hell is going on? Did the Americans get to Esser?"

"There's a complaint that you're interfering with their security preparations for the president's visit, yes; then there is—"

"Interfering, what the hell are they—"

"Shut up, Gunter. Will you for once back down and use your head! Then Esser's mad as hell about the leak of the documents, and finally he says you made a big blunder releasing the only captured terrorist you had."

Stark took a deep breath, then said, "There's something else going on, don't you see? What the hell is Equinox? And why are the CIA so hot under the collar? Tell me!"

"I'll talk to you tomorrow. Pull out now, and return to your office. Your department will continue with the case, but you are relieved as of now. Sorry."

The rain and hail woke up Gaby. She sat on the bed and looked at Fontana and Benn; her panic at the strange surroundings cleared the sleep from her system in a hurry. The men stopped their murmured conversation and looked at her.

The room lay in near darkness even though it was only late afternoon. The rattling on the windows was very loud.

"What . . ." she said. "Oh God. I've been dreaming." She sat crosslegged in her jeans and blouse, rubbing her eyes like a child.

"Dreaming about what?" asked Fontana. He got up from the chair, crossed the room, and sat on the foot end of her bed.

She looked at him bleary-eyed, her mouth slack with childish despair. "About father . . . and Mahmoud. Bicycles, coveralls . . ." She straightened with a start, suddenly wide awake.

"*Bicycles, coveralls* . . . what do you mean, Gaby? Who wore coveralls?"

"Mahmoud! The first time I saw him. It was in the very early morning in the pad in Deutz. He wore a coverall and he'd arrived there by bicycle. The clips were still on his ankles. And the coveralls—"

They stared at her, and from the chair Benn said impatiently, "What? What about it?"

Fontana put out his hand to quiet him. Gaby was staring at the wall, then she blinked and looked at Fontana. "There were wood slivers on it. And the rag he'd wrapped up the machine pistol in had some splinters too. I noticed it but didn't think anything about it."

"What kind of wood slivers? Fresh and white or old gray oncs?"

"White. They were sticking into the fabric as though he'd brushed against some sort of—"

"A stack of lumber, recently sawed boards?"

She nodded.

Fontana turned on the light and went to the map of Cologne which he and Benn had taped to the wall while the girl was asleep. Red pins already stuck on Kassemattstrasse; where the barge had been; where the old man's body had been dumped, at Mendelssohn's; at the day-care center, and at the airport parking lot. All the red pins were on the right side of the Rhine; the only green pin was stuck on Neumarkt, at the site of the abduction.

Fontana waved Gaby to the map, and Benn stepped closer too.

"You see the pattern, Gaby?" asked Fontana. "The only time they ventured across the river was for the snatch itself. The hiding places, the cars, the bicycles, all that was on the other side. Clearly they feel more at home over there. You say Mahmoud bicycled to the apartment on Kassemattstrasse, so it's unlikely he came from very far, say a couple of kilometers. See this?" He pointed at Kalk.

"The Kalk hole," she exclaimed. "But what could it be?"

The map was the overview sheet from a taxi driver's sectional large-scale booklet. Fontana folded out the isolated Kalk page and they went over it square by square.

Then the answer stared them in the face. In the center of the page, occupying a fair chunk of property, sat the Kalk Sawmill and Lumberyard. The map even showed the entrance to the site and the orientation of the two existing buildings.

Fontana looked up and met Benn's gaze. He said, "I know, it seems almost too easy and obvious, but what else have we got to go on?"

Benn said, "There's a strike on in the lumber industry. That fits, too. And it's on the way to the airport. Mahmoud could have flown in with a guest worker's pass; there're lots of Turks and Arabs here now. On his way to the Deutz pad, he stopped off in Kalk to survey the scene for a day or two. The coveralls could clearly have come from the sawmill. Underneath it he wore his traveling clothes."

"And the machine pistol?"

Benn looked at Fontana. "Come on, you know how that's done. Checked baggage, wrapped with film in an X-ray-proof bag just to be sure. It's only boarding with a gun that's difficult. He probably left his suitcase and jacket at the sawmill before bicycling to the Kassemattstrasse address."

As he had been told to do, Fontana strolled casually over to the window and said loudly, "So it's the sawmill and lumberyard in Kalk." He looked out into the downpour, hoping the AT people could hear him all right. Where was the transmitter? He searched the lampposts, then saw it dimly in the rain and dusk; a steel tube like a muffler, strapped to the pole.

Fontana turned around and said to Benn, "Have you decided whether you're coming along? Remember, we're just showing the cops the way. But who can ever say for sure how things turn out?"

Benn asked, "I'll come along as the driver. I want to be there when those bastards are caught. And I want to see Dietrich's face."

Gaby said, "Please . . . take me along too."

Fontana asked, "Are you sure? You'd be safer with the cops. If the terrorists see you with us . . ."

She said, almost smiling, "Please."

Fontana and Benn had talked while she was asleep. He had predicted that she would want to come along. Now he repeated, "Are you quite sure, Gaby?"

Benn asked, "You know Paul's and my reason for going. What's yours?"

She looked at Fontana but remained silent. And looking into her eyes Fontana understood, and he felt a fleeting stab of pride in her. Almost gently, he asked, "Can we trust you, Gaby? Can we really trust you not to suddenly change sides?"

"You *must* let me come. It's the only chance I have . . ." She looked away, then added, "I want Uncle Dietrich to see me there with you. So he knows . . ."

Both men understood what she meant by "only chance," and they went along. It was a late, desperate act of contrition.

There was just one gun between them. Fontana's Agency .38, but the AT people would have all the firepower in the world.

Suddenly it all seemed so simple. They went downstairs, left through the delivery entrance, and walked in the pouring rain to where the police had delivered the Peugeot. They were soaked to the skin by the time they got there. In addition the driver's window had been left open, and Benn, who took the wheel, sat as though on a dripping sponge.

It was 5:15, and because of the weather rush-hour traffic was a nightmare. It took them nearly half an hour to get across the Deutzer bridge. Fontana sat next to Gaby on the backseat. The whole time she was looking blindly out the window, and he watched her, wondering what he could say to her. At times, he was tempted to reach out and squeeze her hand on the seat. The windows were steamed up and Benn had the defroster going full blast. Behind them was a sea of headlights; it was impossible to say which cars belonged to the AT people. At any rate, thought Fontana, the Peugeot was moving slowly enough for them to keep up.

He turned to Gaby and said, "No matter what happens, you stay in the car. Do you understand? Stay with Mr. Benn, at least until I come back to the car. I want to check out the situation first."

She stared, then turned away. Beyond the dripping windows, both lanes of traffic had come to a complete stop. Her hands lay folded in her lap. They were small and chapped; the fingernails were chewed. Somehow, with her newly laundered jeans and blouse, with the rain pouring down, she looked like a kid going off to summer camp. In her plastic purse was Vicky's picture.

From the driver's seat, Benn said, "I can't see anything of those cops, Paul. I hope you're right. I'm a journalist, not a—whatever. We're just leading them there, right? I mean, I want to be there when Dietrich is freed, but we certainly can't do it alone."

"We won't have to. Stark was going out on a limb. I trust him."

"And if not?"

"Shut up, Attila. And stay with Gaby till I call."

Traffic got going again. Six trucks full of soldiers passed them in the opposite direction. They sat in the rain on the truck beds like swamp creatures. They were in full battle gear; net helmets, fatigues, assault rifles with muzzle caps poking up like a picket fence.

Shifting up into third, Benn said, "So that was the holdup. Maneuvers or something."

Fontana sat still. Impatience and anger were burning inside him like a flame. But he was also worried about the outcome of this operation—most of all he was worried about Gaby. On reflection he knew that he should have insisted on her staying with the cops.

Shortly after three o'clock Helm had heard a whooping "Hooray" from the other room, then Mahmoud had turned the radio up loud. Seconds later he had come dancing into the saw shed yelling, "Hear this? Theo got to them and they're broadcasting us. Who needs to talk to those lying politicians when we can talk directly to the people? The people, man, hear this." He put the transistor radio on Helm's stomach and stood back grinning, hands on hips, his face glistening with sweat.

In the self-important tones of young professional know-it-alls, the announcer was saying, ". . . All-News Radio has learned that the kidnappers of the Green Party strategist Dietrich Helm have found top-secret documents in his possession. Top secret usually means *military,* and in this day and age military usually means *nuclear.*

"In a minute our news director will take an in-depth look at these new developments—but first this word from our sponsor . . ."

Helm heaved his belly and twisted so that the radio fell to the ground. There was the sound of shattering plastic and the jingle for HB cigarettes stopped abruptly.

He regretted his action immediately as premature. The baling twine on his wrist was loose, but not loose enough yet to slip out. And his ankles were still tied down firmly. He needed another half hour.

Mahmoud's face had drained of all blood when the radio broke. His eyes had become completely round and his hands had left the hips and turned into talons. Helm knew himself to be suspended on a whim between life and death.

"Sorry, Mahmoud. I'm very sorry. I didn't mean to do that. Perhaps we can fix it. I can fix things really well, Mahmoud!"

"Fucker," Mahmoud said in a low, deadly whisper. He bent to pick up the pieces of the radio.

Helm said eagerly, "It's just the battery that's come off. See that clip—put it back on."

Mahmoud did, and the little radio screeched on top volume. He turned it down, and they heard the sonorous conjecture of the news director, filling air time. Mahmoud turned it up again, then held it very close to Helm's ear. Grinning, he yelled over the speaker, "Don't you wanna hear that, fucker? They've got your number. They know you're a fat-cat politico powermonger!"

Helm closed his eyes, like a diver. Diving not into water but into waves of hatred.

Eventually Mahmoud became tired of it. He turned off

the radio and left to join Banigan in the other room. From the door he yelled, "Wait till I tell Theo you didn't wanna hear it. Maybe he should clip your ears, man. I'll lend him my knife." He cackled insanely, then was gone.

Helm went back to work with renewed fury on his wrist. Ten minutes later the first strand was worn through. He loosened the whole tangle just enough so that he could slip in and out. Then he took heart, sat up and untied his ankles, fixing the baling twine so that it lay across but was held in place only by the weight of his feet on the conveyor.

He lay back, nearly delirious with adrenalin and anticipation. He did not care if he died in the process, but he would teach these cretins a lesson they would not have the opportunity to forget.

Stark sat in the Porsche, his mind restlessly sweeping the band of possibilities. He already knew what Fritz would tell him once he got off the radio. *They had lost track of the Peugeot with Fontana, Gaby, and Benn.*

Fritz clicked off the gooseneck mike and, in anticipation of Stark's chagrin, murmured, "Sorry. They lost them, Gunter. And with the rain slapping on the window, they couldn't understand a word. But the Peugeot is gone, and somehow no one saw it leave."

"Say you're kidding, Fritz! I mean this is so bad it's ridiculous. They're gone? She's leading them to the hole, and we've no idea where they're going!"

The rain was hammering on the car, and waves of water ran down the windows. The world outside looked like footage from an underwater film.

"What should we do, Fritz? You tell me," Stark said in a novel tone of resignation. "I mean, I'm off this fucking case anyway. Why should I be upset, right?"

Fritz looked at him sideways, then murmured something about the weather and other excuses. But he had the sense not to say it in a tone resembling conviction.

Stark clapped him on the knee and said, "Shut up, Fritzi. We don't need condolence prizes. Because of an unfortunate combination of circumstances we screwed up; but screw up we did. So there." He fired the engine and turned up the fan. Before he swung the car around, he said, "There's one last thing we can try. Perhaps the CIA guys were less clumsy than we were and somehow hooked into the Peugeot. You never know. Wolff is a very clever devil. Try scanning their favorite channel!"

They drove in silence, Stark only half-listening to the hiss on the bands and the snap of communication fragments on the other channels.

Once they got past the railroad bridge, traffic became a snarl, then it stopped altogether. At the corner of Frankfurter and Heidelbergerstrasse two cars had collided. One was a Renault, and a fire department crew worked with a blow torch to free someone trapped inside. It looked like a wreck under water; the firemen wore glistening rubber clothes, and the acetylene cutter was like a bright blue knife. Only fish were missing.

"Hey . . ."

"Hey, what?" asked Stark, snapping his face round to Fritz.

"Who's that?" In the speaker they heard American voices, and they listened impatiently to the fragmented conversation.

"They're using a hopper channel," said Fritz. "But isn't that Teagarden? That drawl."

"Listen!" Stark pulled over onto the sidewalk so as to be able to concentrate on the radio.

Then they clearly picked up the words "Fontana" and "Peugeot," and they sat staring at the radio, willing it to tell them more.

"Come on, sweet mother. Just once in three days, give me a sniff of luck," Stark whispered. *"Where* are they?"

*   *   *

Theo had obediently taken the detour Mahmoud had told him to take, and as a result he pedaled for nearly an hour through the rain. It soaked through his heavy coverall, which hung on him, weighing him down. His boots filled with water, and his hair and beard were plastered to him as if he had just been swimming.

Understandably he arrived at the lumberyard in a foul mood. But Mahmoud knew how to handle him; the first thing he did was to give him a benny to reward him for a job well done.

"Hey, it was on already?" Theo was cheering up quickly. "Was it good stuff? They got the gist all right?"

"Great, Theo," said Banigan. "Not just good. You did *great*, man. This'll put the squeeze on the government to negotiate with us. We'll hit them again tomorrow after they've stewed for a while."

Theo grinned, pleased with himself. Where he stood, a great puddle was spreading on the rough-sawed floorboards.

Mahmoud added generously, "You can dry off for a little while, man. I'll keep an eye on the outside. After a communication, it's always good to be doubly careful." He pulled on the big yellow oilskin that he'd found in the shed and checked for his knife and his gun. Grinning, he said to them, "Keep an eye on the fat cat. Though now that we have the papers, he's the lesser bargaining tool."

"By the way, where's those papers? Are they safe?"

Mahmoud patted his inner jacket pocket. "Safe as can be, man. Best spot for them." He pulled up the hood and stepped out into the rain.

He had not been in the fresh air since they got here the previous afternoon. Bending forward he breathed deeply a few times, then hurried across the opening to the first row of stacked lumber. If the rain in its force and cleansing freshness reminded him of the cloudbursts of Beirut in spring and fall, the smell was something else. Beirut, the whole of Lebanon, always smelled of rotting vegetables and wet clay bricks. It was the smell of his childhood, and the thought of his childhood propelled him back into the turbulent mainstream of the dark force that drove him. Disdainfully, he sniffed the wet air, smelling only the sourness of wood greedily absorbing the moisture that days of heat and sun had evaporated.

He passed the spot between the stacks where they'd hidden the car and moved on carefully. Not that he expected any trouble, but at this stage in any squeeze one was the most vulnerable. Too much communication had gone out, too many traces could be followed back to the source, the pigs had too much to go on.

In a few days he would be back home, the freed comrades in safety once more, each with a great deal of pocket money to help them get back on their feet.

Moving along slowly from stack to stack, Mahmoud thought that he should have worn the oilskin with the green side out, not the yellow. It was too bright. He considered reversing it, but the thought of getting soaked stopped him.

At that moment two cars turned off the main road onto the drive to the lumberyard. The first switched off its lights and the other followed. Mahmoud's pulse began to fly. He crouched down behind a bush, loosened the knife in his sleeve, and felt for the gun.

The cars were dark sedans, and in the dim light and the rain they advanced virtually unseen and unheard. He watched them crawl past the gate. When he lost sight of them, he whipped off the clumsy oilskin and rushed among the stacks to see where they had gone. His shoes squelched in the mud, but now Mahmoud was oblivious to dirt and rain. Sneaking around the stacks, he felt but ignored the big slivers that ripped into his hands. The cars were gone.

He cursed passionately and silently. He ran to the far end of the yard; pausing, then hurrying, as he'd been taught years ago in training camp. When he still could not see the cars, he circled around, back to the gate. The envelope fell out of his jacket pocket and he put it back, soaking wet. Then he stumbled on one of the cars, a Peugeot. It had been parked next to a tall stack of lumber just inside the gate, and in the dim light from the faraway street lamps Mahmoud saw that there were only two people—a man in the driver's seat and a woman in the backseat.

Somewhere a siren wailed. The woman raised her head at the sound, and in that instant Mahmoud recognized *Marion*. He understood immediately: she was betraying them once again—betraying the brotherhood, the family.

The thought flashed through his mind that Theo had been right about her. Already moving, he loosened the knife. The execution would take only a few seconds, then he could worry again about the other car.

Driven by the same force that had raised him above others and made him what he was, Mahmoud whipped open the rear door. Because the fools had not thought to tape up the switches, the dome light came on. The man in the driver seat turned around; he was an older man in suit and tie, and from the panic in his eyes Mahmoud knew immediately that he would pose no danger.

Marion screamed and raised her hands in defense, and while the old man struggled to turn around and help her, Mahmoud jammed his knee into Marion's belly and yanked back her head by the ponytail. He implored Allah to condemn her, then slowly brought back his fist to give her the first taste of the curved blade.

He looked with elemental joy into her wide-open eyes, anticipated with wild triumph the first signs of death—the darkening of the iris, the freezing of the pupils. Her blood would gush like that of any of the hundreds of goats he had slaughtered, first in Bir Bakeim, then in the backyard of the mud house in the Beirut suburb, then in the vile, filthy communal yard at Sabra.

But the old man in the front seat was clutching his knife hand, screaming. Mahmoud twisted and punched to free his hand, then clambered off Marion. He dragged her out of the car into the open where the old guy could not interfere with the ritual slaughter.

Marion tumbled out, head first, her ponytail still wrapped around his hand. She struggled and screeched, bleated like a goat. She fell into the mud, and he kicked her in the head to stop her hysterical screams. Now the old man came around the back of the car. Mahmoud pulled the gun from his belt, pointed it, and fired. Now the moment was his.

Kneeling on Marion's belly, he showed the blade to Allah omnipresent. His knife hand raised into the streaming night sky, Mahmoud forced his left into the traitor's mouth. He dug his fingers into her tongue, to yank it out, expose its quivering root to the blade. She was unconscious but the pain would wake her in time for her to see her own blood spurting from her mouth, in time to see the knife slashing her throat, in time for her to recognize the error of her ways. This was how traitors died.

Suddenly thunder and lightning struck his knife hand, shattering it, and he stared at it incredulously. Someone was yelling something, and Mahmoud turned to find himself looking into the muzzle of a gun. The .38 was in the unwavering hand of yet another old man—but this one had a thin hard face, and the cold light of killing shone in his eyes. The lips barely moved when he said, "You goddamn little swine," and the bony finger curled on the trigger.

Mahmoud screeched *"Allah akbar!"* and threw himself forward. At the same moment the muzzle blew up in his face, and the fire and wind struck him like a speeding train and carried him away.

Fontana stared for a second at Mahmoud's shattered face, then stepped over him.

He presumed that the car that had followed them here had been part of Stark's team, but now he did not know where they were, and he did not care either.

Gaby lay half under the Arab and he heaved and yanked at his body to free her. Mahmoud's jacket fell open, and Fontana saw the manila envelope protruding from the material. He picked it up, peered inside, and pocketed it himself. The action took only seconds but it filled him with a grim satisfaction; then he knelt by Gaby's side.

She was coming to, dazed, muttering. He felt her pulse,

and it was strong and regular; then she opened her eyes and recognized him. There was blood around her mouth, but the rain was washing it away, and he heard her whisper, *"Oh God."* She looked white and tiny, and somehow years older.

Fontana put his cheek next to hers and cried tears of anguish and relief that he had no longer known he was capable of. On the horizon of his life he saw the first glimmer of hope in years, a ray of light to focus on.

He pressed Gaby to himself, and seconds passed like years before he realized again where he was.

Then he heard Benn behind him and he left Gaby to see what could be done for his friend. Benn had dragged himself into a sitting position — he was leaning against a stack of lumber. Blood welled from a bullet wound in his right side, but Benn was still breathing, even talking. "Paul . . . Paul come here," he said.

Fontana knelt next to him. "I'm sorry, old friend—"

"No, no, quiet," murmured Benn. "Listen, Paul . . ." he spoke slowly, panting with each word. "Listen, I'll give you a name. About your Vicky . . . in Pankow . . . Colonel Karel Ostropov . . . he owes me a favor . . . KGB East Berlin section. Remember, Paul: Karel Ostropov . . ."

"All right. I'll remember. Don't talk anymore, now."

"Where're those cops, Paul?"

Fontana stood up and screamed, "Police! Stark, where the hell are you? Come on now!" Then he remembered why they had come here in the first place, and he turned on his heel and ran towards the shack.

At the end of the driveway a Porsche with a flashing blue light veered off. Its high beams swept the yard momentarily.

Both Theo and Helm heard the shots and looked up at the same time. Even though the rain made a hellish racket on the roof, the shots had been so close that they had rattled the window in the saw shed. Helm pulled his hand from the loop.

Theo leaped up from the floor next to the saw and stared like a wild man. He raced to the freight door and pushed it open a crack. All he saw was darkness and the rain pouring from the eaves.

But then there was a scream, and it whipped Theo into action. Yelling, "Banigan, watch out!" he turned and flung himself towards the saw.

Helm saw him coming, lunging for the red switch. At that moment the freight door opened again, and Theo half-turned his head. His hand touched the switch just as Helm brought up both feet, smashing the tips of his shoes against Theo's chin. Helm rolled off the conveyor and was back on his feet in no time to see the apparition of Paul Fontana pick up a piece of board and swing it against Theo's head. The conveyor belt was moving now and the band saw ripped the air with a high whine.

Helm bent down and with all the strength left in his arm, hoisted Theo's torso onto the conveyor. The steel links bit and grabbed the shirt, then the belt.

Someone screamed something, but Helm could only watch with wild triumph in his heart as Theo regained consciousness in time to recognize the slicing blade. His hands went out in defense, but the saw kept coming; then the finger fell on the hairy face and the saw traveled in the blink of an eye from Theo's shoulder through his chest to the opposite hip. The sliced torso tumbled heavily off the conveyor, but the legs caught on the upright which pushed them around so that the band saw ripped through both knees before the bloody freight was thrown clear of the steel links.

Helm sat down heavily, looking up in a daze. There was Paul by his side saying something, and two steps away stood Banigan screaming words that were drowned by the whine of the saw. The Englishman's face was a wild mask of desperation and the MP5 in his hands was pointing straight at Helm and Fontana, ready to spit out enough bullets in a half second to kill ten men, not just two.

Helm tried regretfully to clear his mind of the euphoria.

There was a fourth man entering the room, a man he had never seen.

The man came through the door to the other room, and under cover of the noise from the saw he kept on walking, raising a big police Walther at the same time.

Banigan never saw him, nor did he see the gun or feel the heavy bullet that slammed into his head from behind, collapsing him forward over his machine pistol. From the pressure of his dead finger the gun went off, riveting a full five-second burst into the floorboards under his body.

The man with the Walther stepped over to the saw and shut it off. It died with the whine of a turbine slowing, and the first few seconds of silence were like a grave.

Then Fontana said, "Damn it, Stark, you took your bloody time."

The man put away his gun, then pointed a stiff index finger at Fontana. "You'd better be off right away. I don't want you figuring in this on the records. Get into your car and be off. We've got ambulances and support on the way now. We'll look after Gaby and Benn."

"And you'll remember our deal?"

"I will. Now get out of this before it's too late. I'll be in touch with you. Trust me."

Fontana rose, touched Helm's arm, and said, "I'll see you in a day or two." Then he walked out the freight door the way he had come in.

In the yard, Fritz had put Gaby into the Porsche, out of the rain. Fontana saw her dimly behind the streaming window, and he gave a little wave. On the car the blue light still rotated. He made the sign with a thumb and forefinger that things would work out all right. Gaby looked at him, immobile and pale.

Sirens were wailing not too far away and coming closer. Fontana walked over to Benn, who was still leaning against the stack of lumber. He was covered with a blanket up to his shoulders, and Fritz was by his side.

Fontana asked, "How is he?"

"Can't say. Shot in the shoulder—should pull through."

Benn made an effort to half-raise his hand and wave Fontana away.

The sirens were much closer now. Several vehicles with red and blue dome lights turned from the main street into the industrial drive. Fontana quickly went to his car, backed out of the lumberyard, and sped off. Moments later he passed the ambulances and squad cars without getting stopped. He continued on to the hotel.

He was soaking wet; shoes, suit, and all, as though he had fallen into a pool. But he felt triumphant, wonderful— he'd rarely felt better. He patted his pocket for the envelope; it was still there and he sped on.

Dornier was at the desk. Taking in his friend's dripping, disheveled appearance, he gave him a questioning glance.

"Dietrich's free," grinned Fontana. "Attila unfortunately got wounded but it looks as though he'll be okay. We'll talk later . . ." He held out his hand for the message in his pigeonhole. It said, *Wolff, Bonn 54-63-51.*

Squelching toward the stairs, Fontana asked, "Can you send me up something to eat, old friend? I'm starving."

He took a long hot bath, and when he came out a tray with sandwiches and tea was on the table. Eating and drinking he began to shuffle the four ingredients of his plan—a plan that was no more than his response to a once-in-a-lifetime opportunity. What made Fontana hesitate was that it was such a bold departure from the rules that had governed his professional life that his heart and mind were in great conflict.

Still, he knew already that his heart would win out. He hid the papers, put on dry clothes, and went downstairs to have a good stiff drink with Herbert Dornier. Herbert was an important part of his past, and even if in his present circumstances he could not offer much practical help, he could nevertheless be relied on for companionship and understanding.

But when Fontana got down, he found that, since his arrival, the lobby and lounge had filled with religious travelers marooned by the rain. Dornier was bustling back and forth, helping the waitress fill all the various orders for mulled cider, wine, and food.

Fontana caught him on the run and said he wanted to talk to him, but it would keep until tomorrow.

Dornier's eyebrows went up. "Sure?"

"Sure, Herbert. Meanwhile, can I borrow an umbrella?"

"You want to go out in this rain?"

Fontana nodded. The final shape of the puzzle was suggesting a solution that had sent his pulse flying. It had induced a state of near-exultation, and in this state there were two things he did not want to face: the one was a crowd of wet pilgrims, and the other was to be alone.

He took Fontana's big doorman's umbrella and went out in search of a bar.

21

The morning papers called it a brilliant undercover operation; they carried file pictures of Mahmoud, Theo, and Banigan. But not of Gaby: Chief Inspector Stark so far had kept his word.

Dietrich Helm was reported safe but weak from his three-day ordeal. He was pictured shaking hands with the young leader of the Green Party—the old, experienced strategist being welcomed home by the much younger party boss whose college-boy face was lately on many billboards. In the newspaper photograph they both smiled at the camera: youth and experience in one image.

In a separate story the papers reported that the terrorists never had been in the possession of any secret documents; clearly, the paper said, this had been no more than an attempt by Mahmoud's splinter group to get more bargaining power. This report was either goodwill journalism or a coverup, thought Fontana.

The opposition party demanded an investigation, and the minister for the interior, Dr. Karl Esser said that his government would be happy to comply.

Fontana was reading the morning papers in his room. On the table lay the manila envelope with the targeting file; the photograph of Vicky which he had again taken out of Gaby's purse; the slip of paper with Wolff's Bonn number; and another slip of paper on which Fontana had written "Colonel Karel Ostropov, KGB East Berlin."

At nine o'clock, Fontana called Stark to thank and congratulate him. Stark made no reference to the documents which supposedly no one was missing. But chances were that Stark had not been truthfully briefed on that aspect in the first place. Still, it was puzzling, and Fontana decided to get his plan in motion.

Stark said, "About Gaby, I'm not sure just how it will be played. But you'd best find a good lawyer. At any rate our deal stands, and perhaps we can give her a crown witness status as well. Time will tell. Give it a day or two."

Next, Fontana called the general hospital, where he was told that Benn was off the critical list, but was still in intensive care after last night's operation to stop the bleeding in his shoulder.

After that Fontana sat back, reshuffled the components of his plan, and took action. It was 9:30 when he placed his call to Colonel Karel Ostropov. He had anticipated endless bureaucratic problems in getting through to the colonel, but Attila Benn's name worked amazingly like a secret key. When the connection was established, Fontana hooked on his digitizer.

"Attila Benn," chuckled the colonel, "what mother would today call her infant son Attila?" He had a deep, even voice and spoke precise, unaccented German. "But seriously, we value Mr. Benn as a good, neutral journalist and friend. If he has given you my name then I shall be glad to hear you out, sir."

Fontana read between the lines and came straight to business. He described in detail the good news he had to offer and the bargain he wished to make.

The colonel heard him out, then asked, "With maps, you say?"

"Yes. In detail."

"Hm. Even if we agree, sir, why do you assume that your daughter would want to leave East Germany to join you in the West?"

"Just give her the choice. As long as she is released from Pankow jail."

"Hm. Very well. Let us proceed to step one. Listen carefully, please . . ."

Twenty minutes later he dropped off the packet at the DDR trade commission, then returned to the hotel to wait for the verdict. If the papers proved to be false, or if Benn had overestimated his contacts . . .

The rest of the day was mental and emotional torture. He was still unable to speak to Benn at the hospital, but he telephoned the Helm residence and spoke to Dietrich at length. Dietrich insisted that he come that same evening for dinner and stay for the weekend. Fontana happily agreed.

At 4:45 P.M., fifteen minutes before closing, he went to the Moskvich dealer on Behnstrasse, as instructed by Ostropov. He walked past the ugly cars on the showroom floor and introduced himself to the man with the black moustache.

"Mr. Fontana," the man said, "one minute please."

He walked behind a dividing curtain and a moment later returned with an envelope.

Fontana took it, left the showroom, and walked for three blocks before he dared to look inside. His old heart beat alarmingly hard and loud. He felt like a Christian must have felt looking toward Caesar: would the thumb point up or down?

The map he pulled out was of West Berlin, and Fontana went to the nearest bench, sat down, and wept with joy..

Passers-by looked at him strangely, and a policeman asked if everything was all right. Fontana said, yes, yes, it was, and walked quickly to the hotel.

22

The payoff in Equinox came on Tuesday, after Henry Wolff had spent four days watching the phones and the Telex in the castle at Olpe and reading a dozen newspapers each day front to back, searching for the Russian response.

On Tuesday morning the *Kölnische Rundschau* and the *Herald Tribune* carried precisely the information Henry Wolff had hoped for.

Among the personal announcements in the *Rundschau* he found this notice:

THIS IS TO ANNOUNCE THE EARLY RELEASE OF VICKY SCHOTT, NEE FONTANA (40) FROM PANKOW PRISON, PANKOW, EAST BERLIN. HER RELEASE DOES NOT CONSTITUTE A PARDON FROM HER CONVICTION, AND ACCORDINGLY VICKY SCHOTT HAS BEEN EXPELLED FROM THE GERMAN DEMOCRATIC REPUBLIC. SHE WAS HANDED OVER TO THE AUTHORITIES AT MARIENFELDE REFUGEE CENTER, WEST BERLIN, WHERE INTERESTED PARTIES MAY CONTACT HER. SIGNED:
THE ADMINISTRATOR OF PANKOW PRISON
IN ASSOCIATION WITH THE
SPECIAL CIRCUMSTANCES REVIEW COMMITTEE

Henry Wolff looked up the airline schedule, then put out a call for Jack Teagarden, who was still in charge of the team covering Fontana. While he waited for the call-back, Henry Wolff buzzed the kitchen and asked for fresh coffee.

Teagarden called promptly.

"Where is Fontana now?" asked Wolff.

"In his hotel room."

"You're sure?"

"Yes. He just had a phone call. Jackson found a way to neutralize his digitizer. The lawyer told Fontana that the magistrate agreed to release Gaby into his supervision. They waived the usual bond, and the only condition is a three-part psychiatric examination and perhaps a period of treatment. Fontana was very pleased."

"Hold on . . ." The knock on Wolff's door came again, and he called, "Who is it? Come in."

The housekeeper entered with a tray, looking around for a place to set it down.

"Here, Mrs. Cook," Wolff said, "Put it right here."

She approached his desk and began to set out the coffee service. She was a plumpish, cheerful woman with a fresh and clean aroma, like laundry dried on the line.

Wolff said into the phone, "Fontana is going to drive to the airport. My guess is he will take the PanAm flight at twelve-thirty to West Berlin. It's the only possible flight there from Cologne today. Stay with him but don't go into the departure lounge. I'll be there."

"Don't go into the—you don't want us to cover you?" asked Teagarden.

Wolff sighed. "Jack . . . listen, Jack—"

"All right. All right."

When Henry Wolff hung up the phone, the housekeeper said to him, "Those Russians are really something, Mr. Wolff."

"What?" Usually Wolff hated it when people stood by his side, reading things on his desk, even if it was just the newspaper. But this was different: the *housekeeper* noticing it was proof positive that the public reaction would be just what Washington was hoping for. To make sure, he asked, "What exactly do you mean?"

"Well, this here. This headline in the *Tribune* . . . about Moscow calling us liars . . . claiming we have far more missiles than the number that the peace talks are based on."

He looked up at her. "Ah, well, those Russians. What can one expect, Mrs. Cook? And look—" he tapped the second paragraph of the story. "Even though we know that their accusation is simply not true, they're already talking about deploying a third line of SS-30s. See, it says so right here."

She shook her head, clucking her tongue at those bad Russians. "Surely they can't get away with that, can they?"

Serenely, Wolff said, "Well, Mrs. Cook—we will have to respond in kind. Even the score again."

He watched her weigh his words, then nod in agreement. Having dealt with world peace and the nuclear balance, she returned to a topic of more immediate interest to her. From the door she said, "Dinner tonight is roast pheasant with fresh garden peas and wild rice. Are you going to eat in, Mr. Wolff?"

He charmed her with his smile. "Pheasant! . . . how can I say no, Mrs. Cook? Is it all right if I invite Mr. Thompson to dine with us here?"

"The American ambassador in Bonn? Oh, Mr. Wolff, of course! We'll be honored."

"Good," smiled Wolff. "Have them set a table for two in the small dining room. I'll be selecting the wine personally." He winked at her. "You see, we have cause for a little celebration."

"Oh? A birthday, Mr. Wolff?"

"Well, no. Just a little private—shall we say, success."

When she was gone, Wolff poured himself a cup of coffee. Then he made a last file entry and signed it with a flourish.

In the corner, one of the Telex machines began to clatter. Wolff looked up—it was the black machine, the coded line from Langley. He set down the coffee cup and went across.

Because praise was so rarely given in the Agency, the message filled Wolff with pride. He savored the congratulatory words as they appeared and formed sentences. When the machine had stopped, he tore off the paper and read the entire message once again.

Then he folded it and put it in his pocket.

At the PanAm ticket counter Paul Fontana pocketed his credit card and the open return ticket to West Berlin. He was still in a state of euphoria. Turning away from the counter he was only dimly aware of the crowd in the main departure hall. Even though he still had lots of time, he moved towards the security check and the PanAm gate.

Suddenly Henry Wolff stepped into his path like the embodiment of his worse fear. Fontana felt a wave of nausea, something like death, the end of all hope.

But Henry was smiling. "Hi, Paul," he said. "Going on a little trip?"

Fontana had no words.

Henry reached out and touched his arm. "Relax, my friend. It's all right. I know everything."

Fontana watched as Henry reached into his pocket, took out a folded piece of paper, and proffered it. They stood amidst a solid stream of passengers. People shouldered past them and bumped them with suitcases. The PA system announced departures and arrivals. Life bustled on.

Fontana unfolded the piece of paper and read:

TO OLPE-HEAD FROM LANGLEY EURO-HEAD . . . HENRY, CONGRATULATIONS ON FINE OUTCOME OF EQUINOX. HAVE POSITIVE REPORTS FROM MOSCOW RESIDENT THAT EQUINOX DATA ACCEPTED AS GENUINE . . . STEPPED UP DEPLOYMENT OF RUSSIAN SS-30s IMMINENT . . . EARLY RESPONSE OF NATO HEADS NOW IN FAVOR OF OUR LONGARM DEPLOYMENT . . . EQUINOX GONE EXACTLY AS PLANNED . . . EXCELLENT WORK BY YOUR SECTION. EMERSON

Fontana read the Telex again, then gave it back to Wolff. He was beginning to understand, but the complexities were overwhelming. His fear gave way to indignation.

"So?" asked Wolff. "Do you understand?"

"Can we get out of this crowd, Henry? There's—"

Henry shook his head. "Let's stay right here. I like the noise, the commotion. It's safe."

Fontana let his hands hang idly. With a sense of helplessness he said, "The documents were a plant . . . deliberate *dis*information. What's Longarm?"

Henry stepped even closer. He murmured, "Paul, I'm just a little wheel in the machine, you understand. The big boys don't tell me too much about the tactical aim of any operation. We work on the need-to-know principle. All I know is that we Amerians have this brand-new type of missile, called Longarm. And we want to deploy it here in Europe—"

"Deploy more nuclear arms here in Europe? I don't think the civilian population, the *voters* here, will go for that. Even back home there'll be a lot of opposition to it."

"Not any more. Read the *Herald Tribune* today, or wait for the *New York Times* tomorrow. That's what this whole operation was all about. Equinox is the preparatory stage for the deployment of Longarm."

"And what about the peace talks?"

"The peace talks . . . they'll go on. Of course they'll go on. But Washington will have a stronger position, both in terms of public opinion and in terms of our defense capability."

"But if they are deploying more—"

Wolff said, "Deploying what? Longarm is so fast and so accurate that it will make the Russian SS-20s and -30s look like flying turds."

"You're setting them up . . ." Suddenly the entire operation was clear to Fontana. It was so complex, so daring, it literally took away his breath.

Wolff watched him, narrowing his eyes. "Got it? And now you understand why this thing could *not* get into the hands of the press. Imagine the field day the media would have with it.

There was a lot at stake, Paul. For Germany, for NATO, and for Washington." Wolff brightened. He stepped aside for a young woman with a baby in a stroller. Moving closer again, he touched Fontana's arm. "Hey, Paul. Don't feel badly. You were simply looking out for number one. Which is human, and I *counted* on you trading those papers for Vicky. I'm sure you've guessed by now that you only did what Benn was *supposed* to have done."

"Since when has Benn been a Russian agent? I had no idea."

Wolff shrugged. "The Russians got Benn the same way and the same time we got you—1945, long distance sleepers. Except that we wised up to Benn fifteen years ago. And without knowing it he has performed some useful work for us. In order to get Equinox into Russian hands without making them suspicious we had Carl Stolz feed Benn the file. Stolz's antinuclear and anti-American stance was well known, so his motive was acceptable. We figured that Benn would happily run off to East Berlin with Equinox—"

"But he gave it to Helm instead. How did you get Stolz to leak it in the first place?"

Wolff wagged his head. "Delicate, these things. Let's say Stolz was prompted by us and by Bonn. He was reluctant, but he obeyed."

"And to show your gratitude you had him killed."

Wolff managed to look genuinely sorry. "Paul . . . that's about the only development I regret. Our guy fucked up. I swear he was only told to *scare* Stolz. I wanted to make sure that Stolz didn't go blathering to everybody how he was pressured by the Americans and by his own government to leak things to the Russians."

"That day in Olpe, when you set me up with the news of Vicky's being alive . . . why didn't you just say to me, 'get those papers and then I'll let you trade them in for Vicky' ?"

"Paul, that was an option I could always come back to. But I know you. You work best under pressure and with your own motivation. Your tone of voice on the phone to Ostropov, the whole chemistry of your deal with him would have been different." Wolff grinned. "Don't get me wrong, Paul, but a guilty man sounds different."

"Guilty . . ."

"Well, you know what I mean."

The PA system announced that PanAm 212 to Berlin Tegel was now available for boarding.

"There you go, Paul," said Wolff. He extended his hand.

Fontana kept his eyes on Wolff's face. "But Vicky *is* alive—that picture is not some grisly retouching job?"

Wolff lowered his hand. His face took on an expression of honest surprise. "Hey Paul. Would I do that to you? You and I go back a long time. Remember?"

Fontana remained silent. Did he remember? Had he even once in all these years not been driven by the chain of events that began that June 4th 1944? He searched Henry's face and recognized himself. The decades of duplicity and secret intentions. Puppets and puppeteers.

"Goodbye, Henry," said Fontana slowly. Speaking the words was like closing a heavy door behind him.

The P.A. system announced the final boarding call for PanAm Flight 212.

"Goodbye, Paul. You better not miss that plane. I guess she'll be waiting." This time Henry was not smiling, not play acting—he was merely offering his hand again, and this time Fontana shook it.

Vicky was alive—he was sure of it now.

Fontana released Henry's hand, then he simply turned and walked away. After a few steps walking became easier—he moved more quickly, lighter. Had the terminal been less crowded, he would have broken into a run.